Like a Thief
in the Night

Like a Thief in the Night

A Christopher Worthy/Father Fortis Mystery

❖

DAVID CARLSON

coffeetownpress

Kenmore, WA

coffeetownpress

A Coffeetown Press book published by Epicenter Press

Epicenter Press
6524 NE 181st St.
Suite 2
Kenmore, WA 98028

For more information go to:
www.Camelpress.com
www.Coffeetownpress.com
www.Epicenterpress.com
www.davidccarlson.net

Cover watercolor by Kathy Carlson
Interior design by Melissa Vail Coffman

Like a Thief in the Night
Copyright © 2021 by David Carlson

ISBN: 978-1-60381-799-8 (trade paper)
ISBN: 978-1-60381-384-6 (ebook)

Printed in the United States of America

*This mystery is dedicated to Nils Y. Olson (1917-87),
who offered his generosity and support at crucial crossroads
of my early life journey. Nils was more than my father-in-law.
He was a dear friend. He taught me how to be a better fisherman
and a better human being. It was in composing his eulogy that I
first realized that writing would be my way of listening to my heart.*

The Day of the Lord so cometh
as a thief in the night.

I Thessalonians 5:2 (King James Version)

✝

ACKNOWLEDGMENTS

———— ◆ ————

I OWE SO MANY PEOPLE FOR THEIR role in the publication of *Like a Thief in the Night*. Firstly, I am indebted to my wife, Kathy, for her tireless reading, rereading, and editing of the novel. Her belief in the Christopher Worthy and Father Fortis series is something that I count on but never want to take for granted.

Secondly, I wish to thank Sara Camilli, my literary agent, and Jennifer McCord, my editor at Coffeetown Press, for their friendship, guidance, and constant support.

Thirdly, I am indebted to so many friends at Holy Trinity Greek Orthodox Church, Carmel, Indiana, who over the past twenty-seven years have shown me the love that is at the heart of Orthodox Christianity.

Finally, this sixth mystery in the Christopher Worthy and Father Fortis series would not have been written without Olivier Clement's inspiring and visionary work *You Are Peter: An Orthodox Theologian's Reflections on the Exercise of Papal Primacy*. I hope this novel honors Professor Clement's memory and courageous stance.

NOTE TO READERS

---◆---

*L*IKE A *THIEF IN THE NIGHT* is set in the indefinite future, but the mystery was, of course, written at a definite time. I finished the mystery while the coronavirus epidemic was raging, when no one knew how long the pandemic would last. As will be clear from the novel, the story assumes a time in the near future when the pandemic is over. No one in the novel has to socially distance or wear a mask. I hope and pray that this is truly the case when you, the readers, open to the first page of *Like a Thief in the Night*.

The religious sites mentioned in this novel are real places, their descriptions based on visits I have made. I am indebted to Gordon College in Massachusetts and especially Franklin College in Indiana for offering me the opportunities to accompany college students in visiting these sites.

There is a brief glossary of terms and titles at the conclusion of the novel.

CHAPTER ONE

———————◆———————

JUNE 29: ST. PETER'S SQUARE: ROME

FATHER NICHOLAS FORTIS PAUSED AS HE stepped through Bernini's columns to gaze upon the fountains, the obelisk, and St. Peter's Basilica, the largest church in the world. *Built so that any pilgrim, any visitor, would remember it forever. And they were right*, he thought. Yet, what struck him about the famous square was that it seemed more Roman than Catholic. He couldn't imagine Peter, the fisherman from Galilee, feeling any kinship with this immense space named after him and built atop his bones.

Father Fortis' observation didn't betray some Eastern Orthodox bias against Rome, the heart of the Catholic faith. He'd visited the city before and loved Rome, but his love was not grounded in her massive churches. It was walking the ancient Appian Way where he felt the presence of the early Christian martyrs—the famous ones like St. Peter, St. Paul, St. Lawrence, St. Anastasia, and the unknown ones. And it was most often in the smaller churches where he felt a spiritual kinship.

The massive St. Peter's Square, however, did serve a practical purpose, as it was one of the few places on earth that could hold the throngs who showed up for major holy days. This day was one of the holiest, June 29th being the feast day of Saints Peter and Paul. The feast day was also one of two celebrated together by Catholic and Orthodox Christians, this year by Pope Gregorio and Ecumenical Patriarch Michael.

A helicopter flew over, drawing Father Fortis' attention upward to where he could make out the word "Polizia" on the craft's underbelly. It was a precaution he approved of as he looked around the massive open space and felt a shiver pass through him. Yesterday, in his meeting with Ecumenical Patriarch Michael, head of the worldwide Orthodox Church, Father Fortis learned that a surviving offshoot of ISIS had posted vague threats on the Internet. Vatican security officials had assured the Patriarch that the threat didn't seem credible even as they outlined the extra precautions they'd taken.

As Father Fortis stood in line leading to the metal detectors, he couldn't help but remember the assassination attempt on Pope John Paul II in this very square in 1981. While that had brought major changes to Vatican security, he couldn't stop assessing how an assassin might still succeed. He studied the people in front of him in line, all having tickets which entitled them to one of the chairs closest to the canopy set in front of the basilica. Father Fortis realized that someone planning a sensational murder might manage to secure one of those tickets, but he didn't think it likely.

But what about the thousands without tickets who'll stand toward the back in the square? he asked himself. Then, looking over the top of Bernini's columns to the hills of Rome beyond, he thought, *Is even that distance beyond the range of a sniper?*

He took out his photo ID badge and placed its cord around his neck as he arrived at the metal detectors and the guards manning them. *My worrying isn't going to change a thing,* he told himself as he turned his attention to the other piece of information that Patriarch Michael had shared with him the day before.

In that conversation, Father Fortis was stunned to learn that the new Pope and new Ecumenical Patriarch had been fellow doctoral students at one of Rome's universities back in the nineties.

"That's a little-known fact some enterprising journalist is bound to uncover sooner or later," Patriarch Michael had said. "Serg and I were friends, friends who joked about converting one another, as I remember."

Father Fortis knew that Ecumenical Patriarch Michael and Pope Gregorio were not the first in the line of popes and patriarchs who'd formed a bond of friendship. Father Fortis knew that many of the most conservative Orthodox and Catholic hierarchs, those in power in the two Churches, would be surprised to know how many popes and patriarchs had prayed regularly for each other. And he still remembered the previous Ecumenical Patriarch, Bartholomew, being invited to pray over Pope John Paul II's body at his funeral, a sight beamed around the world. On "sunny days" of Catholic-Orthodox relations, such as today's feast day, Pope John Paul II's description of the Catholic and Orthodox communions as the "two lungs" of the ancient Church, meant to breathe together, seemed nearly achievable.

But not all days were so sunny. Deep theological differences between Catholics and Orthodox remained, leading Father Fortis to wonder what the new Pope, Gregorio, had in mind when he'd requested a private meeting with the Patriarch after today's ceremony.

Father Fortis appreciated why Patriarch Michael never made his friendship with the Pope public. Yes, there would be some leaders in both Churches like Father Fortis, who would be cheered by the news. On the other side, however, would be the hierarchs who'd be apoplectic with the revelation. Even further to the right would be the conspiratorial types who'd imagine a diabolical plot that brought these two former friends into the highest offices in their churches at nearly the same moment.

Until Patriarch Michael told him about the friendship, Father Fortis had heard only rumors of an opposite nature. Before being elected to the papacy just months before and taking the name Pope Gregorio, Sergius had been Cardinal of Kiev in the Ukraine. In the decades after the fall of the Soviet Empire, the Ukraine became a region known for bitter accusations and recriminations between Catholics and Orthodox. One Orthodox pundit suggested that the Catholic Church's elevation of a Ukrainian Catholic cardinal to the papacy signaled a hardening of anti-Orthodox attitudes.

All those rumors dissipated like smoke when Father Fortis heard the tender way Patriarch Michael had uttered the name Serg. He thought it likely that the upcoming meeting between the two leaders would produce yet another pledge to pursue closer relations, but he wondered if the meeting would lead to something more substantial.

Father Fortis hadn't even been born in 1964 when relations between the two Churches first changed for the better. That was when Pope Paul VI and Ecumenical Patriarch Athenagoras met in Jerusalem and embraced, that gesture ending nearly nine hundred years of mutual anathemas. *But how much progress has been made in the sixty years since that historic gesture,* Father Fortis wondered. Yes, there were public expressions of goodwill such as this feast day of Saints Peter and Paul, but the journey toward reconciliation had too often stalled because of thorny theological disagreements.

Father Fortis' musings ended when he located his reserved seat among other invited Orthodox bishops and metropolitans. Many he recognized were from North America, reflecting Michael's own background as the previous Archbishop of North America and earlier, as the Metropolitan-Bishop of Detroit. The surprise in the group was the appearance of one of the abbots from a monastery on Mt. Athos in Greece. Mt. Athos tended to be the hotbed of conservative Orthodox thought, and denunciations of the Catholic Church continued to emerge from that isolated spot despite the historic embrace between the Pope and Ecumenical Patriarch in 1964. The conservatives among the Orthodox wouldn't be satisfied until a pope came to Mt. Athos on his knees to beg for forgiveness.

Keep your friends close and your enemies closer, Father Fortis thought. Was that why Patriarch Michael had invited the abbot from Mt. Athos to Rome? He

watched as the abbot ignored the cardinals and monsignors who were slowly filling in the larger Catholic section. *So much for Christian charity*, Father
Fortis mused.

Father Fortis' fears about security eased as the beauty and pageantry of the
service unfolded. The celebration began with the seating of Pope Gregorio and
Patriarch Michael, each with a crozier, or staff, indicating authority. Neither
gave any hint of their shared past friendship, which didn't surprise Father
Fortis. The service, after all, was a formal occasion.

The sun overhead was shielded for a moment by a passing cloud. A cool
breeze wafted over the square, and Father Fortis no longer felt his black robes
sticking to his skin. He was struck once again by how the differences between
the two Churches were reflected in their vestments. The Orthodox wore basic,
though flowing, black robes, with metropolitan-bishops and patriarchs adding
golden robes that could weigh another ten pounds. It would take a strong wind
to cause those robes to billow.

In contrast, the Catholic cardinals, monsignors, archbishops, and bishops
wore red or crimson robes with lacy white albs. The slight breeze of the moment
was lifting their robes like sails. Even Pope Gregorio, clad in white, seemed
buoyant compared to the gold-encased Patriarch Michael seated next to him.

Heavy and light, black and white—were those preferences of costume sug-
gestive of inner differences? Was the traditionalism of the Orthodox Church
proof of its loyalty to the faith of the Apostles, or was it evidence of a kind of
frozenness in time? Similarly, was the Catholic Church's willingness to change,
especially since Vatican II in the mid-sixties, a responding to the winds of
change, or rather a never-ending reaction to Western culture?

For a moment, Father Fortis felt the heavy burden of history and the over-
whelming differences between the two Churches. *What if the two Churches
could never agree?* he asked himself.

Maybe that worry, one related to theology rather than security, was what
brought tears to his eyes when the gospel was read. Two deacons, one Catholic
and one Orthodox, approached matching podiums to read the text from the
gospel of John. It was a text Father Fortis knew well, where Jesus prayed that
His Church to be united. As Father Fortis heard the text first in Greek and then
in Latin, he thought, *This is what the future should hold, each Church loyal to her
distinctive traditions but blessing the other.*

The sun reappeared in all its intensity as if heaven agreed. His optimism was
interrupted, however, by a sudden stirring in the crowd. Everyone seemed to
be pointing to something off to the west. Father Fortis looked over his shoulder
and saw an object hovering above the square. The object, obviously metallic, in
the shape of an X, and with a fluttering tail, flew from over Bernini's columns
toward the obelisk in the square's center.

As soon as Father Fortis realized everyone was looking at a drone, he felt a wave of anger. *A stunt*, he thought. *A stunt by the media.* Drones came in all sizes, from the military type that resembled a small plane to the cheap, toy-sized ones favored by children. The drone hovering over St. Peter's Square seemed mid-sized, each of its four arms about two feet long.

As he wondered what the uninvited object would do next, Father Fortis remembered a recent notorious flyover of such a device, the one that halted a soccer match in England when fireworks on the drone detonated and sent a cascade of colors down on the pitch. In all the cases Father Fortis could remember, publicity-hungry newspapers or techy companies had been responsible for the annoying occurrences.

Father Fortis glanced at the Pope and Patriarch underneath the canopy and saw Pope Gregorio gesture to the deacons to proceed, even as security personnel moved behind the two men. Several of the hierarchs seated nearby stirred nervously, with some rising from their seats.

Yes, Father Fortis thought, *don't let these tricksters have the satisfaction of stopping this event. Ignore the drone, and it will soon fly off.*

The buzz in the crowd, however, didn't subside as the Orthodox deacon continued to intone the gospel reading in Greek. Sensing the challenge facing him, the deacon chanted louder, but the drone continued to hover over the obelisk, red lights blinking, its tail sporting words in Italian that danced in the breeze. Suddenly, with a speed not shown until that moment, the drone seemed to make up its mind. As it shot toward the canopy, Father Fortis and others present there received a clear view of the drone with its two intersecting arms and its hovering blades.

"This stunt has gone too far," Father Fortis uttered aloud just before the drone landed on the front of the canopy. The last sounds Father Fortis heard before everything went black were the shards of metal and fabric debris from the canopy falling around him accompanied by screams from those under the canopy.

CHAPTER TWO

Mr. Demetrius Angelopoulos stared dumbly at the package on the floor of the mailroom. He still felt groggy from the anesthetic his dentist had administered that afternoon, and, at first, he had no memory of the package. Only when the fog in his head began to clear did he remember with a groan that the item had arrived four days earlier.

So, he wondered, had the package somehow fallen off the mailroom shelf? While the return address was smudged beyond recognition, he could make out that the postage had been paid on Hydra, a Greek island not far from Athens that was the ancestral home of Patriarch Michael. Turning the package over, he uttered a second groan when he saw that the package had been stamped with the Greek word for "perishable." This would not be the first time that the Patriarch's distant relatives had sent him almond pastries, one of the island's specialties.

He nodded to himself as it dawned on him how the package had been mislaid. For the last week, the Phanar, the headquarters of the Ecumenical Patriarch, had been consumed by Patriarch Michael's trip to Rome. The halls had been buzzing, voices expressing mixed hopes that the visit would go well or fail miserably.

Mr. Angelopoulos gingerly felt his jaw. The right side of his face felt swollen, and he had difficulty resisting his tongue's desire to visit the crater left by the extracted molar. He looked at his watch. It was nearly four o'clock, late afternoon in Istanbul, stubbornly still called Constantinople by the Orthodox. In fewer than fifteen minutes, he would be sitting down over glasses of retsina wine with Father Timos, who would fill him in on the gossip that he'd missed that afternoon.

Forgetting how long the dentist had told him to avoid alcohol, Mr. Angelopoulos reasoned that a glass of wine couldn't hurt. Anyway, he'd take the bus rather than drive home to his wife and their supper. But as he turned the package over, he admitted to himself that he was hungry now. Eating a few of the pastries shouldn't be a problem if he chewed slowly and carefully on the other side of his mouth. Anyway, the Patriarch would hardly want the contents to go bad.

He heard the slow and methodical steps of Father Timos, his closest friend, coming down from the third floor chapel to meet him. He smiled at the surprise it would give Father Timos when he showed him the almond treats. He fiddled for a moment trying to untie the package's string, but his hands were still a bit shaky from the anesthetic. Using scissors, he cut away the string and lifted the package to his nose. *Funny, I don't smell almonds,* he thought.

Mr. Angelopoulos pulled away the paper and saw that the container was a shoebox that had been taped securely. Again using the scissors, he cut the tape on one end and raised the lid halfway.

Mr. Angelopoulos' eyes melted before he could see what was nestled beneath the padding in the shoebox. The explosion removed all traces of his smile, his beaked nose, his front teeth, upper and lower, and his still-numb jaw. His faceless body was thrown across the room where it twitched and continued to spasm even after Father Timos managed to open the door of the smoke-filled mailroom. The smell in the room was not of almonds, but of burning flesh.

CHAPTER THREE

---◆---

JUNE 29: DETROIT

AFTER FOUR DAYS OF RAIN IN DETROIT, Christopher Worthy felt the gloom had settled in his bones. What awaited him in precinct headquarters was a dark cloud of a different sort, one he'd been under for the past two weeks.

He should have expected the inevitable to happen. Nine years before, he'd worked with Father Fortis on the homicide of an elderly priest. Father Fortis had testified at the killer's trial, his testimony along with Worthy's providing the key evidence that sent the accused away for life.

The accused's team of lawyers had now petitioned for a retrial on the grounds that their client's hypothetical admission of any crime to Father Fortis should have been protected under priest-confessor privilege. Without Father Fortis' testimony, the killer's lawyers could argue that there was no hard evidence linking their client to the elderly priest's death. And because of the accused's previous status in the community, the petition for retrial had become a front-page story in the media. Worthy's old nemesis in the department, Lieutenant Phillip Sherrod, had quickly weighed in on the conversation, offering his own perspective that Worthy, in acting on what Father Fortis claimed to have heard from the killer, had clearly violated the rights of the accused. Worthy considered the lawsuit frivolous and consequently remained mute when the media outlets sought his response.

A follow-up story on the impact of the accused's incarceration on the family had noticeably swayed public opinion. The story centered on the oldest son's overdose of fentanyl, a tragedy the family believed could be traced to the father's unlawful conviction. The police commissioner's first comment, that he stood squarely behind Worthy's handling of the case, changed quickly. Now, the commissioner's office was saying that the department would not comment further on the case at this time. Worthy could only shake his head when he heard of the department's flip-flop on the ten-o'clock news.

The next day, the family's lawyers announced they were suing Worthy for procedural misconduct and Father Fortis for violating privileged information. The lawyers demanded that Worthy be placed on administrative leave until the case could be retried. To Worthy's surprise, the department refused to comply.

Nevertheless, the lawsuit that Worthy believed should have been immediately dismissed wasn't. This meant that he spent more time in the captain's office than at his own desk. In those meetings, he sat across the table from the commissioner, the departmental lawyers, Internal Affairs, and the department's public relations officer. He was tired of the endless "what ifs" that he was forced to answer, not to mention the numerous excerpts of TV coverage that he was forced to watch. Most of all, he hated the odious phrase "maybe we can tweak the story a bit if you'd say x, y, or z to the press." Nobody seemed to believe him when he said that he had no intention of commenting on the case. Over and over, Worthy argued that he'd break his silence in the trial but not before.

That late morning when he arrived at the precinct, Worthy deliberately avoided looking down the hallway in the direction of Captain Betts' office. How he wished he could somehow focus on the current case assigned to him, ironically that of a trucker who'd either overdosed or been helped to overdose at a truck stop out on I-69, also with fentanyl. In his world of homicide, such a case seemed the closest thing to "normal." What had happened years before on the elderly's priest murder case was just that—something that was long past and could never be changed no matter how often it was rehashed. But Worthy had only managed to hang up his sport coat before he heard Captain Betts call his name.

What if he refused, he wondered. What if he said, "Enough is enough; do with me what you want, but I'm done with this." He seriously considered that option, but decided that such words needed to be said face to face.

As he entered Captain Betts' office, he was surprised to see a group huddled around a TV screen. Captain Betts saw him and told the others to let Worthy through. Sherrod was the last to give way, and he did so grudgingly. *Now what are the lawyers up to?* Worthy thought.

In an instant, he realized his error. On the screen were photos of Father Fortis and Ecumenical Patriarch Michael. Above their photos were their names; behind them as backdrop, a postcard view of St. Peter's Basilica in Rome; and below their photos, a trail of words scrolled across the bottom of the screen. "Church leaders caught in bomb blast in Rome. Conditions unknown. Early reports from Vatican describe tragedy and chaos at religious festival; at least two dead, identities unknown."

Worthy grabbed at the corner of the captain's desk to keep from falling.

"Worthy, what can you tell us?" he heard someone ask him. The question was repeated, now from a voice he recognized as Captain Betts'.

What do I know? he thought. He took a deep breath and tried to slow his racing thoughts. "I knew that Nick—I mean Father Fortis—was going to Rome. I knew that he was set to be with the Patriarch at the Vatican for some big deal, some feast. When did this happen?"

As if to answer his question, the words at the bottom of the screen changed. "Time of bomb's detonation: 3:00 pm Italian time. Preliminary reports suggest a drone delivery of the bomb. Two confirmed dead; many others wounded."

As his daughter Allyson once derisively said, "My father is in the death business," and she was right. His chosen career brought him routinely to kneel over corpses—some shot, some knifed, some strangled, some run over by automobiles, some poisoned, and some partially decomposed.

For almost every case, Worthy had been able to fend off the chill of death by treating his cases as puzzles deserving a just solution. That was the best gift he could give the victims and their families. If he couldn't remain detached, he knew he'd be worthless.

But one case had been the exception. A little over a decade before, his career tumbled down what seemed to be never-ending stairs. On the very day when he arrested the Eagle Scout who had killed the young prostitute, his wife of nearly twenty years had walked out on him, and their marriage ended. In the months that followed, as he tried to adjust to the tiny apartment where he slept, watched one video after another, and drank more than was helpful, he slowly realized that the face in the mirror was that of another victim, someone who'd had the life he'd known ripped away.

It was only in meeting Nick, known as Father Nicholas Fortis to the world, that he'd let another person into the tight confines of his new life—the routine of rising, showering, driving to work, trying with varying success to concentrate on the case before him, driving home, microwaving a dinner, pouring Scotch or Rye, lying down on the second-hand couch, pouring more Scotch or Rye, watching a video, and, as often as not, falling asleep on that couch rather than in bed. He dreamt quite often of being with his wife and daughters again, their life as it had been: going on trips, fishing at the cabin up north, or—and this was when he would wake up—when he was about to be caressed by his wife.

Staring now at the screen in those first moments and trying to imagine Nick as one of the casualties, Worthy felt abandoned again. And that made him instantly angry—angry at the world, angry at whoever had set off the bomb, and angry at himself for focusing on himself. His closest friend could be in some hospital fighting for his life, or he could be one of the two dead, his body lying in some morgue in Rome.

Worthy felt dizzy with the questions circling around him. "Where would Father Fortis have been seated at such an event?" "Where was the epicenter of the blast?" "How soon would the Vatican confirm or deny if the Pope has been assassinated?" "Could a terrorist group have drones?" "We hear bells tolling in the background—what does that mean?" The worst part was that he felt every question was being directed at him, and he had an answer for none of them.

"Worthy," the department's public relations officer said, "The press keep calling, wanting to know what you can tell them. This time, please, will you talk to them?"

The room grew quiet, waiting for Worthy's response. "Tell them I've heard nothing. Tell them they know more than I do."

Captain Betts looked sternly at Worthy. "Chris, you owe the public this. You know Father Fortis better than anyone. Tell them what he was like . . . what he *is* like," she commanded.

He waded through the crowded room, feeling that he could clear his head if he could just get away from the screen with its ever-repeating words scrolling at the bottom. Catching up with the department's P.R. person, he followed her down the hall to her office. On the walls were headlines praising accomplishments of the precinct. Worthy could see that two with the largest headlines included his name, but now he only felt numb.

"Can I just give a statement?" he asked.

The middle-aged woman nodded as she sat behind a desk. "A statement is fine in the short run," she said. "But when we get further news, they'll want more, probably some on-air interviews."

"How do I know they won't turn an interview back to the other case?" Worthy countered. "I'm not commenting on that."

"Look, Lieutenant, we've both dealt with the media long enough to know we can't predict what they might ask. But I don't think you have to worry about that today. This bomb story is something global with a significant local connection. You might recall that Patriarch Michael was once Metropolitan-Bishop of Detroit."

Worthy sat down and rubbed his chin, his mind empty. He couldn't shake the idea that he might be composing Nick's obituary.

The P.R. director looked over her half-glasses at Worthy. "How about I ask you some basic questions, and then I'll cut and paste to make an initial statement?"

Worthy nodded in agreement.

"Okay, I'm going to record our conversation, Lieutenant. That's standard procedure for accuracy." She pushed a digital recorder across her desk in Worthy's direction. "Let's start with some easy ones. How long have you known Father Nicholas Fortis?"

Worthy's brain couldn't seem to understand the simple question. Or maybe the truth was that he could hardly remember when Father Fortis hadn't been in his life. "That would be about ten years, I guess."

"Good, ten years. And Father Fortis has helped on several homicide cases, is that right?"

The lump rising in his throat made it difficult to answer. Finally, he was able to collect himself. "Yes, I think we've worked at least six cases together."

"I'm sure you've been asked this many times, but how did your partnership . . . your friendship begin, Lieutenant?"

Why __did__ I let a Greek Orthodox monk into my life? Worthy asked himself. It certainly had nothing to do with wanting some priest rooting around in his spiritual life. His bankrupt faith had remained unfunded, and Nick had always seemed to respect that. And their seemingly odd relationship was certainly not based on any likeness between the two. If Nick had been repeatedly reprimanded by his abbot for his gregariousness as well as his girth, Worthy had been censored for his propensity to communicate less and less as a case unfolded.

No, the reason for their partnership was harder to explain. On their first case, when the body of one of Father Fortis' fellow monk had been found floating in a river, Worthy had found himself consulting Father Fortis more and more as the case went on. And almost immediately, Worthy recognized that Nick's tendency to chatter with one and all never led him to spill confidential information. Rather, Nick's talkativeness was his cover, his way of gauging others while hiding what needed to remain hidden.

The P.R. director broke into his thoughts. "Let me put it this way. What would you say that Father Fortis has contributed to solving those cases?"

Worthy appreciated that the P.R. director had glossed over the fact that their third case together had been the one related to the recent lawsuit. He looked out the window at the dark clouds scuttling by. "What has Nick contributed? Well, that's not easy to describe." He paused for a moment, and then the words seemed to flow without thought. "Nick has an unusual ability to feel compassion not just for the victim and the victim's family, but also for the perpetrator. He doesn't excuse the killer, but he doesn't demonize that person either. Whenever we solved a case, Nick never gloated. That a case was closed didn't change the fact for Nick that the suffering was far from over."

"I'm not sure we should share that," the P.R. director said. "People want justice. Mercy for killers doesn't go over very well."

Worthy turned his attention back to the woman. If this was going to be a eulogy for his friend, then he was going to make it an honest one. "No, I think that is exactly what we should let people know about Nick."

CHAPTER FOUR

————◆————

JUNE 29: ROME: THE HOSPITAL OF SANTI ANGELI

FATHER FORTIS AWOKE TO FIND HIMSELF strapped to a gurney in the back of a racing ambulance. It took him a few moments to remember that he was in Rome and that he'd been attending a service in St. Peter's Square. To be in an ambulance, to hear voices around him echoing as if from deep in a cave, and to taste blood meant that something traumatic had happened. But what? He wanted to ask the ambulance attendants to fill him in, but English wasn't what he was hearing.

Slowly, the events of the afternoon returned. He lurched up from the gurney and called out, "What happened to the Patriarch and Pope?"

"Che?" one of the medical staff asked. "No speak English."

At the hospital, Father Fortis saw the staff bustling from one gurney to another. *All victims from St. Peter's?* he asked himself. After a wait of about ten minutes, he was checked out by a team of doctors and nurses. By the way the doctor kept checking the movement of his eyes, he suspected that he had a concussion. He pointed to his neck, which was also sore.

He was propped up in bed in a room with two other men and told in broken English that he would be spending the night at the hospital. "Precaution, precaution," the nurse who had the best English told him.

Two hours later, he was awakened by the same nurse to find two tall men in suits standing by the side of the bed. "Father Fortis, we're from the American Consulate. Do you feel up to answering a few questions?"

When the nurse objected, Father Fortis gave his permission. "Before we do that," he said, "will you please tell me what happened to Patriarch Michael and Pope Gregorio?"

"Certainly, sir," the older of the men replied. "Security men threw themselves on them both just before the blast. The Patriarch and the Pope are uninjured."

"And the security? What about them?"

"Injured with shrapnel, but nothing serious," the other American added.

"So no one was killed?"

The two men paused and looked at one another. The older one nodded to the younger. "Two people under the canopy were killed in the blast. They were the two standing toward the front."

Father Fortis groaned. "At the podiums?"

"Apparently so, sir. One was a young man from Greece; the other was a young man from Italy. Neither American, but still, most unfortunate."

Father Fortis made the sign of the cross and said a prayer for the two deacons. So young, no doubt feeling honored to have such prominent roles in the service. And their families had probably been watching on TV.

"Father Fortis, can you tell us what you remember? Besides the drone, was there anything else that seemed odd?" the older of the two asked.

Father Fortis tried to recall what happened just before the blast. "I think several on the platform party moved away when the drone approached."

"Catholic or Orthodox priests?" the younger one asked.

It seems to Father Fortis that the two were alternating questions. "I can't exactly remember," he said.

"Maybe more details will come back to you later," the older one added. "We know you've been with the Ecumenical Patriarch since he's been in Rome. Did the Patriarch express any reservations about attending this service today?"

Father Fortis shook his head. "Not really. He was looking forward to it."

"Nothing he was alarmed about?" The older one asked out of turn.

Father Fortis' head was aching. He sighed and repeated his previous comment.

The younger man now stepped forward. "Just one more question, sir. Did the Patriarch seem relieved to be away from Istanbul?"

"We refer to the city as Constantinople," Father Fortis said. "And why would he want to be away from the Patriarchate?"

"His headquarters in Constantinople, you mean. That's the Phanar, right?" the younger one pursued his line of questions.

"Yes, that's its formal title, but how did you know? And why is that important?"

The two men exchanged glances again, and the younger one coughed. The older one delivered the news. "The Patriarchate was bombed this afternoon, not long after the bomb in St. Peter's Square."

"What? That's not possible."

"Yes, it is possible, sir. A mailroom worker was killed in the blast."

Father Fortis held up his hand to halt the questioning. He offered a silent prayer for the victim before looking up. "Do you think a group like ISIS could have done both?" he asked.

"What makes you say that, sir?" the younger one asked. "Did the Patriarch or anyone else say they were worried about an attack from that kind of group?"

"Not exactly," Father Fortis replied. "Vatican security said there'd been threats on the Internet, but nothing out of the ordinary. So it wasn't some group like ISIS?"

"No one has taken credit," the older man cut in. "And we'd ask that you don't share your speculation with the press."

Father Fortis didn't answer, but nodded his agreement. "I need to rest, gentlemen," he said.

"Of course, of course," the younger one replied. He stepped forward and laid a folded sheet of paper on the bed. "This is a message from Patriarch Michael. He asked me to give it to you."

"Thank you, gentlemen. I assume I'll be seeing you again."

The two men left the room. Father Fortis wanted desperately for his head to stop pounding, so he could return to sleep. But before that, he reached for the piece of paper.

He unfolded the sheet and read the three words sent by the Patriarch.

"I want Worthy."

JUNE 29: DETROIT: ALONE WITH A BOTTLE OF SCOTCH

WORTHY SAT AT THE EDGE OF his sofa with an unopened bottle of Scotch in front of him. He'd been staring at the bottle for two hours. To open the bottle would be to wash away the last ten years and return to the half-life that he was then enduring. To open the bottle would be to tell the lawyers in the lawsuit against him to take their best shot.

Now might be the time to resign, he thought. "And do what?" he asked himself. In the immediate wake of his divorce, the question hadn't been "Should I resign?" but "Will I be fired?" He had come close to that outcome, with the worst part of that living nightmare being the way he embraced the booze and the booze embraced him.

"So why is this bottle still unopened?" he said to the empty room as he rose and walked to the window. He wondered if he hadn't opened the bottle because he doubted he could keep Scotch or anything else down. He turned toward the table and addressed the bottle. "Maybe when the pain sets in tomorrow or the day after, I'll be back."

The real reason for his sobriety was that he didn't want to accept that Nick could be gone. He was not superstitious nor any longer religious, but he owed it to someone or something to stay hopeful.

He had tried to sleep but only managed to doze on the sofa. He lay awake for another hour before he found the strength to turn on CNN. Just as the commercial break was over, his phone rang.

His heart raced as he answered and heard his name. Nobody would call him at five in the morning except for life-or-death news. Maybe it was his daughter Allyson, who was serving in the FBI somewhere and would have heard about the attack. But it was a voice he knew very well, yet not so clear as to remove all doubt for the first few seconds.

"Christopher, is that you?" the voice repeated.

Worthy bent over and tried to stifle a sob. "Christopher, it's Nick. Are you there? Hello?"

"Just a minute, Nick," he managed to say and then pulled the phone away from his ear. *Nick is alive. Nick is alive. Nick is alive.* Until that moment, he hadn't admitted how sure he was that his friend was dead. "Another minute, Nick," he said.

"Are you all right, Christopher?" Father Fortis said on the other end of the line.

"Nobody told us what happened, Nick." He looked at his TV screen and read that the dead were identified as two deacons who were participants in the service. "Until this minute, we thought you might have . . . you might not have made it."

"Christopher, my friend, I'm so sorry. Two did die, but they were—"

"The deacons," Worthy said, finishing the sentence. "Are the Pope and the Patriarch okay?"

"Yes, thank God. Just very shaken by the day. I've seen a number of the injured here in the hospital."

"So, you are injured, Nick?"

"Nothing serious, my friend. A minor concussion and a sore neck. It's ten in the morning here, and I'm expecting to be released before noon. You can reach me at the Maximillian Kolbe Hotel. That's across the street from where Patriarch Michael is staying."

Worthy had no idea who Maximillian Kolbe was, but he didn't care. After a moment, he did manage to say, "I assume that you'll be coming back home as soon as possible."

"I guess you haven't heard all the news then, Christopher."

"All I've heard is what's been on the TV. What else are you talking about?"

"More sadness, my friend. Christopher, the Patriarch's headquarters in Constantinople was bombed soon after the explosion at St. Peter's."

"What? Are you saying the Patriarch was the real target of both attacks?"

Worthy could hear other voices in the background, in what sounded like Italian.

"No one knows, and that's the real reason I'm calling. I have a message from the Patriarch. Because of what happened at the Patriarchate, the American

Consulate gave him a choice: he can stay here in Rome under heavy protection or fly to the States. For many reasons, the Patriarch has chosen to remain in Rome where he would be closer, at least, to Constantinople."

"You said there's a message for me, Nick."

"Sorry, my friend, my head is still groggy. Patriarch Michael has asked you to come to Rome; he wants your expertise. I know that we're both named in that crazy lawsuit, but can you get away?"

Worthy rose from the couch and turned off the TV. *Can I take a break from Detroit and the media circus swirling around the lawsuit? In a heartbeat,* he thought.

"They're telling me to hang up, Christopher. The doctors want to look me over. Will you at least think it over, my friend? The Patriarch is in dire need of someone he can trust."

Before Worthy could answer, the line went dead. He returned to the table by the sofa and retrieved the bottle of Scotch. In the kitchen, he opened the bottle and poured its contents down the sink. "There goes the best fifty bucks I've ever wasted," he said as he dumped the bottle in the trash. "And I hope I never see the likes of you again."

CHAPTER FIVE

•———————•

JULY 1: ROME: ABBEY OF THE THREE FOUNTAINS

WHEN FATHER FORTIS AWOKE TWO DAYS later, he took stock of his body before letting the confusing thoughts and questions flood back in. His neck's slight whiplash had eased with the prescribed muscle relaxants. Today, even though he still had headaches, he wouldn't bother with the neck brace.

He now knew that he would likely be in Rome as long as the Patriarch chose to stay. The housing arrangements were convenient, Father Fortis remaining at the Maximillian Kolbe Hotel while Patriarch Michael was lodged across the street in an apartment connected to the church of San Teodoro. That ancient 6th century church had been a gift from Pope John Paul II to the Greek Orthodox community in Rome in 2000, evidence of one of those sunny periods of Catholic-Orthodox relations. In his apartment, the Patriarch would be protected by bodyguards, both Americans and Italians, at least six of them always on duty whenever Father Fortis was called to a meeting with the Patriarch.

So far, no one had accepted blame or credit for the incidents in Rome and Istanbul. Middle Eastern terrorist groups had, however, praised whoever had "struck at the roots of the Christian heresy." While such groups couldn't be eliminated from consideration, their responses were uncharacteristic and raised the possibility that the attack was planned and carried out by someone unknown.

While the global news cycle had moved on from the Rome and Constantinople incidents, Father Fortis felt time stand still in his personal world. The media interviews were over, but he'd been visited by one intelligence agency after another over the past two days. The Italians had dedicated at least twenty investigators to the crisis; the Greek government had sent a team of four; the Vatican officials had interviewed him each day, hoping that he would remember more of what had happened from his vantage point; and then there were the Americans, the ever-present Americans.

Father Fortis stepped out of the bed slowly and looked out the window to another sunny Rome morning. He showered and offered his morning prayers, aware that in an hour he had to accompany the Patriarch to another meeting scheduled with Vatican officials. Father Fortis wondered if the Patriarch was as tired of the questions as he. He ended his morning prayers, asking for safe travel for Christopher Worthy, arriving later that day. *Perhaps Worthy's coming will be mentioned during the morning's meeting*, he thought.

Father Fortis had breakfast before walking across the street to the church of San Teodoro. After showing his credentials, he knocked on the door of the Patriarch's apartment. As Father Fortis entered the room, he found Patriarch Michael in a whispered conversation with a man he didn't recognize.

"Ah, Nicholas, yes, please come in. I want you to meet George Pappas, one of our lawyers from the United States. George has kindly offered his services more than once to the Phanar."

A middle-aged man, clean-shaven, with graying hair and a slight paunch, approached Father Fortis. He bent down, out of respect, to kiss Father Fortis' hand, though his expression showed no sign of pleasure in their meeting.

"It is an honor, Father. I know of the high esteem in which you are held by His Holiness."

He certainly speaks like a lawyer, Father Fortis thought, *but which kind?*

"I pray the Phanar in Constantinople is secure," Father Fortis said.

The man nodded his assurance. "The Patriarchate is safe. The authorities say they are hunting the culprit or culprits, but, based on the Turkish government's responses to previous violence, we don't hold out much hope."

Father Fortis could see that the Patriarch was monitoring their conversation.

"Mr. Pappas, are you part of our legal representation with the Turkish authorities?" Father Fortis asked.

Mr. Pappas shook his head. "No, I'm not that kind of attorney. I'm a canon lawyer."

Father Fortis looked over at the Patriarch, who returned his look with a raised eyebrow. *Interesting*, Father Fortis thought. Part lawyer, part theologian, Mr. Pappas was an expert on Orthodox Church law.

"Are you in Rome in your official capacity, Mr. Pappas, or here to relay conditions at the Phanar?"

The lawyer shrugged in a gesture of neutrality but avoided Father Fortis' gaze. "Maybe a bit of this, a bit of that."

Father Fortis would ask the Patriarch later, but he sensed the lawyer was being coy.

"Mr. Pappas will be joining us today at the meeting," the Patriarch explained.

There was another knock on the door, and a new face appeared. "The car is here, Your All Holiness."

The car? Father Fortis thought. *The meeting won't be here?*

In the limousine, the Patriarch asked the Vatican official in the passenger seat if the meeting would be at St. Peter's. The man answered in English with a German accent. "The Holy Father said you'd remember the place. Apparently the two of you have been there before."

Patriarch Michael smiled but didn't say anything. In contrast, the canon lawyer retained his stony expression as the limousine came to the end of the narrow street where it was met by two other black cars. One of the vehicles preceded and one followed as they headed away from the heart of the city. Father Fortis recognized some of the oldest parts of Rome, but not the neighborhoods they were passing.

After a half hour of dealing with the honking of cars and the whine of scooters, the three vehicles approached a quieter neighborhood of the city. The only landmark that Father Fortis recognized was the Basilica of St. Paul's Outside the Walls, a massive church that housed the relics of the Apostle Paul. But the cars passed the basilica without slowing, proceeding further west until they came to an open gate in a high wall.

"Nicholas, have you ever been here?" the Patriarch asked.

"Oh, yes. This is one my favorite places in Rome."

"A Catholic site," Mr. Pappas observed.

"Abbazia della Tre Fontane, the Abbey of Three Fountains," Patriarch Michael said without commenting on Mr. Pappas' observation.

The driveway curved to the left and approached a medieval stone archway. Beyond, Father Fortis could see a complex of buildings, which he knew were three ancient churches. The noise of Rome seemed miles away.

In a small parking area to the left, the limousine's doors were opened by waiting men with earpieces. Behind them stood two men with assault rifles. As Father Fortis exited the vehicle, he could see other armed men positioned discreetly around the grounds. One of the men with an earpiece approached Patriarch Michael and bowed in respect before speaking to him in a low voice. The Patriarch nodded and turned to the others. "Before we have our meeting, we have time to take a short walk around. Gentlemen, we are not here by happenstance," he said, as he led the others toward the small church closest to the medieval archway. "We are in a special place, a holy place for all Christians, Mr. Pappas."

Over the next half-hour, the Patriarch guided Mr. Pappas and Father Fortis around the grounds and inside the three churches. He explained that the first small chapel was built over the cell where St. Paul had been imprisoned. The second church was where the Pretorian guards were housed. Some of those, the Patriarch pointed out, were converted by the apostle.

But it was the third church at the end of a long path bordered by eucalyptus trees and boxwood that the Patriarch was intent on visiting. As the three entered through the door, Father Fortis heard the sound of running water. It had been several years since he'd been in this church, but Father Fortis immediately felt at home.

The three men stood before a grate from which they could hear flowing water. Father Fortis knew they would find a similar grate in the middle and at the end of the far wall. He waited for the Patriarch to explain the odd sounds to Mr. Pappas.

"According to tradition, when St. Paul was beheaded, right here, his blessed head dropped to the floor and bounced three times. At each of the three spots, a fountain began to flow."

Outside, Patriarch Michael inhaled deeply before turning to Mr. Pappas. "George, I would be interested in your impressions of this place."

Creases appeared on the lawyer's forehead as he looked from where they were standing back down the pathway to the other two churches and the medieval archway. After a moment, he turned back toward the Patriarch. "Rome for me is too noisy, but I can see how visitors would find relief, some peace, in this place."

"But it's a site of incredible suffering, George, is it not?" the Patriarch asked with a slight smile. "St. Paul, let us remember, could very well have spent his last living minute right near where we're standing. How can such a place be peaceful?"

"I'm sure I don't know," Mr. Pappas replied, his tone implying that he wasn't that interested in the question or the place.

"What do you think, Nicholas?"

After a moment's pause, Father Fortis replied, "I believe it's the faith of the apostle we feel. I believe he died in complete calm."

The Patriarch closed his eyes as if soaking in the peace of the place. "That's why we graduate students at the university always welcomed the chance to visit this place. We even took one of our student-led retreats here. Here at Tre Fontane, love overcame fear and hate, and that love can still be felt. I want you to remember that, Mr. Pappas."

The lawyer stared dumbly at the Patriarch. "Sorry, I don't quite see your point."

Patriarch Michael approached the lawyer and placed a hand on his shoulder. "There is no peace, George, without love, and that love must be sacrificial."

From the direction of the medieval gate, a Vatican official approached the three of them and nodded to the Patriarch.

"Yes, yes, lead on," the Patriarch said.

Approaching a set of low buildings, the four entered what was obviously an artist's studio before passing through to a meeting room beyond. Here comfortable chairs formed a semicircle around a small table on which was a lit candle in front of an icon of St. Paul. The official led the Patriarch to one of the two leather chairs before pointing to adjoining ones for George Pappas and Father Fortis.

The Patriarch caught Father Fortis' eye and offered a brief nod. "Patience, Nicholas. Everything will become clear in a few moments."

Father Fortis heard the distant sound of a helicopter and soon realized from the thud-thud of the rotors that it was approaching. A shiver passed down his spine as he remembered the drone hovering over St. Peter's Square. He glanced over to see Patriarch Michael's reaction and detected a slight movement forward in the chair. *He expected this,* he thought.

After a few moments, the copter's blades wound down. The room remained eerily quiet until Father Fortis heard footsteps approach. As the outer door creaked open, Patriarch Michael stood. Mr. Pappas and Father Fortis stood as well, as a tall monsignor led others into the room. It was only when two Vatican officials and the monsignor moved to the side that Father Fortis saw Pope Gregorio, all in white, enter.

The Pope stopped in the entranceway and gazed around the room until he spotted Patriarch Michael. He marched solemnly to stand in front of the Patriarch. For a moment, the two men, standing and holding their croziers, looked as if they might begin jousting. But then they both grinned as they passed their staffs to those sitting nearby.

"Michael, we are back at Tre Fontane," the Pope said as he kissed the Patriarch on each cheek.

"Serg, that we are," the Patriarch replied with a smile. "To see you, especially here, is to turn back the years. Sadly, our hearts are filled with sorrow."

The Pope nodded and closed his eyes. "I am so sorry that security reasons prevented you from attending the funerals of the deacon and the worker in Constantinople. But thank you, thank you, my friend, for attending Deacon Alphonse's funeral here in Rome."

"May their memories by eternal," the Patriarch replied.

"May their memories be eternal," the Pope repeated.

After another moment of silence, the Pope spoke softly, as if the two were oblivious to the others in the room. "Police and others are working without a break to discover who killed our friends and why we were targeted. That's their proper concern. But ours must be different. We must answer another question—'Why did God spare us? Is that not so, my friend?'"

Patriarch Michael responded by embracing the Pope again. Father Fortis could detect tears in both men's eyes.

"You missed my tour of Tre Fontane," the Patriarch said in a brighter tone before turning to introduce Mr. Pappas and Father Fortis. Mr. Pappas' stiff bow seemed perfunctory to Father Fortis, and, perhaps reacting to that, he chose to approach the Pope, bow, kiss his ring and say, "Holy Father, I ask for your blessing."

When Father Fortis heard Mr. Pappas clear his throat behind him, he took it as a reprimand. The Pope made the sign of the cross over Father Fortis and patted him affectionately on his head.

"I deliberately postposed my arrival, Michael, to give you some private moments at Tre Fontane. I come here often to pray, but I don't imagine that you've been here since our student days."

"Yes, this is my first time back, but I was surprised how much I remembered. Only the artist studio we walked through seems new."

"Ah, but this room. Do you remember? This is where Herr Professor Guentzel lectured on our retreats. On 'Redemption,' wasn't it, or was it Marian studies?" the Pope asked.

"No, Serg, you were right the first time. Only he pronounced it *ray-deem-schon*, as I remember."

The Pope's head flew back as he laughed loudly. "Guentzel, Herr Doktor Guentzel, of course. Our professors, at least most of them, have gone on to their heavenly reward." He paused for a moment, then added, "I wonder what they're thinking as they see the two of us sitting here."

"Not to forget what St. Paul is thinking of us," Patriarch Michael added.

"Ah, yes, we are certainly surrounded by the Biblical 'great cloud of witnesses,' are we not?"

The Patriarch nodded and looked solemnly at those assembled in the semicircle. "And we are surrounded by these witnesses here as well. We have Church historians with us, systematic theologians, liturgists, canon lawyers, and monastics, both monks and one nun, I'm happy to see. All different, but I'm sure you all have the same question in mind—'Why are we here?' As a brief word of explanation, let me start by saying that the Holy Father and I have prayed for Ecumenical Patriarch Athenagoras and Pope Paul VI to intercede for us as we come together. They too are part of that great cloud of witnesses of this gathering, and both the Holy Father and I feel the weight, yes, the burden, handed down by that monumental embrace in 1964."

Patriarch Michael nodded in the direction of Pope Gregorio, who spoke next. "Please do not consider what Ecumenical Patriarch Michael just shared as some pious phrasing. It is now almost sixty years since Patriarch Athenagoras and Pope Paul VI, both of blessed memory, met in Jerusalem, the city of Our Lord's Death and Resurrection, to begin to heal the breach between our two Churches. We both share the burden they have bestowed on us: why has so little been accomplished in the last sixty years to bring our two communions into closer friendship?"

Pope Gregorio raised his hand as if to ward off anticipated opposition. "We are not fools, other than fools for Christ's sake, as St. Paul advised. Consequently, we haven't brought you here to announce some secret breakthrough in the dialogue that has been occurring, on and—too often—off, between our best theologians over the years. But we are here together in this holy place, as Patriarch Michael and I once were as fellow students. Circumstances at the Patriarchate in Constantinople remain unstable, and so Patriarch Michael will remain in Rome for perhaps several weeks. We will seize the opportunity of these days for what they are—an incredible opportunity to pray together and seek God's will. We are here at Tre Fontane to follow the leading of the Holy Spirit, wherever that may lead us."

Father Fortis noted George Pappas and several on the Catholic side shifting nervously in their chairs. He knew various leaders of both churches viewed the split between the two churches in 1054 as a divorce, a shattering of relations beyond repair unless one side capitulated completely to the other. In the tense atmosphere, Father Fortis wondered if this pope and ecumenical patriarch, even with the Holy Spirit on their side, could convince their flocks that what happened in 1054 wasn't an irreparable divorce, but rather a tragically long marital separation, one able to be healed.

And then another thought, one more troubling, crossed his mind. *Had the bombs in Rome and Constantinople been meant to thwart such a thaw in the relations of the two Churches? If so, did that mean that someone opposed to progress had tried to assassinate not one, but both supreme leaders of the Christian Church?*

Father Fortis looked around at the faces of those sitting in the semicircle. *Is there a Judas here among us?* he wondered.

CHAPTER SIX

⸺◆⸺

JULY 2: IN FLIGHT, DETROIT TO ROME

CHRISTOPHER WORTHY'S READING MATERIAL ON HIS flight across the Atlantic included notes on the two bombings, the known details of which had been forwarded by Vatican security and the Turkish authorities. There was also a note from Patriarch Michael, delivered to him personally by the Metropolitan of Detroit.

"Dear Lieutenant Worthy,

You are undoubtedly wondering why I request your presence here in Rome. Certainly, there is no shortage of security officials swarming around us, and you might consider yourself an outsider with nothing to contribute. I ask for your help because you are that outsider. We do not know the scope of the horrific attacks in Rome and Constantinople (could there be more?) or, if these attacks are part of a conspiracy, who is behind them.

On a personal note, when I became Metropolitan-Bishop of Detroit in 2016, I learned how you helped our Church by finding Father Spiro's killer. And even from Constantinople, I have kept abreast of the recent lawsuit which has returned you to the media's spotlight. In reviewing all the documents that our Church was given after that tragedy, I found your behavior at the time commendable. You served our Church in the past, and I believe that our Church needs you once again. Of course your expenses will be covered by the Patriarchate."

Worthy was impressed not just with the support of the Patriarch, but his realism. The search for the launch site for the drone, the reviewing of CCTV from St. Peter's Square, and the interviewing of the witnesses in both Rome and Istanbul would be better handled by the Italian and Turkish authorities. Italian officials had already discovered witnesses who saw a white Ford transit van, large enough to contain the drone, parked behind an abandoned factory within two miles of St. Peter's on the morning of the bombing.

The only role that Worthy felt he might play was that of a consultant, someone brought in to ask different questions, the unexpected ones, the ones that might lead nowhere or to breakthroughs. *So, where should I begin?* he asked himself.

He jotted down his initial impressions.

Outcome of two bombings: the same—the death and wounding of innocents, yet innocents attached to two major religious leaders.

Motive: the same for both bombings? Yet to be determined.

Delivery Systems: Radically different. A quadcopter drone in St. Peter's Square. A shoebox in Istanbul. High-tech in the first, old school in the second. Does the difference in delivery system suggest anything?

Target: In Rome, solely the Pope, or was the Patriarch the real target in both attacks?

Worthy paused to think about that last possibility. If the Patriarch, not the Pope, were the target of both, why would the assassin, striking at the Patriarch in Rome, have bothered with a second blast in Istanbul? But that, Worthy realized, depended on when the shoebox was delivered to the Patriarchate in Istanbul. He wondered if the shoebox bomb package had arrived earlier, and the killer, hearing nothing of a detonation, set in motion a second attempt in Rome. No, he thought, that didn't make sense. The bomb in Rome had clearly needed months of preparation, not days.

Worthy looked up from the folder, wondering if they were looking for a clever, high-tech plotter, a bungler, or, if the two bombs were separate incidents, different assassins. Then another thought struck him. *If the drone bomber had been this audacious and innovative, what else would he, she, or they be capable of?*

Worthy turned the page and wrote "Will the culprit try again?" He'd read online that in the wake of the two bombings, the Dalai Lama, the chief Imam of Iran, the Sheik of Mecca, and the Chief Rabbi of Israel had increased their security in case of copycat attempts. And he knew that security in Rome for the Pope and Patriarch would rival that at the White House in Washington, DC.

Worthy knew that the question of "what could be next?" was related to "who is the target?" And the answer to those questions would also settle the question of motive.

In a normal attempted-murder investigation, the two initial questions were always "Did Mr. X have any enemies that we know of?" and "Did Mrs. Y receive any recent threats?" In this case, Worthy suspected that the response to those queries would be a hearty laugh, followed by a reply of "Do you have a few years to study the lists?"

Worthy reasoned that both men regularly received death threats, mostly from the lunatic fringe. But those who sent such messages would hardly have been able to mastermind a drone attack, though a shoebox bomb would have been within the perpetrator's capabilities.

Worthy wrote next: "Who benefits from the deaths of the Pope and Patriarch?" before considering the multiple possibilities, which ranged from Middle Eastern terrorists to North Korea. No, unless someone or some group accepted responsibility, that question would likely remain unanswered until they caught the perpetrator.

Without knowing the identify and motive of the perpetrator, Worthy knew he had to start with the intended victims, the Pope and Patriarch. Had the two hierarchs written or said something recently that could have incited an extreme response from an individual or group with global reach?

Worthy knew that pursuing that question might lead to nothing. Perhaps the rage behind the event went back decades, not aimed at the two men, but at their two offices. But wouldn't the Vatican know of such groups or individuals? Wouldn't such groups have already been investigated?

He sat back in his seat, closed his eyes, and listened to the plane's engines. The thought that had kept him awake the night before returned to mind. He would be in Rome, the city he'd wanted to visit ever since he took first-year Latin in ninth grade. The Colosseum, the Tiber River and its ancient bridges, the Imperial Forum, and the Palatine Hill—all illustrations in his Latin text-book and now sites he would actually see.

First, Father Nick survived a bomb attack, and now I will see Rome for myself. What have I done to deserve this? he thought.

JULY 2: ROME: FIUMICINO AIRPORT

THIRTY MINUTES BEFORE WORTHY'S PLANE WAS TO ARRIVE, Father Fortis was already sitting in the waiting area in Rome's Fiumicino Airport. He'd taken a cab directly from Tre Fontane and was now reflecting on the meeting with Pope Gregorio, the Vatican representatives, Patriarch Michael, Mr. Pappas, and himself.

Father Fortis couldn't deny that the Pope and Patriarch Michael had spoken with both candor and commitment. The two were united in believing that any healing of the long-standing division between their churches demanded con-crete expression. For that reason, both men had committed to pray together in private for the remainder of the time Patriarch Michael was in Rome.

He remembered the faces of the others at the meeting at Tre Fontane. On one side were three Orthodox representatives, including himself; on the other side, at least fifteen Catholic representatives. Father Fortis could guess what was in the mind of Mr. Pappas, that the Orthodox Church had survived the last thousand years not only by preserving its faith under Islamic and later Communist rule, but also by resisting advances from the mightier Catholic Church of the West.

A disturbance in the waiting area broke into Father Fortis' musings. Marching in was a group of nearly thirty brandishing hand-painted signs. He was surprised to see that many of the signs were in English. "Welcome, Mother Cleery." Chants of "Mother Cleery, Mother Cleery" rose from the group.

Why did that name seem familiar to him? Was Mother Cleery a nun? The Irish flags were a clue, as was the raucous noise from the group—sometimes a chant, sometimes loud applause and cheering, and sometimes a lull before the sound would once again swell.

Three Italian police assigned to the airport, two women and one man, walked behind the group, obviously curious about the uproar, but they gave no indication that they felt a need to intervene. After nearly ten minutes of this, a short elderly priest with a megaphone asked for quiet and addressed the crowd.

"Mother Cleery's plane has landed," he said to loud applause. Again, the priest with a lilting Irish accent calmed the crowd before inviting all to kneel and say the rosary together. Everyone in the group did as requested, while a nun led the group in the recitation.

After a few minutes, someone with a cellphone came up to the priest and whispered something into his ear. The priest rose, tapped the nun on the shoulder, and the chanting died out. "Mother Cleery and those traveling with her are in the baggage area. We expect her to come through customs in just moments. Praise be to Our Lord and His Holy Mother, the Ever-Blessed Virgin Mary!"

The group rose from their knees and repeated the phrase. They strained against the cordons holding them back from the automatic doors that were just now opening.

Standing on his tiptoes, Father Fortis was able to see over all but the tallest in the group. In a moment, Christopher Worthy came through the door and, like the other passengers who had preceded him, looked surprised by the group with the banners and the Irish flags.

Father Fortis waved to him, and in a moment, Worthy surprised him by giving him a hug. Although it wasn't the bear hug Father Fortis was famous for giving, the hug was something Worthy hadn't initiated with him before. "I can't tell you how good it is to see you, Nick," Worthy said in a quavering voice.

"Ah, my friend, I am the one who's pleased. I feel so much better just seeing you."

Worthy smiled awkwardly before looking over his shoulder. "I take it that crowd isn't for me."

"It's for someone on your flight. Did you notice a celebrity on board?" Father Fortis asked.

Worthy shook his head and stifled a yawn. "There was one person, a red-haired woman wearing a yellow scarf, who seemed to have a small group of followers in tow."

"Was she a nun?"

Worthy laughed. "She didn't sound like one. As she passed my row, I heard her say something about the 'bloody seats' being 'too bloody narrow.'"

Before Father Fortis could comment, the group began to shout and wave their banners and flags as a red-haired woman exited through the doors. She smiled broadly as she raised her hands and blew kisses to the crowd. "Bless you, my dearest friends," she yelled over the crowd in a thick Irish brogue. "Bless you all."

"A word, Mother Cleery, a word!" someone yelled from the middle of the group.

"Bloody cheeky you are," the woman replied with a laugh. "I just gave you a blessing, and you ask for more!" The group laughed with her. "You all know that I can't utter a sentence without swearing. And yet, and yet, that hasn't stopped our sweet Lord from speaking to me right here," she said, pointing to her heart.

Father Fortis nudged Worthy. "That's where I've heard of her. She's the Irish woman who curses like a sailor but claims that Jesus speaks to her. Christopher, do you mind if we listen just a bit to her? I've heard she has a knack for giving the media all they can handle."

The two of them stood behind the group, while a reporter spoke to Mother Cleery in rapid Italian. She shrugged before smiling to the crowd. "I've been told the Italian press are a bunch of wankers."

Her admirers responded with an appreciative hoot at her irreverence.

"But we should at least give this young man a chance. Anyone here able to translate?" she called out to her followers.

A small woman raised her hand and was ushered to the front. She listened intently to the reporter before speaking to Mother Cleery. "He wants to know why you've come to Rome."

"Ha, as if Catholics don't come to Rome every day! Isn't that a good enough reason, Father Rory?" she said, looking in the direction of the priest with the megaphone.

The reporter asked another question. The translator nodded before turning again toward Mrs. Cleery. "Does your arrival have anything to do with the bombing this past week in St. Peter's Square?"

Father Fortis heard a few in the crowd whisper, "I knew it. I knew it." Mother Cleery paused until the crowd hushed. Her smile disappeared. "Rome is the source of my faith. This is where St. Peter, St. Paul, and so many others have been martyred, including the two deacons just days ago. I come to Rome for one simple reason: I'm a Catholic, an owner of a laundromat, and a mother of six, who's come to pray."

Which completely avoided the question, Father Fortis thought.

The reporter understood enough English to realize he still hadn't gotten tomorrow's headline. He rattled off a longer question before pushing the mic closer to Mother Cleery's face. Eventually, the translator said, "Did the Pope know you were coming to Rome, and, if so, did the Pope invite you?"

Mrs. Cleery fixed her gaze on the reporter. "This is my last comment. The answers to your questions are yes and then no."

With that, her companions on the flight made a circle around Mother Cleery and pushed toward the airport exits. Father Fortis and Worthy watched her admirers give way before moving in behind her as sheep following a shepherd.

Outside in the warm afternoon, Father Fortis and Worthy walked toward the taxi stand. "My friend, I'm quite sure Pope Gregorio did *not* ask that woman to come," Father Fortis said. "In fact, she might be the last person he wants to deal with right now."

"The Pope doesn't have to pay attention to every crackpot who comes to Rome, does he?"

"Hmm" was all that Father Fortis said, but to himself he thought about the ancient phrase "all roads lead to Rome." For two thousand years, Rome had drawn not just apostles, martyrs, mystics, and prophets, but also charlatans. Some of those had been laughed out of the city; others had been forced to leave by police or mobs; some had lived in tents while a few had attracted huge followings and purchased sizeable estates. What Father Fortis understood was that the vast majority of these eccentrics had made little impact on the Church. Yet, he could not deny that a few had changed the course of Church history.

Thinking about the Irish woman, Father Fortis thought, *Only time will tell.* Yet, he felt uneasy as he entered the cab with Worthy.

CHAPTER SEVEN

JULY 3: ROME: CIRCUS MAXIMUS

CHRISTOPHER WORTHY AWOKE THE NEXT DAY AT NOON, Italian time, and felt he could have slept another eight hours. But he was in Rome! He showered and looked out the bathroom's west-facing window onto a narrow street that zigzagged between two old churches before joining a major thoroughfare. The sun was shining brightly on a flock of cars, trucks, and scooters zipping in both directions on the main road.

"Maybe I should pinch myself," he said aloud to the room. He thought back on his childhood as a Baptist minister's son growing up in northern Kentucky. Rome was not only the city in the black-and- white photos in his Latin textbook, but also the home of the Catholic Church. His father had preached at least once a year on the errors of Catholicism, giving Rome an aura of the taboo about it to the young Christopher.

He dragged himself away from the window and put on his clothes, wondering as he did so what his father would think of his being in Rome to help protect a pope and a patriarch.

The phone rang in Worthy's room. "Christopher, did I wake you?"

"Morning, Nick, or I guess it's afternoon. No, I'm up and showered."

"Are you hungry, my friend?" Father Fortis asked.

"Now that you mention it, I am."

"I thought you might be. We have a meeting at two o'clock, but there's a deli down the street. How about I meet you in the lobby in ten minutes?"

"Sounds good, Nick."

The two walked from the hotel south to where the street ended at a site that made Worthy stop in his tracks.

"Did you forget something, my friend?" Father Fortis asked.

"No, I can't believe I'm standing in front of the Circus Maximus, Nick. It's huge, much bigger than it looked in my Latin text. It makes the Kentucky Derby track in Louisville look small."

"Why don't you sit down on this bench and admire the site, Christopher. I'll buy us some sandwiches."

When Father Fortis brought back panini and sodas, the two men ate in silence as they looked out at the massive ruin. Finally, Father Fortis said, "I read in a pilgrim's guide to Rome that Christians didn't actually die in the Colosseum. They died in Nero's circus on Vatican Hill, where the two deacons died, and Christians died right here, in this circus. Now it's just a place to let Fido do his business or a place for joggers. Rome has changed, and then, in other ways, it hasn't."

The two men sat in silence for a moment before Worthy asked, "Did you know either of the deacons who were killed?"

"No, but I remember their faces—young and earnest."

"How about the old man at the Patriarchate in Constantinople? Worthy asked.

Father Fortis shook his head. "I might have seen him when I visited the Phanar several years ago, but I don't think we ever talked."

Neither man said anything for a moment until Worthy asked, "Has there been any progress on the case while I was sleeping?"

"Yes, but some of that is so bizarre that I don't know what to make of it," Father Fortis replied, "so I'll leave that piece of news to whoever we're meeting with. The good news is they found the white van and the drivers. They're in police custody right now."

Worthy took a swig of soda and nodded. "So I could be flying home before I even unpack."

"Probably not, Christopher. There seem to be rumors of their innocence."

"Ah, well, I can't say that I'm in any hurry to get back to Detroit."

"The lawsuit mess, I take it? I felt so guilty being here while you've had to face that alone."

"'Mess' is a polite word for it, Nick. But I'd do the same thing all over again."

"Which is a big reason why you're here. The Patriarch asked for you because you're not the typical, go-by-the-book investigator, my friend."

Worthy shrugged. "I won't fight you on that, Nick."

They finished their sandwiches and sodas, but Worthy wasn't ready to leave the Circus Maximus. "Did you ever see the movie *Ben Hur*, Nick?"

"Oh, yes. Charlton Heston, if I remember correctly."

"That movie made a great impression on me as a boy," Worthy said. "My dad disapproved of Hollywood films. He always said that going to a movie theater was supporting the immorality of Hollywood. By immorality, he meant the unholy trinity of divorce, alcohol, and drugs. But my dad did take us to see *Ben Hur,* and from then on, I was hooked on movies. Of course, I had to find a way to sneak out and see them secretly. So I invented a friend named Ben Hurley, in honor of the film, and I'd tell my folks I was going over to his house to shoot baskets."

Father Fortis laughed loudly as he slapped Worthy on his back. "People think it's monks and nuns who take 'Be ye separate from the world' seriously. But it's the fundamentalists who really run with that idea. I wonder what your father would think of our movie nights at the monastery—always with beer and wine, by the way."

Worthy smiled as the two began to walk back toward hotel. "You don't want to know, Nick. You don't want to know."

FATHER FORTIS AND CHRISTOPHER WORTHY were ushered into a meeting room within the church of San Teodoro, a small room with a rectangular table that would seat six. Father Fortis nodded toward three Vatican officials whom he met at Tre Fontane two days before, but he didn't recognize the woman in the room. From her stylish suit and makeup, he knew she was no nun.

If he expected Italy to still be traditional, he was surprised that the lone woman, Professor Lena Fabriano, introduced herself first. Father Alessandro and Mr. Gracci followed by offering their names. Worthy had just introduced himself when the door opened, and Patriarch Michael walked into the room.

The two Catholic men and the professor stood and bowed respectfully, which Patriarch Michael acknowledged with a nod and then a brief gesture of blessing before he approached Worthy.

"A good trip, Mr. Worthy?" he asked.

"Yes, sir," Worthy replied. Seeing Worthy's look of confusion, Father Fortis reminded himself to instruct Worthy on how to address the Ecumenical Patriarch.

"And knowing Father Nick, I suspect that you've also eaten well?"

Worthy smiled. "Never a problem there."

The Patriarch laughed softly as he glanced at Father Fortis. "Never a problem indeed. Everyone, please sit down, and we shall begin."

"I've had the privilege of meeting Father Alessandro and Mr. Gracci before, but perhaps they're new to the others here," Patriarch Michael said. Looking at the two he mentioned, he said, "You both work closely with the Italian and international media, if I'm not mistaken, Father Alessandro."

"That's correct."

The Patriarch gestured toward the professor. "Doctor Fabriano and I have had a brief conversation before, and her expertise will be evident shortly.

Lesser known to the three of you is Father Fortis, who is a trusted friend of mine from the United States—in fact, from near Detroit, where they make cars not quite as impressive as your Italian models. Finally, I'm happy and relieved to welcome Lieutenant Christopher Worthy, a homicide investigator whom I've invited to Rome."

Father Fortis noted the sudden interest in Worthy from the three Italians sitting on the other side of the table. Professor Fabriano took out a pen and pad of paper from her briefcase and began writing. Occasionally, she would glance in Worthy's direction and then return to writing. After she repeated this several times, Father Fortis noticed that Worthy fidgeted.

The Patriarch continued with his opening remarks. "I should add that Lieutenant Worthy and Father Fortis have successfully worked together on previous homicide cases, one even here in Italy. I hope you two will take it as a compliment if I describe your success in these cases as having something to do with working well together."

Father Fortis smiled appreciatively and noted that Worthy too seemed grateful for the vote of confidence. *Outsiders we may be,* Father Fortis thought, *but we're <u>his</u> outsiders.*

Patriarch Michael cleared his throat and opened a folder. "We all know the tragic circumstances of the bombing in St. Peter's Square and the subsequent bombing at the Patriarchate in Constantinople. One of the Patriarchate's most senior workers, a faithful Christian, loving husband, and doting grandfather, was killed in that blast." He paused for a moment before continuing. "Both investigations are moving forward, but we still don't know if a connection exists between the two tragedies. Father Alessandro, perhaps you will give us the latest on the St. Peter's incident."

"Certainly. As is now common knowledge, we have brought in the two men, both local technology engineers, who controlled the drone until the last few seconds. The men claim complete innocence, saying they were hired by what they thought was an Italian ice cream company. They're saying the drone was given to them on the morning of the attack. We have determined the make of the drone. It is, as is already known, a quadcopter. What wasn't known until this morning is that the remains of the housing unit suggest it was one previously used by the Swiss government for mail delivery to remote villages in the Alps. This quadcopter can carry a payload of approximately four pounds or two kilograms, so it is quite able to transport a bomb. Several of the Swiss drones have gone missing over the past year and were assumed to have flown off target and been destroyed in crashes. We now suspect that one of those was stolen, not destroyed. It would take minimal knowledge to reprogram it for purposes such as this one."

"Hmm. So these two men claim no knowledge of a bomb on board?" the Patriarch asked.

"Precisely. Both men have referred repeatedly to the tail on the drone that advertises a gelato company. They assumed the whole thing was just a publicity stunt," Mr. Gracci replied. "And, to be fair, publicity stunts aren't that rare in Rome."

"What's their reason for not reporting what happened immediately?" Worthy asked.

"They admit to being frightened, Lieutenant. They assumed no one would believe their claim of innocence. And given the fear and anger in the city right now, their fears might be well-founded. Even if the two men are innocent, it will be safer for them to remain in police custody for the time being."

"And this gelato company?" Worthy asked.

"They're completely panicked by the news. Their employees are in for long rounds of questioning, and the longer that takes, the more likely the company's fear of bankruptcy will become a reality," Mr. Gracci said.

Father Fortis noticed that Professor Fabriano hadn't contributed anything but continued to take notes of the meeting. *What kind of professor is she?* he wondered. *Forensic profiler, perhaps?* He wondered if Worthy also noticed that she wore no ring on her left hand. *Now who's profiling,* he thought.

Father Alessandro sat forward and addressed the group. "The authorities will soon have an artist's sketch of the person the two men claim they met. They are adamant that this man spoke fluent Italian but with an accent from maybe somewhere in the Middle East."

Patriarch Michael frowned as he looked at Father Fortis and Worthy. "That's not good news."

Dr. Fabriano looked up from her notes. "I don't mean this as a jest, but did these men receive payment in advance?"

Father Fortis noted her English was better than Mr. Gracci's, who tapped his fingertips together as he replied, "They were promised two thousand Euros each, which, even if they'd received it, would not even cover one day of their legal fees."

Patriarch Michael thanked the two Vatican officials before turning to Dr. Fabriano. "And now to our other problem. Help us put our visitor into perspective, Professor," he asked.

Dr. Fabriano turned a few pages in her notepad. "Margaret Cleery is an interesting person, but someone we may all wish had remained in Ireland."

Recalling the red-haired Irish woman from the airport, Father Fortis could think of no reason why the Cleery woman would be of any interest in the case.

"If I may, I would like to show you what our Irish visitor has been up to, and this is just her first day in the city." Dr. Fabriano rolled a TV monitor to the end of the table.

When she turned on the monitor, Father Fortis was able to identify one of the fountains in St. Peter's Square. Judging by the number of people in the background, the scene wasn't from the day of the bombing. After a few seconds, Mother Cleery was seen standing on a wooden box that served as a podium. There were as many people surrounding her as Father Fortis remembered from the airport. They cheered loudly until she gestured for them to stop.

Professor Fabriano adjusted the volume to pick up what Mrs. Cleery was saying. At first, the Irish woman said nothing, but instead raised a small silver and glass container above the crowd. She held it out and slowly moved the object from right to left and then back again.

"The blood of martyrs," she said. "Behold, the blood of martyrs."

The crowd hushed, and the only sound that could be heard was the rushing water from the nearby fountain.

Slowly, she raised her gaze toward the sky, and with the glass and silver object made the sign of the cross over the crowd.

"Now comes her big surprise," Professor Fabriano told the group.

"As we all know, a horrible tragedy occurred in this very square just days ago," Mother Cleery began. "I was folding sheets in my laundromat in County Wicklow when I saw the first reports about the bombing. Even before I knew that anyone had been killed, Our Lord told me to come to Rome, what Our dear Lord calls 'this holy city, the city of martyrs.'"

"Holy Mary, Mother of God," someone started saying in the crowd, and Mother Cleery bowed her head as those around her completed the phrase from the rosary.

When her admirers had finished, Mrs. Cleery again raised the silver and glass object. "This is a reliquary containing the blood of martyrs. Not from St. Peter's Basilica behind us or from some other site of this great city. Inside this reliquary is the blood of the two deacons who died in this square."

Some in the crowd immediately knelt while others made the sign of the cross.

"Two martyrs, one from our Holy Church and one from our sister Church in the East, the Orthodox Church. But look hard at this reliquary," she said, as she again slowly showed it to the crowd, now grown larger with curious onlookers. "You won't see any separation, one side for each deacon martyr. No, this is the blood of the two martyrs as it was found, already flowing into each other on the pavement of this very square."

Patriarch Michael sighed and asked Professor Fabriano to pause the video. "Is what she is saying credible? Could she really have their blood?"

Dr. Fabriano nodded. "I don't believe she would deliberately lie about that, but how she got possession of the blood is a bit of a mystery."

"But it's possible the blood was collected at the time?" the Patriarch continued.

Father Alessandro interrupted. "I'm certain that relics of the tragedy were collected."

Dr. Fabriano agreed. "Think of all those who've investigated the scene, not to mention all those in charge of cleaning up the area. I find it likely that their blood was not only collected but even offered for sale."

"And there would be a market for this?" Worthy asked, looking at Father Fortis.

"Definitely so, my friend."

"May I continue with the video?" the professor asked Patriarch Michael as if Worthy's question irritated her.

The Patriarch nodded, but Father Fortis noticed the worried look on his face.

The video started up, with Mrs. Cleery speaking to the ever-enlarging crowd. "In our catechesis, we all learned that the Holy Church was built on the blood of the martyrs. Our Lord is asking, 'Could it not be so again?'"

Father Fortis noticed how the woman paused to give her adoring fans time to respond. *She's good at this,* he thought.

"Our Lord has told me that He wants to honor the sacrifice of these two deacons, men so young, men who didn't live long enough to offer their first mass but who lived to offer their own blood. As with the blood of Abel, their blood cries out from this holy ground, and now I understand why Our Lord ordered me to come to Rome," she said, pausing again.

"Tell us what Our Lord wants," a woman from the crowd called out. "Tell us Our Lord's plans." The words occasioned nods from those standing closest to Mother Cleery.

"Woe to the person who claims that Our Lord caused these deaths," she replied. "Our Lord did not cause their deaths, but Our Lord will redeem their deaths, as He did with Sts. Cosmas and Damian, Perpetua and Felicity, and Felix and Adauctus!"

Her statement brought applause from the crowd. She waited a moment before speaking again.

"Our Lord has not given me permission to share all that He has told me over the past few hours, but I am to say this. 'Thus says Our Lord, The blood of the two deacons that has flowed together,'" she said, pausing to raise again the silver and glass object, "is a sign. It is a sign for our Holy Father and the Orthodox Patriarch that the Holy Church of Rome and the Holy Church of the East are to flow together, are to become one. That is what Our Lord has told me."

Worthy looked over to see that the Patriarch's head was in his hands. He was no longer watching the screen.

On the video, those in the crowd looked at one another and began murmuring. Mother Cleery asked for quiet.

"Even I did not understand the sign until I asked a priest within the last hour, 'What can Our Lord mean?' My friend told me that the differences between the two Churches have been difficult to resolve. So I said, 'If that is what Our Lord wants, then it's a damned shame for *anyone*, and I mean anyone, to stand in His way."

With that, Mother Cleery stepped down from the box and was immediately surrounded by her followers. Dr. Fabriano turned off the video and moved back to her chair.

"What you just saw will be all over the news tonight and tomorrow," she said. As she closed her notepad, she added, "Of course, Mother Cleery is totally unpredictable, as is often the case with her type. She may make another pronouncement at any time."

"What would you say is her type?" Worthy asked.

Dr. Fabriano's eyebrow raised, as if Worthy had asked an impertinent question. "Perhaps, I spoke imprecisely. Rome has seen hundreds of self-styled prophets and mystics. All claim their messages have come from God the Father, Jesus, the Holy Spirit, the Blessed Virgin Mary, or some saint. Mother Cleery isn't even the first in this new millennium to broadcast her message from St. Peter's Square. I must admit, however, that it's unusual for someone like her to swear while she shares her revelations."

The professor paused again and looked at Worthy for a moment. "Does that answer your question, Lieutenant?"

Worthy didn't flinch. "What I'm asking is if she believes what she says, that she hears voices."

Dr. Fabriano took off her glasses and let them hang from a pearled string around her neck. "I don't think she's conning her followers, though she might be exaggerating various aspects of her message." After a pause, she added, "I hesitate to speak too specifically about Mrs. Cleery until I can study her more thoroughly, but I will say she doesn't fit the usual pattern of mystics. Authentic mystics normally—although using the word 'normal' in this context may be problematic—go through various stages of purification and illumination before they offer messages. Given Margaret Cleery's penchant for theatrics and her foul language, I find it hard to believe that she has passed through even the first stage. And yet, she claims to receive these messages. Is this possible? Yes, but highly irregular."

"Could she be mentally unbalanced?" Worthy asked.

Dr. Fabriano offered a slight smile as if she had replied numerous times to this question. "If she is disturbed, I would guess she has a borderline personality disorder, possibly caused by childhood trauma either remembered or suppressed. Some have suggested Joan of Arc suffered from the same condition—I don't have an opinion one way or another about that—although the Church has declared Joan of Arc a saint."

"And the other possibility or possibilities?" Worthy pressed.

Again, Dr. Fabriano looked Worthy full in the face, and Father Fortis had the impression that Worthy's question irked her. *Does she think he is competing with her in some way?* he wondered.

"Mr. Worthy, I can't be of use to the Vatican if I believe that true mystics have never existed. I am completely willing to say it is possible, though I would emphasize that true mystics are rare."

"But possible," the Patriarch added.

For a moment, no one spoke before the Patriarch dropped his head into his hands again and said softly, "I will admit that I'm praying that Mrs. Cleery is a fraud, but even if she is a fake, she could do immense damage. I say this because, although I can't see how the woman would know this, her timing couldn't be worse."

WHEN THE MEETING DISBANDED, Worthy nudged Father Fortis. "Nick, ask the Patriarch to wait a minute."

Father Fortis did so, and the three sat down again.

"I'm not sure what's expected of me," Worthy said, addressing the Patriarch. "This business with the Irish woman is miles outside my expertise."

Patriarch Michael managed a smile. "Of course. Lieutenant Worthy, I requested your help long before any of us knew about Margaret Cleery. What I'm hoping is that you and Father Nicholas will have the success you've had before. I won't deny that Father Nicholas is going to be busy. I'll be looking to him to advise me on my talks with Pope Gregorio, but I'm counting on the two of you doing whatever you can to find out who is behind these attacks. And I'm sure you've already thought about where you'll start your investigation."

Worthy nodded. "I'm sure Nick agrees that we need to begin by looking into recent public statements by Pope Gregorio and by you."

"Hmm, that's interesting," the Patriarch said. "Are you thinking it's something one or both of us have said that triggered this violence?"

"It's a possibility," Worthy replied. "But even as we dig into that, I want the three of us to be clear about one thing. As you know, Nick and I have worked together on other cases dealing with church matters. But we've never worked a case on this scale or with so much at stake. I think it's clear from the questions I asked in the meeting that I'm a fish out of water when it comes to high-level church politics. Nick, I want it to be clear that you're the lead on this case. And I need both of you to pull me aside if I start stepping on toes and making a mess of things."

"Of course, but I'll let Father Nicholas answer that for himself."

"Christopher, let's agree that we'll share the lead on the case."

Worthy sensed that the two thought he was requesting a vote of confidence. "No, Nick, I'm deadly serious about this. You know better than anyone that there have been times when I've jumped ahead of the evidence and gotten in the way on an investigation. We can't let this happen on this case."

CHAPTER EIGHT

————————◆————————

July 3: Somewhere in Northern Europe: Faith and Wrath

THE CHESSMASTER, AS HE THOUGHT OF HIMSELF, sat in his spacious library and watched for the tenth time the news video from Rome. His crystal tumbler of whisky reflected the light from the fireplace. Even though it was early July, he was glad for the fire and for the wool sweater, for in his country, the season was only technically summer.

He could almost feel the heat of Rome in the news clip. For that and more telling reasons, he had no desire to visit the city. His aversion to Rome was linked closely to his distaste for the Catholic Church, a distaste that was complex rather than simple. He had inherited his northern European country's sense of Catholicism as foreign, but that reaction, though ancient, was hardly deep. Through history and geography classes in his youth, he accepted his country's preference for Protestantism as similar to its need for parkas and fur hats in winter—as a natural adaptation to conditions.

As an adult, the Chessmaster had attained a more educated religious palate, and that had led to his more nuanced and informed hatred of the Catholic Church. A recent decade-long study had led to his encyclopedic knowledge of "the errors of Rome," and those errors filled the bound volumes on his library shelves.

He swirled the ice cubes in the glass before taking another swig of the whisky. The warmth of the liquid was pleasing on the raw evening, even though nearly all his "clients" would frown at this habit, even this sin, if they learned of it. Not that his clients would ever enter his library or even know on what continent he was sitting by his fire. He had established multiple layers of security, impenetrable walls of code, and diverse routing channels known only to him.

His thoughts moved to his clients and their frustration over the outcome of events in Rome. He had received numerous messages, once decoded, that complained of "the debacle at the Vatican."

The Chessmaster didn't reply to those messages. *Let them stew*, he thought. *Let them direct their complaints, frustration, and exasperation at the proper person, God Himself.* He knew from his study of ancient texts that frustrated hopes only raised expectations for the future. His clients were like addicted gamblers who, after losing a bundle at a craps table, put down even greater stakes on the next roll.

No, he thought, no one would back out; that wasn't how his clients would react. His entire business depended on them believing that what transpired in Rome had not been God saying "no," but rather "not yet."

In a few days, he would break his silence and communicate with his clients around the world. His one-sentence message—"Surely God is testing our resolve and commitment"—would give him at least weeks to finalize the next step.

For his own edification, the Chessmaster reread the reports from his sources in Rome to determine how the June 29th plot failed. He concluded that the canopy over the Pope and the Patriarch had somehow detonated the bomb a mere two seconds early. The plan had nearly worked but still left room for improvement on the technological side in the future.

The bomb in Istanbul had also been a miscalculation in timing. Had the mail sorter at the Patriarchate performed his job conscientiously, the Ecumenical Patriarch would have died on June 26th, two days before his scheduled flight to Rome. If that had happened, the world would just be getting over the shock of the Istanbul bombing when the Pope was killed by the bomb on June 29th. The media would have been forced to spread the cryptic message that he intended to send to them, that the countdown for the world's end had begun. A post-script would deliver a threat of more events to follow.

Even though the June 29th plot failed, the Chessmaster knew that some of what he hoped would be the aftermath of the papal assassination had become a reality. The world was on edge, an edge of his own making.

The Chessmaster leaned back and looked into the fire. He could feel its heat from ten feet away, and that brought thoughts of hell. He had no doubt that some of his clients would end up there, roasting with their Qur'ans and their Hebraic scribbles. In his own mind, there was only one door into heaven, and that bore the name of Jesus Christ, the Lord of history, Savior of the predestined, and the Judge of the world who was soon to return.

Because he was in the business of faith and wrath, however, he presented himself as a bone fide interfaith agent. Working with Jews, Muslims, and a wide assortment of alt-right Christians who were convinced of the world's imminent end had not been as difficult as he once believed. Yes, it was true; five years before, he had no dealings with anyone he considered apostate, but that was before he detected their interest in certain websites and publications.

Even though these interested parties hadn't changed his view of them, they had inspired him to study their texts. That study had taken him nearly five years to complete, but the conclusion he arrived at had changed his life. He laughed at much of what he read from those texts, but he also discovered how those texts could support a conviction that Armageddon was imminent.

Gazing again into the fire, he recalled how easy it had been to stoke the passion of these groups. From there it had been a short step to convince such groups that they were ordained by God to "hasten the end."

With that short step, his business had flourished. The Chessmaster smiled as he remembered the night, sitting in this very room, when it dawned on him: *I have been called to bring these disparate groups together to perform God's will.* Not that any group would ever learn of its counterparts in other religions— no, that must never happen. Until the cataclysmic acts that would lead to Armageddon, the final battle that would bring the end of the world, Christian survivalist groups wouldn't even know of other Christian-based groups, much less radical Islamist and Zionist groups. He, and he alone, would be the go- between for groups that hated one another but shared a similar dream. He, and he alone, would orchestrate the various players who, following his direction, would bring down the curtain on this sorry world.

Did he believe without any doubt in the imminent end of the world? There were moments when his faith wavered, but the fear and hatred that were gain- ing momentum around the world had arisen from somewhere, and he was as willing as his clients to believe that God was in charge of this surging wave.

That was the genius behind targeting the Roman Pope and the highest patriarch in the Orthodox Church. They were recognized religious lead- ers by billions of doomed followers. They, along with lamas, rabbis, imams, rinpoches, and gurus, were the main messengers of what the Chessmaster and his clients could not tolerate—false hope. He shared with his clients the con- viction that these false shepherds had brainwashed their followers to believe this evil world had yet a hopeful future. Were such people simply not paying attention to the news?

It was this lie, that religions could build bridges of understanding and pro- mote peace, that the Chessmaster felt a divine call to expose. And what better way to silence that feeble hope, to replace it with fear and hatred, than to kill both Pope and Ecumenical Patriarch?

Which was why, the Chessmaster understood as he finished his whisky, the Pope and Patriarch remained priority targets. The next plot must again bring the two together on a global stage. How to accomplish this, after the June 29th mishap, had now, praise God, become less fuzzy to the Chessmaster.

He pushed the button on his remote and watched again a recent news clip from Rome. *The Irish woman claiming Jesus speaks to her—is she an ally or a foe?* he wondered. It was too early to tell, but he recognized in Margaret Cleery a volatility that excited him. *This woman,* he thought, *may be unpredictable, but she's someone who won't be easily dismissed.*

He'd always assumed someone would arise to bring matters to a head, but to this point he'd thought he would fulfill that role. Margaret Cleery, however, was a strong gust of wind that came out of nowhere, the kind that sent a sailboat flying across the water. He would gladly let her provide the energy, as long as his hand was the one controlling the tiller.

JULY 3: ROME: COLOSSEO HOTEL

LATE THAT AFTERNOON, MARGARET CLEERY ROSE from the bed where, the night before, she'd kicked off her shoes and lain down, fully clothed and exhausted. Looking out the nearest window, she could see the uppermost tier of the Colosseum peeking over the neighborhood buildings. Her feet throbbed, no doubt her diabetic condition reacting to yesterday's flight and then the uneven cobblestones of Rome.

Rome. Was she really here? Drummed into her by the nuns who'd taught her back in County Wicklow was that Rome, the holy city, was her true home as a Catholic. But until three years before, Rome was as distant as the planet Pluto. A single Mom from Greystones who owned a laundromat, a struggling business at that, had to be realistic. Dublin had been as close as she had gotten to Rome, and Dublin was not Rome.

Yet, now that she was in Rome, she'd expected to feel more. Not that she was the emotional type; in fact, she detested those who wept before statues of the Blessed Virgin Mary or knelt with the older women in the wee hours of the morning to repeat the rosary. Didn't they have kiddies or grandkiddies to see off to school? Didn't they have work awaiting them in one of the shops?

Even when she'd stood in St. Peter's Square, she'd felt numb more than anything else. Yes, the place was grander than she'd imagined, but she'd been told that would be so. Perhaps, she wondered, the very size of St. Peter's had simply been too much to take in.

The strongest feeling she'd felt was one of connection—not a connection with her faith, but a connection with death. The small container of blood in the silver case given her by Monsignor Corrigan had felt all too much like the bloody crucifix taken from the neck of her cousin, killed during "the troubles" in Northern Ireland. St. Peter's Square, Skankill Road—blood was blood, death was death, whether in a Catholic pub in Belfast or in the heart of Rome.

Where the words that flowed out of her mouth in the square came from remained the biggest question, the mystery she couldn't solve. They certainly hadn't come from Father Corrigan. The vial of blood had come with just a note listing the names of the two deacons, the date of their deaths, and the fact that they had died together. She may have heard of Cosmas and Damian, as well as Perpetua and Felicity, from her catechesis class when she was a lass, but where had the names Felix and Adauctus come from?

What she told her parish priest three years before, when the messages started, remained the same. The messages never came when she was in church; instead, she was always working in the laundromat or corralling her six kids at home when a warm sensation would begin around her heart. The warmth would intensify until she began to feel uncomfortable. The first time it happened, she assumed she was having a diabetic spell like her mother experienced, but that faded once she sensed that Jesus was in the room.

As she told Father Ambrose back in Greystones, she never saw an image of Jesus; she just knew he was present. When these experiences coincided with her cussing at her kids, she expected Jesus to scold her, but Jesus waited patiently until she removed herself to a private space—often her tiny bathroom—before she felt words rising in her ears, words that she both understood and didn't understand. The messages left her exhausted, as she felt now in her hotel bed.

After three years of reading articles and watching newscasts that hypothesized that she was schizoid, an epileptic, a con-artist, demon possessed, or just a great actor, she no longer cared what people said about her. If she at first felt the thrill of being special, that feeling had evaporated long ago. She'd wished, indeed she'd prayed, for the burning feeling and the messages to stop. She'd even tried drinking more than usual to quiet the voice. But on those occasions, Jesus had always waited for her to sober up. She now considered the days, weeks, and even months when she felt or heard nothing as the "waiting days." She also gave up long ago trying to decide if she were mentally unbalanced. What did being unbalanced feel like if not what happened to her? And the growing following that called her "Mother," meant as a title of honor, couldn't that point to their childish mental state and their longing for a divine sign? That her parish priest and her bishop hadn't condemned her didn't mean much necessarily, as they hadn't acknowledged her experiences as genuine either. In one of His messages to her, Jesus had called them "Church politicians," priests who were cautious, concerned as much as bankers and estate agents about advancement in their careers.

As she ran water for a bath, Margaret Cleery remembered the numbness she'd felt in St. Peter's Square. Did that feeling have anything to do with a suspicion that her latest message meant something special? Did her coming to Rome mean the end of her "texts from heaven," as her followers had started to call them? Or was it just her hope that, even as her episodes had a beginning point, they might have an ending point here in Rome?

CHAPTER NINE

WORTHY AWOKE, FEELING BOTH GROGGY AND FRUSTRATED. What possible importance, he wondered, could the Cleery woman have for their investigation? Leaving the meeting the day before at the church of San Teodoro, he felt the hour had mainly been a waste of time. Well, not completely, he admitted to himself. The heart to heart with the patriarch and Father Nick had been important, and, if he were to be honest, he found the exchange with Dr. Fabriano—she must have a first name—had been stimulating, even though he sensed that she found him annoying.

Keep in mind that both Margaret Cleery and the professor are distractions, he told himself. *You are here to identify and catch the people behind the two bombings.* As he'd learned long ago, the worst way to deal with a distraction in an investigation is to let it distract. *And that,* he cautioned himself, *is as true for the attractive professor as it is for Margaret Cleery.*

After a shower, Worthy entered the hotel dining room, where he found Father Fortis enjoying a lunch of sausage, eggs, toast, prosciutto and melon, two pastries, and a cup of hot chocolate.

"I'll wait for you to finish, my friend," Father Fortis said, "and then we have the next few hours free. I'll leave it up to you to decide what we see."

"What, no update this morning on what the Irish mystic has said?"

Father Fortis shook his head. "Not on an empty stomach, Christopher. There will be time for that later. So where shall we go?"

"I saw on a map that the hill just behind the church of San Teodoro," he said, pointing out the window, "is the Palatine Hill. I remember from my Latin class that the emperors lived up there. Are you up to a climb, Nick?"

"Lead on, my friend."

As the two men began the walk up the quiet hill, Worthy welcomed the cooler air and the break from the noisy Roman traffic. When they were halfway to the top, he felt Father Fortis' hand on his shoulder.

"I hope you don't mind if we stop so I can catch my breath. You're a faster walker than me, my friend."

Worthy sat down next to Father Fortis on a bench and exhaled slowly. "I can't believe the two of us are sitting here. Just days ago, I thought you might be dead." He paused, feeling the lump in his throat. "But you're alive, and this all seems like a dream. We're walking where ancient Romans walked."

Father Fortis smiled. "Quite a place for someone who likes history."

"It's more than that for me, Nick. I know they call Paris the city of love, but that's what Rome is for me. If a thirteen-year-old can fall in love with a city, I fell in love with Rome."

"Judging by the tourists, you're not alone, Christopher." Father Fortis stood and said, "I think I've caught my breath."

As the two continued up the cobblestone walkway, Father Fortis said, "Before breakfast, I read through the folder—the one about Margaret Cleery— that Dr. Fabriano left with Patriarch Michael. It contains all that the Vatican knows about the woman. Quite fascinating reading, actually."

"It may be fascinating, Nick, but I can't see how it's relevant. At least not for me. I'm here to find out who wants the Patriarch and the Pope dead. Anyway," he added, trying to sound nonchalant, "what kind of professor is Dr. Fabriano?"

"You didn't like her?"

"I didn't say that, although I thought it was pretty clear she didn't particularly like me."

"Sorry to say, I thought the same thing—that you somehow irritated her. I wouldn't let it bother you."

Worthy leaned back and gazed up at the clear sky. "Bother me? Would you think I'm crazy if I said I enjoyed her edginess?"

Father Fortis laughed. "Well, that's not what I thought you were feeling."

Worthy laughed as well. "I'm not used to a woman returning that much emotion—even if that emotion was likely negative. For some reason, I got under her skin, and I'm curious as to why. But I think her investigation into Margaret Cleery will have nothing to interest me."

"You might be right. The Patriarch told me before the meeting that the professor is a consultant with the Vatican. An historian, apparently, with a specialty in female saints, mystics, charlatans, and fakes. Thus, her interest in Mother Cleery."

"And, as I said, nothing to interest me," Worthy repeated.

They walked in silence until they passed a couple poring over a map. "My friend, I need to tell you a few behind-the-scene facts if you're going to understand why Patriarch Michael was so despondent yesterday afternoon."

"I must have looked the same when I thought you might be dead."

Worthy hadn't meant to blurt that out, true as it was, but he appreciated Nick's hand resting on his shoulder. He realized that those words had tumbled out not only because of Father Fortis' survival, but because he felt freer being out of the pressure and tension of Detroit. The successes he had in Detroit with difficult cases had spawned envy, while his notable failures along with his divorce had brought glee to his detractors. This wasn't the first time he'd recognized that he was most relaxed, and most effective, when he was working a case outside Detroit, especially one with Nick.

He had to smile at how odd their partnership must seem to anyone who knew them separately. Father Fortis was an Orthodox priest and monk; Worthy was a Baptist minister's son who'd lost his faith. Worthy could no longer pray; Worthy knew that Father Fortis prayed a lot and included Worthy and his broken family in those prayers. Worthy was taciturn, increasingly so when he was no longer working a case but when a case was working him. In contrast, Father Fortis was outgoing, talkative, and easily excitable. Father Fortis was celibate, bearded, a ponytailed monk, sumo wrestler in size—with a bear hug to match. Worthy was fair-haired, taller by two inches over Nick, lean, clean- shaven, and the divorced father of two girls.

His ex-wife, Susan, often remarked on what she called "odd couples," two people no one could predict would be together. Perhaps, at the end of her marriage, Susan concluded that the two of them had become simply too different. But the odd friendship of Worthy and Father Fortis worked uncommonly well. Father Fortis was able to listen to what was going on below the surface even as he was talking, which meant that Worthy nearly always felt understood by his friend. Nick simply "got people," while Worthy was accused—perhaps rightly—of understanding the dead better than the living.

As the two approached a barricade on the top of the Palatine Hill with ruins beyond, Father Fortis said, "Do you know anything about this House of Livia? It looks like it could have belonged to some wealthy Roman."

The two studied the sign in front of the ruins. "I remember studying the Emperor Augustus in a college history class," Worthy replied. "Livia was his wife."

"And the house is named after her, not her husband? That surely says something."

Worthy read more of the English translation on the sign. "Ah, it says that Augustus had a separate house here on the hill, one even bigger than Livia's."

"Like I said," Father Fortis added, "that says something. My guess is that says something about power."

"Or perhaps an understanding between them. This sign mentions Livia was his third wife."

Father Fortis was quiet for a moment, started to say something, and then stopped.

Worthy heard the catch in Father Fortis's voice. "What is it?"

"Something I don't need to say."

Worthy laughed. "What? Since when do we have secrets between us?"

Father Fortis nodded. "You're right. I was just thinking about what you said when we were sitting on that bench. By the time you were a teenager, you'd fallen in love with Rome. I don't think I've ever seen you look so . . . so happy. And that made me wonder if you've ever thought of . . ."

"What? Moving to Rome?"

"No, my friend. I was thinking about remarrying."

The smile died on Worthy's face. No one since his divorce had asked him that. And it wasn't any easier to hear it for the first time now, even from his closest friend.

"I flunked the course on marriage, Nick, remember? I don't have what it takes, or maybe what I would need to give, to even imagine trying again. I think it was you who said once that I live in the graveyard of broken marriages."

"Ah, another time when I should have kept my mouth shut. By that, I never meant you had to remain in that graveyard." After a moment, Father Fortis added, "You deserve happiness, my friend. You do."

Worthy started walking away, hiding his face from Father Fortis' view. He felt like lashing out at his friend and saying that a celibate monk was hardly in a position to judge anyone's marital ability. But he didn't say anything. What hurt the most was not what his friend had said, but the obvious love that it had taken Nick to say it.

If asked, Worthy would have to admit that he hadn't thought about the word "happiness" since the day Susan had said the words that, for a time, destroyed his world. He had settled for being satisfied, as if happiness was too high a goal to aim for. His homicide cases continued to take him out of himself and away from his unanswered questions. He'd found in Father Nick a friend who understood and valued him. He'd worked hard to recover something of a relationship with his daughter Allyson.

In short, Worthy felt that if he couldn't find love and happiness again, he had all that life was going to give him. He turned to see that Father Fortis hadn't moved from the barricade in front of the House of Livia. "Why did you ask me that now, Nick?"

Father Fortis did not meet his eyes. "It isn't the first time that I've wanted to say something, Christopher. I wanted to ask you back in New Mexico that first time, when I saw how well you worked with Sera Lacey."

Worthy allowed the image of Sera Lacey to come back into his mind. The police officer had been beautiful, no doubt about that.

"Sera wanted—no, she needed—someone exactly my opposite," Worthy said. "When we first worked together, I could see that her faith was what held her family together during some pretty tough times. And the second time, I could see how vulnerable she was. All I could do was pity her."

Father Fortis walked toward Worthy, his hand clasping the crucifix around his neck. "The real reason I never asked you about this before was that I knew the question would hurt you. That's not what I ever wanted. But when I saw how your face glowed when you talked about Rome, about loving this city, I pictured you loving another person."

I must still be jetlagged, Worthy thought, as tears welled up. He turned to his right and took in the panoramic view of Rome from the top of the hill. The two men stood silently at a railing before Father Fortis said, "It's mind-boggling, isn't it?"

Worthy was grateful that the topic had changed. "It's a history book opened right in front of us," he said. After another pause, he added, "Nick, you were going to explain why the Cleery woman is important."

"Ah, so I was. The question is, 'Where to start?' I guess I should begin with Pope Gregorio and Patriarch Michael knowing each other almost thirty years ago in Rome."

Father Fortis explained how the relationship between the present Pope and Ecumenical Patriarch went back to their days together as doctoral students in Rome in the nineties. "But this year's feast day of Saints Peter and Paul, when the bombing occurred, was the first time the two had seen one another since those days. What some of the more progressives, like me, are hoping is that their past friendship might translate into something more significant than a photo op or a vague commitment to pray for one another."

"You know, Nick, I don't think I ever understood what the split between the Catholic and Orthodox Churches was about in the first place."

"There were some minor issues caused because they didn't speak the same language. We're talking about the 11th century. One side spoke Latin, and the other Greek. Then there were some more serious theological disagreements. They disagreed about some wording in the creed, but particularly about the power of the pope—had God placed the pope of Rome at the head of the whole Church or just the Western Church?"

"Okay, now I'm confused," Worthy said. "If there's a chance that the friendship between the Patriarch and the Pope could improve the relationship of the two Churches, why wouldn't they welcome the Cleery woman's message?"

"Timing is everything, my friend. We're talking about a schism that has lasted for nearly a thousand years. Orthodox and Catholic Christians have had a long time to get used to distrusting each other."

Worthy looked down on the small church of San Teodoro and then to the distant dome of St. Peter's. "Like a long-standing divorce."

"When Pope Paul IV and Ecumenical Patriarch Athenagoras embraced in Jerusalem in 1964, I believe it was their way of reframing the schism as a long and regrettable marital separation," Father Fortis replied.

"I think I understand," Worthy said. "Something both leaders would want to do behind the scenes has now been broadcast by Mother Cleery. So she's an unwelcome headache."

"The least she has become is a headache. Her message is going to activate the conservatives who want the two churches to stay at odds. I can see that some might believe Pope Gregorio or Patriarch Michael—or both—put the woman up to it," Father Fortis said.

"So one step forward and two steps back," Worthy said. "But you said that was the least she had done. What's the most she has done?"

Father Fortis scanned the panorama in front of them. "If the motive for the attack in St. Peter's Square was an attempt to sabotage talks between the two Churches, then Mother Cleery's message accomplished something she probably never considered. And that is, she's put herself in real danger."

CHAPTER TEN

WITHIN THE SECRETIVE CORRIDORS OF THE VATICAN, Margaret Cleery's pronouncements were already having an effect. Father Fortis was notified just two days after the first meeting of the Pope and Patriarch that a second meeting had been called. This one was to take place at neither the Vatican nor at Tre Fontane, but rather at the church of Santa Sabina, another ancient site considered sacred by both Catholics and Orthodox.

Patriarch Michael asked that Worthy accompany Father Fortis to the afternoon meeting, so the two men stood outside their hotel only seconds before a black Italian sedan pulled up and a man jumped out to open the back door for them. One of the men spoke a few words in Italian into a communication device attached to his lapel before motioning for the driver to proceed. At the end of the block, their car was joined by two others of the same model.

In no more than five minutes, the three identical cars turned off the busy Via Ostiense to begin climbing the winding residential streets of the Aventine Hill. On the summit, the three cars passed several churches before stopping at a massive rectangular edifice on the western edge of the hill. Stepping from the vehicle, Father Fortis first noted the quiet of the place, much as at Tre Fontane and atop the Palatine Hill. Apparently, the twisting streets leading up the Aventine Hill discouraged all but the most determined pilgrims, and, today, even they would be turned away at a barricade manned by Vatican security.

To Father Fortis' relief, Worthy seemed relaxed. Perhaps Worthy's excitement at being in Rome helped him forget Father Fortis' unfortunate comment about Worthy remarrying. Of course, there was another possibility, Father Fortis admitted, and that was that Worthy had simply forgiven him.

As the two men walked toward the church of Santa Sabina, Father Fortis' introspection was interrupted by a voice from his right. "Buongiorno." He looked over at the smiling face of Dr. Fabriano.

She shook the two men's hands before remarking on the cool breeze. "It's the elevation," she added. "And the shade trees, of course. But down by the Tiber, it will be very hot today. I studied in America, so I know that summers can be warm there as well."

"Professor, where did you study?" Father Fortis asked.

"Please call me Lena. Both of you, please," she added, looking with a smile at Father Fortis. "I have my doctorate from Notre Dame. Maybe you know where that is?"

"Everyone knows Notre Dame," Father Fortis replied. "And please call me Nick, or Father Nick, if you must."

"I'm Chris," Worthy added. "And since I'm from Michigan, I know all about Notre Dame football, at least."

Lena Fabriano fell in beside Father Fortis as they entered the outer portico of the church. "The American version of football was something my ex-husband eventually grew tired of explaining to me. I guess I never grasped the point of the sport," she said.

"Are you against all sports, or just our football?" Worthy asked.

"Ah, our football, what you call soccer, is different. For one thing, soccer doesn't have to have a lot of scoring to satisfy the fans. I suspect that says something about Americans, but maybe I'm biased."

Father Fortis waited for Worthy to answer. The prickliness he'd felt days before between the professor and Worthy hadn't abated. The only question was how Worthy would handle it.

"Did you like anything in the US?" Worthy asked, not gazing in her direction.

And that was meant to sting in return, Father Fortis thought.

"Actually, I liked many things American. I was very impressed with American women, particularly those in politics; or should I say, the women American men let into politics. I like your national parks, particularly those out west. And I like American literature, especially modern writers. I'm sure, if we weren't being directed to enter the church, I could think of others."

But not American men, Father Fortis thought, reading between the lines.

JULY 4: ROME: CHURCH OF ST. PETER IN CHAINS

MARGARET CLEERY AWOKE FROM HER NAP with a splitting headache and a burning feeling in her chest. "If I'm lucky, I'm just getting sick," she said to her hotel room. But she knew she wasn't sick. No, this was the feeling that came over her whenever Jesus spoke to her.

"Why? Why? Why?" she asked the crucifix set on her end table. Why was she receiving another message so soon after the one only days before? Was this what her time in Rome would be like? She toyed with the idea of packing her bags and flying back to Ireland, the messages be damned. But she knew if she flew back to her home that Jesus would simply tell her to return to Rome.

From within her, she heard, "In the Garden of Gethsemane, I prayed three times to be spared my suffering death. I too was tempted to run away from my mission."

"But I'm not you," she said to the figure in the crucifix.

"No, you are not me. But I am He who created you. I am He who called you, Margaret. I am He who will be with you until your end. You are in me, and I am in you. What more is needed?"

Margaret rose from the bed to look out the window. Below her, on Via Cavour, the afternoon traffic was struggling to make progress. She raised her eyes to the top tiers of the Colosseum and thought that if she were simply a tourist, she could visit the site and spend the morning writing postcards to family back home. *But I'm not a tourist.*

"What is it you want of me?" she asked with resignation.

The room was quiet as she waited.

"Open your heart. Do not fight me as Jonah did."

The voice was right. She knew there was a wall in her mind, a wall she kept re-building in the hope of cutting her off from the voice, the invitation, the command. But every time she admitted her resistance, she felt the wall begin to dissolve.

She heard the voice again. "Take your followers and pray in the church near you. I am waiting for you."

She looked out in exasperation at the busy city. "I don't see a church. Since you're God, can't you be more specific?"

No answer, even after a few minutes. "So that's it? Nothing else?" she asked. "I have to find a church in Rome, a city of maybe a thousand churches? What am I supposed to say when my friends ask where we're going?"

But now, there was no answer.

By three p.m., Margaret Cleery's entourage had congregated at her hotel lobby, awaiting instructions for the afternoon. She hadn't spoken to them or anyone the previous day, a day she needed to be alone to recover her bearings. But now, the voice had spoken to her again, and she knew her followers would be excited, thrilled to be on a divine adventure with Mother Cleery.

Maybe they have more faith than I do, she thought. *Or maybe, they're just more gullible.*

In the end, it was nothing miraculous, but rather the common sense of a young priest who provided direction for the afternoon. When she asked the group what churches were close to the hotel, a young priest named Father Aiden O'Malley stepped forward, introduced himself as a doctoral student at the Irish College in Rome, and pointed out churches in the area in a guidebook.

Margaret took an instant liking to the short, freckled priest. He spoke to her with respect, but not in that quivering pious tone that set her nerves on edge. Father O'Malley explained that news of her arrival had spread through the Irish College, and he came, hoping he might be of some help to her.

Father O'Malley suggested that Mother Cleery's group visit the church of San Pietro in Vincoli, St. Peter in Chains, which was no more than two hundred yards from the hotel. Margaret agreed immediately and was happy to walk behind her admirers as they crossed the busy street and walked up the stairs of a walkway.

Walking ahead, Father O'Malley raised his hand, which brought the group to a halt at the entrance to the church. The church was clearly larger than Margaret Cleery's in Ireland, but not overly impressive in her eyes. However, the numerous tourists and pilgrim groups that were streaming in and out of the church suggested the interior might hold a surprise.

Father O'Malley turned to Margaret, shading his freckled face and light blue eyes while asking what her wishes were. *I'll tell you what I want to do*, she thought. *I want the two of us to split off from the group for a couple of pints. Let Jesus speak to someone else and give me a rest.*

With Margaret not answering the priest's question, the group hushed. Hearing no further message from Jesus, she gestured for Father O'Malley to lead the way. Her legs felt heavy as she climbed the steps in the heat of a late summer afternoon in Rome. *How many more churches are we going to visit today before I can soak my feet?* she wondered.

The church's interior was blessedly cool, and Margaret began to relax. She took note of a considerable crowd six or seven deep in the right aisle that was huddled around a massive sculpture. *I hope no one asks me who the figure is*, she thought.

As if on cue, Father O'Malley told the group in a soft voice that the sculpture was of Moses and was a celebrated work of Michelangelo. Feeling no burning sensation in her heart, she found it easy to dismiss the sculpture. Art appreciation was nothing Jesus' voice seemed to care about.

But her breath caught in her throat and the burning sensation returned when she turned to face the altar. She walked purposefully, drawn to steps that led down to a glass case displaying chains.

Margaret Cleery sensed immediately that the chains were what she was meant to find. As the burning increased, she felt ashamed of her earlier irritation. Jesus had graciously sent Father O'Malley to her, for she was hardpressed to imagine how, without his assistance, she would have ended up in this particular church. *I must find a way to keep the little Irish priest around*, she thought.

She turned to face her followers. "These chains are what Jesus has led us to see today," she said. "That doesn't mean that I know what Jesus wants us to understand. But we have benefitted so much already today from our new friend Father O'Malley that I cannot believe he's joined us by accident. Jesus has brought him, and so I would ask Father O'Malley to explain what we're looking at."

Father O'Malley's pale complexion turned a bright red, and for a moment, Margaret Cleery thought that he'd refuse. But when she gestured for him to join her at the front of the group, he followed obediently.

"I'll have to speak quietly," he began in a hushed voice. "I'm not an official guide, you see, and the Italian authorities are quite adamant about that." But with a mischievous smile, Father O'Malley said, "I don't think I'll be fined for sharing a story, especially if I talk softly. This is a story about St. Peter, one that I think you'll appreciate, given where we're standing. Is that okay?" he asked, looking at Margaret.

"Sounds perfect to me," she replied.

Father O'Malley moved into the center of the group. "You might remember that St. Peter was arrested in Jerusalem in the early days of the Church. He was imprisoned and was due to be killed as St. James and St. Stephen had been earlier. But then an angel came and set him free of his chains. Not surprisingly, those chains were venerated as relics by the early Christians and were brought to Constantinople before ending up in Rome."

He paused and waited until the official guide standing by the statue of Moses continued with his talk. In his same soft voice, Father O'Malley said, "As we know, at the end of his life, St. Peter came to Rome, serving the Christian community until the time of Nero."

Margaret was relieved to see that her group was listening intently to the little priest.

"Now we come to the end of the story. St. Peter died by crucifixion, being nailed upside down to a cross very near where St. Peter's Basilica now stands. Once again, Christians procured his chains from where he'd been imprisoned, and they were safeguarded here in Rome as sacred relics. Can anyone guess what we're looking at here?" he asked, gesturing toward the display case.

As everyone in her group craned their necks to stare at the chains, Margaret Cleery experienced such a fire in her chest as to make her suddenly dizzy. Out of her mouth came the words "These are the two chains of my servant, Peter, which I joined when they were brought together in Rome."

Father O'Malley gave her a strange look, but he seemed to understand that Margaret was becoming agitated. "Let's go outside," he said quietly, "where

Mother Cleery can speak more freely." As before, the group obeyed his instruction, and Margaret was only too happy to be led.

A blast of hot air hit Margaret Cleery as she left the church behind Father O'Malley. At the far corner of the church's courtyard, the group sheltered in the shade of a high wall. As if on cue, a news crew appeared and began filming the event.

Margaret focused on the priest and her followers instead of the media. "The message I shared inside came from Our Lord. Was the message correct, Father O'Malley?"

The little priest nodded quietly.

"Praise Jesus," someone in the crowd spoke.

"Praise His Mother and St. Peter," another follower added.

"But what does the message mean?" a woman with an Australian accent asked.

Margaret felt like she was melting. The temperature was much hotter than what she was used to in Ireland, and the heat emanating from her heart doubled her discomfort. Both would become more bearable, she knew, once she completed sharing her message.

"What I shared with you inside is linked—just like those chains are— to the message Jesus gave me in St. Peter's Square. There, Jesus told me that the blood of the martyred deacons meant that He longs for the Catholic and Orthodox Churches to reconcile and show the power of God to bring about unity. Today, Jesus used Father O'Malley, not me, to lead us to chains that God miraculously joined together. Remember what he said. One of the chains was in Constantinople, the home of the Orthodox Church. The other chain was here in Rome, the home of our Holy Catholic Church. When I saw those two chains linked together inside this church, I heard the words 'What God has united . . . what God has united . . . let no . . . let no man divide. . .'"

Her legs gave out beneath her, and she felt herself falling as if from a great height. Before she lost consciousness, Margaret heard a woman scream, "Oh, my God; Oh, my God" even as a news camera looked down on her.

JULY 4: THE CHURCH OF SANTA SABINA

INSIDE AND AT THE BACK OF THE CHURCH, Worthy focused on Dr. Fabriano and considered their exchange outside. Worthy knew that many people resented him, especially colleagues back in Detroit, but rarely had someone disliked him without even getting to know his quirks. He wondered if he reminded her of her ex-husband or American men in general. She certainly seemed to relish the opportunity to slap him down. Yet, there was something about her, something that intrigued him, something he couldn't shake.

Looking around the huge space, he noticed security from both the Vatican and the Italian police.

The first topic was an update on the investigation of the bombing in St. Peter's Square. In their halting English, Italian counterterrorism experts shared that the two men who'd flown the drone agreed on an artist's rendering of the man they'd met. The image was put up on a screen where Worthy along with everyone else could study the face. The suspect appeared to be in his late thirties or early forties, of olive complexion, sporting a close-cut beard and receding hairline. Worthy's first impression was that the man could be Italian, Greek, Middle Eastern, or Pakistani. Yet, he knew that if the beard and skin tone were false, the man could even be Russian or Scandinavian. About the only certainty was that the man was not Asian or Black.

The authorities had played the entire spectrum of accents for the two men. The two disagreed on which accent seemed closest to what they remembered. The older of the two thought it was the Italian spoken by someone from Lebanon or Palestine, while the younger was just as certain that the man's diction as much as his accent suggested he was from Chechnya or one of the Balkans. Either possibility could point to an Islamist group, but Worthy knew that the accent could be as phony as the beard might be.

More information followed from other security personnel on the bomb's composition. The ingredients could be easily bought over the counter in most countries or online. The conclusion was clear even as it was muddy—the bomb could have come from any number of terrorist groups.

What intrigued Worthy the most was that no group had taken credit for the attack. Perhaps, if the plan was to kill the Pope, the Patriarch, or both, the silence was explained by the plot failing. Or worse, perhaps the group wasn't posting anything because it was planning another attack.

On a short break, Worthy walked outside to where others were congregating, some smoking. He looked down from the Aventine Hill on the hazy afternoon in Rome. Cars were jammed on the streets below, while scooters buzzed in and out of the traffic like bees. Before he could stop himself, his thoughts shifted from the threat to the Pope and the Patriarch to Lena Fabriano.

CHAPTER ELEVEN

THE BITTER TASTE IN AIDEN O'MALLEY'S MOUTH overpowered the soda he purchased at a kiosk outside the Colosseum. As he sat and gazed at the ancient arena, he couldn't escape the feeling that he'd been used. The only question was who had used him the most.

Yesterday at this time, he'd been sitting contentedly in the library at the Irish College working on his dissertation. His thoughts at the time were divided between his topic, "The Suffering of the Righteous in the Apocalypticism of Joachim of Fiore," and his desire to return as soon as possible to the west coast of Ireland.

As everyone had told him and kept telling him, his time in Rome would open doors for the rest of his priestly life. A doctorate from Rome meant assignment to one of the larger parishes, and that could mean advancement up the ladder to the bishopric and even higher offices.

The allure of Rome, however, had worn off quickly for Father O'Malley. The city had brought essential but hard-won self-knowledge, such as his difficulty in learning Italian. His fatigue at having to ask Italians to please speak more slowly had increased with every passing month of his three years in Rome. He'd grown up with Gaelic and English, and until he came to Rome, they had been sufficient. He'd met and observed enough of the Vatican higher-ups to know that everyone in a prime position was a polyglot, fluent in Latin, Italian, German, French, and even other tongues. His limitations with language meant his priestly career would never go beyond Ireland, and he was more than content with that.

The heat of Rome, which could last from May until mid-October, had also worn him down. His thought as a youth that he might have a calling to be a missionary in Africa or Southeast Asia had evaporated in the swelter of Rome's summer. God had made him for Ireland, and to Ireland he longed to return.

His time left at the Irish College was now down to months. He was on the last chapter of his dissertation, which meant his committee would soon set a date for his oral defense. After that, God-willing—and it seemed clear that God so willed it—he would be back in Ireland, where he would never have to ask another person to please speak more slowly.

His three years in Rome had also soured him on the pageantry of Vatican life. The elaborate services at St. Peter's and the other major churches of Rome, which seemed so beautiful in his first months in the city, now struck him as competitions between the various religious orders or the various members of the Curia. He realized in his first year that some cardinals and monsignors traded their highly prized presence in the processions on feast days of the major churches for favors. Of course, these favors were not monetary, as nothing like that was permitted after the Vatican's most recent financial scandals. No, the favors were paid off in invitations to speak at banquets, to lead "missionary" cruises to the Caribbean, or to be invited to lead pilgrimages for the wealthy to Assisi.

Ego—that was what Aiden O'Malley most longed to escape by leaving Rome. He didn't deny that ego was present everywhere, even in his small town in Ireland, but at home he'd seen ego confronted by faith. He would never forget what one of his professors in Ireland said to him before he left for Rome. "In Rome, it will be hard to remember that God gives gifts, undeserved gifts, not rewards that have been earned."

The longer he stayed in Rome and observed Vatican matters, the more he was convinced that here faith had made a deal with ego, rather than overcoming it. At the underside of his study desk, some past student had taped a cryptic note which read, "Churchmen in Rome have scratched each other's backs so often that it's a wonder anyone has any skin left." When Aiden found the note, his first thought was, *I wonder where that priest is now.* His second thought was, *I wonder if whoever wrote that is still a priest.*

There were, of course, notable exceptions to the egoism of the Church, and Aiden believed that, by some miracle of God, the recent popes had been truly and deeply humble. But below that within the Curia, in his opinion, the structure was rotten.

All these observations and feelings Aiden had managed to hide. He hadn't even recorded his thoughts in a private diary, as no one could guarantee that such honest observations wouldn't surface at an inauspicious time. Instead, he'd learned to wear a mask while in Rome. To others, he was a capable if not distinguished doctoral student, one destined for parish or seminary duties in Ireland. If his language skills were limited and if his preaching abilities weren't stellar, his organizational skills were notable, and the hierarchy recognized that those could be of service to Christ and His Church.

For his final act of duplicity in Rome, Aiden had to pretend that he, like all students coming to the end of their stays, was heartbroken at leaving the Eternal City. Consequently, when he crossed paths with his fellow doctoral students, he had to accept their condolences on his return to Ireland.

He had been actually daydreaming of his village of Belmullet and the waves of the Atlantic washing onto the shore at the edge of his town when one of the librarians laid a note next to him. He opened it to find that Monsignor Britter, the Dean of the College, wanted to see him at his earliest convenience.

Monsignor Britter, along with everyone at the Irish College, had no idea how eager Aiden was to escape Rome. Aiden O'Malley accepted that the Dean saw him as a quiet and mature student, someone who "did Mass" reverently and, more importantly, without embarrassing slip-ups.

The meeting with Monsignor Britter later that same day had been brief, its sole purpose to enlist Aiden's cooperation in keeping an eye on Margaret Cleery and her followers. Aiden understood immediately that Monsignor Britter hadn't initiated the request. Instead, someone in the Vatican, aware of Mother Cleery's presence, had contacted the Irish College to find someone trustworthy and capable of representing the Church's interests.

Aiden O'Malley had once again hidden his feelings, specifically his anger at being selected. As with other requests from the Vatican, "trustworthy" was used to describe someone who was its opposite—someone who'd betray the trust of others. The Vatican wanted a "mole" in the Cleery camp, and Monsignor Britter had chosen him.

"Yes, of course, Father, if that is what's necessary," he had replied to the request. "I have, of course, heard of Mrs. Cleery, from back home."

"What do they say about her in Ireland?" Father Britter had asked, his eyes looking at a place on the far wall.

Aiden answered as he knew he was expected to answer. He shared how the older faithful believed in her while the youth of Ireland viewed her as a novelty.

"We don't know how long she will be in Rome, and maybe she doesn't know herself," Father Britter had said. "But please know that your doctoral studies need not suffer." Aiden had offered a humble bow, even as he pocketed Britter's assurance that his doctoral committee would be made aware of his extracurricular service to Mother Church.

"Please understand, Father Aiden, the Vatican is not saying that Margaret Cleery is a fraud. She may very well believe that the voice she is hearing is from Jesus, whatever its actual source. Put simply, the Vatican needs to know what she is saying and how her followers are taking her messages, so that the Vatican can respond appropriately or . . . or not respond at all. In addition, the Vatican would find it useful to hear if her following grows or dwindles while she's here in the city."

Consequently, that afternoon found him in the hotel lobby mixing with the Cleery group until their leader appeared from her room. His first impression was that the woman looked like one of his favorite aunts. She seemed to find his face in the group and smile directly at him, as if they'd met before.

In that smile, he realized the opportunity presented to him. His hidden frustration with the Vatican now had a potential outlet. Hadn't he enjoyed the evening's news from several days ago of Margaret Cleery calling out the Church's slow pace of reconciliation with the Orthodox Church? Hadn't he felt she was a kindred spirit when she baldly said, "If that is what Our Lord wants, then it's a damned shame for *anyone*, and I mean anyone, to stand in His way."

Instead of lurking at the back of her followers, Aiden had decided to edge his way to the front to introduce himself. With luck, he could make himself indispensable. With luck and planning, he could quietly encourage the woman to express her frustration with Vatican politics. And then, he thought, the games could begin.

The opportunity came almost at the same moment he began to move toward the front. Margaret Cleery asked if anyone in the group could tell her where the nearest churches were. He pushed his way to the front with his pilgrim's guide to Rome open.

"The closest church would be San Pietro in Vincoli," he said. "That's St. Peter in Chains."

"Can you lead us there?" she asked as she put her arm on his shoulder.

With a bow conveying just the proper appearance of humility, he agreed.

But now, after the woman's swooning followed by TV coverage of her being lifted into an ambulance, he realized that all the cleverness he felt earlier that day was an illusion. He thought that he was leading Margaret Cleery. He now realized that she had been leading him from the first moment.

The first hint of the woman's duplicity had come inside the church, when she had unerringly finished his short explanation of the chains being miraculously joined. That was when he first suspected that he'd been set up so that she could offer one of her so-called divine messages.

He realized immediately that Margaret Cleery intended to make a scene in the church, as she had days before in St. Peter's Square. That led him to suggest that the group leave the church. But Margaret Cleery had outsmarted him. As soon as the group reassembled outside, a news crew appeared. *Coincidence?* he asked himself. Hardly. No, they'd been tipped off about her intention to visit this particular church.

The final straw had been when Margaret Cleery communicated the remainder of her so-called message. As she spoke the words "What God has united, man must not divide," Aiden had immediately recognized that the words weren't the more familiar "What God has joined together, let no man put asunder." Margaret Cleery, not Jesus, had quoted from some modern version of the Bible. So it was long before Margaret Cleery swooned that Father Aiden O'Malley was convinced that she was a fake. Yet, she was very clever. The news crew had caught the whole scene and would have just enough time to edit it before the evening news.

As he crushed the soda can in his hands, Aiden welcomed the raw rage that flowed through him. His anger at the Cleery woman's deception stoked rather than slaked his anger with the Vatican, yet he would not let his anger overflow its banks. No, he would control his feelings as he always did, hiding them from view.

But he saw the next days and weeks in greater clarity. If infiltrating Margaret Cleery's circle postponed his return to Ireland, so be it. He wouldn't pass up this once-in-a-lifetime opportunity to wield his anger like a double-edged sword against these two deserving targets: this fake mystic from Ireland and the Vatican. *Perhaps*, he thought, *I'm a double-agent. No*, he corrected himself, *a double agent favors one side in the depths of his heart. I have allegiance to only one master—the truth.*

✝

July 4: Rome: Santa Sabina

Reentering the cool interior of Santa Sabina, Worthy saw Lena Fabriano standing in front of the group. Her gray suit and modest scoop-necked blouse suggested to Worthy that she dressed for style but also for respect from men. Her medium brown hair turned up at her collar, while her half-glasses dangled from a jeweled necklace. Worthy guessed her age as mid-forties, his same generation.

She appeared poised as she raised her half-glasses to her face, the room accepting the gesture as a cue to be quiet.

"I'm here to provide an update on Margaret Cleery, our Irish visitor to Rome. First, let me offer a little background. Margaret Mary Cleery was born in 1971 in Greystones, Ireland, where she still lives and operates a laundry business. She attended Catholic schools where she was considered an unexceptional student. She was expelled twice, once for fighting with a boy and the second time for smoking in a janitor's closet."

Lena Fabriano looked up and smiled. "That's one thing she and I have in common, getting caught smoking in school, I mean." A ripple of light laughter echoed through the hall. Looking down at her notes, she continued. "Margaret Cleery is the single mother of six children, some grown, her husband having died of alcoholism shortly after the birth of their last child. She attends Mass semi-regularly at her local parish and did nothing to attract attention until three years ago. That was when she reported receiving her first message from Jesus. She freely admits that she has a loose tongue and was cursing one of her daughters when Jesus first called her name."

Worthy looked around the hall and saw where Father Fortis. His friend along with everyone else was giving the professor their full attention.

"Margaret Cleery describes the voice coming with a warm, even burning sensation near her heart. She reports seeing no image, but instinctively knowing the voice to be that of Jesus. The first message she received was not widely reported in newspapers in the British Isles and elsewhere until subsequent messages followed. In that first message, Jesus reportedly told her that a new spiritual vitality would soon arise throughout the world. Until quite recently, her other messages have been of a similar tone, always with the promise of an imminent spiritual renewal."

Lena Fabriano paused to turn a page in her notes. "By her own account, Margaret Cleery has never received a message from the Virgin Mary or any another saint. Only from Jesus, whom she refers to by that name. Never Christ, or Jesus Christ, or Lord, just Jesus."

Worthy realized that had Lena Fabriano not been the one offering the information, he would have excused himself. He still saw no way that Margaret Cleery mattered to his investigation, but he wouldn't miss this chance to listen to a woman who fascinated him.

"There is no history of mental illness in the family," Lena Fabriano shared matter-of-factly, "although that can't be dismissed as an underlying condition in the alcoholism of her father, an uncle, and her husband. Her only brother described their family of origin as observant of Irish saints' feast days, but no more than their neighbors in Greystones. Neither Margaret nor her brother remembers books about mystics in the house. Margaret did write a paper when she was twelve about Joan of Arc, but the paper didn't receive more than an average grade."

Lena paused again, as if to let the information be absorbed before proceeding. "There's been considerable media attention to her messages as they have continued, as well as one scholarly article by a Church historian from Trinity College, Dublin. That article is of considerable interest, as Margaret Cleery's messages from Jesus bear some resemblance to the revelations of St. Julian of Norwich, St. Catherine of Siena, and St. Theresa of Avila. Yet, we have no evidence that Margaret Cleery has ever read the accounts of these saints. For a revealing contrast, Margaret Cleery's demeanor is nearly the opposite of St. Theresa of Liseaux's. There is a different vibe altogether with Margaret Cleery, something that I would describe as more earthy, less heavenly."

Worthy didn't know the other female names being cited, but he couldn't help being impressed with the research capabilities of the Vatican. *And, as a researcher, Lena Fabriano would make a good detective,* he thought.

There was a sudden commotion in the proceedings, as a Catholic priest approached Lena Fabriano. She stopped talking immediately and listened attentively as he spoke in her ear. She nodded several times and shrugged once.

After the priest retreated, Lena removed her half-glasses before addressing the group. "There has been a recent development, two developments, actually. Firstly, approximately one hour ago, Margaret Cleery walked with her followers from her hotel to the church of San Pietro in Vincoli, known in English as St. Peter in Chains, where she began to deliver another message. What she said has not been reported, so I cannot share that with you or offer any analysis. Secondly, you may have noticed that I used the words 'began to deliver.' It seems Margaret Cleery, outside the church, continued sharing her message when she abruptly fainted. She has been taken by ambulance to a nearby hospital as a precaution. Our sources also said the sequence of events was captured by a news crew, so we can expect to see the episode tonight on television. That is all we know at the present time, but we are obviously following Margaret Cleery's visit to Rome with keen interest and concern."

For Worthy, what mattered in that moment wasn't the Irish mystic fainting but Lena Fabriano's use of the word "sources." What he realized in that moment was that the reach of the Vatican was both the good news and the not-so-good news for Father Fortis and his investigation into the bomber or bombers. Yes, Father Fortis had been given several files containing public statements by both the Pope Gregorio and Patriarch Michael. Reading through those files was slow, but essential, work. But the thoroughness of Lena Fabriano's report made him realize that the Vatican would undoubtedly have other files, these on hate groups obsessed with the papacy. The not-so-good news was that Worthy wondered what he could discover about groups like that that the Vatican didn't already know.

FATHER FORTIS STUDIED THE NOTE HANDED TO HIM at the close of Professor Fabriano's presentation. Delivered by a Vatican official, the note was written in Patriarch Michael's handwriting. "Please remain after the updates." Given that neither the Patriarch nor Pope had attended the meeting, Father Fortis wondered when the note had been written.

The note said nothing about Worthy remaining as well, which led Father Fortis to assume that whatever the note referred to was unrelated to the investigation. He looked around the hall, hoping to see Worthy, but he couldn't spot him. He did, however, see the Vatican official who drove them both to the meeting.

"Would you please find my American friend, the policeman, and tell him I won't be riding back with him?" he asked.

The official nodded and replied, "I saw him leave about the same time that Dr. Fabriano left."

"Oh?" Father Fortis said with surprise. "More power to you, Christopher, and may God bless you," he muttered to himself.

"Excuse me?" the official said.

"Just a prayer, just a prayer," he said with a smile.

He returned to his seat and looked around to see who else was remaining. He saw Mr. Pappas as well as several people from the Vatican who'd been at the previous meeting at Tre Fontane. Yes, this would be a theological discussion. Thanks to Margaret Cleery, the work the two prelates, the Pope and Patriarch, had committed themselves to had been almost forgotten.

When all the other participants of the meeting had departed, about twenty people—priests, monks, nuns, and laypersons—remained while security personnel scurried about as they whispered into lapel microphones. After ten minutes, Father Fortis noticed chairs were being arranged in a semi-circle in front of the podium and altar. After another five minutes, two large chairs were placed next to one another within the open space. At the same moment that Father Fortis heard the helicopter circling overhead, two papal coverings were placed over the larger chairs, and a red carpet was placed in front of them.

There was a buzz in the room as everyone anticipated what was to follow. The group stood respectfully as more Vatican security entered the room, followed by Ecumenical Patriarch Michael and Pope Gregorio together. They were a perfect contrast to one another, Pope Gregorio tall, slightly balding, and clothed in white robes; while the Patriarch shorter, bearded, and wearing the traditional black. Father Fortis was struck with the ornate pectoral cross worn by each man, the common symbol of a faith that hadn't been able to avoid division.

Father Fortis remembered the promise made by the two prelates at the first meeting, to pray together and follow the leading of the Holy Spirit, wherever that might lead them. But Father Fortis knew that the longer the Patriarch remained in Rome, the greater the concerns and fears of conservative Orthodox and Catholic leaders would be.

Father Fortis searched the group for the face of Mr. Pappas. He expected the canon lawyer to be the first to remind the Ecumenical Patriarch that Constantinople, when facing greater threats in the past, had consistently rejected Rome's offers of help.

In Father Fortis' view, George Pappas was treating the Catholic Church as if it hadn't changed in five hundred years. How could this fear of Rome remain viable in the face of the humility of Pope John Paul II and Pope Francis? Both had confessed the past sins of the Roman Church in its dealings with the Orthodox, had treated Ecumenical Patriarch Bartholomew as a fellow Christian, not an adversary, and had fostered a dialogue of love that continued even when theological dialogue between the two Churches had broken down.

From numerous Catholic friends whom he'd met at ecumenical conferences, Father Fortis had heard the quip "If the Orthodox won't accept Pope John Paul II or Pope Francis, what kind of pope would they accept?" While both clever and overly simplistic, the question did strike Father Fortis as containing a truth. Would any pope be acceptable to George Pappas and those whom he represented? And what about the Catholics on the far right who felt no love for the Orthodox? Was it simply too late for reconciliation for these factions?

These questions led Father Fortis to appreciate what he was witnessing, the two prelates sitting once again side by side. Yes, the sight was symbolically important as well as a good photo op. But given the resistance lurking in both communities, would Patriarch Michael's extended stay in Rome lead to something more substantial?

After a Catholic cardinal had offered a prayer for divine guidance, Patriarch Michael nodded to Father Fortis, indicating that he should offer a prayer as well. Because only he and George Pappas represented the Orthodox, Father Fortis perhaps should have anticipated the request, but it surprised him nonetheless. For a moment, he stood in silence in front of all assembled. His brain was full of prayers that he had learned for almost all occasions, but for an occasion such as this, he knew no fitting prayer. He remembered Jesus' advice that a person should not be afraid to offer short prayers, prayers that trusted in God knowing our needs better than we do.

"In the name of the Father, the Son, and the Holy Spirit," he began, making the sign of the cross as he did so. He paused again, took a deep breath, and prayed from his heart. "We pray that we who are assembled here will not let our historical grievances, our theological differences, and our inertia overwhelm our faith in your guiding Spirit."

He paused again. Yes, that was what was in his heart, but what should he add? "Our Lord has said that if we have faith, we can move mountains," he began again, grateful that his mind had cleared. "How tempting it is for those of us present to believe that the other community is the mountain obstructing the path ahead. Forgive us our sin of pride, that mountain within our hearts that is the only true obstacle blocking Your power and Your will. As St. Ephraim the Syrian has taught us to pray, 'grant us to be aware of our own sins, and not those of our brothers and sisters.'"

As Father Fortis closed the prayer, he heard to his right Pope Gregorio whisper, "Amen, amen, amen."

Father Fortis made the sign of the cross again and bowed to both the Patriarch and Pope before walking toward his seat. As he was praying, he'd hoped he wouldn't say anything that would add to the tension in the room. He passed Mr. Pappas on his way to his chair and saw that the lawyer wouldn't meet his eye. *Did I pray too candidly?* he wondered. *Was my prayer too confronting?*

He realized that he might never fully understand the objections George Pappas and his ilk had to mixing with Catholics. But he also understood that the canon lawyer, and those in the ultra-conservative Catholic faction, wouldn't be able to ignore the relative youthfulness of both Patriarch and Pope, their media consciousness, and their charismatic styles of leadership. If the two found agreement, they would make a formidable team.

Father Fortis' musings were interrupted by Ecumenical Patriarch Michael addressing those assembled. "Holy Father and I are confident the investigation into the two bombings is in good hands. To speak more specifically to the other matter under discussion, we want all to know that what Mrs. Cleery says and does while in Rome will not affect our efforts. Over the past few days, the media has repeatedly asked us to comment on her messages, and we will truthfully respond that we have nothing to say in that regard."

He continued, "We've also heard that some of you are troubled by our praying together. We only ask, 'Have you also been praying?' Have you been pondering Jesus' prayer that His Church would be one?'"

Father Fortis could feel the tension in the room. The Pope and Patriarch would have to be careful not to move faster than their advisors could follow.

"I don't have to remind a room of theologians that disagreements have always threatened the unity of our faith. Even now, Pope Gregorio and I have different views on a number of issues, including the conception of the Theotokos, the Blessed Virgin Mary, and the infallibility of the Pope."

Father Fortis was glad that Worthy wasn't in the meeting. His friend would likely have found the Patriarch's comments to have no bearing on the investigation. But Father Fortis wasn't so sure. If the motive of the assassin or assassins was theological, as odd as that would seem to the secular press, what Patriarch Michael was saying could lie at the heart of the investigation.

Pope Gregorio nodded vigorously as he rose to stand by Patriarch Michael's side. His deeper voice reverberated through the ancient church as he began to speak.

"Since the blessed embrace of Pope Paul VI and Ecumenical Patriarch Athenagoras in 1964, numerous proposals have been offered to move our two Churches toward reconciliation and full communion. History since 1964 has shown that such proposals are of limited value; they help us understand one another's position but have led to few breakthroughs. So, dear brothers and sisters, Christ's prayer is for us to be one Body, His Body on earth, but history and theology continue to divide us. Is there no way forward?"

The Pope paused before continuing. "Ecumenical Patriarch Michael and I believe history has given us a new chance to consider this vexing question. What the assassin or assassins meant for evil, God can redeem. Please remember that reconciliation should never be confused with uniformity. The Holy Spirit breathes through every word of the Divine Liturgy in the Orthodox Church even as the same Spirit is experienced in every word and gesture of the Mass. In this truth, the two of us sense a guiding principle. Nothing given by the Holy Spirit should ever be given up. I repeat, nothing given by the Holy Spirit should ever be given up."

To Father Fortis, the silence in the room that followed the Pope's pronouncement seemed charged with electricity. He felt that even looking at others in the room might set off a spark.

"The Ecumenical Patriarch and I ask you to treat this unexpected opportunity to be together as a time of boldness, of innovation, and of trusting in the Holy Spirit to move among us. It is not for Patriarch Michael or me to dictate the outcome of this time of prayer and listening with open hearts to one another. Let each of us and all of us be open to the surprise of God."

Without allowing for questions or comments, the Pope finished by saying, "I now ask my friend Michael to dismiss us with a blessing."

Patriarch Michael invited everyone to rise. "Before I give the blessing, I implore everyone to keep in confidence what has been said in this room. The curiosity and intrusion of the media will only impede the work of the Holy Spirit." Raising his right hand to make the sign of the cross, he offered a brief prayer, and then the room was quiet as people waited for the Pope and Patriarch to recess.

Father Fortis' legs felt like lead. He and everyone present had witnessed a new moment in Church history, an invitation to move beyond debate to pray together and to think boldly together. But was this a moment of genuine hope or a moment of supreme naiveté?

CHAPTER TWELVE

---◆---

JULY 4: ROME: THE CHURCH OF SANTA SABINA

OUTSIDE SANTA SABINA, WORTHY FOUND LENA Fabriano leaning against a wall.

"Ah, Lieutenant, I see I'm not the only one disinvited to the next meeting."

"You're ahead of me. I didn't even know there'd be another meeting." They walked out to the parking lot. "Could I ask you a question before you leave?" Worthy asked.

The professor looked warily at him. "About Margaret Cleery?"

Worthy shook his head. "No, not about her. I wanted to ask you about Vatican resources for our investigation."

"I see," she said, turning away from him to walk toward her car. "I assumed the Vatican would have already given you pertinent files." She stopped and looked at Worthy. "By the way, do you smoke?"

Worthy shook his head again. "Sorry, no, I don't."

"Don't apologize. I gave it up two years ago. I ask because so many Italians smoke, and being around them still presents a temptation for me."

"About the files. We've been given the public statements made by Pope Gregorio and Patriarch Michael since they came into office. Reviewing that is slow going, though it might lead to something. But what you said inside the church made we wonder about other files the Vatican might keep, files on hate groups, I mean. Nick—Father Fortis—and I need to review those as well."

Before Dr. Fabriano could answer, the Vatican official who'd driven Worthy and Father Fortis to the meeting approached. "Excuse me, please. Your friend, Father Fortis, asked me to tell you that you shouldn't wait for him but go back to your hotel on your own. I can, of course, drive you."

"Why don't you let me drive our American friend to his lodging?" Lena Fabriano suggested. She turned to Worthy and gave him the beginning of a smile. "Is that okay with you?"

For a moment, Worthy felt panic grip his chest. Was he just setting himself up for further ridicule? Trying to return the smile, he said, "That's very kind."

Lena Fabriano said something to the driver before turning to Worthy. "My car is just over here."

While she drove expertly through Rome's late afternoon traffic, Worthy and she made small talk about the driving habits of Italians compared to Americans. "Americans are better," she conceded. "But almost everyone in the world is better than Roman drivers."

As they neared the Circus Maximus, she glanced over and said, "Coffee?"

Worthy felt the atmosphere in the car shift. "That would be great." As they looked for a parking spot, Worthy pointed to one partially hidden to the right.

"Ah, you are a genius, Mr. Worthy. Or maybe you are lucky? I can't believe you found a spot so close to the café."

She ordered expresso for both of them before nodding toward a table outside. "More luck, Mr. Worthy, a table in the shade," she said, offering her second smile.

They sat for a moment in silence as both looked out past the traffic to the Tiber River beyond. When the expressos arrived along with a plate of complimentary cookies, Lena said, "Can you feel that hint of a breeze?" Looking up at the branches overhead, she added, "There, the leaves are moving. It will be cooler tonight."

Worthy realized she was waiting for him to say something, but he couldn't very well share that he'd noticed the breeze's effect on her hair. Diverting his attention to a cookie, he said, "Call me Chris."

"Chris, short for Christopher, the English version of Cristoforo. Do you know what your name means, Cristoforo?" she asked, as if testing him.

"For me, my name has always meant I was named after an uncle, my mother's favorite brother."

"Cristoforo means 'Christ bearer,'" Lena explained.

His cup stopped halfway to his lips, as he laughed. "Then I probably have the wrong name."

"Not a man of faith, then?" she asked in a mocking tone. "Don't worry. I work for the Vatican, but I promise not to report you."

"So what does Lena mean?" he asked.

"It is short for Magdalena, the saint who some say was a prostitute," she said with an easy laugh. "As you said about your name, I will say about mine: 'no, that's not me.' "There," she said, patting the table, "now we have been properly introduced." She took off her suit jacket and hung it on the back of the chair. The silky move gave Worthy the delicious feeling that she was prepared to stay awhile.

He decided to try teasing her in return. "So, Lena, not the prostitute, how did you come to work for the Vatican?"

She accepted the joke with a nodding smile. "I'm more of a consultant, really," she said, waving one hand to suggest the irregularly of her service. "They call me when they need me. My real position is at the University of Rome."

Worthy tried to relax and take in the perfection of the moment: the breeze, the shade, the ancient city that he'd dreamed about since he was a boy, and the beautiful woman across the table from him. But he didn't trust Lena Fabriano, at least not yet.

"What does it take to become an expert on female mystics?" he asked.

Lena sipped the expresso. "Odd, isn't it," she said, "how refreshing a hot drink can be on a hot day? Yes, female mystics. When I tell people about my specialty, even other academics, most think my area is religious studies, which it is to some extent. But I had more courses in psychology and medieval history than in religion."

"So you've met someone like Margaret Cleery before, someone who believes God is talking to her?"

"Yes, yes, many times. No, that is not quite right. Perhaps twenty times."

"All here in Rome?" Worthy asked, surprised at the number.

Lena shook her head. "No, no. I've consulted all over Europe as well as once in the Philippines and another time in Russia."

"So, tell me, of the twenty you investigated, how many were on the level?"

"By 'on the level,' do you mean did they believe that they were receiving messages from God, from Jesus, from the Virgin Mary, from St. Francis, or other saints?"

"No, how many of the twenty were, in your expert opinion, true mystics?" Worthy pressed.

Lena took another sip of expresso, her brow furrowed as she considered the question. "I'm curious to know why you're so interested, but my answer is I didn't think even one was genuine. But six of the twenty truly believed that they were receiving messages, while the rest, I concluded, were frauds. Of the six, I should say that I could draw no conclusion. I didn't quite believe them, but I could never establish that any of them was psychologically compromised."

Worthy nodded, and the two of them sat in an easier silence before he asked, "Do you hope someday to meet a true mystic?"

"Good Lord, yes. I would love to interview such a person."

"Will you interview Margaret Cleery?"

Lena frowned. "I think the Vatican would prefer me to observe Mrs. Cleery from a distance. Women like Margaret Cleery can be very charismatic. But tell me, why are you interested in this woman?"

"Speaking professionally, what you do seems similar to what I do when I interview and study suspects. I'm trying to imagine who's telling me the truth and who's lying."

"So that means you're not offended by my skepticism?" she asked as she caught a wayward strand of hair and hooked it behind an ear.

"I'm a detective, Lena, so if I'm offended by skepticism, I'm in the wrong profession. I'm paid to be skeptical: skeptical of witnesses, skeptical of family members of the deceased, skeptical of suspects, even skeptical of the victim, and always skeptical of my own theories."

Lena looked at him for a moment so directly that he had to turn his eyes away. "You're not the first police officer I've talked with, Chris, but you're the first American police officer I've sat with socially. Why did you become a homicide detective?"

Worthy couldn't remember the last time a woman had expressed interest in his career. Certainly, his ex-wife, Susan, hadn't asked a question about his work for months before she demanded the separation. And his older daughter, Allyson, had made it quite clear that his obsession with work had been, in her opinion, what had destroyed their family.

"How did you know I work homicide?" he asked. "Is that how they described me?"

Lena smiled. "Actually, it's how the Ecumenical Patriarch introduced you when we met in the church of San Teodoro. But I also did my research."

"Ah, now I remember. I'll give you the short answer about why I do what I do."

Lena raised her hand in protest. "No, no, why do Americans always want to give the short answer? As if you're in a hurry to be somewhere else. Are you in a hurry, Lieutenant?" she asked.

Worthy shook his head and took another sip.

"So, Lieutenant, give me the long answer."

Embarrassed, Worthy looked back to the river, the famous Tiber from his Latin textbook. The river of Caesars, kings, popes, and dictators. For some reason, he thought of all the men and women over Rome's long history who, like Lena Fabriano and he, had sat by this same river. Maybe it's true, he pondered, that there's nothing new under the sun.

"Okay, the long answer then. That starts with my family. We were very religious; in fact, my father was a minister. Religion was the business of not just my father, but of all of us. I learned very early that religion was about having answers, not questions. Unfortunately for my father, I was full of questions.

Most of my questions I knew better than to ask out loud, but when I went away to college, they all came out. I was still a person of faith, I'd guess you'd say, but I soon realized that my father's absolute certainty didn't mean much to me."

Lena nodded as she continued to look at him. "I remember something like this from when I was a teaching assistant at Notre Dame. So many undergraduates were wrestling with questions that European young people, I think, dealt with earlier. Maybe it's because any person growing up in Europe tastes cynicism long before university time. We're raised to be cynical about politics, of course, especially in Italy. Perhaps we're cynical about leaders of any sort, so most of us are ambivalent about the Church, the police, marriage, our professors, and even our football teams. When our team has a losing season, the first assumption we make is corruption. Most of the time, we're right. Sorry, I think I got us off track."

"No, no, that's quite all right." Worthy took another cookie before speaking. "I see we're back talking about football again. I mean soccer."

"No, no, I don't want to talk about football!" she said laughing. "Tell me more of the long story."

Worthy broke the cookie in his hand in two. "Once I was allowed to question everything, as we all were in college, I realized the questions weren't enough for me. I wanted to solve them," he said, "not dismiss them with some sense of false certainty. I suppose that's what led me to be a history major, art history minor, with a goal of going to law school."

"An advocate? I mean, a lawyer? I wouldn't have guessed that about you," Lena said.

"Why's that?"

She laughed. "I said we Europeans are cynical. We're especially cynical about the courts. Italians see lawyers as having little interest in finding the truth. Instead, we see lawyers as those who cover up the truth for a living. I can't see you being very good at that."

Just when he thought this woman might be viewing him in a positive way, Worthy wondered if she was simply amused by him.

"Are you sure you want to hear all this? I mean, what I'm telling you bores even me."

"I thought all American men liked to hear their own voices," she said. "Sorry, that was catty of me. Please, go on," she said.

Despite the apology, Worthy found himself paying attention to how his words could be misconstrued. "I had an internship in a law office my third year of college. Instead of solving cases, the firm seemed to be interested only in winning them. So, after graduation, I didn't head for law school, but joined the police force instead."

"Where you dig for the truth, yes?"

"As best I can, in the way that works for me."

"That's a mysterious answer. What's your way?" she asked.

Worthy looked out toward the busy street and the river. He knew he was giving her all the ammunition she'd need to dismiss him as typically American and supremely foolish. But something told him to risk telling her the truth. "Let's say there's a car crash right there where those two streets meet."

"That's often true," Lean added.

"That's how I understand murder. The victim and the perpetrator come together, a murder occurs, and we have the scene of a crime," he said, slapping his hands together, "which is a kind of intersection. There's nothing really innovative there. In fact, I don't consider myself innovative at all, just persistent or stubborn."

He thought of the antipathy that his colleague Philip Sherrod had for him. "Some homicide detectives, when they first get to the crime scene, take off at full speed in whatever direction they think the perp, the perpetrator, is headed. I usually let my partner take that approach. I try to uncover as much as possible where the victim was in the days, weeks, and sometimes months before death."

"Yes, I see. Quite a different approach," Lena said.

"In the way I approach a case, I don't give much credence to the answer friends and families give to the question, 'Did John Doe have any enemies?' In fact, I don't usually ask that question. Instead, I ask families and friends questions to help me create a timeline moving backwards from the murder."

Worthy paused but could see that Lena was still paying close attention to what he was saying.

"Is that another way of saying that most murder victims know their killers?" she asked.

Worthy felt he'd shared too much to stop now. "Actually, I go one step further, but bear in mind that my method is controversial. I believe the victim did, said, or decided something in the days, weeks, or months before the murder to arouse the fear, anger, hatred, or jealousy of the killer. That's what I dig for."

"Ah, that's different," Lena said, frowning. "I thought you were saying victims cause their own deaths."

Worthy nodded. "I hear that criticism a lot. It sounds like I'm blaming the victim for his or her death, but I'm not. What makes sense to me is that the victim, quite innocently and unknowingly, said or did something that set him or her on a collision course with the killer. Looking back from the murder, the crime was in some sense probable, if not inevitable."

Lena didn't say anything for a moment, and Worthy wondered if his working philosophy made sense to the woman. "Father Fortis is one of the few who understand my approach."

"No, I think I get it. And it's certainly not how I'd imagined most American police approach a murder. Your patience, I mean. But certainly, your superiors must appreciate how you work."

Worthy shrugged. "When my approach works, yes. But my approach also allows a killer time to do whatever he or she needs to do to feel secure after the crime."

"Such as create a better alibi?" she asked.

"Yes, or time to dispense with the weapon or incriminating clothing, or clean a car that might have been used in the crime. In short, my approach allows the killer to fade into the background. So the criticism is that my approach too often abets the perpetrator."

Lena smiled. "Sounds like politics to me. They love you when your approach works and distance themselves from you when you fail. Hmm, sounds a lot like life in university as well." She paused and offered what Worthy understood to be a knowing look. "You must have some stormy times with partners."

Worthy was momentarily dumbfounded. Had the professor made a lucky guess, or had she read him that well?

"More than one of my partners has complained. They say I ignore them and work alone. I can't really say that they're wrong," Worthy admitted.

"Well," Lena said, rustling in her purse for sunglasses. "I will say this. I didn't expect you to tell such a captivating story."

"I feel like I should apologize," Worthy said. "Nick will tell you that I'm usually a quiet person. Sorry for the rambling."

They stood and Lena put down six Euros for the bill and tip. "My treat," she said with a smile. "You can pay next time."

Next time? he thought. *I can take that.*

As they walked to her car, Lena said, "I now understand why you want to know about hate groups. That fits your approach perfectly. But the files that the Vatican has on hate groups might be even more helpful than you think."

"Oh?"

She stood on her side of the car and looked over the top at him. "Yes, the Vatican keeps a record of anti-Catholic hate groups, of which there are many. But the Vatican would also have a record of anti-Orthodox hate groups. Of course, some of those groups are the same."

"Really?"

"The Vatican may seem cut off from the world, Chris, almost as if its thoughts are in heaven. Many have made that mistake and paid dearly for it, including Russian czars, European kings, Middle Eastern emirs, numerous dictators, and even American presidents. The Church has lost much of its power, but the Vatican continues to have a very sensitive ear trained on the world. We like to say that when something happens anywhere, the Vatican knows about it before the BBC and CNN."

"Good to know. I'll have Nick ask for those files in the morning and hope there won't be a lot of red tape in getting access to them," Worthy said.

"Italy is held together with red tape, Chris," she replied as she unlocked her car door. "But I will call someone tonight. I don't foresee a problem. Can I reach you tomorrow?"

His heart skipped a beat as he replied, "Sure. I should probably break down and get a phone that I can use while I'm here. It's just that I'm not sure what my schedule is for tomorrow, so maybe you should just leave the message where I'm staying. That's the . . ."

"The Maximillian Kolbe Hotel," she said, finishing his sentence as she stepped into her car and reached across the seat to unlock his door. "I told you; I've done my research."

JULY 5: EVENING, KOLBE HOUSE

HAVING FINISHED READING THROUGH the Vatican files containing the encyclicals, formal addresses, pronouncements, and audiences that Pope Gregorio and Ecumenical Patriarch Michael had given, Worthy and Father Fortis returned after dinner to find that Lena Fabriano had, as promised, managed to obtain the files on hate groups that targeted the Catholic and Orthodox Churches.

Throughout the day, Father Fortis had been his chatty self, talking while at the same time waiting, should Worthy wish to share how his time with the professor the night before had gone. But noticing no reaction from Worthy when the hotel receptionist handed him the bound files after they returned from dinner, he'd tried to temper his curiosity while they spent the next three hours reading some of the vilest language and most paranoid beliefs about the Catholic and Orthodox Churches. At ten-thirty in the evening, Father Fortis suggested they call it a day and walk down the block to a gelateria.

After ordering, Father Fortis couldn't contain himself any further. "Christopher, you know I'm nosy. But I also care about you, so please end my suffering. How was your time with the professor?"

Worthy looked puzzled. "Did I spend time with her?"

"I know you did because the driver told me she offered to take you back to our hotel. But if you don't want to tell me, I understand."

Worthy shrugged. "Not a great deal to tell. We stopped to have coffee. And if you insist on details, we also shared a plate of cookies."

Father Fortis smiled. "Coffee together is good. Yes, that's very good."

"Nick, it was fine, but it was simply a friendly conversation. She expressed interest in detective work, which might have been feigned or genuine. She can be a bit sarcastic, as you know, especially about the US."

"Interested in detective work or interested in a detective? Sorry, I don't mean to pry . . ."

"Oh, yes, you do, Nick. You're curious as hell. But you know my luck with women, so let's not make a big deal of two people having coffee together."

"She didn't give even one snarky comment about American men?" Father Fortis asked.

"Nothing like earlier outside the church."

Father Fortis waited for Worthy to say more, but he was mum.

"Just answer me one question, Christopher."

"Look, Nick, one question, and I'm not promising to answer it."

Father Fortis took a moment to construct his one permitted question. "My friend, as you look back on yesterday, did your time with her leave you happy?"

Looking up from his gelato, Worthy took at least a moment to offer an answer. "I'm happy" was all he said.

Father Fortis breathed a private sigh of relief. Ever since his divorce, Worthy had remained on his personal cross, feeling ashamed and guilt-ridden. Consequently, the simple "I'm happy" from Worthy gave Father Fortis the first hint that his friend was finally coming down from that cross.

Father Fortis' reverie was interrupted by Worthy saying, "Did you hear what I asked?"

"Hmm? Oh, sorry, my friend. I was miles away."

"I was saying, while I was reading the files on the hate group this evening, I began to wonder if there's a connection between the public addresses the Pope and Patriarch have given and the hate messages they both received. But here again, I need you to take the lead and cut me off if I'm showing my ignorance about Church matters."

"I'm happy to listen to your theory, Christopher. If you're off-track, I'll tell you."

"Good. All day, we read through everything the two of them have said in public, and a lot of that dealt with political and social issues. Then tonight, we read hate mail and anonymous threats directed at both of them. A lot of the hate mail accused them of acting like kings or rulers, butting in on matters that shouldn't concern them. I couldn't help thinking that if the Pope and Patriarch did stick to religious matters, they'd be safer."

Father Fortis took the last bite of his cone and noted that Worthy was only half finished with his. "You pose a fair question, Christopher. Popes and patriarchs have frequently been accused of abusing their power, drifting from Churchy matters into politics. You have to remember that there are Catholics in nearly every country of the world, and we Orthodox are scattered far and wide as well. When a pope or patriarch comments on a global concern—such as climate change or the destruction of the rainforest—their positions are broadcast everywhere. What I'm trying to say is that both of them see issues like climate change and the rainforest not as abstractions, but as affecting the lives of real people, often the poorest of souls."

Worthy nodded. "So, terrorists and hate groups can easily follow what the Pope and Patriarch are saying, on the internet, I mean."

Father Fortis pondered that thought. "Yes, I take your point. Those groups would know that any attack they made on the Pope or the Patriarch would be seen almost instantaneously around the world." He shivered. "Thank God, they failed this time."

"Not totally, Nick."

Father Fortis glanced at Worthy and saw that he'd finished his gelato. "What do you mean?"

"Take the bombing in St. Peter's Square. The perpetrators' goal was to kill the Pope, the Patriarch, or, more probably, both men. But another part of their plan was likely to send tremors through the entire world."

"Such as the Islamic State did with beheadings," Father Fortis mused.

"Or suicide bombers, or the killing of Abraham Lincoln and JFK or, to cite an example from my high school Latin class, the assassination of Julius Caesar."

"Christopher, are you saying that support for the perpetrators hasn't fallen off after their failure?"

"Nick, look at how that so-called failed attempt has become a headline around the world. Millions of people have seen images from that day, and everyone is still feeling jittery."

"I see what you mean. Even with the failure, the world seems less predictable, more unsettled."

"Well, it's brought Margaret Cleery and me to Rome, right? I've seen reports that security surrounding world leaders, particularly other religious leaders, is probably at an all-time high. Regular people with no notoriety are afraid to travel, especially to places like Jerusalem, or Mecca, or Rome. So, the ripples are still going out."

"The world teetered a bit on its axis last week, didn't it, Christopher? It's not as if Italian and Vatican security forces thwarted the plan."

"But if we catch them before they try again," Worthy said, "the media will splash their faces across TV screen around the world, and people will breathe a huge sigh of relief. That's the sole reason I'm here with you, Nick—to catch whoever is behind the attacks."

"But if we don't catch them, and they try again, the world will teeter even more," Father Fortis added. "I must pray that we're not too late this time."

JULY 6: ROME: COLOSSEO HOTEL

MARGARET CLEERY WAS ON THE LAST of her three days of doctor-ordered rest. She was tired of the knitting she brought with her from Ireland, tired of making little sense of Italian TV, and tired of the confines of her room. As she'd expected, the cause of her fainting spell was attributed to being off schedule with her diabetes medications in all the hoopla of being in Rome.

If Margaret suffered from feeling idle, she also appreciated the time to think. The usual gap between messages was months, and to have two visitations so close together concerned her. *Clearly, my system can't take this pace*, she thought, hoping that Jesus agreed. After the messages began in Ireland, she read about the few people who'd experienced something similar. From those accounts, she knew that Jesus, the Blessed Mary, or some saint often didn't so much use people as "used up" people like her. Many died young, younger than her own fifty-three, and often because of being physically pummeled by the ecstatic experiences.

When she first read the accounts of St. Francis receiving the stigmata, she remembered blurting out "Jesus, don't even think about that with me." In subsequent messages, Jesus hadn't commented on her demand, which made her wonder if others like her had pushed back. Did Jesus, the Virgin Mary, or the saints just laugh at the futility of resistance? Did they even care about wear and tear on the human body and mind? She didn't know, but until fainting outside St. Peter in Chains, the most she had ever suffered from the experiences was occasional headaches or a sense of fatigue in the aftermath.

As she lay in her hotel bed and gazed out at the sunny morning, she admitted to herself that Rome might not be the healthiest place for her. If Jesus was going to show up so frequently, how could she weather the messages?

As she'd slept, eaten off trays, and gone to the bathroom over the past two days, she'd felt a bitter feeling rising within her. She imagined that her followers, her devoted followers, cared little about her physical well-being. Father Aiden, the one visitor whom she looked forward to seeing, told her how excited the group was when she fainted. They thought she was in a trance, her soul in ecstasy. If she had died, she now wondered, wouldn't they have felt blessed to witness the moment of her passing? Would they have told stories to their grandchildren of clouds hiding the sun, of hearing angelic voices, of seeing her soul depart her body?

In contrast, Father Aiden shared in a very matter-of-fact voice what had happened when she fainted. She knew that she could trust him; he wasn't agog with wonder at her, nor was he the dripping pious sort. He offered to bring the

Eucharist to her on her first day of recovery, but when she replied, "If you must, go ahead," he gave her a smile of understanding and asked if she wanted a pack of cigarettes instead. When Father Aiden told her that she had gained followers since her fainting, he shook his head as if he could sympathize with what she had to put up with.

That was the worst part of this message business for her—the loneliness. Even as people would press to get nearer to her, she knew they were not with her so much as with themselves, wondering if they would feel the Divine in her proximity. She had observed very early in the experiences that she exerted a power over her followers, but that wasn't something she desired. Her old drinking gang in Greystones immediately cut themselves off from her, as did old schoolmates. She was now the odd one, the eccentric. And not one person who'd joined her band of followers had ever offered friendship. Apparently, mystics didn't have friends.

But friendship was what she sensed Father Aiden was offering her. He'd stepped forward and taken the pressure off of her at St. Peter in Chains, and he was the only one to visit her daily since her mandated bed rest. Others knocked softly and tiptoed in, whispering their prayers for her recovery as if she were too frail to manage a normal conversation. The flowers they brought filled the air with a sickening smell, and, as soon as they left, she would throw them into the bathroom waste bin.

Father Aiden never brought flowers. Yesterday, he arrived for his visit with a small bottle of whisky. In sharing the bottle, Margaret welcomed the other more familiar warmth in her chest. And the two of them found opportunities to laugh together more each day. *This man, this wee priest*, she thought, *is someone I can count on. Finally!*

She dreaded what the next day would bring, sensing that Jesus was just pausing before speaking to her again. That was the problem, she thought, with having God talk to you. You couldn't keep a secret from Him, couldn't make plans of your own that would be honored. All she could do was wait.

Unless . . ., she thought, *unless Father Aiden can help*. As a teenager, she was the sassy one in her family, the one who said that priests were those that knew how to keep God at a safe distance. She no longer said that, but she still thought it. Priests had been the first to doubt her, the first to give her the fisheye, as if they assumed she was one of them, one of those who knew how to use God to make the people cower. A few, she knew, looked at her with jealousy, even hatred, wondering why Jesus spoke to a foul-mouthed Irish washerwoman and not to them. She had despised them in return, wanting to tell them that she would gladly trade places with them in a moment, that they could have the messages, and that she would return with her mates to the pub.

But Father Aiden seemed to immediately understand her, and consequently, she was certain he would never turn on her. He offered respect for her unique calling, but she knew he also pitied her, knowing that her gift was a handicap, like a hunched back or a withered arm.

She would ask Father Aiden, she decided. Today, she would ask how the two of them together might gain some control when the burning began and the voice followed. She knew that she couldn't put Jesus on a schedule, but were there not ways to space the messages out? And could gaining control lead someday to truthfully announcing to her followers that the messages had ceased?

Margaret rose from the bed and, in the bathroom, stood before the mirror. "Finally," she said to her reflection, "I have someone who will share this burden. Finally," she said more adamantly, "I will recover control of my life. I will. I will."

CHAPTER THIRTEEN

July 7: Rome: Maximillian Kolbe Hotel

T HE NEXT MORNING, FATHER FORTIS WAS surprised to see George Pappas sitting in the lobby of the hotel. The lawyer rose when he saw Father Fortis and approached.

"Might we breakfast together, Father?"

Father Fortis had hoped to have breakfast with Worthy, to find some way to ask his friend if he intended to see Lena again. He admitted to worrying about Worthy, but his worry wasn't about Worthy's safety—or perhaps it was. Father Fortis knew that Worthy could take care of himself physically, but in affairs of the heart his friend was battered and bruised. He didn't know whether to hope that Lena genuinely liked Worthy or not.

Father Fortis gestured toward the breakfast room and followed George Pappas to a table. The two exchanged comments about the traffic noise and the smog of Rome's summer until their food arrived. As he'd been the previous times that the two men had met, George Pappas was dressed immaculately. His gray polo shirt and black slacks set off his Mediterranean complexion and salt-and-pepper hair, every strand of it neatly in place.

"I feel an obligation, Father," George Pappas began, "to share with you some of the emails and texts I've received over the past four days. Perhaps you have received them as well?"

"I assume you're not talking about credit card offerings and appeals from charities."

The hint of a smile from George Pappas looked like he allowed it over inner opposition. Shaking his head, he said, "Nothing so prosaic, I'm afraid."

"Ah, you say 'afraid.' That's a bit concerning."

The lawyer pulled apart a roll and began to spread jam on it. Having meticulously covered the roll, George Pappas took a bite and chewed slowly. He swallowed, took a sip of tea, and touched the cloth napkin to his mouth.

He wants me to feel some nameless fear before he tells me, Father Fortis thought. *Well, I can wait out his game.*

"Associates of mine, some of the most respected leaders of our Church, I should add, are quite disturbed by the news coming out of Rome," he said.

"Well, we all are. His Holiness' life was threatened not once, but twice."

George Pappas shook his head. "No, I'm not talking about the attacks, which, as you say, are serious threats. I'm referring to what is happening now, since the attacks."

Father Fortis looked squarely at the lawyer. "Unless someone has violated the confidentiality that we were asked to respect, they shouldn't know about any news coming out of Rome."

George Pappas looked surprised, as if he hadn't expected Father Fortis to speak so forcefully. "I resent your implication, Father," he said, returning the look.

"I am implying nothing, Mr. Pappas. I thought I was just stating a fact."

George Pappas sat silently for a few moments, concentrating first on the roll and then on a bowl of muesli. "I'm not referring to the discussions between our Patriarch and the Pope. No, I'm talking about these messages from the Cleery woman."

Father Fortis considered apologizing, but rethought the urging and let his accusation remain as a warning. He wondered why the lawyer's attention was centered on an Irish so-called mystic instead of the danger to the Ecumenical Patriarch's life. "Your associates, as you call them, should know that Margaret Cleery is a 'loose cannon.' Why would they give her messages any credence?"

"Father, think about it from their point of view."

"I can't do that, as I have no idea whom you've heard from."

"It is enough to know that I've heard from lay leaders of our Church, from clergy, and from monastics," George Pappas clarified.

"Monastics?" Father Fortis asked. "Ah, you must mean monks from one or two of the monasteries on Mt. Athos."

"It is enough to know that these are significant leaders of our Church, those at the highest level of authority and influence."

Father Fortis refused to be intimidated. "That still leaves me in the dark, but please illumine me on their point of view."

George Pappas chose to pour himself a second cup of tea and add both cream and sugar. After slowly stirring the tea, he wiped his hands on his napkin before looking up. "A canon lawyer in our Church is, what should I say, corrective rather than prescriptive. My role is to observe and offer correction when and where needed, based on the holy and ancient canons of our faith. Which brings me to another point worth considering. Has it never struck you as an extraordinary coincidence that this woman arrived in Rome almost precisely when our Ecumenical Patriarch and the Pope were to begin their . . . what should I call them . . . their dialogues?"

"If I can offer some correction to you, it's fairer to say that Margaret Cleery arrived in Rome in the aftermath of the bombing in St. Peter's Square," Father Fortis said.

"Yes, fine, that too. My associates are smelling intrigue with the entire sequence of events."

Father Fortis checked the anger rising within him. "They think the Vatican has put Margaret Cleery up to what she's doing, is that it?"

George Pappas looked across the street to the church of San Teodoro. "We shouldn't be too trusting, Father Fortis, about the papacy. History advises against that, do you not agree?"

"This is not the 11th century, and it is not the 13th, 14th, or 15th century. We cannot continue to blame recent occupants in the chair of St. Peter for the duplicity of their medieval predecessors."

When George Pappas gave no indication that he was ready to relinquish that suspicion, Father Fortis added, "You've been with this new Pope, Mr. Pappas. Can't you see that he's as upset by Margaret Cleery's presence and grandstanding as Patriarch Michael?"

"How well do any of us know this new Pope? Can you be absolutely sure that the Cleery woman isn't a plant, a tool of the Vatican to accelerate the capitulation of our Holy Orthodox Church to Rome?"

It wasn't until a table of priests from across the room looked over at the two of them that Father Fortis realized his fist had come down harder on the table than he intended. "You are close to calling Patriarch Michael a fool! He has known this Pope for decades."

Mr. Pappas responded in a flat voice, "No, he knew a doctoral student in Rome back in the nineties. That student is now the Pope of Rome. Pope Gregorio's allegiance is not to an old friend, but to his Roman Church."

Father Fortis took a deep breath and tried to calm his racing thoughts. "Surely, Mr. Pappas, you recognize paranoid fantasies when you receive them from these so-called associates. I have no doubt that some in our Church are so suspicious of the Vatican that they will even accuse the Curia of staging the bombing. Please tell me that you have more sense than that."

Mr. Pappas ignored the request. "Perhaps my associates sense a level of trust, a naïve trust on the part of the Ecumenical Patriarch, that is unwarranted. Have you never heard of the circus trainer who spent ten years transforming a savage bear into a cuddly pet? The animal no longer desired to bite the trainer, but one day the bear hugged the trainer so hard that he killed him, nonetheless."

"Of course, I've heard that story. It's a story based on fear. First, you or your friends accuse the Catholic Church of duplicity, and now you accuse the Catholic Church of suffocating us with love."

George Pappas gave a sly smile that irritated Father Fortis. The lawyer was clearly comfortable going toe to toe with him. Father Fortis fought the urge to reach across the table and grab George Pappas in a headlock, mussing that perfectly coiffed hair.

"My associates and I do not dispute Our Lord," George Pappas said. "Far from it, but any reconciliation must be the result of Rome admitting her sins, her false doctrines. For nearly a thousand years, that's what we've been waiting for. I haven't heard one admission of error yet from this Pope."

"And I'm not hearing one ounce of flexibility, not to mention humility, from you or your associates. You clearly care more about Church politics than the attempt on His Holiness' life."

George Pappas didn't say anything for a moment as he wiped his mouth. "Of course I'm concerned about the bombings at the Phanar and here in Rome. But as you know, there have been other attacks on the Patriarchate in Constantinople, and they have always been traced to Turkish Muslims, to extremists. I believe that is the case this time too. And the drone attack in St. Peter's Square? Isn't it obvious that the target for that was the Pope?"

Father Fortis stared dumbfounded at George Pappas. "But the two attacks happened almost at the same moment. Surely, that can't be just—"

The lawyer interrupted him. Can't be a coincidence? Yes, that is exactly what it was—a coincidence. Now, Father Fortis, let's agree that our roles are different. Finding the person behind these attacks is the job of your detective friend, the security forces, and you. My role, not yours, is to safeguard the traditions of our Orthodox faith. And in that role, let me give you this warning. Have you never heard of the man who was so open-minded that his brains fell out, Father Fortis? Could that be describing you? I don't say this out of spite or meanness, but in recognition of how much Patriarch Michael values your perspective. I am pleading; remember your role and help him proceed cautiously. We are both aware of the consequences for our Church if he does not."

And there, Father Fortis realized, was the trump card. Any Orthodox leader who drew too close to Rome risked splintering the Orthodox world. He remembered when Pope John Paul II had visited Greece on pilgrimage, how some of the monastic leaders from Mt. Athos had advised the Archbishop of Greece not to meet with the "heretic."

"Mr. Pappas, I see you are a treasure trove of pithy sayings. I also know that I won't convince you, and you won't convince me. But I'm so tired of this 'if I don't like the game, my friends and I are going to take our ball and go home' stance of some in our Church; I don't care if they're in Moscow, Jerusalem, or in monastic seclusion on Mt. Athos. I beg of you one concession."

George Pappas folded his napkin carefully and placed it next to his plate. "And what is that?"

"I ask you to choose one Catholic priest or nun from all those who were with us at Santa Sabina and invite that person—no, invite that Christian—to pray with you for the safety of the Patriarch *and the Pope*."

The lawyer rose from the table and for a moment stood in silence. "Ah, well, we can't all be like you—asked to pray in the presence of the Pope. I promise to pray, but whom I pray *with* is for me inconsequential. But I will tell you what I am praying *for*. I'm praying that Patriarch Michael will return as soon as possible to Constantinople. It's there, not here in Rome, where he belongs."

Father Fortis watched the canon lawyer stroll out of the hotel and cross the street in the direction of the church of San Teodoro. He had no idea if George Pappas' associates even existed, but then he realized that it didn't matter if the man had actually received emails and texts. The truth was that leaders sharing his perspective did exist, and George Pappas was not inventing their suspicious attitude about events in Rome.

How, he wondered, had the will of God become synonymous with inertia? What was the Bible but a series of stories of people called to step out on journeys, stories of persons willing to take risks? Hadn't that been the case from Noah to St. Paul? The Biblical God seemed to Father Fortis to be antsy, dissatisfied with the status quo, luring people of faith toward a reality yet to come, the Kingdom of God.

In contrast, Father Fortis felt at times that the Church had become the fearful person in Jesus' parable of the talents, the one more afraid of losing ground than advancing toward God's future.

As he buttered a second roll, Father Fortis realized that he needed to reevaluate Margaret Cleery. George Pappas and his ilk imagined her to be in league with the Vatican. Patriarch Michael and Pope Gregorio saw her as a dangerous distraction even as he thought of her as a "loose cannon." In the opinion of the Vatican and the Patriarch, the best thing for God to do would be to tell this woman and her entourage to leave Rome. *But what,* Father Fortis was just allowing himself to wonder, *if God has other plans?*

JULY 7: ROME: THE IRISH COLLEGE

FATHER AIDEN LOOKED AT HIS REFLECTION in the mirror. He approved of the short-sleeved clerical shirt, given the projected heat of the day. He thought about visiting Margaret Cleery without the "dog collar" and decided he would don one while on public transportation and wait until he stood outside her hotel door to remove it. The look he wanted to project was that he was comfortable with this woman, that they knew each other well enough for him to show her his relaxed side. That would be an invitation for her to trust him even more.

He smiled before turning away from the mirror and heading for the door. His campaign to gain the woman's confidence was on track; no, the campaign was working better than he had expected. He'd started with some carefully constructed asides, comments that showed that he knew what she needed. To his surprise, he had no competition for this role. He'd expected Father Rory, who'd traveled with her from Ireland, to vie for her confidences, but the old priest was filling a different role, that of being her scribe. When Father Aiden visited with Father Rory at the hospital while Margaret Cleery was being checked out by the E.R. staff, he saw the journal that the old priest carried with him. When he asked about it, Father Rory reluctantly explained that he was recording the messages of Jesus. Father Aiden found it easy to put the old priest's fears to rest, praising Father Rory for his service and hinting that, one day, people all over the world would be gratefully reading his account of the Irish mystic.

The city bus was crowded and, because of his slight stature, he found himself once again assaulted by those around him who never considered using deodorant. The Irish weren't much better, he conceded, but the climate was cooler and perspiration less common. While this and the foul exhaust fumes were why he hated public transportation in Rome, he was willing to put up with the unctuous smells for his new opportunity to play both sides, Vatican and Margaret Cleery, against each other.

The work on his dissertation was suffering, as his updates to Father Britter, Principal of the Irish College, and his visits to Margaret Cleery gave him little time to work in the college's library. He knew, however, that his committee had been apprised of his new responsibilities and, besides, he was enjoying his new covert life too much to worry. He had kept his report of what happened at the church of St. Peter in Chains sparse, leaving out the telling fact that Margaret Cleery had quoted from a recent version of the Bible. The Vatican, for his plan to work, had to be left uncertain about the veracity of Margaret Cleery.

Before entering the hotel, he stopped at a newsstand to buy a copy of the *Daily News*, the trashy take on news back in Britain that he figured Margaret Cleery would enjoy after being cooped up in her room. Father Aiden wanted to please Margaret Cleery especially today, as he needed to hear her plans for tomorrow, the day her followers expected her—because he'd leaked the information—to resume her activities.

His overall plan was simple. Having visited her every day and earned her trust, Aiden O'Malley expected her to share her plans for the next days in Rome, and in this way, he'd begin to understand how she engineered her messages. If she slipped at all and revealed how the scam worked, he'd offer a complicit smile. *I will be the magician's assistant, and, as the days wear on, I'll come to know all her tricks.* And then? And then he'd plot the great reveal, when the world would know two truths at the same time: that Margaret Cleery is a fake and that the Vatican pressured him to spy on her. In one glorious moment, both Mother Cleery and the Vatican would be discredited.

He gave his name as he knocked softly on her door. He heard her rustling around in the room before telling him to enter. When he did so, he found her sitting in a chair and smiling up at him.

"Well, well," he said, as he handed her the newspaper, "aren't we looking perky today."

"Ah, the *Daily News*. How did you know?" she asked, beaming at him.

"We're Irish, aren't we? What's better than reading about the shenanigans of the English? I think one of the royals was caught with a woman of the night again."

"Lovely, lovely, Aiden. Sometimes I think they do it on purpose, just to see their names in the news."

You of all people should understand that, he thought.

"So, today's the last day of being cooped up here. That must feel good," he said, then waited for her reply.

Margaret Cleery continued to look through the newspaper for a moment. "We need to talk, Aiden, about tomorrow. I need your help," she said.

Oh, this is too easy, he thought. He knew she welcomed his presence, even as he knew many of her followers tired her when they came to her room for a visit. He hadn't expected her to take him into her confidence so quickly, though.

"You know that I'm your friend, Margaret, above all else." He left the "all else" to be filled in by her, but he saw her relax in the chair as he said this. The mood in the room seemed perfect for her to offer a first hint of her method.

"As you know, I feel a burning sensation around my heart when the messages come to me. Before I collapsed, I had received two of these since coming to Rome. The thing is," she said, then paused.

Go ahead, let me peek into your scheming brain and your dark soul, Father Aiden thought. "Yes, Margaret?" he asked when the pause extended so long he thought she might be changing her mind.

"In Ireland, I'd have these messages maybe four or five times a year. That I can handle, but you saw what happens when these messages come close together." She looked up at him.

Despite being confused by her words, he smiled pastorally.

"I need some way to control the messages, Aiden, to not be so powerless in the face of them. There, I've said it. Is that selfish?"

He marveled as he realized what she was doing. *Oh, you are good*, he thought. *You want to play me, to ask my help in controlling your messages that you and I both know you've always been in control of? Fine.*

"No, no, that's not selfish, Margaret. I know you are fully submitted to God's will, but we are weak vessels, flesh and blood. Sorry to say, most of your followers wouldn't understand, though."

Margaret laid the newspaper on a side table and sighed. "No, they wouldn't give a tinker's damn if I dropped dead, as long as they believed I died in ecstasy."

Aiden sat down in the chair next to her. He took her hand in his and said, "Margaret, I hope you know that I'm not one of those followers. I'm here to be of service. How can I help you with this?"

Margaret sighed again. "Just your saying that helps me more than you can know. But tell me, is there anything I can do when the burning starts? I feel so helpless."

He had to stop himself from laughing. What a performance! He realized that whatever advice he offered would work. If he told her to drink green tea, stand on one leg, and then fall to her knees to offer a Hail Mary, she'd accept his "advice." So would telling her to gargle with vinegar, sing the Irish national anthem, or throw a book at a wall.

His admiration for Margaret Cleery's talent was growing along with his anger. Whatever he suggested would be a placebo, only this placebo was intended to be known to the patient but not to him, the doctor. So to play along, he realized he must offer something that sounded plausible.

"Margaret, I'll study what other mystics have used in the past. You certainly can't be the first mystic who has had this . . . " he paused, wondering if the term "problem" was too strong, "who had this concern," he offered. "But this might take me a few days. Can I ask you a question about the burning feeling?"

"Of course, Aiden. You know I trust you."

Like hell you do, Aiden thought. "Do you have any physical sensations before the burning begins?"

He watched as Margaret Cleery decided how best to respond. He was forcing her to think quickly, and the quicker she had to think, the more likely she would be to trip herself up.

"Now that you mention it, I sometimes have a premonition, no, not a premonition but an odd sense, like I'm expecting something, right before the burning begins. Have you ever felt that you knew when someone was going to telephone, just before the phone rang?"

"Hmm, that's interesting," Aiden replied. He had to say this for this woman: she was a pro. "May I suggest something?"

"Oh, please, Aiden. Anything."

"Margaret, do you remember the story of Moses and the burning bush? Or the account of Isaiah the prophet as he prayed in the temple?"

"Aiden, please. I went through confirmation and first communion, but I don't much read the Bible."

He patted her hand again. "Fine, fine. When Moses felt the presence of God near to him, he heard a voice tell him to take off his sandals. When Isaiah found himself drawn up into the heavenly temple, he felt just as afraid as Moses did. He closed his eyes and prayed for relief."

That last bit was a slight tweaking of the story, Father Aiden realized. But it sounded plausible, and that was all that mattered. "When that feeling you described begins, before the burning starts, immediately take off your shoes and pray for relief."

She stared at him for a moment so hard that he thought she knew that he was onto her game.

"Really? Do you think that will work?" she asked.

"I'm not promising anything, Margaret. But until I find something in my research, why don't you try that?"

Margaret nodded before frowning. "Sometimes that queer feeling begins when my shoes are already off. What should I do then?"

God, he thought, *what a worthy opponent! What an artist!*

Pretending to consider her question seriously, he offered, "Then you must put your shoes on and immediately take them off again."

Once again, he expected her to say, "Look, Aiden, let's both drop this charade." Instead, she laughed, but he could see that he'd passed the test. The act would continue, with him in the role of Sancho Panza.

CHAPTER FOURTEEN

THE CHESSMASTER STRODE ACROSS THE TREELESS MOORS on his estate. He was what some countries called a laird, others the lord of the manor. His inherited lands were so extensive that since his childhood nanny died, he'd never let anyone get close to him geographically or personally. Had his nanny lived, he would have some cause to worry, as she knew him better than anyone, including his father.

It had been nine days since the bombing in St. Peter's Square, and messages from his clients were no longer demanding to know what went wrong. Yes, in the immediate wake of the failure, he'd received demands for a quick follow-up event, but those messages dwindled to a trickle within days. All major networks continued speculating about who was responsible for the drone flight. As the Chessmaster expected, the Italian media presented a hodgepodge of rumor and press conference analysis. With no group claiming responsibility, some people were convinced that a Middle Eastern terrorist group was behind the attacks, while others suggested North Korea, and yet others floated the rumor of a California death cult's involvement. *Not even close*, the Chessmaster thought as he leaned on his horn-handled walking stick and admired the sunset.

The Chessmaster knew that he would soon need to offer his clients a hint of the next operation. Little did they know how close he was to setting into motion not just a next step, but his grand plan. This one would make the Rome and Istanbul bombings look like warm-ups, which was precisely how he saw them.

Within an hour of the bomb in Rome missing its intended target, the Chessmaster had accepted that the survival of the Patriarch and Pope was the will of God. He remained convinced that the two prelates were pawns of the Antichrist, but he saw now that their deaths were not, as he'd assumed, precursors of the End, but even something grander. God had allowed the two to live so that their deaths in the imminent future would have greater, even apocalyptic meaning.

As he'd done for the past ten years, he returned nightly to the book of Revelation and the Dead Sea Scrolls. Sometimes he felt so gripped by what he was reading that he failed to sleep. And over the past three nights, as he prayed and flagellated himself with a prickly reed, he found the Irish woman's face increasingly coming to mind.

More and more, he accepted that Margaret Cleery had some part in the long game. That she was a thorn in the side of the Vatican and the Orthodox Church was obvious, and he had no doubt that this was also part of God's purposes.

God's purposes. Yes, he believed God's purposes were being worked out through the Pope, the Ecumenical Patriarch, and Margaret Cleery. There were no other world figures with such symbolic value as the Pope and Ecumenical Patriarch, and their staying in close contact with one another in Rome could only be taken as part of God's design. All he would need, he reasoned, was one or two more weeks of preparation before the world's final drama would begin. The last thing he needed was for the Ecumenical Patriarch to return to Istanbul.

The Chessmaster had his own sources of information in Rome, so he knew the Irish woman had been silent for nearly a week, initially because she was re-cuperating from a minor malady and then because she'd begun using an Irish-American priest as a buffer and surrogate. The priest, a Father Aiden O'Malley, led the group on tours daily to various catacombs and a host of churches in Rome, tiring her followers and giving Margaret Cleery time in seclusion sup-posedly to pray.

Pray, my ass, he thought. *The woman is doing exactly what I am doing: plan-ning ahead.* Even as he knew that he had to keep his clients engaged and fo-cused, he knew the Cleery woman had to offer a new message soon or risk defections.

If only I'd thought of this myself, planting a fake mystic in Rome, he thought. How he would have enjoyed sending "messages" that would move the Pope and Ecumenical Patriarch like pieces on a chessboard. But it was too late for that, as God had taken charge, sending the Irish woman to fill that role. He would wait for Margaret Cleery to tip her hand. Then, he would act accordingly.

He began his descent off the moor to return to the warmth of his hearth. After a few steps, he stopped to lean on his walking stick as a new thought sur-faced. Perhaps he could do more than simply wait for this Cleery woman to act. What would happen, he wondered, if he anonymously sent her funds—not too much but enough to be an unexpected surprise—along with a note describing his admiration for her courageous stance?

He returned to his loping gait, feeling satisfied with what had been accomplished on the walk. He had read somewhere that walking promoted creativity, and he often found that to be true. This was not the first time he'd returned from a solitary stroll with a clearer idea of the way forward. After he walked another five minutes, he sensed a second piece of his plan falling into place. He laughed so loudly that he heard his echo from the nearest hill. *Of course*, he thought, *I know exactly what I can do to force the Patriarch to stay in Rome.*

✝

July 8: Rome: The Church of San Teodoro

On the fourth day following her fainting spell, Margaret Cleery didn't leave her hotel room until Father Aiden took her followers away on one of his morning tours. Then, on her own, she blended into the crowds of tourists at Rome's more popular sites, visiting Piazza Navona, the Pantheon, and the Trevi Fountain. To her relief, she felt neither the burning sensation around her heart nor the preceding wave of foreboding.

On her first outing, Margaret Cleery felt exposed, but she soon realized that few tourists watched Italian TV news. To them, she was just another red-haired Brit seeing the sights. To be safe, however, she avoided the famous churches of Rome, but then she had no desire to visit them anyway. She relished the feeling that she was living a normal life for a change.

She knew that she owed all this and more to Father Aiden. How quickly he'd become a trusted friend, someone who anticipated many of her needs. It was Father Aiden who suggested she have some time on her own in Rome. It was Father Aiden who arranged with the hotel staff for her to have a conference room set aside where she could join with her followers nightly in praying the rosary. Instead of her followers staring at her all day long as they hoped for another Jesus message, she was with them for only an hour every night as she recited, rather more quickly than the others, the decades of the rosary.

Being away from the group during the day gave her time to imagine life after the messages ended. But that was the question: *Do I want a completely normal life? Do I really want to return to boring Greystones and the laundromat?*

Her ruminations were prompted by an envelope handed her that morning by the desk manager. Inside, she found five one-hundred Euro notes along with a note: "From someone who believes in your gifts and prays for your success."

This was new. She'd received an endless amount of media attention over the years of her messages, but never money. To this point in her stay in Rome, her room and basic board were covered through the generosity of several long-term followers. This generous gift, however, seemed to come with no strings attached.

As she left the hotel and walked down one of Rome's quieter side streets, she thought of the money in her purse. Five hundred Euros was a considerable sum, and she wondered how best to spend it. "I'll buy a sun hat," she said to herself. Reaching the major thoroughfare of Via Nazionale, she entered a shop where she found a hat that offered protection from both the hot sun and from prying eyes.

Later, as she walked past other shops, she looked for something appropriate for Father Aiden. Her first thought was to buy him a new rosary, but then she smiled, knowing Father Aiden would prefer something more practical. She passed kiosks that offered aprons for men with Michelangelo's *David*, penis prominently displayed, printed on them. No, she smiled again, that would hardly do either. Finally, she entered an art and paper store and bought Aiden a fountain pen. It was far costlier than her sunhat but expressed, she hoped, her gratitude. While her fans would follow her anywhere, she needed someone in Rome to share the burden of leading of the group, and Father Aiden was a godsend.

Returning to her hotel, she was depressed, feeling like a dog after a walk, confined again to her cramped room. On the spur of the moment and without knowing exactly why, she returned to the hotel desk and asked the young woman if there were any Orthodox churches in Rome. Expecting a "no," she watched as the woman typed into a computer and then nodded that there was one not that far from the hotel. The young woman unfolded a map of Rome's center, circled the hotel's location and then put an X at a spot several blocks away on the other side of the Imperial Forum.

"San Teodoro, yes? It is no more than a ten-minute walk," the young woman assured her. "I do not know the church," she said, pronouncing that word as "shursh," "but it must be very old to be at that location."

Margaret Cleery asked if she could take the map with her.

"But of course," the woman replied, as she folded the map neatly and handed it to Margaret with a smile.

Margaret went first to her room to fetch her water bottle as well as weigh her impulse more carefully. Did she run a risk visiting that church? While she thought it unlikely that she would run into Father Aiden and her followers, was there a chance that someone from the Orthodox community would recognize her from the news?

She stood in front of the mirror. She donned her sunglasses and then her new sunhat. Her distinctive red hair was completely hidden by the hat, and she thought it likely that she'd be taken as just another tourist.

The walk to the church of San Teodoro took her almost twenty minutes as she had to pay an entrance fee to pass through the Imperial Forum. She could see from the map that she might have taken a different route to arrive at the church and saved sixteen Euros, but she didn't want to risk getting lost.

Exiting the forum on the opposite side, she realized that she was walking on Via di San Teodoro. Despite that, she was surprised when she arrived at the gate of the church. Inside the gate, stairs on two sides took the visitor down to a lower level and to the door of the ancient church.

From the outside, the circular-shaped church had little to commend it, but she stopped at the entrance and read the plaque in its various languages. In ancient times, the little church was a "diaconia," a Christian center that distributed food to the poor of Rome. Later, the church had been the home of a Catholic confraternity. Finally, in 2000, the little church was gifted by Pope John Paul II to the Greek Orthodox community of Rome.

"Well, isn't that bloody interesting," she said aloud. "The Vatican gave this church to the Orthodox a little more than twenty years ago. Maybe my messages aren't so crazy after all."

She entered through the front doors and found herself in the perfectly round room. On the far side, however, an ornate wooden screen was placed before an altar by the back wall. On the circular ceiling above, she saw frescoed figures, most with beards and in long robes.

The air was cool in the church, and she sat down, happy to find herself alone. On the wooden screen hung a grouping of icons, the icon of Jesus and the icon of the Blessed Virgin Mary being the only ones she recognized.

The small church reminded her more of her home parish than St. Peter's Basilica or the church of St. Peter in Chains. After a few moments, she concluded that it was the quiet. The visit to St. Peter's Basilica on her first day had been with the noise of at least two thousand other people in the massive church, cameras clicking and people bumping into one another. Her twenty minutes in St Peter in Chains had been in the presence of fewer people, of course, but there was no sense of solitude.

If I was better at praying, she thought, *I'd like to pray in this place.* In interviews she'd given the media since the messages began, the interviewers tended to focus on her admission that she'd never found praying easy. They seemed to find it an oddity that Jesus would speak to a woman who rarely spoke to Him.

She looked around the church to make sure she was alone as the thought came to her, *Why don't I pray?* It was as if she were daring herself, or maybe she wanted Jesus to know what it felt like to have someone barge in on His thoughts. After clearing her throat and false-starting several times, she managed to start with part of the rosary, then the Lord's Prayer. She recited as much of the 23rd Psalm as she could remember before giving up and sitting in the quiet.

Her legs and arms felt heavy, leading her to wonder if she should have stayed in her hotel room after all. But then she felt a soft breeze on her face and wondered if someone had entered the church. Turning around and seeing no one, she sat for a moment as the sensation of the breeze continued.

Fearful that the burning feeling near her heart was about to return, she felt instead a wave of something else wash over her. Without understanding, she realized she felt shame.

"Why have you come to me this way?" she whispered.

She waited for a moment before hearing a familiar voice. "I am always this near, Margaret. I'm this near in your laundromat, in your kitchen, and when you're taking a chance on the Irish Sweepstakes. I was this near to you when you were seventeen and found out you were pregnant. But sometimes, people don't want to know how near I am to them."

"Well, that's me, I guess," she said. "These people that follow me around— they think the two of us are best mates, but a lot of the time, especially lately, you seem more like Liam. You know, the clutching guy at the pub who wants to drink with me. Sometimes I think you chose me just to punish me for being such a bad person."

"No, that's not what I do. People hardly need me to punish them; they do such a good job punishing themselves. People think I see them as bad, but the truth is, I just see them. I see Margaret. Just Margaret."

Margaret Cleery felt tears begin to trickle down her cheek. "Jesus," she said, not sure in the moment if she were cursing or still praying, "the way I've been acting since I got here. I've been a fool, haven't I?"

"I'm just glad you didn't take off your shoes this time," she heard the voice say.

She laughed. "That's just a load of shite, isn't it? Aiden was just trying to help me, so he made that up, I guess."

The voice was silent, and once again she felt alone in the quiet. *He sees Margaret, just Margaret*, she thought. She knew Margaret the mouthy Mom, Margaret the pushy broad, and she knew Margaret the cussing woman whom Jesus sometimes speaks to. But it dawned on her that she didn't know "just Margaret."

She rose from the chair and took another look around the church. What an odd place for Jesus to be waiting for her. And this time He gave her a message just for herself, not for her followers, the Pope, or the Patriarch. As she exited the church and walked across the small patio to the steps leading up to the street, she turned and looked up at one of the windows off to the side of the church of San Teodoro. From it, she saw a man with a long black beard and an ornate cross looking down at her. She stopped and returned his gaze. In a moment, he turned back into the room and disappeared.

No doubt one of the priests, she thought. Did he recognize her, she wondered? And then it hit her. She no longer cared who recognized her or who waited for her to share some message from Jesus. She felt the weight of that lift from her shoulders as she headed back to the hotel.

JULY 8: ROME: EVENING AT THE COLOSSEO HOTEL

FATHER AIDEN WAS SURPRISED WHEN MARGARET CLEERY didn't rush through the evening rosary with her followers. Not once did she glance in his direction and give him her knowing look. Instead, she remained behind with those who wanted to spend a few more minutes with her.

What's her game? Aiden wondered. Yesterday, she had thanked him profusely for getting her followers "off my back, out of my hair," as she put it.

He remembered a public-school friend who once showed him a picture of a three-dimensional chessboard. Now he felt he was in a three-dimensional play. On the surface was Mother Cleery, the Irish mystic, sent to Rome by Christ. On the second level, below public gaze, was Margaret Cleery's relationship with him. At this level, she let him believe he alone knew how she felt being adored by her followers.

Now he realized that there was a third level, the level occupied solely by Margaret Cleery, the scheming actor. Not being invited to share in this level was what made him furious, for, at this third level, he sensed she felt perverse joy in scamming not only her followers but him.

Never mind, he told himself, *her day is coming.* At some point, she would make the tiniest slip, and he would have the damning evidence he needed. He fantasized about the look on her face when she saw that there was a fourth level to the drama, one she didn't know existed. That was the level where he alone was in charge.

Aiden waited outside her room until she arrived. It was now ten o'clock, and Margaret looked worn out. Not the first time, he wondered if she'd had formal theater training. She invited him in and seemed to be looking for something in her purse before sitting heavily in a chair.

"How about a whisky?" he asked.

"Not tonight, Aiden. I'm much too tired. Do you mind if we call it a day?"

"Of course, Margaret, of course," he said, and wished her a pleasant night's rest as he left her room. Tired? How can she be tired? He was the one who sorted out public transportation to take her followers to the neighborhood of Trastevere, and that was no easy feat. He was the one, not she, who arranged a visit to the church of San Crisogono and convinced the sexton to let them visit the early Christian ruins below. From there, he'd walked the group to the church of Santa Maria in Trastevere, another of the early churches of Rome. It was he, not she, who found a modest-priced restaurant near the church where the group clearly enjoyed themselves. By the time the group returned in late afternoon to the hotel, everyone agreed that a rest was in order. While the gullible followers rested, he called Principal Britter to update him on yet another day of inactivity by Margaret Cleery.

The principal was clearly frustrated with the lack of developments. "I'm being contacted every day," he said. "How can she give two messages and now nothing?"

Aiden remained silent, deciding not to share the "remedy" he'd given Margaret Cleery for her visitations.

After a long pause, the principal lowered his voice and, in nearly a whisper, asked, "Father Aiden, what sense do you have of her? Is she . . . well, is she a fraud?"

Aiden knew that someone higher up the ladder had ordered the principal to ask him that. He paused, wondering what response would be most advantageous.

"As you say, there've been just the two messages," he began. "And that's not enough for me to form an opinion one way or another. I'm sorry I can't be more helpful. I can only imagine the worry of our superiors—the not knowing, I mean. I hope you don't consider me a failure."

"No, no, Father Aiden, not in the least." The principal was then silent for a long moment. "But it's been an entire week since her last message. A full week."

I can count, Aiden said to himself. *He's suggesting I could do something to push Margaret. Well, I will, but I'm not going to tell him my plan.*

Instead, he decided to make the principal and his superiors more anxious. "Principal, you do know that often the gap between her past messages has been months. If Jesus is truly speaking to her, we can only pray." He smiled at that last touch—so pious.

"Of course, you're right, Father Aiden. But if she is a fraud, won't she need to present another message soon?"

"I'm afraid I don't follow, Principal," he lied.

"I've been told that the number of her followers is decreasing."

Well, well, Aiden thought. So the Vatican had someone else keeping an eye on Margaret. And that meant that this second person was also keeping an eye on him. *This is getting even more interesting*, he thought, as he wondered who in the group might be the second mole. Whoever it was, that person was keeping a low profile.

"Yes, yes, that's true about her followers," Aiden replied. "I honestly don't know if Margaret Cleery has noticed that, though."

He heard the principal sigh heavily, as if he knew he'd soon have another uncomfortable conversation with his Vatican contact. "As you so wisely said, Father Aiden," the principal said, "let us pray for . . ."

Aiden waited with a smile for the principal to finish the sentence and share what the Vatican was hoping to discover about Margaret Cleery.

"Yes, let us pray, then," the principal finished the sentence without finishing the thought.

CHAPTER FIFTEEN

---◆---

THE PHANAR, THE HEADQUARTERS of the Ecumenical Patriarch, was situated in the old Greek area of modern Istanbul, though the days were gone when Greek families populated the area. The Turkish government, while giving lip service to religious freedom, had done little to counter Muslim fundamentalists who wanted to eliminate the Christian presence in Turkey.

Even before the bomb that killed Mr. Angelopoulos, there'd been other attacks on personnel of the Patriarchate. With the recent bombing, however, the Turkish government had placed security at the various gates to the compound. All mail was now being scanned for bomb components. Clearly, the explosion at the Patriarchate had embarrassed the Turkish government.

Archdeacon Andreas sat in his office on Monday morning, reading through the most recent communique from George Pappas. Pappas' worry, that Ecumenical Patriarch Michael's stay in Rome was becoming a concern, was a sentiment with which he wholeheartedly agreed. After the anathemas between both Churches were withdrawn in 1964, the visits of Orthodox patriarchs to Rome had been short, usually only for the feast day of Saints Peter and Paul. But the Archdeacon agreed with George Pappas that the embrace in 1964 did not give Ecumenical Patriarch Michael the right to act on his own.

The longer Patriarch Michael remained in Rome, Archdeacon Andreas believeed, the more the Orthodox world would question the Patriarch's leadership. At what point would he be seen not so much as a guest of the Vatican, but rather a willing hostage?

It was clear to Archdeacon Andreas that George Pappas didn't have the ear of the young Ecumenical Patriarch. That was not the canon lawyer's fault, but rather the result of Patriarch Michael's inexperience and naiveté. As someone older and more knowledgeable of Church politics, Andreas wanted to urge the Patriarch to heed the advice of Pappas, who represented powerful forces in the Church. In contrast, the American monk and confidante of the Ecumenical Patriarch, Father Nicholas Fortis, represented a much smaller fraction of the Orthodox community. "The monk is becoming a Rasputin," he said aloud to the empty room. The problem was that no one, not even Father Fortis' abbot, could overrule the Ecumenical Patriarch and demand that Father Fortis be sent home.

He went to the rickety window and opened it to enjoy the morning air. Looking out, he saw minaret after minaret piercing the skyline of Constantinople and thought of how much the Muslims had confiscated from the Orthodox. Would Patriarch Michael naively give away even more, this time to Rome?

Two pigeons flew in and lit, cooing, on the window sill. He recognized both and returned to his desk where, from a drawer, he extracted a crust of bread. Breaking the bread into small pieces, he placed them in a row so the pigeons would be forced to come closer to receive their treat.

"If only I could fly like you," he said to the birds. "I'd fly to Rome and bring Patriarch Michael home." He paused for a moment and asked himself, *Why don't I?* He could be in Rome in a matter of hours, and surely Patriarch Michael would not rebuff the advice of his archdeacon. His message to the Ecumenical Patriarch would be blunt: if he did not consult with the other Patriarchs and the Holy and Sacred Synod of the Church before further meetings with the Pope of Rome, he risked division in the Church.

He looked down to see the lead pigeon peck at the last piece of bread, no more than inches from his own hand. Soon, he realized, the birds would be so tame that they'd take the bread directly from his gnarled fingers. If only humans could be so tamed.

Zssst! The first bullet hit the lead bird, exploding the hungry pigeon into a mass of feathers. Archdeacon Andreas instinctively leaned out as if to catch the feathers as they flew into the air. A long-buried memory of a pillow fight with his younger brother was Archdeacon Andreas' last thought as the sniper's second bullet ricocheted off the window's stone lintel and entered the Archdeacon's occipital right lobe before it exited the back of his skull.

JULY 9: ROME: THE CHURCH OF SAN TEODORO

LATER THAT SAME MORNING, FATHER FORTIS and Worthy threaded their way through a throng of media camped outside the church of San Teodoro. Father Fortis took the lead and, by lowering his shoulder, managed to break through the wall of microphones aimed in their direction.

Within the gate, the security at the church of San Teodoro seemed to be doubled as Worthy and he were patted down and Worthy's briefcase searched. In the conference room adjacent to the Patriarch's apartment, they found George Pappas, clearly grief-stricken, sitting on the far side of the table and looking down at his hands. He didn't look up to meet Worthy's or Father Fortis' eye. Also present was a Catholic priest whom Father Fortis had noticed sitting close to the Pope at Santa Sabina. Father Fortis remembered his name as Father Gilley. He did meet Father Fortis' eye and give him a slight nod.

No one said anything until Patriarch Michael entered the room. Everyone except Worthy approached and kissed his hand. The Ecumenical Patriarch then approached Worthy and shook his hand before inviting them all to take their seats.

The four waited for the Patriarch to speak. "There must be an end to this misery," he said, and Father Fortis wondered if he was speaking to those in the room or to God. "But we still don't know who is behind everything, do we, Lieutenant Worthy?"

Worthy cleared his throat. "I owe you an honest answer. We'd be a lot further ahead if the perpetrator or perpetrators had taken credit for the attacks. That hasn't happened, but we do know that the Orthodox community was the sole target in Constantinople." After a pause, Worthy added, "and it's possible you, as the head of the Orthodox Church, were the sole target outside St. Peter's."

Patriarch Michael pursed his lips. "Lieutenant, assuming you are right, why do you think these attacks are taking place now?"

Worthy met the Patriarch's gaze. "Father Fortis and I are working on the theory that something you said or did triggered the attacks."

Sighing heavily, Patriarch Michael asked, "That hardly narrows things down, does it? And if Pope Gregorio is also a target, does that mean he said or did something to trigger the attacks?"

"Your Holiness, Lieutenant Worthy and I have the files of every official statement that Pope Gregorio and you have made," Father Fortis said. "We think it likely we'll find a clue to the perpetrator in those files."

The Ecumenical Patriarch folded his hands in front of him and looked from Worthy and Father Fortis to the other three men. He seemed about to say something but then did not.

"You are clearly still in danger, Your All Holiness," George Pappas said. "We have to concentrate on protecting you."

"I am protected, George. Just look out the window. Half the Roman police force is out there."

"But Rome has proven not to be any safer, Your Eminence, than the Patriarchate," Mr. Pappas insisted.

"And your suggestion is what?" Father Gilley asked, his tone acidic.

Patriarch Michael raised both hands to ask for peace. "Security in Rome has been excellent since the bombing, George. Certainly, you can see that."

"But for how long?" Mr. Pappas pressed. "Friends of yours and our Church believe you'd be safer in Athens, or back in New York City."

Father Fortis couldn't hold his tongue. "So the Patriarch is to go into hiding, is that it? Perhaps you'd recommend plastic surgery."

Worthy sat forward. "I know how you feel, Nick, but moving Patriarch Michael to the States is a reasonable suggestion."

Father Gilley sighed in disgust but seemed to know that the decision was entirely in the hands of Patriarch Michael.

The Ecumenical Patriarch looked from one man to another before speaking. "I agree with Father Fortis. To go into hiding would betray our faith. I don't mean faith will magically keep me out of danger, but many of my predecessors faced similar threats and were willing to die." He paused for a moment until he heard George Pappas clear his throat.

"Before you try to argue me out of it, George, I want to make my position clear. Since hearing the tragic news from the Patriarchate about Archdeacon Andreas, I've had time to think about my future and the future of our Church. I am choosing to remain in Rome not because I wish to court martyrdom, but because I have work to do here with Pope Gregorio."

George Pappas stared at the Patriarch. "Your words give me no peace. As I have tried to tell you before, the longer you're here, the more nervous grows our Church."

The Patriarch rose from his chair and came behind George Pappas. Resting his hands on the lawyer's shoulders, he said in a very soft voice, "George, you are the brakes on the car, and Father Nicholas is like the jumpy gas pedal. One of you wants to proceed full-speed ahead; the other wants the car to stop, if not turn around. George, I make this promise to you and to God. I won't sacrifice one element of our Orthodox faith, and I beg you to communicate that to our worried friends. But I also promise to continue to pray that Pope Gregorio and I will discern what the Holy Spirit is calling us to do. Pope Gregorio and I can do that best if I remain in Rome."

"But with what goal?" George Pappas pressed, his voice strained. "The Orthodox faithful do not wish to be united with the Roman Church. If you insist on that, you will create further division. You can't deny that the 2018 schism between Constantinople and Moscow is still a raw memory. Do you want the spirit of disunity to grow?"

"You know I don't, George. If now isn't the time for our two Churches to discuss how we may join in Jesus' prayer that His Church be one, then the Holy Spirit will make that clear."

There was silence in the room as Patriarch Michael returned to his seat.

"Father Nicholas, do you have enough control of your emotions to make a contribution, a positive one, to this conversation?"

Father Fortis felt his face turn red. All his life, he'd been scolded for his quick anger and his hasty words, but he'd never felt this level of shame as he accepted the reprimand of the Patriarch.

"I beg everyone's forgiveness. I spoke without thinking. I was wrong."

Patriarch Michael waved in the direction of Father Fortis, as if he were shooing away a bee. "You can do penance later, Nicholas," the Patriarch said with a soft smile. "Take a moment, and then please share what's in your heart."

Father Fortis nodded. "Our world is terribly broken. That's nothing new, but the level of anger in the world is dangerously high. Politicians refuse to compromise, factions and terrorist groups can be found in all faiths, even as the religions of the world have always pleaded for peace. My own country is so divided that some people joke—though the humor of it escapes me—that we're headed toward another civil war. There doesn't seem to be one nation that hasn't split into bitter factions. It's no wonder so many people believe the world is coming to an end. The world hungers for hope, but where is hope to be found?"

Father Fortis paused and glanced at Worthy and then at Patriarch Michael. For some reason, Worthy was busy scribbling something in a notebook. The eyes of the Patriarch, however, had a faint gleam in them.

"Please go on, Nicholas," he urged.

"The world is desperate for a sign of healing, some hope that what separates people, tribes, groups, and nations can be overcome. I believe what you and Pope Gregorio are seeking offers an example of healing and hope." He took a deep breath before adding, "And I believe what you both are seeking is the will of God for this broken world."

The room was again silent. Worthy continued to write furiously, but the others in the room didn't move or say anything.

Finally, Patriarch Michael rose and with a gesture invited the others in the room to rise. He offered a blessing to the room before saying, "Father Gilley, please convey to the Holy Father my appreciation for his condolences on our Church's loss, and please tell him, after a respectful time of mourning, that I will again be meeting with him to continue our journey."

Patriarch Michael walked toward the door that led to his apartment. Turning, he added, "And may the will of God be done on earth in this hour as it is in heaven."

JULY 10: A NORTHERN EUROPEAN ESTATE

THE CHESSMASTER LISTENING TO THE FIRST report out of Turkey on BBC

World Service when a confirming communique came in from one of his sources in Istanbul. He studied the stern face of the archdeacon on the screen and
set down his coffee. The plan hadn't been to kill anyone, but rather to simply
frighten those in the Orthodox compound. Such a simple act would have been
enough to convince the Patriarch to remain in Rome for safety reasons.

But the Chessmaster realized that God sometimes has other plans. "The
Lord giveth, and the Lord taketh away," he said to the empty room. There would
be oceans of blood when the final battle of Armageddon began.

Did he feel guilt over the death of the archdeacon? No, that would show
a lack of faith. God had delivered a very direct and uncomplicated message
through events in Istanbul. That message was "Never doubt Me."

As he sat in his library and contemplated the update from his operative in
Istanbul, he knew God's intervening action was also meant as a warning to him.
"Never doubt Me" was a message for him to ponder as well. Studying texts from
other religions about the end of the world had left him with a growing sense
that these texts were mainly nonsense. But to secure his clients' support, he pretended that their beliefs were well-founded. Jesus said, "Be wise as serpents,"
but the Chessmaster had found it difficult to hide his true feelings.

Take Dabiq, a minor city in northern Syria. From long hours of research,
going to websites sponsored by Islamists and analyzed closely by the CIA and
others, he'd gleaned where ISIS and its surviving offshoots believed the world
would end.

When he first read of ISIS' apocalyptic belief that the end of the world
would be centered on little-known Dabiq, he could only laugh. After study of
both ancient and modern apocalyptic groups, however, he realized that groups
as ancient as the Essenes of the first century BCE had also believed that the
final battle with evil would take place on their home turf, insignificant as it was
in the world's eyes.

Dabiq, Qumran, Jerusalem, Megiddo, or a desert site in Southern California.
The Chessmaster was no gullible fool. He recognized that all apocalyptic groups
were narcissistic, each seeing itself as the most important and beloved in God's
eyes and therefore the site where the end would come. But facing that narcis-
sism had made the Chessmaster wonder, in his weaker moments, what other
elements of those prophesies were simply proofs of human hubris.

Consequently, the death in Istanbul, while not making him feel guilty, had
shaken him. If there was even the slightest chance that he could lose faith in
God's ultimate purposes, wouldn't God destroy him as certainly as God had
destroyed the archdeacon?

Yes, the Chessmaster realized that God was testing him. *I do believe the end
of the world is near*, he told himself, even though he'd been careful to this point
never to predict when the end would come. What he had promised his clients

was that God was using them to complete the penultimate steps, the events that he kept telling them would happen before the end.

This hadn't kept various client groups from pressing him to make a precise prediction. He always waited several days before responding to these demands, and then he would reply that after deep study and prayer about the question, he'd been led to say that the end of the world was near, even very near.

Now he wondered if the unexpected death of the archdeacon in Istanbul had been a divine sign that the end was, in fact, close at hand. Certainly, his clients would be buoyed to hear the news. And wasn't he also buoyed by what had happened?

The Chessmaster decided that a solitary walk on his hills was in order. He turned off BBC Worldwide, found his walking stick, and headed out. The sun was warm for his clime, and that made him think of Rome and the Irish woman. One of his operatives in Rome had left the money along with the note and then followed Margaret Cleery on her impromptu shopping spree. Being an Italian woman, his operative had been able to follow Margaret Cleery into the shop where she bought the sunhat and then later into the paper store. *So the Irish woman likes a bit of cash,* the Chessmaster thought. *Good to know.*

He would have been happier, however, if Margaret Cleery had tipped her hand with another one of her messages. Instead of acting, the Irish fake seemed to be taking a break, which led him to wonder why Margaret Cleery was letting her followers slip away.

Coming over a rise, the Chessmaster scared a rabbit from its warren. The animal raced away from him as if he were the angel of death.

"I will give our Irish con-artist two more days," he said. "Then, if nothing happens, I will give her a push. A gentle one, to start with, but a push nonetheless."

CHAPTER SIXTEEN

———————◆———————

JULY 10: ROME: THE CHURCH OF SAN BARTOLOMEO

"**W**HAT IS THIS?" FATHER AIDEN ASKED. Margaret Cleery and he were eating together in the hotel's breakfast room when she passed him a small box with a gold ribbon around it.

Margaret Cleery smiled. "Open it and see," she said as she spread marmalade on a roll.

Aiden felt himself blush as he removed the fountain pen from its presentation box. "But why?" he asked.

"Because you're a dear friend. And for giving me a few days to get my bearings. I see things more clearly now, and please, no jokes about Cleery seeing more clearly."

He fingered the pen and tried it out on one of the paper napkins. Would he feel guilty in the future when he used it, he asked himself? "I'm only glad to help. You're under a lot of pressure, Margaret."

Margaret took a sip of tea before speaking. "I realized yesterday that a lot of that pressure has come from me, Aiden."

He returned the pen to its box and put it into his shirt pocket. He would not let her gift, whatever its motivation, disturb his focus. "Oh? I'm not sure I understand."

"I can be a cantankerous bitch, Aiden. I know that, so don't play nice and contradict me. And when I'm like that, I forget . . . how should I put it? I forget how blessed I am. I mean, here I am, an Irish washerwoman, in Rome, Italy. And why? All because Jesus decided to speak to me."

Aiden didn't contradict her, but listened intently for where she was headed on this new tack. He wondered if he should have anticipated this repentant phase of her plan. Had she adopted it because she suspected that he was on to her game?

"Jesus talked to me the day before yesterday," she said in a softer voice than he'd heard before.

Ah, he thought, *that's what she's about. She's losing support and has decided to throw her adoring fans a bone.*

He sat forward in his chair. Should he bother to ask if she'd removed her shoes when she felt the burning begin? Instead, he asked. "What did Our Dear Lord say?"

"It wasn't like before. I stopped into a church and was sitting quietly when He spoke to me. No burning sensation, no headache later, just the voice."

He fought an urge to laugh in her face or to slap her. But he'd let her play out her little scenario a bit longer. He folded his hands in front of him as if in prayer.

"No message. Well, that's not true. Yes, there was a message, but it wasn't for our group. He simply said that He was near to me. And, Aiden, I felt He was just that, near to me. And the feeling hasn't completely left me. Does this make any sense?"

Yes, you are a clever bitch, he thought. *You want to take your drama in a new direction? Okay, let's do that. Point the way; I'll be right behind you until that delicious moment when the trap snaps.*

"I want to understand, Margaret," he replied. "That's all I've wanted to do for you, to understand." *Not bad,* he thought. Those words were both the truth and what she would take to be his continued gullibility.

"So I have something to ask you, Aiden. While I've been hiding in my room like a spoiled brat, you've been out with the group. Where do you think I ought to go next?"

Well, he thought, *if she's stopping short of admitting that she's making up this whole drama, she's at least moving in that direction. She's as much as admitting that her Jesus doesn't know Rome.*

"Aiden, I ask that because I trust your judgment. You were the one to suggest that first church, the one near the hotel, and you were right. Plus," she added, "you know that the two messages I received last week were both about the Orthodox and Catholic churches coming closer together. Is there some site, another church, one that would fit with all that?"

Father Aiden wondered if Margaret already had a specific church in mind. Was she that organized in her scheming, or was she willing to turn over that part of her performances to him on a more permanent basis?

He thought of a church that Margaret would not know existed. Her response would reveal how she was playing with him. Would she subtly turn down his suggestion, indicating that she was, in fact, planning every step, or would she accept whatever he proposed, meaning that she was focusing only on the messages and he could do the rest?

"There is a church on an island in the Tiber River that comes to mind," Aiden said. "San Bartolomeo all'Isola is a church especially devoted to modern martyrs. I remember visiting there for one of my classes at the college. I know there are altars or shrines there not just for Catholic martyrs, but also at least for one Orthodox martyr as well for a few non-Catholics. Does that sound appropriate?"

He watched as Margaret pretended to ponder his suggestion. After a moment, she nodded her agreement. "I'll follow your lead. Even if we're wrong, I'm at peace now about making mistakes. I know the people who are supposed to understand my intentions will do so, and my critics will always think I'm a fraud."

Aiden could feel his face redden. *She's making me feel like Judas at the Last Supper.* "One of you will betray me," *Jesus had said. How dare she do this,* he thought, anger rising within him.

"Can we go there today?" Margaret asked.

"Of course, Margaret. Can you give me an hour to prepare the group? I can't begin to tell you how thrilled they'll be to hear the plan."

"Oh, one other thing, Aiden. Some anonymous person sent me some money, and I've arranged through our hotel to have a private bus today. I think the group will appreciate that."

"Yes, I'm sure they will, Margaret."

In his room, Father Aiden took the pen from the box and looked at it again. "With this pen I will sign my accusations against her. That will be the end of Mother Cleery, her death warrant as a seer." He didn't so much speak those words to the empty room as hear them. And he heard them with satisfaction.

As MARGARET CLEERY WATCHED FATHER AIDEN negotiate with the bus driver, she felt another wave of shame. He'd proven indispensable in so many ways, but how had she shown her gratitude? By whining about the voice she heard and about the group. *Always about me, me, me,* she chided herself.

She remembered her mother's saying—"No use crying over spilt sins." Despite priests whom Margaret had known growing up in Greystones, who told her that her mother's advice was heretical, Margaret had grown up taking comfort in the thought. Until she was a teenager, she went obediently to confession, but after she'd said her piece and the priest had delivered God's verdict through the grate, she'd accepted her penance and promptly forgotten about her sins. Once she become pregnant with Molly, she'd gone less to confession but continued to forget her sins rather than hang on to them. Molly had been too obvious a sin to forget, but even as her teenage belly swelled, she'd comforted herself that she was still doing God's will by not traveling to Glasgow or Liverpool to terminate the pregnancy.

But Margaret knew that something was changing within her in the past forty-eight hours. She felt both a need and a desire to treat Father Aiden differently. How she could treat Jesus differently, that voice that came tenderly the day before, was also something she wondered about. But what can a human being give God?

The followers still with her were happy to see her enter the bus and were solicitous of her needs. Did she want help climbing into the bus? Did she want a bottle of water or a banana smuggled out of breakfast in the hotel? Did she want help coming off the bus?

Only days before, such concerns would have irritated her. Now the people surrounding her seemed like vessels of some love, the same love she'd felt in the quiet darkness of the church of San Teodoro. *Is that it?* she wondered. *Could simple gratitude be all that God wants of me?*

Father Aiden led them into the church of San Bartolomeo and handed out English visitors' guides available on a table just inside the doors.

Margaret again invited Aiden to offer whispered comments about the site. He described how the main altar contained the remains of St. Bartholomew, a fellow missionary of St. Paul who was known for miraculous cures. After that, he pointed to the numerous side altars, each one dedicated to a modern martyr or saint. He looked in Margaret's direction as if expecting her to say something, but she just shook her head.

"I suggest we walk around on our own for twenty minutes or so before we gather outside for questions or to hear what Mother Cleery will share with us," he said. The entire group looked at Margaret, but again her feelings had changed. She didn't feel her skin crawling with their desperation for a message but only pity at their hunger.

To her surprise, the group let her walk around the church on her own. Her heart was ready, but she heard nothing as she moved from altar to altar. She knew of Archbishop Romero and his martyrdom, but Alexander Mem, the Orthodox priest who was killed in the waning days of the Soviet Union, and Franz Jägerstätter, who was beheading by the Nazis, were new to her. Both filled her with a sense of being an unworthy intruder in their presence. The meaning of martyr, which the guide said meant "witness in blood," had never struck her so powerfully.

Outside, the group closed in around Margaret before she saw the TV crew. *These simple folk want to protect me,* she thought. *Oh, well, maybe it's for the best for them to see that I have nothing to offer, no message to give.*

She stood silently and waited. Then, without warning, it came, not a burning, but a soft warmth that joined a feeling that she could only describe as regret. *I have done so little*, she thought. No, she corrected herself, *I have been so little.* And yet, for some reason, Jesus had chosen her for this purpose.

Despite the warmth, she felt no message within her. *They are so hungry*, she thought, as she looked with pity at the faces in her group. Even Father Aiden looked as if he needed something from her.

"I have nothing to share," she said, "but would you all join in saying the Lord's Prayer with me?" She was as surprised by her request as her followers were, but the group members bowed their heads and began. "Our Father, Who art in heaven. Hallowed be Thy Name. Thy kingdom come; Thy will be done, on earth as it is in heaven."

"Stop!" she heard someone say in almost a shout before she realized the voice was hers. Some of her followers made the sign of the cross while others backed away from her. Father Aiden stared at her with a slight smile on his face. *Bless you, my friend*, she thought.

Margaret heard no voice, but she somehow knew that she was supposed to lead her followers back inside the church. She said nothing, but, as she moved toward the doors, she heard the group following behind her. Inside, she approached the steps below the main altar. Turning around, she looked not at the group, but at the altars along both side aisles of the church.

"Your will be done on earth as it is in heaven," she said, again feeling that she was not so much speaking as hearing the words. "We are in heaven here. Yes, we are in heaven."

She glanced back at her group and saw that some of them were looking at her with clear unease. Others, including Father Aiden, had moved first to the sides of the group and then to the front as if to protect her from the TV camera.

"These martyrs are not here," she said. "They are under the throne of God in heaven." She looked away from one camera's lights and paused, waiting for her thoughts to clear. "Jesus is telling me that in heaven, there is no east or west, no Catholic martyrs and saints, no separate Orthodox martyrs and saints, and no separate Protestant martyrs. Just as these martyrs, east and west, Orthodox, Catholic, and Protestant, are together here in this church, so they are together in heaven."

Again she paused to look over at the altars. "I think I finally understand that Jesus' messages to me in Rome have all been leading to this. In the joined blood of the two deacons in St. Peter's Square and the miraculous joining of St. Peter's chains, the world has been given a glimpse of heaven. And in this church associated with healing, with its community of martyrs, undivided by the sin of separation that still plagues our churches and our world, are we not tasting heaven? Here, we enter the truth of the Church triumphant, the Church in heaven."

Where is this going? she wondered. She waited again, and she felt her followers waiting with her. Several tourists, those curious about her and the TV crew, had joined the group, while other tourists, apparently convinced they were in the presence of a madwoman, had bolted for the door. *No matter,* she thought.

"Jesus hears the prayer that He taught His disciples offered millions of times a day. But Jesus is asking, 'Do we believe what we say?' Do we believe that what is true in heaven is to be true on earth? If so, how can these two Churches continue to dawdle and frustrate Jesus' prayer for unity?"

She felt suddenly worn out and accepted the help of two group members as they led her to a chair. She felt more than saw that her followers had gathered around her, cutting off the lights of the camera.

She looked up and searched the faces for Father Aiden's. "Father Aiden, Jesus led you to bring us here. Do you see, my hungry followers? Jesus is using Father Aiden as much as He is using me. I want you all to know this. And the words of Jesus that you are hearing are not coming from me, but from these altars. The innocent blood of these martyrs cries out to us from this holy ground. The martyrs who are united with Jesus in heaven are asking us and asking both the Pope and the Patriarch to heed this message. And what is that message? It is found in the Lord's own prayer. May God's will be done on earth as it is in heaven . . ."

A wave of fear coursed through Margaret's body. As she heard herself automatically repeat the phrase, "May God's will be done on earth as it is in heaven," she faced for the first time the thought *What if my journey is to end in martyrdom?*

CHAPTER SEVENTEEN

———— ✦ ————

JULY 10: ROME: TRASTEVERE

After a little prompting from Father Fortis, Worthy called Lena to invite her to dinner. It had been a long time since he'd had dinner with a woman, outside of a police colleague on a case, and he could hear the tightness in his voice. Lena didn't respond immediately to the invitation, and Worthy chastised himself for making assumptions.

"I was about to ask you if this was a good idea," she'd said, "but then I realized you wouldn't have called if you didn't think so. Where would we go?"

"I'll leave that completely up to you. And, if you say yes, you'd also have to pick me up. I realize I'm putting you out, so feel free to say no."

Again, Lena didn't say anything for a moment. "Tonight?" she asked.

"Yes, yes, I was thinking tonight," Worthy blurted out.

"Are you one of those Americans who need to eat at five in the afternoon?"

There it was, he thought. *She's really got a thing about Americans, especially men.*

"No. You set the time."

"Okay," she said, sounding professional rather than warm. "I'll pick you up at 7:30."

Worthy had come to Rome to investigate, not to dine with a beautiful woman, and consequently he was faced with wardrobe issues. In his younger years, he'd prided himself on looking smart, the definition of that being to imitate Ralph Lauren by wearing blue oxford cloth shirts and khaki pants with a variety of ties. But in Italy, he'd noticed that both men and women valued fashion much more highly than he ever had. In comparison, he looked both bland and clearly American.

After noticing that Italian men didn't wear khakis, he settled on an off-white linen shirt, fashion jeans, and a pair of comfortable light brown loafers.

His goal wasn't to pass for an Italian, but rather to avoid embarrassment when he walked into the restaurant with Lena.

As he showered and dressed that afternoon, he was reminded of Henry David Thoreau's advice—"Beware of ventures that require new clothes." But if Thoreau had met Lena Fabriano, Worthy reasoned, the philosopher might have made an exception.

Lena smiled warmly from the driver's seat when she picked Worthy up, giving him the feeling that he looked more than passable. Lena, in Worthy's opinion, looked both casual and stunning in a silky light blue dress. And as they drove to the restaurant, Worthy could smell a hint of perfume.

Despite Rome's rush hour being over by early evening, it took them nearly an hour to drive to Trastevere, find parking, and walk to the restaurant. Worthy counted at least five near mishaps, but Lena expertly avoided them all. The place she'd chosen was at the quiet end of a dead-end street, and, to Worthy's eyes, not one attracting the tourist crowd.

They were shown to a table in an outside area, one separated from the street's walking traffic by greenery. He sat and for a moment saw the scene as if from above—the two of them sitting together on a warm summer evening in Rome, Italy. Feelings of contentment and nervousness vied with each other, and he gave himself time to think of something to say by looking across the narrow walking street to an old church where a disheveled beggar with several plastic bags was settling in for the night.

"I'm getting used to seeing monuments and ruins," he finally said, "but this whole neighborhood looks old."

"Trastevere is old, which is part of its charm," Lena said.

He took a deep breath. "I love that smell," he said, looking at the greenery. "Is it boxwood?"

"Yes," she said, in a tone that suggested she was impressed. "It's my favorite smell in the spring and summer. I remember when I found a hedge of it at Notre Dame." She inhaled deeply. "Whenever I felt homesick, I'd retreat there and just breathe the scent in." She reached out, squeezed a sprig of the bush in her hand, and brought her hand to her nose. She closed her eyes before asking, "So, Christopher, are you a gardener?"

Worthy shook his head. "My ex-wife was the gardener in the family. I think it's still her favorite hobby."

"Ah, I live in an apartment, but I have access to a loggia. Ah, I see you don't know what that is. How can I describe a loggia to an American? It's a covered area, usually small and intimate, on the roof of a building. Inside, there might be chairs, a bar, or, in my ex-husband's case, a small garden. He could make anything grow. Maybe we should write a book together on how gardeners make lousy spouses."

Worthy tried to smile but failed.

"Please forgive me," Lena said, sitting forward and catching his eye. "I didn't realize your divorce was recent."

The contentment he felt a few minutes before seemed to be slipping away. *Of all the topics*, he thought, *why are we talking about divorce?* "No, not recent," he said, looking out at a couple walking hand in hand on the street. "I've been divorced for over a decade, but sometimes it still seems like ten minutes."

"So she divorced you. Hmm," she said, as if that explained something.

Worthy waited for the obvious next question from the woman who'd already made it clear she didn't like American men. Had he been unfaithful? Had he been abusive? Was he an alpha male? Wishing to move the attention off himself, he asked, "And you? How long have you been divorced?"

"Four years," she replied. "But, in my case, sometimes it blessedly seems like twenty years. My ex-husband is American, but he's Italian-American. Truthfully, I think he's more Italian than I am. He's as tied to his mother and family as Italian men can be. When we visited them, in an Italian neighborhood in St. Louis, he'd ignore me or insult me, all to please his Momma."

Lena shook her head. "To a point, I was okay with how he treated me. You see, it's typical of Italian as well as American men. And I took solace in our agreement—our form of a pre-nup, I'd guess you'd say—to live either in Rome and spend vacations in the US, or live in the US and spend our vacations here, after we finished our programs. But when we both received our degrees, he announced that his life goal was to find a teaching position in the St. Louis area. Nothing against St. Louis, but I knew what that meant in terms of his dear Momma. That was the deal breaker, as I think you Americans put it."

Worthy nodded at several points in her story, but he had no intention of sharing the details of his divorce. Their waiter arrived at that moment to take their orders for antipasti and Worthy, feeling grateful for the interruption, reminded himself to be generous with the tip.

"What's the Vatican making of the Cleery woman's . . . I'm not sure what to call it. Her most recent stunt? Her vision?" Worthy asked.

"You don't mind talking about this?"

"No, Margaret Cleery is starting to interest me," he lied. It wasn't the Cleery woman who interested him but Lena.

"Well, certainly the location is new," she said. "The church of San Bartolomeo is quite far from her hotel. Her group hired a private coach, so someone is putting money into her stay. I have no doubt that the Vatican is checking into that."

"I think I get it. If someone is funding her, then some person or group could be putting her up to this."

"Don't assume so quickly," she said, and Worthy detected the sudden hard edge in her voice. "Funding could also be coming from someone who believes in her. A true follower, you might say."

The waiter brought a basket of bread along with a bottle of Pellegrino and glasses. Worthy vowed to approach the topic of the Cleery woman with more care, rephrasing his opinions as questions. "Her coming to Rome, her messages while the Pope and Patriarch are in talks at the same time—does that seem a bit too well-timed to be coincidental?"

Worthy offered the basket of bread to Lena, who shook her head. "In Italy, we don't touch the bread until the food arrives."

"Then why did the waiter bring the bread?"

Lena laughed. "Don't try to make sense of everything in Italy. "That's why I'll never live outside the country again. It's the small, crazy things I'd miss."

For a moment, Worthy wondered if Lena was drawing his attention to a line she wouldn't cross. A second later, however, he dismissed the thought as egotism. Sometimes a rose is just a rose, and sometimes a comment is just a comment.

The waiter brought the antipasti and a bottle of Pinot Grigio. He poured out a small amount for Lena to sample. She brought the glass to her nose before swirling it and taking a sip. "Perfetto," she proclaimed, as much to the wine as the waiter.

"When I phoned you, you commented on Americans eating early. I think that's because we're always thinking about where we're going afterwards—a movie, a ballgame, or even back to work. Italians seem to take more time for the small things, like waiting to taste the bread."

"But you were the one who first mentioned the boxwood, Chris. Is Italy rubbing off on this American?"

"You're so not crazy about America, are you?" he said, being sure to say it with a smile.

Lena looked away, as if there were more to answering the question than she wanted to provide. "Ah, maybe I know your country too well after my three years there, or maybe you'd argue I don't know it well enough. Your politics are . . . what is the word? as zany as ours."

Worthy nodded. "We can go off the deep end, no doubt about that."

"Dio mio, I never understood how your country could hate the Russians for so long and then suddenly want to become best friends," she added. "But Italians have no room to talk. We had Berlusconi. Anyway, you were asking about Margaret Cleery. She seems to have picked up a young Irish priest to co-lead the group."

"Why do you say 'picked up?' I came in on the same flight as her, and I was sure there was an old Irish priest with her."

This time, Lena didn't seem to mind the challenge. "Not this one. This is a Father Aiden O'Malley, a doctoral student at the Irish College here in Rome. I've asked my friends at the Vatican to get me background information on him, but I've heard nothing so far."

"And you say this Father O'Malley leads the group. Isn't that a bit odd?"

Lena shook her head. "He co-leads, but no, mystics and frauds often have a priest partner. Sometimes he's the confessor, and other times he's a go-between with the hierarchy of the Church. A priest, especially one from Rome, gives credibility to someone like Margaret Cleery. Of course, there's always another possibility, and that is that he's a spy for the Vatican."

Worthy nodded. "I hadn't thought of that. But if she's a true mystic, wouldn't she see through a spy?"

Lena laughed, then took another sip of wine. "Mystics have no necessary abilities to see into people. Margaret Cleery's type conveys a message based on what she claims is a supernatural experience. It's usually frauds who believe they have to be more than the messenger. In fact, frauds are often those who read people well, who surprise others with what they seem to know about them. But that's the characteristic of an insightful or intuitive person, not a mystic."

"So if Margaret Cleery claimed to look into the hearts of people, you'd smell a rat?"

Lena made a face. "That's one thing I wouldn't miss about Rome, and that's the rats down by the Tiber. And God help us when sanitation workers go on strike. The rats take over the city. But the question I'm struggling with is this: Is Margaret Cleery a rat? All my training suggests she is, but that might simply be my academic bias."

"Ah, cynicism," Worthy said. "I know it well."

"I'm a skeptic, but I'm not sure I'm a cynic in this case," she said, and Worthy wondered if he had once again made a false assumption. "As someone who's spent her career studying mystics and fakes, I know about the law of averages. Margaret Cleery's chances of being authentic are about two out of a thousand. But when you consider that percentage over the past century, the chances of her being authentic are less than one in ten thousand."

"But the law of averages can't be all that you take into consideration," Worthy replied cautiously. "Don't you have to analyze her messages on their own merit?"

Lena looked up to the evening sky, and, for a moment, Worthy thought she had decided to forego the rest of the evening. "He really gets it," she said with a laugh, as if addressing the clouds. "Lieutenant Worthy from the United States of Male Arrogance, you amaze me."

His cheeks warmed even as his racing heart subsided. "Careful," he said. "I have a track record of disappointing as much as amazing."

He could feel Lena studying him, perhaps seeing him in a new light. "Is that what Father Fortis would say? Your friendship with the monk is part of what intrigues me."

"Our friendship amazes *me*," he replied. "An Orthodox monk and an agnostic. A Greek who has an aversion to the briefest of lulls in a conversation matched with a cop who craves silence. As my older daughter, Allyson, once said, I should be the monk, and Nick should be the homicide detective."

"I'm glad you're not a monk," Lena offered, without a hint of embarrassment. "If I've learned one thing from my research, it's this: throughout history, the Church has stolen the very men that intelligent women long to find. Men who are well-educated, thoughtful, cultured, and, most importantly, passionate about life. And to make matters worse, a lot of Churchmen love the company of bright women."

"Nick is certainly all of that, especially the point about being passionate about life." He paused as he was struck with a realization. "I'm not exaggerating when I say that Nick is the friend I always wanted to have." He felt his cheeks burning. "I'm sorry if that sounds weird."

He looked up to see a different expression on Lena's face, one he couldn't read. "No, not at all. That's one of the big lessons I learned about American men through my marriage to Tony. Men in America have a lot of what I call 'bullshit' male friendships. A lot of teasing, a lot of posturing, a lot of talking about sports or how their wives nag at them. Italian men, of course, also try to be very macho, but they know it's all a front. So beneath all that, most Italian men have mates, or what Americans call buddies."

Lena paused before continuing. "I took Tony to Venice once, and one night after we left a restaurant and were walking back to the water bus stop, we passed four or five young men, all about twenty years old. They were laughing and teasing one another, but they had their arms linked. Just linked, nothing else. But I bet you can guess what Tony's reaction was."

"He assumed they were gay."

She nodded. "I was shocked. They must be gay because their arms were linked? But after I thought about it, I realized Tony had misunderstood something about Italian men and I'd learned something about American men. My ex wouldn't admit it, but he longed for such a friend—and Tony desperately needed a different kind of male friend—but that longing was so missing in his life that he had to dismiss it when he met it. For a long time, I felt responsible for this hole in Tony, but I eventually saw I wasn't the one to fill it."

"There are a lot of people in police work like your ex. We'd take a bullet for our partners, but we joke about partners who've worked together being 'married.' Sometimes it takes a funeral before a cop says out loud that he loved the guy."

"Wow, Lieutenant Worthy, man-love. Are you sure you're an American?"

Worthy smiled. "Back to that, I see. Okay, I can take it."

Lena laughed easily again. "Hmm, I'd point out at least ten more reasons you're different from American men I've known, but I don't want to embarrass you." As the waiter set the main course before them, scallops for Lena and lamb for him, Lena added, "So tell me where you and Nick are in your investigation."

Worthy was so focused on Lena that he didn't notice that the beggar from across the street was now standing by their table, shaking his bowl, just as Lena had asked that question. Worthy reached into his pocket and brought out a Euro, failing to notice that the beggar left his plastic bag behind the boxwood as he moved to the next table.

"If I'm going to tell you where we are in the investigation, I have to ask a favor," Worthy said.

He thought Lena looked a bit wary as she said, "Okay."

"I have a new theory about my investigation into the attacks. The problem is that Nick is now the skeptical one. I asked him to rein me in when he thinks I'm jumping too far ahead of the evidence, so he has my full permission to doubt my theory. As long as you know you can agree with Nick that I'm way off base, I'd like to run that theory by you."

"I'd love to hear it. It might explain why you're a famous detective," she said with a smile.

"Ha. No, far from famous. Here's the background to what I'm thinking. As you know, Nick and I read through the Vatican files on what the Pope and Patriarch have spoken about publicly. There was the environmental debate, but we couldn't see climate-change deniers being willing to kill for that. Famines in Africa were also a shared concern; both men spoke on several occasions about them. But again, it's hard to see how that could lead to such a carefully-planned assassination attempt. Both men have also taken stands on protecting and caring for refugees streaming into Europe, but so have numerous political leaders of the world including the UN Secretary."

"Did you consider human trafficking?" Lena asked.

"We did. The Pope and Patriarch have each issued calls for action on the issue. I could see how international crime groups might find that threatening. Trafficking of children and women is, sorry to say, the most lucrative business in the world."

"Our Mafia certainly agrees," she said. "I can see how that topic could trigger a violent reaction."

"And to tell you the truth, I'd feel hopeless if that were the motive. Sorry to say, I don't think there's an agency in the world that can stop trafficking. If that's the case, the best we can do is isolate those who targeted the Pope and Patriarch."

"You said 'if that were the motive.' And you also said that was where you started. You're pursuing another theory, I assume."

Worthy nodded as he took another bite of his savory lamb. "In our last meeting with Patriarch Michael, Nick said something that got me thinking. He talked about the feeling of hopelessness in the world, how so many people think the world is about to end."

"I've heard the same sentiment here in Italy, which is unexpected. The Catholic Church doesn't go in for 'end of the world' prognostications. If I were to guess why, I'd say it was because those predictions have always proved wrong. The Church doesn't like to be embarrassed. Or perhaps it's because," she said, flashing Worthy another knowing smile, "the Catholic Church knows it has a pretty good thing going in this world."

"You're looking at a Kentucky boy," Worthy said, "which means I grew up with backwoods preachers who claimed that the book of Revelation was unfolding before our eyes. Later, I realized how much money there is in peddling that message."

"Really?"

"Absolutely. Books on the subject sell in the millions, and then there are seminars to attend and charts to buy. But the big money is in selling guns, underground shelters, and supplies to those obsessed with the idea. But I hadn't even thought of this 'end of the world' angle for our case until Nick mentioned how prevalent the belief has become."

Lena took a sip of her wine before asking, "How would killing the Pope and Patriarch be connected with that?"

"First of all, I thought some crazy end-timers—that's what we call them— might have targeted the Pope and Patriarch because they believed that killing them could be one of the 'signs of the apocalypse.' But those folks aren't usually the sophisticated, tech-savvy types. So then I began to look for something more, some statement or stance by the two that might have attracted smarter end-timers to carry out the attacks."

Lena put her fork down and sat quietly. "Now we're talking about a religious Mafia. God, that's all the world needs."

"I've never thought of it in those terms, but yes."

"Have the Pope or Patriarch said something to alarm that kind of group?"

Worthy nodded. "Not that long ago, a group called Christians Dedicated to Peace in the Middle East proposed a pretty radical idea. They suggested that the holy sites in Jerusalem: the Jewish Wailing Wall, Temple Mount with its two mosques, and the nearby church of the Holy Sepulcher be designated a World Heritage Site. Notice that I said site, not sites. The group wants the three sites to be treated as common holy ground, an area accessible to peoples of all faiths and patrolled by UN peacekeepers."

"Ah, now I remember. Didn't Pope Gregorio add his support to this idea as well?"

"Both the Pope and Patriarch are on record favoring the idea, saying it deserves further thought."

"I think I see," Lena said. "This peace group just got the backing of the two most important Christian leaders in the world."

Worthy nodded. "Now think about how such a plan would sit with dedicated end-timers, those wanting to believe Armageddon, the final battle to end the world, is near. When they read of increased tensions in the world, and especially in the Holy Land, they get excited. They fantasize about a final battle there, not peace coming to Jerusalem."

Lena didn't say anything for a moment. "You said Father Nick doesn't agree?'

"Right. He has doubts that groups like that could stage a drone attack with such precision. But as I said before, what he really thinks is that I'm jumping too far ahead of the evidence we have, which isn't much. And, to be fair, I tend to move slowly on cases until . . . well, until I move too fast."

"And I thought my task was complicated. I just have to figure out if Margaret Cleery is putting us all on. But you have to find a killer. Yet, what you said does make me wonder," she said.

"About what?" Worthy asked.

"While you were describing these end-timers, I kept thinking about the mystics I've studied. Yes, mystics can also be bizarre, but most mystics—at least ones accepted by the Church—don't talk about the end of the world. It's just not what they seem concerned with."

"How about Margaret Cleery?" Worthy asked.

Lena shook her head. "It's not a pet topic for her either. In her first message, Jesus told her that a spiritual awakening is coming soon to this world. She's said nothing about some final apocalyptic battle. Actually, in most of her messages, Margaret describes the coming change as positive, as healing, even."

Putting down his knife and fork, Worthy sat silently before speaking. "How much publicity has Margaret Cleery gotten since she arrived in Rome?"

"Every time she has one of her messages, she's all over TV that night."

"Right. What about outside of Rome?" Worthy asked.

"Some publicity, I would expect. I suppose I could find out, but I'm curious why you want to know."

"It's probably nothing, but I'm wondering if whoever pulled off the bombings is aware of Margaret Cleery."

Now it was Lena who sat in silence. "Why would such a group care about her?"

Worthy shrugged. "Like I said a minute ago, I could be way off track, but let's say I'm right about end-timers being behind all this. What would such a group make of her messages here in Rome?"

"Do you mean about the Catholic and Orthodox churches reconciling?" Lena asked. "Would they care?"

"I think they'd hate what she's saying. Think about it. You said her earlier messages were about some spiritual awakening, which is a good thing, right?"

"Of course."

"Could Margaret Cleery be thinking her message of reconciliation between the Pope and Patriarch is part of that spiritual change?"

"Hmm. I think I know where you're going with this. You're wondering if a fanatic might take her messages as hopeful."

"Way too hopeful," Worthy replied. "Groups like this believe the world must go to hell before the end can come. They'd hate her messages, wouldn't they?" Worthy paused for a moment. "What if whoever is behind the bombing knows that the two of them, the Pope and Patriarch, are friends? What if whoever did all this is smarter than we think? What if he or they saw this coming—the meetings between the Pope and Patriarch, I mean."

"Well, it's no secret that an Orthodox delegation comes to the Vatican every year on the feast day of Sts. Peter and Paul," Lena said.

"Which was the very day that someone tried to kill the two of them."

He could feel Lena studying his face. "This excites you, doesn't it? It's like you're solving a puzzle," she said.

"I won't lie. This part of the job—the cerebral part—yeah, it fires me up. But remember, everything I've said tonight about this group could be pure fantasy," Worthy warned.

"Somehow, I don't think so. But maybe we'd better stop before you convince me that Margaret Cleery is a genuine mystic. Her messages certainly seem to be on the side of the angels. How about coffee at my place?" she asked.

Worthy paused, but then thought, *Why not?*

Lena reached across the table and put her hand on his. "Please don't feel any pressure. Even though you're an American," she said with a smile, "I've had a wonderful time tonight. We can leave it at that."

JULY 10: LATE NIGHT: A REMOTE LODGE IN NORTHERN EUROPE

THE CHESSMASTER WAS PLEASED THAT THE LISTENING DEVICE and micro-transmitter in the Trastevere region of Rome worked so well. The sensitive microphone hidden in the plastic bag of the beggar, his agent, picked up the voices so clearly that he felt he was a third party at the table.

Lieutenant Christopher Worthy had become a person of interest to the Chessmaster from the moment he appeared at the church of San Teodoro with the Orthodox monk. Since then, the Chessmaster had amassed an impressive file on both Christopher Worthy and Father Nicholas Fortis. What he read fascinated as well as troubled him.

Of the two, he was especially drawn to the Detroit detective. Clippings from Detroit newspapers and even one from *USA Today* described Worthy as a detective who solved cases that stymied others. He also read a caustic article about Worthy from a reporter named McKenna that described the detective as a stubborn loner, one opposed to cooperating with the media. The Chessmaster had smiled when he read that. *We have something in common*, he thought.

Despite this sense of distant kinship—both of them loners and both highly intelligent—the Chessmaster viewed the detective as a dangerous chess piece in the game. The Clessmaster sat back in his chair, contemplating his options. The Detroit detective had shown that he was a truly worthy adversary, just like his name indicated. Lieutenant Worthy had figured out more about the motive for the attacks than he knew, even as he was also off track at other key points.

In many ways, the Chessmaster regretted that he would need to deal with Worthy. Here was a dream opponent, a skilled player of the intuitive type. But while he'd enjoy watching his unpredictable opponent make his moves, the Chessmaster also knew that it was always best to remove a threatening chess piece as early in the match as possible. Once Worthy was removed, the chessboard would be simpler, victory more certain. No, he would not wait.

CHAPTER EIGHTEEN

———————◆———————

JULY 10, EVENING: OVERLOOKING THE PANTHEON

WAITING FOR LENA TO RETURN WITH THE COFFEE, Worthy sat in the loggia on the roof of her apartment. Vines crawled up the four supports to the roof and a sweet smell hovered over everything. From where he sat, Worthy could gaze over the neighboring rooftops to see the dome of the Pantheon flooded in lights.

The thought came to him that Romans, from senators to slaves, had once walked on the streets below, speaking Latin, the language he barely remembered from high school. But then he recalled the word "Salve," the Latin for "hello," and he whispered it to the warm evening, half expecting to hear a greeting from the ancient streets below. He was in awe of where he was, of what he was looking at, and of the woman he was with. He wished the night would last forever.

An added bonus of the evening was Lena's reaction to his end-time theory. He didn't fault Father Fortis for having reservations about his assumption that the assassin believed the world was in its last days. It wasn't as if the theory had arisen out of the files Father Fortis and he had reviewed. Instead, the new angle surfaced when Father Fortis described the widespread despair gripping the world that led some desperate groups to yearn for the apocalypse.

Worthy would be the first to admit that he was at a disadvantage in a case involving intricate theological differences between the Catholic and Orthodox Churches. He was happy to remember that Father Fortis was in the lead on this case. But Worthy also remembered that Patriarch Michael had specifically invited him because he was an outsider.

As Worthy looked down on the ancient Pantheon, he was pleased that Lena hadn't disagreed with his new theory. Better yet, she hadn't dismissed it.

Instead, as they talked he realized how Margaret Cleery's messages of reconciliation would rile anyone expecting a fiery end to the world.

At that moment, Lena came through the door holding a tray of mugs and a plate of biscotti.

"If I lived here, I'd sit up here every night," he said.

"Even if it rained?" she asked.

Worthy nodded. "Even if it rained."

"Actually, I have come up here in the rain," Lena admitted. "Everything becomes very quiet then. There's not so much noise from the streets below, and usually no one else is on their rooftop. Rome offers so much to engage the mind, especially for someone interested in history, but peace and quiet are harder to find. Have you been to Ostia yet?"

"Ostia? No, I don't think so. What is it?"

"Ostia is a place where you walk on the streets ordinary people walked on two thousand years ago. It's a place where you can feel the men and women who sat together as friends, something like the two of us tonight." After pausing, she added, "Will you let me take you there?"

Worthy felt his stomach clutch, then relax.

"I would love to show you Ostia, Chris."

"I'd like that," Worthy replied.

"I know what we should do," Lena said, sitting forward in her chair. "We'll save Ostia as a reward, what we'll do once we solve our cases. Sorry, I wasn't supposed to talk about work."

"No, you're not violating our agreement," he said. "You're talking about what we'll do when my investigation and yours into the Cleery woman are over." *Over*, he thought with sadness. *Yes, our investigations will someday be over.*

As if she had read his thoughts, Lena asked, "Will you be glad to go home?"

"No. Detroit is where my life is, my job, but after working cases elsewhere, I realize I'm happier when I'm not there."

Lena leaned back in her chair, her eyes closed. "Would it be good for you to leave Detroit? I mean, for good."

Worthy thought how best to answer the question. He'd considered leaving Detroit before. When he was on the case in New Mexico, he thought about resettling there, but what he thought might develop with his partner on that case didn't develop.

"I'm tied to Detroit for a number of reasons, but mainly because of my daughters," he said vaguely, "but I wonder sometimes if Detroit has too many regrets, too many reminders of failures for me to ever feel . . . to ever feel free."

After a moment, Lena asked in a softer voice, "Can you see yourself in another career?"

Worthy exhaled. "I've never wanted to do anything else but police work. I guess that's my dilemma in a nutshell. The problem is that my career, what I love to do, has proven again and again to destroy the closest relationships in my life."

The two sat quietly as an orange moon rose over the rooftops. Worthy wondered if he'd spoiled the evening by speaking too openly.

But even as he thought that, Lena rose from her chair. Standing over him, she reached down and lightly took his hands in hers. "I made a rule after my divorce to never again have a relationship with an American. I viewed every American male through the lens of Tony. I keep expecting American men to try to impress me. But here you are, Chris, an exception to my unbreakable rule," she whispered, before stooping down to kiss him. "Stay with me tonight. We can sit up here and watch the moon, or we can go downstairs. But I want you to stay."

In answer, Worthy rose and kissed her back.

July 11: Morning: Rome: Breakfast Together

"Excuse me, Father," the young woman at the hotel's reception desk said. "I have a message for you."

Father Fortis accepted the envelope and took it with him into the breakfast lounge. Not finding Worthy in his room when he retired the night before, he hoped to meet with his friend over breakfast. But Worthy hadn't answered his phone, and Father Fortis decided to let him sleep in.

He ordered his usual breakfast: muesli, fruit, sausage and eggs, prosciutto and melon, and two pastries as well as juice and coffee. Looking around, he didn't recognize other guests at breakfast, and that reminded him that he hadn't seen George Pappas for the past two days. Father Fortis didn't miss the wrangling with Pappas, but he worried about what the lawyer might be up to.

Settling in at a table by the front window facing the church of San Teodoro, he opened the note.

"Dear Nicholas, there are recent developments. Please meet me at 11:00 this morning at San Teodoro. Lieutenant Worthy need not attend. His humble servant, Michael."

Rereading the short note, Father Fortis tried to guess what the Patriarch meant by "recent developments." Given that Worthy wasn't invited to the meeting, he reasoned that the matter related to the private conversations the Patriarch was having with Pope Gregorio.

He gazed across the street to the church of San Teodoro and thought of the double role he was playing. He was Patriarch Michael's sole confidant as the

Patriarch met with Pope Gregorio, but he was also working with Worthy to
uncover the people behind the attacks before they struck again. He wondered
if he'd be of more help to the Ecumenical Patriarch and to Worthy if he weren"t
being pulled in two different directions.

His thoughts drifted from his two roles to Margaret Cleery and her latest message from the church of San Bartolomeo. Earlier, he'd viewed her as
simply a distraction. Now, he wasn't so sure. He compared the woman's face
in the news on TV last night with the woman he'd seen at the airport. While
her face was paler, it seemed to be less agitated. *Perhaps she's on medication*,
he thought.

He looked up to see Worthy enter the breakfast room and wave in his direction. *I won't ask him how his evening went*, he promised himself. But that didn't
mean he couldn't study his friend's face and manner for clues, even as he had
studied Margaret Cleery's face on the TV.

After Worthy ordered, Father Fortis deliberately turned to look out at San
Teodoro. "Another sunny day, my friend," he said.

"Yes, in answer to the question written all over your face, I had a good time
last night, Nick."

"Last night? What was last night? Good heavens, did I miss something
important?"

"Very funny, Nick. We had a delicious dinner and a stimulating conversation."

And what else? Father Fortis wondered. *No, I will not pry.*

But his friend did look content, calmer, maybe even more settled. Was it
too much to hope that Worthy had rounded some corner, had left some of his
sadness behind?

"I have a meeting in a little over an hour with the Patriarch," Father Fortis
offered. "It looks like Church matters, so you're excused. I'm not prying,
Christopher, but did you and Lena discuss your theory?"

Worthy nodded as he sipped his coffee. "We also talked about Margaret
Cleery."

"Ah, I'm curious what Lena makes of her most recent episode."

"Actually, that wasn't what we focused on. It turns out Margaret Cleery has
become a bit of a puzzle."

"It must be hard for an academic to concede that Mrs. Cleery might be the
real thing."

"Lena admitted as much, Nick. But I did learn something interesting, in
terms of my end-of-the-world theory. Apparently mystics don't usually offer
messages on that topic. The same is true for Margaret Cleery. She says Jesus told
her that a spiritual change is coming to the world, but it's nothing cataclysmic."

"Hmm. Did the professor say how Mother Cleery's messages in Rome fit
with that?" Father Fortis asked.

"Lena interprets Margaret Cleery's pleas for the Catholic and Orthodox Churches to reconcile to be part of that same message of hope."

"Hope? I rarely hear that word these days. Now, about your end-timer theory. There's not much hope in that."

"Actually, Lena thinks I could be right—well, maybe. And I don't think she said that to be kind. Margaret Cleery's messages would be hated by apocalyptic groups. And that's why I think she could be in danger."

"Well, that's something new to worry about. I thought ridicule would be the worst thing Mother Cleery would face," Father Fortis said.

"You know my method, Nick. I'm trying to put myself into the shoes of one of these apocalyptic types. If that's my mindset, then every day I'm on the internet looking for evidence that the world is falling apart; you know, wars, plagues, earthquakes, terrorism, all that stuff. Think how many TV preachers used the coronavirus to reinforce their belief that the world will soon end. If I'm one of those types, the last thing I want to read is that there's hope for this world."

Father Fortis considered this new perspective on Margaret Cleery. "Anything else she said about Mother Cleery?"

"We talked about her picking up an assistant, an Irish priest who's studying here in Rome. She's relying on this priest to organize her visits to religious sites in the city."

"He doesn't sound capable of protecting her, though," Father Fortis said. "You're suggesting she might need something stronger, some protection. Should I pass that along to Patriarch Michael or the Vatican?"

Worthy looked out the window. "How likely is it the Vatican will offer Margaret Cleery something that will only give her greater credibility?"

Father Fortis shook his head. "I'm thinking it's in their best interest to protect her, even if protection brings more attention to her. If Margaret Cleery is a fraud, the last thing Patriarch Michael and Pope Gregorio would want is for her to be turned into a martyr. And on the off-chance that she isn't a fraud, Christopher, then all of us must do all we can to keep Margaret Cleery alive."

✝

JULY 11: ROME: ST. FRANCIS OF ASSISI'S TUNIC

WHEN FATHER FORTIS ENTERED THE CONFERENCE room within the church of San Teodoro, Ecumenical Patriarch Michael was standing at the window, his shoulders slumped.

"I feel a need to apologize, Your All Holiness," Father Fortis said.

The Patriarch turned and gave Father Fortis a questioning look. "Apologize? For what? And didn't we agree that you're to call me Michael instead of 'Your All Holiness?'"

"I will try, Your . . . Michael. It's not something I've done, but something I've failed to do. I haven't been as sensitive as I should be, given all you've been through. Especially the death of the deacons right in front of you."

The Patriarch turned back and gazed out at the city. "Rome is no stranger to tragedy, Nicholas. Our sorrow, as deep as it is to us, is simply another drop in this city's ocean of misery. When I think of all who've been martyred in Rome, I can't help but wonder how God bears all the suffering we humans cause one another."

Father Fortis knew the statement expected no response.

"Perhaps," the Patriarch continued, "when we bear sorrows such as the deaths of the deacons, we're closest to touching the heart of God. If so, it's a broken heart."

The Patriarch continued to gaze out the window, and Father Fortis sensed something else was on his mind.

The Patriarch turned and motioned for Father Fortis to take the chair next to his own. "I have something to share, Nicholas," he said.

"I hope there hasn't been another tragedy."

"No, not another tragedy . . . or at least not totally a tragedy," the Patriarch replied. "George Pappas has left Rome to attend the funeral of the archdeacon before heading back to the States. But he expressed himself very freely before he left."

"Your All Holiness . . . Michael, George Pappas hardly represents—"

The Patriarch raised his hand for silence. "We both know that my remaining in Rome is raising a considerable amount of criticism. George fired both barrels, Nicholas. If I take what he said to be the truth, I'm one of the most naïve persons walking this planet. Some in our Church apparently consider me to be a traitor to our faith. I can take all that with a grain of salt. But his warning that what I'm doing could cause a rebellion in important circles, in Russia again, in Jerusalem, and in Greece, is probably no exaggeration."

He bowed his head for a moment. "George Pappas reminded me that the throne on which I sit as Ecumenical Patriarch balances precariously on 'legs,' and those legs are the other patriarchs of our Church. If I lose the support of one or two of these patriarchs, I as Ecumenical Patriarch will be toppled from the throne. George accuses me of meeting with the Pope without first consulting with the other patriarchs and the Holy and Sacred Synod of our faith. I have to accept that my conversations, prayers, and dialogue with my friend Serg could lead to the worst kind of disaster, one where steps we take to heal the ancient schism could cause a new schism, this one within our Orthodox Church."

"Yes, I see that," Father Fortis said. "And I think we both know what George Pappas will do when he returns to the States."

"His abrupt departure means I must adjust my expectations," the Patriarch said, looking down at the ring of office on his hand, "or adjust my prayers. After George Pappas left, I had to face the question: are Serg and I moving too fast; have we been too open with our hopes?"

Father Fortis struggled to know what to say. Until the Patriarch had said it aloud, Father Fortis didn't realize how high his own hopes were for the dialogue. Finally, he said, "I'm so sorry."

"But not a complete tragedy," the Patriarch said in a stronger voice as he looked up. "I now see that the invitation given at Santa Sabina to think boldly under the guidance of the Holy Spirit alarmed rather than inspired quite a few of those present. It's not just George Pappas and his ilk. There's also resistance on the Catholic side. So, one door closes, but I believe Our Lord has offered a new one, perhaps the right one all along. It may not be everything that Serg and I are praying for, and I suspect the new proposal won't seem bold to you, Nicholas. But whoever said 'Politics is the art of the possible' must have been a churchman."

Father Fortis remained silent but noticed a gleam in the Patriarch's eye. "So, this other door?" he asked the Patriarch.

Patriarch Michael smiled and put a hand on Father Fortis' shoulder. "Assisi, Nicholas, the door is in Assisi and has been all along. Please, let's sit. I have a story to tell you." He folded his hands in front of him. "When Serg and I were in grad school together here in Rome, we had a class trip to Assisi. I know the experience profoundly affected both us both, but maybe not for the reasons you might think. Yes, the basilica dedicated to St. Francis is massive, but that was built after his death."

Patriarch Michael paused for a moment as if caught in the memory. "I remember the two of us pausing together before one of St. Francis' tunics on display. Even now, all these years later, I can see the two of us standing there, our mouths agape. I'm not exaggerating when I say that the ragged tunic was more patches than whole cloth. The image of that ragged tunic is in my mind whenever I put on the robes of my office, which you know are quite ornate. But of this I am sure: Pope Gregorio and I would trade all the robes, miters, crowns, ornate crosses, and jeweled croziers that we have in our offices to don that humble tunic for one moment."

Patriarch Michael paused, and Father Fortis understood that the Patriarch was overcome with emotion.

"Nicholas, here's what has stuck with me after all these years. St. Francis of Assisi didn't found a Church or even a monastic order, but a community of brothers. He even called them 'fraters minor', lesser brothers. That's what I believe the Pope and I can be to one another—servant brothers."

The Patriarch's face radiated such joy that Father Fortis averted his eyes. He didn't have the heart to say it wasn't clear what the Patriarch was proposing.

"Yes, Serg and I are well aware that we are prisoners of history, but we are also men of faith and hope. So many Orthodox and Catholics fear obstacles from the past that no longer exist. Thanks to English, language no longer divides us. Thanks to technology, we have instant communication, which means we can immediately ask for clarification about what confuses us. The papacy no longer has armies or extensive lands to protect. Isn't it obvious that many of the reasons for the initial schism, especially the political factors, have been overcome by history itself?"

Father Fortis remembered Worthy's confession when he first arrived in Rome that he had a tendency at times to leap ahead of the evidence on a case. Father Fortis now worried that Patriarch Michael was making a similar leap. "But surely, Michael, the most difficult sticking points are theological," he said.

"Nicholas, Nicholas," the Patriarch exclaimed as he reached across and grabbed Father Fortis' forearm. "The entire thorny issue of the supremacy of the pope can be circumvented by Serg and me treating one another simply as brothers! Just brothers, Nicholas. We can let go the debate about who is the elder brother or the more important brother. No, we can simply pledge to be loving brothers with one another."

Father Fortis knew that if George Pappas were present, the canon lawyer would cite a host of complex arguments that had slowly, over time, built an impenetrable wall between the two Churches.

"Michael, I think you know my heart is moved by what you're proposing, but sometimes my head, and maybe my faith, is weak. When I think of all the words and books written over the centuries that argue that one Church is right and the other is wrong, I feel paralyzed."

The Patriarch closed his eyes and bowed his head for a moment, leading Father Fortis to wonder if he were praying. Finally, he raised his gaze and offered a smile. "I have felt that same sense of paralysis, and, without a different approach, I believe it would take another thousand years just to respond point by point to all the theological arguments that have been raised since the split in 1054."

"I hate to sound like George Pappas, but what other way is there?" Father Fortis asked.

"Here, dear Nicholas, is where St. Francis offers a better path, a path forward, not backwards. The way of St. Francis is the path of simplicity and humility. Being a brother to one another is the new stance, a stance that is both simple and humble. It is the only way that can cut through centuries of complex arguments."

The two men sat in silence until Father Fortis asked, "Won't there always be people who insist that one of you is more important? The issue of who has first place in Christ's Church won't simply go away."

The Patriarch nodded that he understood the concern. "Remember when James and John asked Our Lord if they could have the best posts in the coming Kingdom? Do you remember what Our Lord said?"

"He that is greatest among you must be your servant," Father Fortis replied.

"Brothers, just servant-brothers," the Patriarch repeated. "That's what Our Lord has led me to see and what Pope Gregorio and I will discuss tomorrow—brotherhood not as an abstraction, but as something real, something concrete."

"What happens when the brothers disagree?" Father Fortis asked.

The Patriarch squeezed Father Fortis' forearm even harder. "As brothers, we commit to communicate with one another, to reason together, and to pray together, but neither brother can veto the other church's decisions. The Pope will still be the head of the Catholic Church, and the Ecumenical Patriarch will still be the shepherd of the Orthodox Church. The commitment is simply to act as brothers, to serve one another by helping the other discover the will of God. But never to dominate. I think Athenagoras and Pope Paul VI as well as Bartholomew and Pope John Paul II were closer to this than many of the critics realize."

The sparkle in the Patriarch's eyes remained. Father Fortis knew the grief-heavy heart of the Patriarch was soothed by this idea of brotherhood. He also knew that if such a relationship could be achieved, the two deacons who were killed on the feast day of Saints Peter and Paul would not have died in vain.

But Father Fortis knew there would still be resistance. "What will George Pappas and his ilk think of this new relationship?"

Patriarch Michael shook his head. "I'm sure he will quote from those books you referred to as well as raise canonical objections. But can anyone oppose a relationship based solely on mutual trust and brotherly love? There will no longer be the question of one branch of Christ's Church capitulating to the other." Patriarch Michael sighed. "Oh, yes, Nicholas, Pope Gregorio and I will undoubtedly be labeled fools, but didn't St. Francis rejoice in being considered a fool?"

Father Fortis exhaled slowly. He wished the Patriarch's enthusiasm could overcome the doubts flooding his mind. "Because the two of you know each other, and I know you also love one another, I don't doubt that you both will commit to this new relationship in good faith. But I worry about the first time one of you chooses to ignore the advice of the other," Father Fortis said.

"Brotherhood isn't real unless it's tested," the Patriarch replied. "When we disagree on an issue—and I'm sure we will—that doesn't mean the advice of the other has been ignored. Brothers don't always agree, but they're still brothers. We will still commit to seek the advice and prayers of one another."

"I hope you're right, but what about when the two of you are gone?" Father Fortis asked.

To Father Fortis' relief, Patriarch Michael didn't seem bothered by his caution. The Patriarch had earlier described George Pappas as the brakes and him as the gas pedal. Now he was applying the brakes.

The Patriarch pointed first to the ceiling and then in the direction of Father Fortis' heart. "If this arrangement is the will of God, the blessing of the Holy Spirit will be so clear . . . so obvious, that it will continue."

Both men sat in silence. Father Fortis pictured George Pappas seat-belted on a plane, nursing a cocktail while methodically recording his scathing reflections on events in Rome. Was it possible that George Pappas and his cronies had misjudged the Ecumenical Patriarch by viewing him as naïve? Was it possible that they'd misjudged God?

CHAPTER NINETEEN

JULY 12: NORTHERN EUROPE: THE MAP OF OLD JERUSALEM

THE CHESSMASTER'S HANDS SHOOK as he opened the safe and extracted the folder. He'd thought of this moment so often over the past two years, but until today he'd had always sensed a powerful "not yet." He opened the folder and looked through bios, maps, and underground schematics so detailed that they would impress the CIA.

But it wasn't Rome that the Chessmaster was studying. Rome had only ever been a lead-up to the finale. He opened the atlas and turned to the maps of the Old City of Jerusalem. The maps were from Biblical to modern times, including a series of annotated Google maps of the same area. As he studied the ancient streets, synagogues, churches, and mosques, he experienced a Godlike feeling. Circled in red were the numerous military and police posts that insured peace in the tensest city in the world. But the Chessmaster knew the peace of Jerusalem was soon to end.

He could almost feel heat rising from the maps, the result of the friction that existed among the three religions of Judaism, Christianity, and Islam. Although the three faiths held the same streets to be sacred, each resented the presence of one another. "All the fault lines of history intersect right here," he said to himself as his finger found the epicenter of Old Jerusalem, where the Western or Wailing Wall, the holiest site in Judaism; the two mosques atop Temple Mount, the third holiest site in Islam; and the church of the Holy Sepulcher, the holiest site in Christianity, uncomfortably rubbed shoulders. "This is where the end of the world—no, the new age—begins."

But even as his hands continued to shake, he wouldn't let his excitement cloud his judgment. He'd continue to work through his encrypted pathways to put the right groups in place, each group knowing nothing of the existence of other groups that would play their parts in the final drama. He smiled at his plan: dedicated believers who wouldn't hesitate to kill one another would unknowingly work in tandem to turn the wheel of history one last cog and bring the curtain down on this world.

"Lord of history, Lord of judgment," he prayed, "my faith in your sword of justice has been the oil that has kept my lamp lit. I am ready for your fearsome coming, as I now see why the two antichrists did not die in Rome. No, You have always had a better plan. The two antichrists must meet their end in in Your Holy City, Jerusalem, not in Rome."

His prayers seemed to flow out of him for the next six hours, as he studied the maps, pored over the books of Daniel, Revelation, and the Dead Sea Scrolls, and listened for God to provide the details of the plan.

Throughout those hours, the parts the Pope, the Ecumenical Patriarch, and the Irish woman would play slowly emerged, leading him to chant repeatedly, "To Your holy and just will, I submit, O God." The only break he took was to contact his most trusted representative in Rome, one of several who'd wormed their way into Margaret Cleery's circle of followers. He authorized the withdrawal of money and dictated a note to Aiden O'Malley that he was confident would contribute to God's plan.

What left the Chessmaster in awe was the inclusion of Margaret Cleery in God's final purposes. He'd had an inkling that her presence in Rome at the same time as the meeting of the Pope and Patriarch couldn't be coincidental. In the last scenes of human history, he realized that there were no coincidences. And that included his own role. From the beginning of the world, God had chosen him for his part in history's conclusion, even as God had chosen the two antichrists of the Pope and Patriarch as well as the two deacons. Now it was clear to the Chessmaster that Margaret Cleery had also been foreordained.

He fasted throughout the day, taking only water when his mouth was too dry to pray. At dusk, he ventured out to see the sunset. He wanted to tell the sun that its brilliance would soon be snuffed out, to proclaim to the hills that they'd be humbled, and to announce that the valleys would soon be exalted.

He waited only for God to reveal how He would lure the Pope, the Ecumenical Patriarch, and Margaret Cleery to Jerusalem. Then, the final act would begin.

JULY 12: ROME: IRISH COLLEGE

AT THE IRISH COLLEGE, AIDEN O'MALLEY reread the most recent chapter of his dissertation. He felt as detached from the research as if it had been written by a stranger.

This should worry me, he thought. *I should be focusing on what I need to do to finish my program and return home.* But even Ireland seemed as distant a reality as his dissertation. He was too deep into investigating Margaret Cleery to care about anything else. All his energy was devoted to figuring out what he could do to expose this woman for the lying bitch that she was.

The visit to the church of San Bartolomeo had been both enlightening and disturbing. Margaret Cleery's style was changing. She was wearing a new mask, a mask of humility and patience, and his loathing for her had tripled.

Yet, he had to give her credit for what occurred at the church. Quoting the Lord's Prayer was pure genius. He wondered how long she'd worked on that set speech.

He closed the folder containing the last chapter of his dissertation and opened the note he'd found under his door the night before. The five hundred euros that tumbled from the envelope had been what first drew his attention, but now it was the note's odd wording that intrigued him.

"We appreciate your role in Mrs. Cleery's visit to Rome. Please accept the enclosed sum as a token of our esteem for your discretion and assistance. Mother Cleery should leave Rome soon, as we believe her final messages would be delivered more effectively in Jerusalem. Do whatever you can to convince her to go there immediately. Also know that similar monetary tokens will follow."

Aiden O'Malley had no doubt that the note and the money—the thirty pieces of silver—had come from the Vatican. Of course, the Vatican was tired of Mother Cleery's unpredictable appearances and aggressive messages in Rome, especially while the Pope and Ecumenical Patriarch were holding their ongoing meetings. No, the note was from someone in the Vatican who understood Mother Cleery's hoax, someone who understood that, after Rome, she would never settle for returning to her small Irish village. She was morphing, creating new poses, becoming more of a media favorite with each message. Whoever wrote the note knew that only a bigger stage like Jerusalem would tempt her.

But what did the words "final messages" mean? At first, the words struck him as ominous—would she be in danger?—but after rereading the note, he interpreted the word "final" to mean that the writer of the note understood something that Aiden agreed with—in Jerusalem Margaret would finally talk herself out, exhaust herself, and realize that her years of fame were drawing to a close.

The five hundred euros and the promise of further tokens of appreciation humored more than excited him. He knew himself well enough to know that money wasn't his temptation, not his drug of choice. It wasn't that he despised money for pious reasons, but rather that he viewed money as important only when it was useful. And what was the most useful for his plans was not the money, but the note itself, a note that he'd share with the world when he exposed both Margaret Cleery and the Vatican.

As he hid the note at the bottom of his toiletry bag, he smiled to himself. The day when he'd turn the spotlight on both the fake mystic and the conniving Curia seemed suddenly much nearer. And all would be revealed in Jerusalem. *How fitting*, he thought.

✝

JULY 12: ROME: IN THE CONFESSIONAL

"A RAW HEART." THAT WAS THE BEST WAY MARGARET CLEERY could describe the feeling that her heart was an open and bleeding wound. She wondered if something would heal the wound within her, or if she would feel this way for the rest of her life.

The rest of her life. What did that mean now? When the messages had first come to her, she'd imagined the phenomenon ending as suddenly as it had begun. But then, at the time she also imagined that she'd spend the rest of her life in Greystones. Even in the first days in Rome, she assumed that just as a plane from Ireland had brought her to Italy, so a plane would one day return her to her home.

Jesus' gentle words spoken days before in the church of San Teodoro, however, continued to have a strange effect on her. For the past two mornings, she'd felt the open wound within her expanding, not closing. With the increased pain came a peculiar image, one where she saw herself on the other side of a river. On the other shore was the person she *had* been, the one who'd always enjoyed shocking people. Long after she became an adult, this version of herself continued to act like the sassy middle-school brat she'd once been. She saw her brash ways as justified because they were both fun and necessary to prick the balloon of the pious types.

That was the version of herself she'd always assumed was who she was. But who this new version of herself was, the one looking across at her old self, puzzled her. All she could say for certain was that it was this new Margaret Cleery who had the "raw heart." That was why she encouraged Father Aiden that morning to return to his college and his studies. She needed time with herself—or her selves—to make some sense of what was happening to her.

Part of what was changing was her sense of the future. There was no logical reason to imagine that she wouldn't return to Ireland, but over the past few days, she'd felt less and less attached to those familiar images of hills, ocean, pub, and neighbors. She shivered with the knowledge that she had no clue what the next weeks or months would bring. Again, she felt a clamminess in her hands and feet as she considered the possibility of martyrdom. Were all these experiences part of her getting ready to die?

With her followers on their own for the day, Margaret pulled her sunhat down and exited the hotel by the back door. In the next block, she found a quiet church on the corner. From a brochure on a table inside the door, she discovered that the church was where the Ethiopian community in Rome met. She stood silently in front of a candlelit icon of a dark-skinned saint before she sat in a pew toward the back of the church. Her hope was that the quiet of the church would somehow help her deal with the new feelings within her. Part of her wanted to remain the old Margaret Cleery, but another part of her felt shame at what she was realizing about herself.

Her thoughts were interrupted by a slender Ethiopian tapping her on the shoulder.

"Madame, have you come for confession?" he asked with a broad smile that she'd have found more appropriate for a maître de. How odd, she thought, that she'd never asked Father Aiden to hear her confession. And how odd that he never offered. No, she admitted, that wasn't his fault. He knew only the Margaret from the other shore, the Margaret of the hard heart.

"Father, I don't think," she said, but then paused, as if no words would follow.

The priest continued to smile, as if he had all the time in the world. In contrast, she felt as if she had only seconds to decide which Margaret she would be. Was confession what she most hated or what she most wanted?

Her heart was beating like a hammer as she heard herself say, "Okay, Father, I'll make my confession, if it's not too much trouble."

The priest offered a slight laugh. "Trouble? No, confession is never trouble. Please," he said, gesturing to a confession booth in the back corner of the church.

Margaret followed him and waited for the priest to enter an older style confessional that resembled a wooden phone booth. She sat on a small stool next to the mesh and waited for him to speak.

"You speak English, yes?" the priest asked.

"Yes, Father."

"My dear, how long has it been since your last confession?"

Without warning, tears blurred her vision. The technical answer to the standard question was three weeks, as she'd made a point of going for confession before her flight to Rome. But that was more a superstitious act, as if confession would ensure a safe journey. Now the priest's question elicited a low groan as she wondered if she'd ever offered an honest confession. As she thought back on the old Margaret, she had to admit that she'd always left the confession booth as the same stubborn and willful person who'd entered the booth.

But how would this priest understand her image of the river and the two versions of herself? What would he make of knowing he was hearing the confession of the famous Irish mystic? Settling for a half-way honest answer, she responded, "Father, it's been too long since I've confessed my sins."

"Then in the name of Christ, I want you to know that you are most welcome," the priest said. "What do you wish to confess?"

The Margaret from the other shore wanted to shout that she didn't wish to confess at all, that confession had never changed anything. The old Margaret wanted to say that until four days ago she had been her own creation.

"I've . . . I've been afraid of God my entire life, Father." She didn't so much say those words as expel them. With the admission came a sense of physical lightness, and she wondered if she would faint. *No matter*, she thought. *I finally told the truth.*

"Why does God frighten you, my child?" the priest asked.

My child. How odd to hear herself addressed with those words by a priest less than half her age. She'd once been a child, but it would be truer to say that she'd once been only young. When her father, in a drunken stupor, ran his panel truck off the road and broke his neck, she was eight years old. Life had been hard for the family before the accident, but life became immeasurably more difficult afterwards. Her mother reacted with rage at her husband from the funeral onward, but she'd included in her anger her passel of eight kids in the months and years afterwards. Margaret had protected herself by creating a thick skin, letting others know that she wasn't someone to be fooled with. Boys had taken her loose tongue as an indication of other looseness, and in the awkward years of development before she dropped out of school, she had on occasion traded access to her body for whispers of love. She'd wanted to believe those whispers, but they'd never settled in her heart. In her life, the word "love" had been a key that boys and then men used to open certain doors and then relock on their way out.

The priest repeated his question. "Why are you afraid of God?"

A flicker of anger from her old self rose within her as she blamed herself for being trapped in this church by this silly, smiling priest. But for some reason the anger released her from its grip, and she understood that she was naked before the question.

"I'm afraid of the future," she began. "No, that's not it. I guess I'm afraid of admitting that the future isn't in my hands. I'm not sure what to do with that . . . that truth, Father."

There was no response from the other side of the grill, and Margaret wondered what sense an Ethiopian priest was making of such a confession. Certainly, her words must sound like the anxieties of a first-world whiner. She thought about bolting from the church, but stopped herself, waiting expectantly for some response.

Oh, God, please don't let him say something sweet and pious, she prayed. *You know what I mean behind my words, and if I am a bitchy whiner in Your eyes, forgive me for that.*

"Before a person can give up control of the future, they often have to let go of the past. I say this because I have struggled with this same issue," the priest said in a softer voice. "You are not alone, my child."

Margaret realized that, in his words, the priest had broken protocol, at least the protocol of her parish priests. In her experience, confession was always when she'd listed her sins and taken her punishment, even as she always assumed the priest did with his confessor, and on and on up to God, the One Who had nothing to confess but so much to punish.

She let herself cry. Again, no words came from the other side of the grill, and she was relieved that the priest didn't know who she was. After finding a handkerchief in her purse and blowing her nose, she managed to gain enough control to whisper, "I don't want to fight God anymore. But that's all I've ever been good at."

"Yet I think you've already begun to surrender. Am I right?" he asked.

There was that word—surrender. For her entire life, that word had been synonymous with failure. Her mother's anger at her husband was that he somehow surrendered to death. He failed with the alcohol, and then he failed with the dying. Her teenage pregnancy—was that not because she surrendered to Ian's lilting words on that moonlit night down on the city beach? Or her dropping out of school right after a teacher encouraged her, despite the pregnancy, to take the A level track that would lead to university—was that not another surrender, a capitulation to what her mother had called "the Irish woman's fate?"

But the priest's tone gave the word surrender an unfamiliar ring. Instead of failing, surrender on his lips seemed to promise a release.

"I know of something that will bring peace into your heart," the priest proposed.

Here it comes, she thought. *Here comes the punishment.* She felt the old resistance within her, the "I will obey, but I won't like it" response she was so used to.

"My child, we all know the Lord's Prayer, but there is another prayer that I believe is the true prayer of Our Lord. It is what Jesus prayed in the Garden of Gethsemane when He too struggled—yes, even Jesus struggled to do the will of God. He struggled so deeply that blood flowed from His brow. But in the end, Jesus uttered a prayer that opens for all of us the door to peace. He offered these simple words: 'Not my will, but yours be done.'"

Margaret felt the aching scraped-out feeling within her press for her to respond, but she felt as she had as a child when she had a splinter. She'd wanted more than anything for the pain to be taken away, but she always pulled her hand away from her mother, not wanting the wound to be touched.

In a trembling voice, she replied, "Yes, yes, I know I have to do something."

"Good," the priest said, and Margaret thought she could hear relief in his voice. Had he sensed how difficult it was for her to give that answer? Or did he know something she hadn't thought of before—that everyone has a wound that fears the healing?

"'Not my will, but yours be done.' Those are the hardest words for anyone to say, even for our Lord," the priest continued. "But whenever you face a decision about the future, I want you to pray those words. Pray them even when you don't believe them, but pray them." After a moment of Margaret's tearful sniffling, he added. "Go in peace, my child. And let us pray for one another, that we will both do the will of God."

CHAPTER TWENTY

———————◆———————

JULY 12: ROME: EVENING IN PIAZZA NAVONA

DRUMMING HIS FINGERS ON AN OUTSIDE TABLE in Piazza Navona, Father Fortis waited for Worthy and Lena to arrive. According to his guidebook, Christians had died here in what was once a stadium, but now families with children laughing and playing around the three Baroque fountains gave Father Fortis the feeling of a county fair.

Father Fortis was anxious to tell Worthy the news of the Patriarch's proposal. Everything that Patriarch Michael had hoped for had been agreed upon, and agreed upon enthusiastically, by Pope Gregorio. The commitment of the two to function as brothers with one another—supportive, consulting, but never demanding—would change the ongoing theological dialogue between the two Churches. The debates and disagreements would not suddenly disappear, but dialogue from this point forward would be under this canopy of brotherhood.

Now, as if the day hadn't given him enough to celebrate, he looked forward to an evening with Lena Fabriano and Worthy. The pair had now been together three nights in a row, leaving Father Fortis to worry that his friend was diving into a relationship too quickly. Yet, every morning over breakfast, Worthy appeared alert and focused on the case.

A seller of a toy that glowed as it was projected high in the air passed by his table. The man, who appeared to be from the Philippines or Indonesia, glanced at Father Fortis before apparently deciding the priest wasn't a likely customer. Father Fortis wondered what had led the peddler and others like him from Southeast Asia and Africa to leave their homes and families to migrate to Rome.

Father Fortis couldn't help but wonder what was more puzzling to these probably illegal workers: the radical injustices in the world based on where a person was born or the sleek sophistication of Italians.

He looked down at his watch and thought if Lena and Worthy did not arrive soon, he would buy one of the toys out of guilt.

From behind him, he heard his name. "Are we late, Nick?"

Rising, Father Fortis smiled at Lena Fabriano as they exchanged kisses. "No, no, not at all. Professor. . . Lena, my dear, so good to see you again."

Unexpectedly, Worthy gave Father Fortis a brief hug before he pulled out a chair for the professor. *Christopher is hugging me again! Will wonders never cease?* he thought.

"Lena, have I chosen too touristy a place for our dinner?" he asked.

"Nick, I live three blocks from the Pantheon. If I find visitors distasteful, even American tourists," she said, smiling in Worthy's direction, "then I live in the wrong city."

Father Fortis noticed that his friend had bought new clothes. *Well, well, well,* he thought.

"You both look very fashionable," he said, "which makes me look decidedly underdressed."

Lena laughed. "Monks and nuns can't be overdressed or underdressed, can they?"

Father Fortis laughed in return before confessing, "Well, I did have my shoes polished this morning."

The three sat down and enjoyed watching two children, obviously twins, running around the tables with their balloons. In a few moments, the waiter approached, and Lena chose the wine to accompany their antipasti orders. Gazing around the oval piazza, Lena said, "There are some places where a person goes when life seems full of happiness. Piazza Navona is such a place. I don't think I've ever seen an argument here, and that's saying something, given that we're Italians."

"More happiness than at the Trevi Fountain?" Father Fortis asked.

Lena thought for a moment. "The Trevi is charming, but it's a bit chaotic, what with the mass of tourists, the pickpockets, and the sound of the rushing water. Here, I can almost believe the world will break out in joy one day. We won't have to sign peace treaties or destroy nuclear weapons; all we'll have to do is decide to be happy," she said, gazing in Worthy's direction.

"If the world breaks out in happiness, I'll have to look for another career, along with psychiatrists and marriage counselors," Worthy observed as he returned a smile.

"And lawyers and cosmetic surgeons," Lena added as if the two of them were children trying to top one another.

Lena's face became serious. "And let's not forget your American weapons manufacturers." Then, the smile returned as she said, "So, Nick and Chris, I've told you why I love this place in Rome. What part of my city do you love?" she asked.

Having enjoyed the exchange between Lena and Worthy, Father Fortis nodded toward Worthy. "You first, my friend."

Worthy shrugged even as he smiled. "I think you both know that Rome has been my 'dream city' since I was a teenager. When I was learning Latin, I imagined that I was living in the times of the Caesars. But I never expected to actually be here. The truth is, there's nothing about Rome that I don't love. Talk about looking through the rose-colored glasses of a tourist, right?" he said, looking at Lena.

Lena reached over and held his hand. "No, I don't think you're naïve. I think you love Rome as much as I do."

None of the three said anything until Lena asked, "And you, Nick? What do you love about my city?"

Father Fortis stopped himself from blurting out the obvious, that seeing the two of them together was what he loved most about Rome. He also decided to save sharing the agreement of the Pope and Patriarch until they were having dessert.

"My favorite part of Rome? That's a tough one. I mean, the history, the art, the architecture, and just look at these fountains," he said, turning toward the three in the piazza. "But I think the older churches, those commemorating martyrs, have impressed me the most."

"'The Church was built on the blood of the martyrs.' That's an old saying, but it's true," Lena said as she pointed to the far end of the piazza. "That ornate façade is the church of Santa Agnese, which probably holds the relics of a saint killed in this very space. I think I'm right in saying that on every block here in the center of Rome, there's at least one church dedicated to a martyr."

Father Fortis nodded. "I feel strange saying this to a true modern Roman like yourself, but I wish the Church after Constantine made the faith official hadn't been in such a hurry to advertise her success."

"Now that's an intriguing comment," Lena said. "Especially from a monk."

"I'm glad I surprised you, then. The Rome I feel closest to isn't ancient Rome or Constantine's Rome, or the Rome of the Middle Ages and Renaissance. What moves me most is the very earliest churches of Rome, the ones that recall when Christians were ignored, humiliated, or persecuted. I can't help but feel that that was when the faith was the strongest."

Lena looked again in the direction of Santa Agnese. "Some historians make the argument that once the Church became the official religion, faith was replaced by power. It that what you're thinking, Nick?"

Father Fortis nodded. "Yes, it is, and it raises the old 'what-if' question. What if Constantine hadn't embraced Christianity—would the Church today be smaller and have made a smaller footprint on history? I think so. But would her faith be purer?"

"If that had happened, the Pope and the Ecumenical Patriarch wouldn't be targeted by an assassin," Worthy observed.

"No, for better or for worse, the success of Christianity meant the two would become global celebrities, especially the Pope," Father Fortis said. "Which is why I find it so strange that no one has taken credit for the killings."

"Are you surprised, Chris?" Lena asked.

"Maybe more worried than surprised. On the homicides Nick and I have worked together, we're used to what's known as 'the hunt.' Last year, we had a case in which the killer literally blended into a forest. He was there, but we were unable to see neither hide nor hair of him. But the hunt on this case is different."

Father Fortis nodded. "Christopher and I have never dealt with murder on this big a stage. Last year's case was centered in a remote corner of Michigan's Upper Peninsula. If that case made the news, it didn't attract much attention outside that area. It's just the opposite on this case. Attempting to assassinate the Pope and Ecumenical Patriarch has made the news worldwide."

"Which is why we'd expect some known group, like Al-Qaeda after 9-11, to take credit and reap the publicity," Worthy added. "But not a whisper, and that's the kind of killer who scares me the most. He or they are in it for something more than publicity."

"You still think it's some apocalyptic group intent on killing the Pope and the Patriarch as part of some bizarre plan?" Lena asked.

"I'm about seventy-thirty convinced of that, but not a typical apocalyptic group," Worthy replied. "Groups like that are generally made up of lower-educated survivalists, religious fundamentalists, paranoid cult members, or TV or radio preachers who don't believe half of what they spew on the air. An exploding shoe-box? Yes, someone from a group like that could manage that. But sniper and drone attacks in foreign countries, and getting away with both? Think of all the organization that takes. And yet, with no one taking credit, Nick and I don't even know where to look for whoever is behind the attacks."

The waiter broke the dark mood by bringing their first course. Lena said, "Congratulations," Lena said. "We almost made it to the antipasti being brought before talking about work."

"My fault," Worthy added.

"I don't see how it can be helped," Father Fortis said. "But maybe we can take a break from all that until dessert."

The three stayed true to their pledge, but Father Fortis found it impossible to block out the thought that the unknown killer could at this moment be plotting another attack in Rome.

JULY 12: NORTHERN EUROPE: OUTGROWING CHESS

AS A BOY, THE CHESSMASTER HAD LITTLE OPPORTUNITY to participate in team sports. Instead, he'd enjoyed walks on the moors or playing chess against his father or friends of his father. His father, a widower and military advisor who was away more than at home, took little interest in his son's development until his son, as an eleven-year-old, defeated a man five times his age in a regional chess tournament.

That evening, his father sat his victorious son down and mapped out a plan that would take the boy to live two hundred miles away with the nation's chess champion. The boy agreed without comment or emotion. Under the champion's tutelage, the boy developed as his father hoped, and by his eighteenth birthday, was ranked in the top twenty-five chess players in the world.

The boy returned to his home on that birthday and, after presenting flowers to his aged nanny, asked to see his father. In that brief meeting, the boy announced that he'd never play chess again. The decision, the boy explained, had been made years before and, now that he was of age, the decision was final.

The few friends of his father found it easy to believe the father's bitter explanation that the boy's decision was made out of spite. The boy, now a young man of age, did nothing to counter that version, but he knew that the truth lay elsewhere.

In the beginning, the boy loved the complexity of chess and the myriad of options open at every moment, limited only by the restrictions of each piece's movement. But after being sent away by his father to live with the chess champion, he learned the truth of the game: the only real limitation in chess is in the mind of the player. As the champion had drummed into him, "The pieces, whether pawns or queens, do not move themselves." The pieces, he was reminded almost daily, were simply carved pieces of wood or ivory, becoming of value only in the minds of the opponents. The trophies were given to the winner, not the pieces. A wooden queen would burn just as readily as a wooden pawn.

On his fifteenth birthday, the boy proved his teacher right by throwing a complete chess set into a fire. By his sixteenth birthday, he'd considered quitting the game, but then realized he'd be sent back to his father, where he'd remain a chess piece controlled by a man he hardly knew. He considered his options and set his sights on his eighteenth birthday, when he'd announce his decision and have access to his inheritance.

It would be too simplistic to conclude that the Chessmaster had quit the game to punish his father. If he could explain his decision, he would have said that chess itself had taught him to quit the game. What is the value of trophies and certifications when what is, in the end, only pieces made of wood?

What he had taken from his years playing chess was the realization that the "juice" of the game for him came not in winning, but in the rush he felt in the minutes before making the decisive move. But by his sixteenth birthday, he realized that the rush would be purer if the decisive moves didn't push pieces of wood or ivory around on a board, but rather moved real kings, queens, presidents, prime ministers, arms dealers, senators, civil servants, and military around on a far different board.

For twenty-five years, until his early forties, he'd developed and honed skills in influencing local, national, and world affairs. He'd begun in small ways, such as stopping a train at a busy intersection in Chicago or in fixing a judicial election in a central African country. Having no political agenda at the time, he hadn't chosen his targets to advance a particular cause, but rather to stretch his capabilities.

In his early forties, however, he experienced a growing sense of discontent, which manifested itself initially as a decrease of the "juice" he would feel when his complex plots succeeded without a flaw. He thought that if he could raise the stakes, the thrill would return, but even that began to feel too much like the final years of his chess career.

One night, in a dream, he found himself walking down a dark street when a figure slowly approached him. As the backlit figure came closer and closer to him, the Chessmaster felt panic increasing. In the dream, he assumed that the figure was someone from the police, Interpol, or CIA who had finally caught up with him. The figure in the dream stopped no more than a foot in front of him, and he realized that the figure was himself. His other self, his dream self, pointed a finger at his chest and said in a hoarse whisper, "Time is running out. Either you figure out what I need, or I'll kill you."

He awakened in a sweat, his breathing rapid. When he reached for his glasses on the side table, he noticed that his hand was shaking. He roused himself and looked in a mirror, surprised to see a reflection that seemed older than he remembered.

He wrote, typed, and even used a calligraphic pen to record over and over the words from the dream, hoping that in doing so, he'd understand what they meant. Yes, he was forty-three, but what did the other self in the dream mean by saying his time was running out? After emancipating himself from his father—not even bothering to attend his father's funeral seven years before—he'd made a point of staying free of entanglements. He'd been with women on a night-by-night basis when younger and then only to prove something to himself, but he hadn't thought of sex for decades. With no siblings and his nanny long dead, no one needed him, and he needed no one.

He was also puzzled by the threat from his other self in the dream. Could he really die if he didn't decipher the dream? Hadn't he thought, until the dream, that he'd attained everything he wanted?

If he hoped that the panic associated with the dream would dissipate over the following two to three weeks, that didn't happen. On the contrary, the words began to have a life of their own within his mind, and he heard them as he drifted off to sleep and then again as he awoke in the morning. He read somewhere about a person's shadow, and that was how the memory and the words felt to him—as close and as inescapable as his shadow.

The dream marked the beginning of his long walks on the moors, walks taken in the hope that he could thereby make sense of his premonition. The first breakthrough came when a question surfaced one day: "Yes, you are clever, but what are you using your abilities for?" He stopped walking and answered, "To see how far I can control events in the world."

A wave of disgust immediately coursed through him. As if someone were walking beside him on the moor, he heard a voice say, "You think I gave you these abilities so you could play pranks on the world?"

What did the voice mean about his abilities being "given?" The Chessmaster had never been a religious person, not out of choice, but rather out of opportunity. His father, as best as he could remember him, never spoke of God, even in swearing, and the chess champion was similarly circumspect. As a boy living in the city, he had, of course, passed churches and an occasional synagogue, but he'd given them no further thought than he had the men's fraternal halls. Religion was a language that he'd simply never learned and never needed.

Abilities given implied a giver, he reasoned. He wouldn't have thought much about God being this giver except that pondering the idea of a God lessened the pressure left from the dream. Not knowing what else to do, he ordered a King James Version of the Bible by mail. When it arrived, he let it sit unopened for almost a week on his bedside table. To open the book and begin to read felt momentous, as if it were a Pandora's box, its ideas never to be safely stored away again.

Eventually he did open the Bible, and, as he always did with novels, he started at the end of the book. He learned to do this after realizing that mystery writers often played unfairly with readers' curiosity. By reading the end of a book first, he could judge his interest in reading what would come before.

That was the reason he started with the last book of the Bible, the book of Revelation, and what he read shocked and stirred him. He felt more awake than at any other time in his life. Here was an ending that didn't seem an end to anything. Instead, the strange book seemed to be the beginning of a great mystery with the entire universe's future at stake. Over the next ten years, the Chessmaster had committed much of his time to puzzling over how the story would—no, should—end.

From the Bible's ending, the Chessmaster had turned back the pages and read other parts. From the Psalms, he gleaned that God separated the righteous from the wicked and had a particular delight in smacking down the latter. He loved the image of the wicked melting like wax in the fire and the righteous bathing their feet in the blood of the wicked. Some of the prophets made little sense to him—he had never been comfortable with poetry—but others reinforced his growing belief that God is a mighty whirlwind about to strike.

Yet, no matter where else in the Bible he read, he always returned to the book of Revelation, and each time he discovered a new clue to the great mystery—where and how history was headed. He read the book daily and treated it as the key to decipher the rest of the Bible. Had he first read Jesus' teachings in the four gospels about loving the enemy and forgiving others, he would have dismissed Jesus as a weakling, a quitter. But having read of the *real* Jesus in the book of Revelation, he understood that Jesus' first coming had been a test, even a trick upon the people who saw Him walking on the earth.

"And I saw heaven opened, and behold a white horse; and he who sat upon him was called Faithful and True, and in righteousness he doth judge and make war . . . And he was clothed in a vesture dripped in blood. And out of his mouth goeth a sharp sword, that with it he should smite the nations; and he shall rule therein with a rod of iron, and he treadeth the winepress of the fierceness and wrath of Almighty God. And he hath on his vesture an on his thigh a name written: KING OF KINGS, AND LORD OF LORDS."

This was the real Jesus. As the Son of God, this Jesus could at any moment in his earthy life have destroyed those who opposed Him. Jesus was always the king on the chessboard even in his disguise as a mere pawn. Yet even in the gospels, the real Jesus peeked out, such as in the story of cleansing the Temple. Here was Jesus acting as God's wrathful judge, tearing into the moneychangers and merchants. And when He hung on the cross and heard the Temple leaders mock Him, laughingly inviting Him to come down off the cross if He could— what blasphemy; of course, he could—the Chessmaster imagined that Jesus' last earthly thoughts had been "just you wait."

The book of Revelation was the salve that soothed his tortured mind. The more he read, the more he accepted that his terrifying dream had been a gift, as it had led him to the book that changed his life. He now understood his dream: he had been confronted by his true self, who'd been waiting, always waiting, for his life's purpose.

He no longer tried to suppress the rage that he felt directed toward him in the dream. Instead, he realized that this rage was the warrior Jesus' own rage to be unleashed on the unbelieving world. And what could the timing of his dream mean but that the return of the Warrior Jesus would be soon?

The Chessmaster continued to test his abilities to affect events around the world, but now with a new sense of purpose. His abilities were gifts to be used for one aim, and that aim was to cooperate with Jesus, the coming Judge.

For the first four years of his intense study, he contacted only Christian apocalyptic sects that were predicting the imminent end of the world. Eventually, however, he understood that Jews and Muslims, whom he considered damned to hell for eternity, could yet be useful to achieving God's ends. This meant that he never tried to convert these groups, but rather communicated with them as someone who, if not a member of their faith, was conversant with and sympathetic to their beliefs. All his clients believed he shared their conviction that the end of the world was near and that their group was a key player in the final drama.

The response that he received from groups all over the world confirmed his belief that his new life's work was blessed by God. Various groups in Judaism, Christianity, Islam, and even some that were eclectic combinations of those faiths welcomed his online presence and were attracted, rather than put off, by his demands for secrecy and anonymity.

Now six years later, as he walked his moors, he was overcome with gratitude for the task that God had given him. Like Paul of Tarsus, he knew that he deserved to be among the damned, but he had been spared and given a special calling. He alone was given the task of orchestrating the beginning of God's final battle in the holy city of Jerusalem. He alone had the role of moving the players into position for the final move. Then, checkmate; the world would end.

CHAPTER TWENTY-ONE

ROME: JULY 13: A ONE-WAY ROAD TRIP

WHEN HIS PHONE RANG EARLY THE NEXT MORNING, Worthy expected to hear Father Fortis' voice. But instead, it was one of the Vatican's security forces, a man Worthy thought he remembered from his first meeting at the church of San Teodoro.

In a distinctive German accent, the caller said, "Lieutenant Worthy, we've located someone who claims he can take us to where the man behind the bomb in St. Peter's Square is sheltering. We thought you'd like to be present when we pick him up."

Worthy looked at his watch. "Yes, I'd like that very much. Should Father Fortis come as well?"

"No, Father Fortis is expected to attend a meeting this morning with the Holy Father and the Ecumenical Patriarch. I will send a car to pick you up at your hotel. Say in ten minutes?"

Worthy dressed quickly and was outside the hotel when the standard black sedan of the Vatican drove up. A man in a dark suit exited from the passenger door and opened the back door.

Entering the vehicle, Worthy found himself sitting beside a slightly older man also in a dark suit. Worthy nodded to him and sat back as the car pulled away. He heard the two men in front say something to one another, but because they were speaking Italian, he couldn't follow the exchange.

"How far is it?" Worthy asked the man next to him. When the man shook his head and said, "Non parlo Inglese," Worthy waited to hear if one of the two in the front would reply.

Finally, the driver said, "Not far, not far. Maybe ten, fifteen minutes."

Worthy looked out at the passing scenery as the car threaded its way through the city center's narrow streets. Passing Circus Maximus, Worthy remembered sitting with Father Fortis on his first day in Rome and talking about the movie *Ben Hur*. He shook his head as he thought of how little progress they'd made on the case in the following ten days. *Perhaps picking up the man behind the drone attack*, Worthy thought, *will lead to our first breakthrough.*

As the vehicle climbed the hill to the east of the Circus Maximus, Worthy looked for evidence that the three men were armed. The suitcoat of the man next to him hung awkwardly, and the shoulder of the man in the passenger seat had the indentation mark made by a shoulder holster. Handguns, he concluded, but maybe something more powerful in the trunk.

There was complete silence in the car, and Worthy noticed the absence of radio equipment. He reasoned one or more of them could be communicating with lapel transmitters, though it surprised him that there'd been no radio chatter.

Having left the ancient monuments behind, the car traveled through residential neighborhoods before coming to a modern shopping area.

For reasons he would never be able to explain, Worthy felt the hair on the back of his neck rise as he had a mental picture of the car's interior viewed from above. There were the three men, all armed security from the Vatican, and he on their way to apprehend a man suspected of orchestrating the bomb attack two weeks before. All that made sense, or did it?

Forgotten until that moment was the thought that had first struck him when the German security man phoned him. From his first days on the case, Worthy had assumed that the bomber had fled the country. He never imagined that the bomber would risk remaining in Italy, much less in Rome.

Worthy glanced over at the man sitting next to him and noticed that his leg was jumping nervously. That too, he thought, might mean nothing. People, even trained security, reacted differently when heading for a potential firefight. When the man saw Worthy looking at his leg, he pushed down on the leg with his hand and turned away to look out the window. He heard the man say something to the two in front and thought he detected a sudden stiffness in the man in the passenger seat.

As Worthy blamed himself for not asking for identification from the three outside the hotel, the words "get ready, get ready" ran through his mind. The car stopped at a light, and as they waited for the light to change, Worthy heard the sound of a siren from behind getting louder. Worthy watched as the cars ahead of the black sedan pulled over to the side. At the same time, the man in the passenger seat wheeled to look out the back window. Worthy did the same and saw a police car approaching at speed. As the man in the passenger seat said something to the man sitting with Worthy in the back, Worthy saw the man's hand move instinctively inside the flap of his suitcoat.

Trying to push down the panic he felt, Worthy thought, *Somehow, I have to get out of this car.* He took a slow deep breath and realized he was more angry than afraid. He'd let his guard down, forgetting that whoever was behind the attacks would have learned of his coming to Rome. He felt the irony of the moment, as he remembered the warning he shared very early when he trained recruits at the police academy: "When you're pursuing an adversary, don't forget that your adversary might have already found you."

As the police car approached and swung around the car, Worthy saw the man next to him turn and stare at him. The man didn't have to say anything for Worthy to know that if he tried anything at that moment, he'd be subdued if not shot.

It was then that he remembered another adage from his teaching at the police academy. "When tempted to panic, never underestimate the power of the unexpected. As he sat back in his seat, he reached in his shirt pocket for the pack of crackers he'd grabbed from the hotel's breakfast room. As the police car shot through the intersection and sped off, he made a show of unwrapping the crackers and putting one in his mouth. When the light changed and the black sedan pulled away, he smiled at the man next to him, who, as Worthy had hoped, physically relaxed.

Without warning, Worthy began coughing and kept coughing, pointing to his throat as if he were chocking on the cracker. Instinctively, the man moved to pound Worthy on the back, and as he did so, Worthy's right fist shot across his body and upward, striking the man just below his nose. The force of the blow brought both of the man's hands to his face as blood spurted out. As the driver reacted by speeding up, Worthy yanked on the door handle, flung the door open, and threw himself out of the vehicle. As he hit the pavement, pain surged up his entire left side, from his head down to his leg. Blocking the pain, he rolled toward the curb. Cars behind screeched to a halt as the black sedan also stopped, then raced away.

Passengers from other cars and pedestrians from the sidewalk ran toward Worthy as he struggled to rise. Nothing felt broken, though he knew from the shooting pain that he'd have road rash down his entire left flank. His first thought was to find a phone and warn Father Fortis. His legs wobbled as a second thought came to him. Father Fortis and he had badly underestimated their adversary, and that mistake had almost cost him his life.

✝

JULY 13: ROME: MAXIMILLIAN KOLBE HOTEL

"NAÏVE, OVERCONFIDENT, NARROWLY FOCUSED, TAKE YOUR PICK," Worthy said with a grimace.

Father Fortis made the sign of the cross as he saw his friend's raw forearm and left leg. "But you were spared," he said, sitting in a chair by Worthy's bed. "That's all that's important."

"I was worried that they'd come for you next. The person on the phone said that you were going to be called to a morning meeting with the Pope and the Patriarch."

"No, I received no message. I think that was just their way of making sure you came alone. Christopher, I think we have to conclude that you're the one who poses the threat to whoever is behind all of this."

"Yeah, yeah, I understand. You don't have to tell me to be more careful. I felt like such a fool, Nick, getting in that car because of a phone call."

"We can focus on that, my friend, or we can focus on what we can learn from the attack."

Worthy exhaled slowly as he shifted in his bed. "You're right, Nick. You start."

"From what you said, it was well-planned. Much like the other attacks."

"I agree," Worthy said with a grimace as he moved in his bed. "I could have sworn the car looked like one from the Vatican. And the black suits on the men, that also shows an attention to details."

"They also know where we're staying."

"And the timing of the car arriving gave them an advantage. I felt rushed." Worthy took a sip of the Coke that Father Fortis had brought to his room. "Did we learn anything in our favor?"

Father Fortis nodded. "Why you, why now? I think we now know the answer to those questions. Until you proposed your end-of-the-world theory, Christopher, the killers were staying in the shadows. Doesn't this attack mean that you're on the right track? You're a threat because you've shone a light on them, and they don't like being exposed."

CHAPTER TWENTY-TWO

JULY 14: QUO VADIS: ROME, IRELAND, OR JERUSALEM?

FOR ONE WHOLE DAY AND A SLEEPLESS NIGHT, Father Aiden felt he was at a crossroads. If he persuaded Margaret Cleery to move on to Jerusalem, he could return to his studies, complete his degree, receive the gratitude of the Church, and be sent back to Ireland.

But he found that option distasteful. He hadn't invested the past weeks in Margaret Cleery just to walk away before exposing her as a fraud. Returning to Ireland would also mean he'd have to forget his other goal of exposing the Vatican as an institution capable of anything, including bribery.

That led to the second option, to convince Margaret Cleery to take him with her to Jerusalem. He thought it fitting that there, in a city older and holier than Rome, he'd have his double revenge.

What kept him awake, however, was a complication with that plan. To expose Margaret Cleery as a fraud in Jerusalem would be as easy as exposing her in Rome, but if he exposed the Vatican at the same time, his doctoral studies at the Irish College and his priestly vocation would be over.

After spending a full day in the library of the Irish College staring at his research without adding a sentence and spending a night of twisting and turning in bed, he began to see another way forward.

The third option, like the second, would bring him to Jerusalem as Margaret Cleery's continuing assistant, but the events there would be significantly different. Jerusalem would be the place of Margaret Cleery's downfall, where he would show the world how she accomplished her tricks. She would be disgraced, even as he would be celebrated as the priest who exposed one of the world's greatest frauds.

At that point, he'd be the darling of the Vatican. He wouldn't return to Rome as the conquering hero, but rather as a humble priest shattered by the experience. He would complain of exhaustion, of sleeplessness, of anxiety, and hint that his taxing service to the Church made it impossible for him to complete his doctoral work. Then his request would come: could he not submit his research to that point—after all, he had been working on the last chapters when the Vatican requested his assistance—and have his prior work, along with his recent service to the Church, be the basis of his degree? The higher ups could hardly deny such a request, could they?

With his doctorate in hand and continuing to act as a withered shell of his former self, he'd return to Ireland with the Church's blessing. His first posting would be to a place where he could regain his strength, somewhere not too demanding but a steppingstone to a brighter future.

Safely embraced in the loving arms of a grateful Church, he'd then arrange for the other trap to snap shut. A hungry journalist eager to uncover the incredible story would be easy to find in Ireland. The travails of the Church, especially after the sex abuse scandals in Ireland, had become a regular beat for enterprising reporters. To such a person, he would reveal even more of what had transpired in his time with Margaret Cleery. Initially, he would keep the Vatican out of the account, but leave enough holes in the story that any journalist worth the title would turn over the rocks to uncover the truth.

Aiden imagined the denouement, the morning when TV cameras and microphones would lie in wait for him outside some Irish rectory. He'd be forced, with his legal counsel at his side, to tell more, but not all, of the sordid story of Vatican intrigue. Tearfully, he would stand, head bowed, as the world's press turned its attention on the Vatican and on the humble priest whom the Vatican had exploited. Then, for the first time and with a great flow of tears, he'd reveal the notes and the money he'd received.

He pondered what the Vatican's reaction would be at that moment. The best-case scenario was that the scandal would force a house-cleaning of the Vatican and the Curia. In that more hopeful scenario, the media and even some in the Church would treat him as an unwilling whistleblower, who was the instrument of God's judgment on the Holy See. And wouldn't that be the truth?

Of course, there was a worst-case scenario as well. The Vatican could turn its rage on him and totally deny its involvement. After all, Aiden had only two pieces of proof that the Vatican was involved—the cryptic comment from the principal of the Irish College, that someone "higher up" wanted him to infiltrate Margaret Cleery's group, and the unsigned notes that accompanied the money.

That scenario frightened him until he realized that he could still have the final word. He would act as the shattered and abused priest for those who saw the Vatican's attack on him as proof of the Church's mendacity. If he didn't panic, he might have multiple offers from publishers for his entire story. He might also have a career as a TV personality, an expert for BBC and ITV on every move by the Vatican in the future.

The more he thought about it, the more the so-called worst-case scenario seemed the best-case scenario. The only lie that he would have to tell, the only mask that he would have to wear, would be that of a heartbroken priest who wished he'd never agreed to be involved in the Vatican's subterfuge, who wished he could have remained a simple priest in some remote parish of his beloved Ireland. But he was very adept at donning masks. This final one would be the simplest of all to wear.

Later that day, Father Aiden found Margaret Cleery sitting quietly in her room reading from a book of prayers. *Good Lord,* he thought, *does she never stop putting on a front? Doesn't she remember that I've witnessed her petty snits and her caustic remarks about her devotees?*

Until a few days ago, his hope that she'd eventually take him further into her confidences seemed likely, but then he began to sense her slipping away as an untethered boat might slip away from a dock. For the twentieth time, he asked himself the question: What's the bitch's game?

But he felt ready for her, no matter what she was trying to pull. He'd spent the morning in the library of the Irish College where fellow doctoral students no doubt assumed he was working on his dissertation's final chapter. He was, in fact, researching, but his focus had nothing to do with his topic. He was building his argument that God wanted Margaret Cleery, expected her, and needed her to bring her messages to Jerusalem.

That afternoon, Margaret Cleery welcomed him with a warm smile and asked him to approach her chair. When he did so, she drew his head down and gave him a quick kiss on the cheek.

"Aiden, you are so dear to me," she said as she released him.

And you are so transparent to me, he thought.

"I've been feeling guilty, Aiden," she continued. "Sometimes, I'm so self-absorbed that I forget you're trying to finish your degree."

He took the other chair. "Not to worry; my research is going just fine, Margaret," he lied. "Being with you has had a very positive effect on me. Our time together has helped me see my future more clearly."

He felt the woman studying his face, but he knew there was no crack in his mask. In his own way, he'd told the absolute truth. He did see his future more clearly, and he saw her future clearly, too.

"I've given up trying to figure out what comes next," Margaret said, looking down at the prayer book. "For the first time in my life, I feel rudderless. It's a new feeling for me, Aiden. Half the time I'm filled with fear, but in the other half, I feel a kind of peace. Or maybe it's just resignation."

Aiden sensed that his Jerusalem gambit might be easier to bring about than he thought. If her talk about giving up control was her coded way of saying she wanted him to determine her group's next step, she might bite on the chance to move on to Jerusalem.

"I have a few thoughts on the subject, Margaret. May I share them?" he asked.

With obvious relief on her face, she said, "Please do, Aiden. I trust you as I would a son."

Inwardly, he let her personal comment fly out of his mind as quickly as it had flown in. "Just this morning, I was reading a passage in the book of the Acts of the Apostles," he began. "Not long after our Lord's ascension, the Mother Church in Jerusalem was at odds with St. Paul. The mother church was still following the Jewish law, while St. Paul saw the Jewish religious law as no longer necessary. I don't mean to preach a sermon, but do you follow so far?"

"Yes, I think so. It sounds like one cluster . . . one big brouhaha."

Drop the pose! Drop the pose! he wanted to yell at her. But he bit his tongue and continued. "The early Church was close to splitting, but then something miraculous—at least in the Church's eyes—happened. The Mother Church in Jerusalem invited St. Paul to explain his message. Everything in the Acts of the Apostles and St. Paul's own letters suggests that the debate was touch and go, but in the end, everyone agreed that St. Paul could continue to preach his version of the gospel to his Gentiles."

"And so what was the miracle?" she asked.

"The Holy Spirit brought the two sides together, despite their differences."

Margaret Cleery said nothing, but she looked intently at Father Aiden.

"Now fast forward nineteen hundred years," he continued. "It's 1964, and Pope Paul VI and Ecumenical Patriarch Athenagoras embrace in Jerusalem. The reconciliation between the two churches begins, though, as your messages make clear, that process remains unfinished and consequently is a disappointment to God."

He leaned forward. "Margaret, the final step toward reconciliation can't take place here in Rome because that would look as if the Orthodox were capitulating. They could have met at the Patriarchate in Istanbul, but that would give the impression that Rome was capitulating."

Aiden waited to see if Margaret saw where he was headed.

"So you think my message won't be accepted unless what—unless I go to Jerusalem?" she asked.

Aiden smiled at her as if she were a prize student. "Jerusalem has always been the apple of God's eye. It's still the place where the Holy Spirit can heal the brokenness of the Church. Of this, Margaret, I, as a priest who agrees with your messages, am convinced."

"And have you prayed about this, Aiden?"

He was surprised by the question, then angered. "Yes, Margaret, I have."

Margaret raised a hand, and Aiden obliged by stopping. The two sat in silence for a long moment before she finally said, "You really think I should go to Jerusalem?"

"Margaret, I think God wants you to go there, and I think your messages will . . . will bear fruit there."

Another long silence followed. Margaret rose to her feet and walked to the window. With her back to him, she said, "Aiden, you know better than anyone that I'm just the messenger. For my messages to be accepted, won't the Pope and the Patriarch have to be in Jerusalem too?"

For a moment, he feared that she had spotted the Achilles Heel in his plan. He took a deep breath, but before he could reply, Margaret spoke again.

"You don't have to answer that. In fact, I don't want you to. If Jesus wants this healing to take place in Jerusalem, I shouldn't doubt what you say. Jesus brought a washerwoman to Rome. He can certainly find a way to bring the Pope and the Patriarch to Jerusalem," she said, as she turned to look at him.

Aiden wanted to laugh in her face, to tell her he knew exactly what she was doing. But his mask never changed expression. Until the very end, when he would expose her, he would remain her unquestioning servant.

"Oh, one last thing," Margaret said as she returned to her chair. "I will need you with me, in Jerusalem, I mean."

Aiden acted totally surprised by the request. "But what about the expense, Margaret?"

"God has provided. Just this morning, I found another envelope addressed to me left at the desk. Inside was ten thousand Euros."

Aiden looked down at Margaret. "Was there a note?"

"No, just the money. Why do you ask?"

"No reason," he replied as nonchalantly as he could manage.

"I hope you see, Aiden, that the money proves that it's God who led you to suggest Jerusalem."

CHAPTER TWENTY-THREE

———————◆———————

July 14: Jerusalem: The Curtain Rises

ARMON LUDD REREAD THE CRYPTIC EMAIL and, despite its contents providing a worthy challenge, concluded that his group would have little trouble fulfilling the assignment. They were all lifelong residents of Jerusalem, and because most of them spent their youth in a gang, they knew the nooks and crannies of the city better than most of the tour guides.

Although religion was ever-present in Jerusalem, faith had come to Armon late in life. Until he became a member of the "vanguard," a secret Jewish group intent on hastening the coming of the Messiah, religion had mainly meant roadblocks, either the physical ones encountered on almost any road of the Holy City or the more stubborn mental ones that separated the residents of Jerusalem.

Growing up, Armon heard that the name "Jerusalem" was related to the Hebrew word for peace, but anyone who lived in Jerusalem knew it was a city of tension. The tension would fluctuate with daily issues, but the tension was always there.

He knew that most lifelong Jerusalem residents accepted the tension as normal. But, as a teenager, when he was becoming too well known to the police, his family sent him to spend a summer with a cousin in Canada. Even though Toronto had its own urban issues, the agent had never felt so safe in his life. In his three months there, he never heard the sound of gunfire once.

When he returned to Jerusalem, he felt both at home and estranged from his old neighborhood and friends. It was then that Armon joined the vanguard, whose goal gave voice to what he'd been wondering since his time in Toronto— why was it impossible to know a day or even an hour of peace in Jerusalem?

Although Armon had become religious, he was not to be confused with the religious crazies on busy street corners who screamed out their messages to passersby who ignored them. Nor was he one of those who sang as they processed with Torahs to the Western or Wailing Wall. He didn't even wear a skullcap, and with his slight build, dark hair and beard, he could pass for a Palestinian. No, the vanguard worked in the shadows, behind the scenes.

In his initiation into the group, Armon learned about historical predecessors to the vanguard—chiefly, the first-century Zealots and, before that, the Maccabees. The vanguard also had allies outside the city, modern-day zealots and followers of the martyr Rabbi Kahani. These allies lived on the fringe of society in the hills of Judea and Galilee where they too were preparing the country for the coming of the Messiah.

Messiah—to the frustration of most Jews, including Armon, the word had been co-opted by Christians who believed something ridiculous, that the Messiah had already come in Jesus. Armon agreed with those who said that any thinking person, by looking at the sorry state of the world, should come to the obvious conclusion—the Messiah had yet to come.

That morning, Armon met privately with his most trusted agent to share the order he'd received. Mordecai Katz, like Armon, had grown up in Jerusalem and consequently could speak a smattering of the city's many languages. Of the two, Mordecai was taller, more muscular, and the one always hoping for a fight. As a teenager Mordecai had been in the same gang as Armon, a gang that prided itself on being able to break into churches, monasteries, and mosques without leaving traces. Once inside, members of the gang would take photos of the site's so-called holy objects to prove they'd completed the assignment. If these break-ins were more pranks than serious achievements, Armon and Mordecai were still proud that they'd never failed an assignment.

The task this time was to break into not just any church, but to break into *the* church in Jerusalem, the church of the Holy Sepulcher, where Christians believed Jesus' crucifixion and resurrection took place.

To Armon's surprise, the first part of the order, breaking into the church, didn't involve taking anything, even photos, but rather leaving something— two notes. The second part of the order, leaving the church and provoking an attack in another part of the city, would be to Mordecai's liking.

Whoever sent the order—the same anonymous person who'd paid them handsomely over the past months—had attached a summary of the church's long history. Armon appreciated the short lessons that routinely accompanied the orders. He felt that the person behind the emails, whoever he was, treated the vanguard as a group with minds, not just muscles. Mordecai laughed when Armon read the part about the Emperor Constantine's mother, Helena, claiming to find the true cross and the tomb of Jesus on the exact spot where the church of the Holy Sepulcher was later built. Armon, however, hadn't joined in the laughter.

Armon read further about the three main Christian groups that now shared the church: Greek Orthodox, Franciscan Catholics, and Coptic Christians. In addition, several other groups, such as the Armenians, controlled other parts of the church complex. What surprised Armon and Mordecai most was found in the last paragraph of the church's history—a list of the riots that had occurred over the centuries involving these Christian groups. The latest of these skirmishes was in November, 2008, when Armenian and Greek Orthodox monks traded punches, ripped down tapestries, and threw objects at one another. *So much for Jesus being the prince of peace,* Armon thought.

Armon realized that this acrimonious history was important to his assignment. Mordecai and Armon were directed to enter the church at closing time and leave two notes. They would leave the first in the Armenian area of the church. The note would describe a plot by the Franciscans and the Greek Orthodox to post a guard in the area known as the Edicule, the supposed site of Jesus' resurrection. The note would say that the Franciscans and the Greeks were plotting to take control over the holiest site in Christianity. They would then leave a second note in the Franciscan area of the church. This note would state that the Armenians and the Greeks were lodging a complaint with the city authorities, accusing the Franciscans of being behind the riot in 2008.

After leaving the notes, the two agents were directed to make their way to the Armenian quarter of the Old City. There they would wait outside a monastery for the Armenian monk who would be walking to the church of the Holy Sepulcher for early morning duty. Armon and Mordecai were ordered to wear ski masks and physically subdue the monk before taunting him, telling him that "we Greeks despise you Armenians, you bloody heretics."

From growing up in Jerusalem, Armon knew that the church of the Holy Sepulcher, like the Western or Wailing Wall and the two mosques atop Temple Mount, was dry tinder. He also knew that the two-part assignment, once completed, would undoubtedly provoke an even bloodier riot in the church than occurred in 2008.

Something Armon didn't share with Mordecai was his disappointment with the choice of targets. *Why start a riot at the church?* he asked himself. *Wasn't the vanguard's ultimate goal to liberate what was only several hundred yards away, the Western or Wailing Wall of the ancient Temple, the holiest site in Judaism?* The vanguard that Armon led shared the belief of the Kahanists, that the true Messiah couldn't return until the blasphemous mosques sitting atop Temple Mount were destroyed and the Jewish temple, demolished in the war against Rome in 70 CE, was restored so sacrifices could once again be offered to God.

Over the past months, since the anonymous person had first communicated with them and offered his support, the members of the vanguard had spent many nights wondering who the anonymous person was and where he lived. Armon's opinion, based on the emails and money he'd received from the donor, was that he was a wealthy zealot, a disciple of Rabbi Kahani from New York perhaps, who shared the vanguard's goal.

I wish I understood what this man is trying to accomplish with this stunt at the church, Armon thought. To break into the church of the Holy Sepulcher, leave notes, and then assault an Armenian monk seemed peripheral, more a distraction than anything strategic for the larger picture—the liberation of Temple Mount.

But Armon knew disobeying wasn't an option, even when the orders made little sense.

JULY 15: ROME: TRASTEVERE

AT THE SAME RESTAURANT IN TRASTEVERE where Worthy and Lena had eaten before, Lena raised her finger and threaded a stray hair behind Worthy's ear. Worthy closed his eyes as her hand lingered on the side of his face; he wasn't yet accustomed to being touched affectionately by a woman. He didn't care if others were watching, but then remembered that loving touches were not uncommon in Italy.

"I have to touch you to remind myself that you're really here," Lena said, her voice quivering.

"Now you know why it's not wise to get too close to a cop," Worthy said.

"Just for the record, Chris, I'm not a woman who gets off on danger. The fact that you can hardly sit down is bad enough, but when I think that you could have been killed . . ."

"And I'm sorry, Lena. I wasn't sure I was going to tell you."

"As if I wouldn't notice the limp," she said as she wiped tears from her eyes. "Is it safe for you to stay in Rome?"

"I'm probably safer than I was yesterday. The people who did this know I'm now on my guard. But if it's all right with you, let's talk about something else."

Lena looked down at a meal that Worthy noticed that she'd barely touched. "Really, I'm okay and I'm as safe as I can be. Nick isn't letting me out of his sight."

"It's not that," Lena said. "It's about Margaret Cleery."

Worthy frowned, wondering why the Irish woman was suddenly upsetting Lena. "What is it?" he said.

"Mother Cleery is leaving Rome and going to Jerusalem," she said, in barely a whisper.

Worthy felt his throat tighten, as Lena continued. "The Vatican is relieved, of course. She won't be here to stir things up with her messages."

"And?" Worthy asked.

Taking a sip of wine, Lena said, "What this means, Chris, is that I've been asked to go to Jerusalem too. The Vatican wants me to continue to track her movements and especially her messages."

Worthy could guess the questions that Lena was afraid he would ask. "Do you have to go?" "Do you have to accept the assignment?" "What would happen to your consulting career with the Vatican if you turned down the offer for personal reasons?" But he couldn't ask those questions, and so he waited, concentrating on the softness of her hand that only moments before had stroked his face.

"Margaret Cleery is a problem for everyone because the jury is still out about her," Lena said, breaking the silence.

Worthy understood what those words meant. Worthy owed his time with Lena to Margaret Cleery's appearance in Rome. Without her messages beginning in the wake of the attack in St. Peter's Square, Worthy knew he wouldn't have met Lena. But now the same person was tearing them apart. *What Margaret Cleery giveth, Margaret Cleery taketh away,* he thought.

Worthy tried unsuccessfully to look Lena in the eye. "Any chance she . . . and you will come back to Rome?"

Again, Lena brushed away her tears. "I doubt it, Chris. It's more likely she'll return to Ireland or head off for a tour of the States." Trying to smile, she added, "Maybe you could invite both her and me to Detroit."

He looked away as he knew Lena had already made her decision, opting for the only thing that made sense. He didn't doubt that their attraction for one another was mutual. But marriage had wounded both of them, him more than her. In the back of his mind, he worried that he'd fallen in love with this new chance at love, which was hardly sufficient grounds for suggesting that both of them change their lives. And once they were separated, he wondered how long it would take for these weeks together in Rome to become a fading memory.

"When will you leave?" he asked, continuing to look away.

"I think in a day or two," Lena said.

"Maybe she'll change her mind," Worthy said, even though he didn't believe his own words.

"No, the Vatican has two very credible sources placed in her group. We know Margaret Cleery is going to Jerusalem along with Father Aiden. We aren't sure how many of her followers will tag along. What I do know is that her decision to leave has really stirred things up in the Vatican. No one is laughing about Margaret Cleery anymore."

Worthy's mouth was dry, the news having sucked all the moisture out of him.

"Look, Chris, I'm not expecting you to say anything. We both knew this day would come, and I think we both know how the other one feels. I don't know any more than you where those feelings will lead, but I know they won't just evaporate."

Worthy nodded slowly.

Her hand once again gently stroked his cheek. He wondered if she was touching him because he was already being to fade.

Lena had had a few more hours to absorb the news than he, so Worthy wasn't surprised that she was beyond him, already beginning to view their situation rationally. He looked down at the empty plate in front of him. For the past weeks, his life had felt like a ride on a rollercoaster. First, he thought Father Fortis might have died in the bomb attack in St. Peter's Square. Then, he received a phone call that told him Father Fortis was alive and that the Orthodox Ecumenical Patriarch wanted him to come to Rome to investigate the puzzling case. As if that wasn't enough, he'd met Lena and fallen in love. Then yesterday, he'd almost been killed.

But now, Lena was leaving for Jerusalem while he would remain in Rome, trying to track down a resourceful and determined killer. He opened his mouth, but no words came out.

"Shh," Lena whispered. "I know."

CHAPTER TWENTY-FOUR

---◆---

JULY 16: NORTHERN EUROPE: FAITH AND FAILURE

WHEN THE CHESSMASTER LEARNED THAT HIS Rome agents failed to kill Lieutenant Worthy, of how the detailed plan had been thwarted by the unexpected appearance of a police car, its siren blaring, he accepted that the failure was his. That Lieutenant Worthy had survived was no credit to the detective; rather, he had survived because it was God's desire.

Not that the Chessmaster doubted God's ultimate purposes. No, the world's end was near, imminent even. He remembered the stories of Abraham, the "friend of God," who nevertheless repeatedly failed to trust God. Yes, God, he realized, was always testing his servants. His own attempt to remove the Detroit detective was a temptation that the Chessmaster had fallen into.

For the next twenty-four hours, the Chessmaster observed a strict fast, consuming neither food nor drink as he walked the moors and prayed for forgiveness and guidance. As his body weakened from the exertion and the lack of food or water, he struggled to return to the manor house of his estate. But with that physical weakness, he felt a mental lightness take its place. He understood that he must have faith that the Detroit detective would disappear, like a cloud passing, when and where God, not he, chose.

✝

JULY 17: ROME: STRANDED

WITH LENA HAVING LEFT FOR JERUSALEM the day before, Father Fortis could only imagine how Worthy was feeling. Was it always true that it is far better to experience love and loss than not to love at all? he wondered.

Father Fortis had no problem admitting that Lena had, in the past weeks, done more to heal Worthy's wound than anyone, including him, since Worthy's divorce. And for that, Father Fortis considered her an answer to prayer.

But Worthy had also confessed that the separation could mean the beginning of the end of the relationship. Father Fortis knew long-distance relationships were fragile, especially ones that had only recently begun. And their divergent tasks, Lena's with understanding Margaret Cleery and Worthy's with finding an assassin, would leave little time for them to connect over email, online, or by phone.

Father Fortis considered telling Worthy that Lena was safer in Jerusalem than if she'd stayed in Rome, but he knew that Worthy would see that for what it was, an attempt to find a silver lining in the gray clouds. He felt helpless, knowing that all he could do would be to hope for the two of them, pray for them, and continue to do what he was doing at that moment over the breakfast table—keep a watchful eye on his friend.

Worthy opened the folder in front of him, a document Father Fortis had seen Lena hand to Worthy as she kissed him goodbye and stepped into the taxi. Father Fortis could see that the folder contained newspaper clippings as well as news summaries off the Internet. He wasn't sure if Worthy was seriously perusing the file or using it as a device to avoid conversation.

"Interesting, my friend?" he asked.

"It's another file from the Vatican, Nick. I've spent most of last night studying its contents, but if there's some connection between these articles, I'm missing it."

"Lena didn't say?"

"She said she was simply asked to pass the file on to me. Apparently, the person who put the clippings together in the first place was an old Austrian priest. Unfortunately, he died three months ago."

Father Fortis took another bite of scrambled eggs. "Well, you've piqued my curiosity. Read me an example."

Worthy turned back to the beginning of the folder. "Here's the first article in the file, chronologically. It's about a militia group, alt-right, white supremacist, and religious, from Barron, Wisconsin. Two years ago, the group was bankrupt and considered defunct. But six months ago, the ATF received an anonymous tip alleging the group was storing a cache of automatic weapons. A raid followed, but no weapons were found. The group is now suing the US government. But the article also suggests that the ATF believes the group received a warning and hid the weapons. In other words, the ATF believes the tip was on the level. And in the margin of the article, the old priest wrote what looks like 'where did the money come from?' Now how would a story from Barron, Wisconsin, end up in a Vatican file?"

"It seems more of a non-story. Read me another one," Father Fortis asked.

Worthy flipped through several pages before stopping. "This one is from the BBC World Service from last year. A jihadist plot in Karachi, Pakistan, was intercepted just before an attack on an Ahmadiyya Muslim funeral. According to the article, the Ahmadiyya aren't considered orthodox Muslims in Pakistan and, like Pakistani Christians, have faced persecution in the past. And here's another underlining, Nick, from the old priest. 'A large stockpile of automatic weapons was recovered, their serial numbers removed. But all indications are that the weapons were Western-made.'"

"Maybe captured in Afghanistan?" Father Fortis offered.

"That was my first thought, but the BBC states the weapons weren't US military issue. A source who wished to remain anonymous claimed the weapons were most likely French or British."

"So, two stories in which something horrible could have happened, but didn't," Father Fortis observed.

"Ready for another? This article describes a YouTube video from Sao Paolo, Brazil, posted eleven months ago. Four statues of the Virgin Mary, large ones, were stolen from churches and then blown up."

"Vandalism, clearly. Was it a gang?" Father Fortis asked.

"Again, the story is small potatoes. But here's something else that connects the stories—no one took credit for any of them."

"Just like here in Rome and in Constantinople."

"Exactly," Worthy said as he passed a fourth news clipping to Father Fortis. "Let me drink my coffee before it gets cold."

Father Fortis scanned the entry. "An Israeli rabbi and peace activist along with his daughter were shot outside a synagogue in Galilee. This was nine months ago. Assumed attackers were Palestinians. Both survived, but the rabbi remains in a wheelchair." He looked up to see Worthy staring out the window in the direction of the church of San Teodoro and the Palatine Hill. He didn't doubt what Worthy was preoccupied with.

"Did you hear me, my friend?" Father Fortis asked.

"Hmm?" Worthy turned back. "Yes, I heard you, Nick. I remember reading that one. Again, no one took credit. I wonder if Lena . . . if Lena left me the wrong folder."

Father Fortis was about to commiserate, saying Lena was undoubtedly upset when they parted, but he held his tongue. Worthy didn't need to hear that, even if it were true. Instead, he pulled out another clipping. "Maybe this will give us a clue."

He read through the article from two months before and realized he'd heard about this event. On Cyprus, an island divided between Turkish Muslims in the north and Greek Orthodox in the south, two bombs exploded within five minutes of one another. He summarized that part of the account and then read the rest aloud.

"One bomb destroyed the chapel of an abandoned monastery, and the other bomb damaged a mosque in the north. An analysis of the bomb fragments established that the bombs were identical.' But the article goes on to ask what I'm wondering," he said. "There have been tensions between the two sides going back to the 1960s, but why would someone want to attack both communities?"

"Unfortunately, we can't ask the old priest why he put this file together," Worthy said.

"Is it possible the file is just a catchall of random events?"

"No, I'm beginning to agree with the old priest. These events aren't random. They're just made to look that way."

"But what's the point of them, I mean, taken as a whole?"

Before Worthy could answer, their conversation was interrupted by a stirring at other tables as residents stood and gathered around a TV monitor on one of the room's walls. A staff member of the house turned up the volume and although the voice spoke in rapid Italian, Father Fortis recognized the word Jerusalem scrolling below the screen.

The scene of chaos made him wonder if there'd been another bomb. But instead of smoke and debris, there were men on screen, obviously monks by their robes, fighting and throwing objects at one another. For a moment, Father Fortis couldn't identify the location, but from the Italian he was able to decipher, he realized what he was looking at.

"Good Lord," he said. "It's the church of the Holy Sepulcher!"

JULY 17: JERUSALEM: THE CHURCH OF THE HOLY SEPULCHER

FATHER AIDEN BROUGHT A CHAIR TO HIS WINDOW in the Catholic hostel and looked down on the parade of humanity below. He believed he'd never see streets older than those in Rome, but the Jerusalem scene below was older than old. It seemed older than ancient. Only the electrical lines running like string of a cat's cradle from one building to another broke the illusion of being transported back in time. No automobile traffic could pass on the narrow and twisting lane, and even merchants' pushcarts had difficulty making their way through the throng of pedestrians.

Had King David used this same street to rendezvous with Bathsheba? Had Jesus, St. Peter, or St. Paul traversed this very street? Had Caiphas or Pilate? he wondered.

In contrast to the streets of Rome, Jerusalem's walkways had heard not only Greek and Latin, but ancient Hebrew, Aramaic, Arabic, Turkish, Armenian, Ethiopian, Syriac, Yiddish, British English, modern Hebrew, and American slang. As Aiden listened, he could still hear many of those languages still echoing along the stone walls and pavements below his window.

Four days before, he had arrived with Margaret Cleery and ten others at the airport in Tel Aviv, where they were met by a dozen new followers. From there, a bus took them to a Catholic hostel, arrangements having already been made by what Margaret referred to as a generous anonymous source.

She works fast, Aiden thought. Sometime in the days between his sharing the Jerusalem option and their arrival, Margaret Cleery must have contacted someone who brokered the deal at the hostel. Then again, Aiden reasoned, the Vatican might have pulled some strings to guarantee that Mother Cleery would be comfortably settled in Jerusalem.

Since they arrived in Jerusalem, he'd had only two meetings with Margaret. In both, she continued to stick with her sickening script of repentant piety. At the airport, she spoke in a soft voice to her followers. She smiled at them all, thanked them for their support, and that was it. She offered no tease, no promises, no cursing, nothing that would indicate she knew her purpose in coming to Jerusalem.

Whatever game Margaret Cleery was playing, Aiden judged, was a dangerous one, capable of gutting her support. This troubled him. He'd expected the move from Rome to Jerusalem to excite her, push her to overreach herself and, in the process, inadvertently reveal her true scheming nature. None of that would happen if she simply faded from view on her own accord.

He'd read enough accounts of mystics and mystic frauds to know that their lives generally led to one of three outcomes. One, both mystics and frauds could become martyrs, dying for their message. Two, mystics or mystic pretenders sometimes withdrew from public view to live out the rest of their days in a monastery or convent. Given her children, some of them still living with her, Margaret couldn't opt for this, and Aiden doubted she could take a vow of obedience to anyone. Three, mystic pretenders who were exposed usually died in ignominy. This is what Aiden saw in Margaret Cleery's future. When he had the proof in his hand and revealed what he knew to the world, Margaret Cleery would have no option but to beg airfare back to Ireland where she'd live the rest of her life in shame.

There was a fourth possible outcome, and this option troubled Aiden the most. In rare cases, a mystic pretender was exposed and driven into obscurity, only later—sometimes long after the mystic had died—to have his or her message verified by subsequent events. Aiden vowed to himself that Margaret Cleery must not become another Joan of Arc, misunderstood in her own time only to be viewed a true mystic later. When the "reveal" occurred, there must be no doubt that she was, in reality, a narcissistic lover of attention. He must guarantee that she not just stumble, but fall from a great height.

Her fall must occur in Jerusalem, he reasoned, even though this was a tall order for someone like him who was visiting Jerusalem for the first time. But the more that he'd thought about the challenge, the more he'd embraced it.

When Margaret Cleery tumbled off the world's stage in a pratfall, he would take her place.

Sirens seemed as common in Jerusalem as in Rome, but now, from the city below his window, the sirens increased, awakening him from his reverie. As he leaned out the window to see the source of the sirens, he heard a knock on his door.

He opened the door to find Margaret Cleery standing before him.

"May I come in?" she asked.

As he stepped aside and invited her into his room, he realized that this was the first time she'd come to his room for a meeting. She looked at Aiden with a puzzled expression before he realized that there was only the one chair in his room. He retrieved it from beneath the window and placed it in the center of the room before sitting on the edge of the bed.

"I just found a note under my door telling me to turn on my TV. I assumed it was from you, so I flipped through the channels until I found BBC. There's a riot taking place right now at the church of the Holy Sepulcher, monks and pilgrims fighting inside and outside the church. The reporter said that early this morning, an Armenian monk was beaten so badly that he's expected to lose the sight of one eye. There were also some notes found this morning inside the church that are being blamed for provoking the riot. The BBC called it a melee, which I take to mean it's a helluva mess, but why did you leave the note for me?"

Aiden was relieved to hear that Margaret hadn't lost her sailor's tongue. "But I didn't," he explained. "May I see it?"

With no apparent self-consciousness, Margaret Cleery retrieved a note from her blouse and handed it to Father Aiden. In typed letters, the note read: "Catholic, Orthodox, and Armenian monks are fighting at the tomb of Our Lord. If Christ has brought you to Jerusalem to bring peace to the Church, won't you do what you can to stop the violence?"

Aiden felt his heart race as he realized events were cooperating with his plan. Instead of trying to figure out how to put Margaret Cleery into public view in Jerusalem, she was doing that task for him.

"Do you think I should go?" she asked.

Aiden piously lowered his head, trying not to reveal that he knew she'd written the note herself. "Yes, Margaret, we should go as soon as possible. Should we inform the others?"

Margaret Cleery was silent for a moment before rising and walking to the door. "Use your own judgment, Aiden. I'll meet you in the lobby in ten minutes."

Although the Catholic hostel was only minutes away from the church of the Holy Sepulcher and despite the constant wail of sirens under Aiden's window, the group under Aiden's leadership had to detour along parallel maze-like streets of the city before they arrived at the church.

The scene they came upon looked like a studio lot for a disaster movie. Bored-looking Israeli soldiers guarded broken chairs, tables, wooden pallets, chains, and stones that littered the square in front of the church. A sure indication that the riot was quelled were the TV crews closing down their operations.

Aiden brought the group to the cordon that kept the crowds back.

"Church closed," a muscle-bound soldier declared, his automatic weapon cradled like a baby in his arms.

Aiden turned to catch Margaret Cleery's eye, wondering what she wished to do. But one of the reporters, accompanied by a cameraman, was already sticking a microphone into her face. Aiden hastened to her side so he wouldn't miss the exchange.

"You're Mother Cleery, aren't you?" the young female reporter asked in a British accent.

BBC, Aiden realized. The Vatican must have sent out some sort of press release about Margaret Cleery coming to Jerusalem.

Margaret tried to shield her face from the bright light of the camera. "Please, I just arrived. I don't even know what happened here."

"But you're here nonetheless," the reporter pressed. "How did you hear about the riot?"

Aiden stepped to Margaret's side, anxious to control the exchange. "Look, Mother Cleery is no ambulance chaser. We received a message at our hostel about a disturbance at the church."

Before he could say any more, the reporter continued, "What hostel are you staying at?"

"We'd rather not say," Aiden replied. "Mother Cleery is here in Jerusalem, like other Christian pilgrims, to strengthen her faith."

"Is it true the Vatican asked you to leave Rome?"

Aiden heard Margaret gasp, even as he was certain the BBC reporter hadn't thought the question up on her own.

"There is no truth in that," Aiden said. "As I said, Mother Cleery—"

"Have you received any messages from Jesus since you've arrived?" the reporter continued.

Aiden glanced over to see Margaret's look of confusion and her face turning red. "No," she snapped, "has he talked to you lately?"

The reporter smiled, apparently pleased that she had gotten under Margaret Cleery's skin. Aiden noticed that Margaret's followers had moved in closer, waiting to hear whatever she would say.

"Your messages in Rome centered on the Pope and Orthodox Patriarch reconciling. Are you aware that today's riot isn't the first time Catholic, Orthodox, and Armenian monks have fought one another at this church?"

Still obviously angry, Margaret Cleery raised her hand to cut off the reporter. "This is the site of Jesus' crucifixion, burial, and resurrection. When Christians stand in this church in front of the cross, there is no Catholic, Orthodox, or Armenian. As St. Paul said, there is no Jew nor Greek, no male nor female, no slave nor free. Those distinctions are made by men and women, not God."

A murmur spread through the group. Was this a message from Jesus, or was this Margaret Cleery's personal view?

"But you're a Catholic," the reporter replied, as if Margaret had forgotten. "Are you saying that God doesn't want this holy site to be divided up by these different Christian groups?"

Margaret wasn't pausing now. She was replying as rapidly as the reporter was presenting her questions. Aiden knew that Margaret would be most likely to slip up when she was ad-libbing, off script.

"Do you think God is pleased this church is the site of riots instead of a place of healing? It doesn't take a mystic to point out that the prayers of monks, with hate in their hearts for one another, cannot reach God even from this holy place."

"Then whose church should this be, Mother Cleery?" the reporter asked.

"Isn't it obvious? This is God's church, only God's."

A jeep pulled into the square, and from it, an older and obviously more senior solder exited to approach the reporter, Margaret, and her entourage. "Your identification?" he asked, addressing Margaret.

Aiden reached into his briefcase and produced Margaret Cleery's passport. The officer studied the document before saying something in Hebrew to the soldier accompany him, who wrote down the documents' names and numbers.

With a frown, the officer turned back toward Margaret Cleery. "This is a restricted area. We cannot have another disturbance. What is your business here?"

Aiden started to explain, but Margaret waved him off. "I received a note that I could maybe help end the riot."

"What note?" the office demanded.

Aiden found the note in his briefcase and passed it over to the officer. "How do I know you didn't write it?" he glanced up at Margaret.

Aiden stared at Margaret. *Is this the moment when she has to admit the truth?* he thought.

"Because I didn't," she said, responding as curtly to him as he was speaking to her.

"Who wrote it, then?"

"I have no idea, but I thought if I could help—"

"My officers made peace without your help," the officer said with a sneer before apparently repeating the comment for the soldier next to him.

Margaret seemed to rise to her full height. "No, captain or general or whatever your rank is. That's exactly what your men and women didn't do. You stopped a riot, for the time being, but I think we both know that you haven't made peace. If you had, this rope wouldn't be here, and my followers and I would be allowed to go into the church to pray."

The officer turned away as if he were finished with her. "No prayers here, today. Probably none tomorrow. And, Margaret Cleery, be careful where you and your group pray in Jerusalem. I won't have you or your followers stirring things up in my city."

The BBC reporter standing to the left of Margaret turned to her cameraman. "Did you get all that?" When the cameraman nodded with a smile, she turned back to Margaret Cleery and Father Aiden. "I'm going to say the opposite. I hope we see more of you, Mother Cleery. Oh, and, welcome to Jerusalem."

CHAPTER TWENTY-FIVE

---◆---

JULY 17: ROME: THE CHURCH OF SAN TEODORO

PATRIARCH MICHAEL LOOKED TEN YEARS OLDER than the last time Father Fortis had seen him. Perhaps, it would be fairer to admit that the Patriarch looked years younger at their last meeting when he shared the pact of brotherhood between the Pope and him.

"Please, both of you be seated." Making the sign of the cross, the Patriarch said, "First of all, Lieutenant Worthy, I am thankful that your life has been spared. When you arrived in Rome, I placed you under the Holy Protection of the Theotokos, the Mother of God."

Worthy's face reddened. "Ah . . . thank you, sir."

Patriarch Michael signaled for those present to sit. "Has there been any word on the men who tried to abduct you?"

"No, and I don't expect they'll be found," Worthy replied. "Whoever is behind this seems to plan for all possible contingencies."

"If you've decided to return to the States, I want you to know that I understand," Patriarch Michael said.

"Actually, I'm safer now than before. They know I won't be so careless in the future."

"I will continue to pray that you're right," the Patriarch said as he looked down at his hands folded on the table in front of him. "You've seen the news coming out of Jerusalem?" he asked.

"We have," Father Fortis replied. "Any updates from this morning?"

"A tremendous amount of confusion, and confusion, as I learned in seminary, is a specialty of the devil." The Patriarch gazed out the window at the relative tranquility of Rome. "Reports coming in describe it as a three-way battle, our Greek monks trading blows with Franciscans and Armenians, with some additional chaos coming from one or two of the smaller monastic orders centered around the church. I can only imagine what George Pappas and his supporters will make of this." He paused before adding with a sigh, "I've spoken with Serg. We'll meet later today to consider what would be the best response."

"Will it be a joint response?" Father Fortis asked.

The Patriarch turned back toward them. "That's my hope, Nicholas. I keep thinking of what Joseph said to his brothers in the book of Genesis, that his brothers meant evil by kidnapping him, but God used it for good. Someone meant this riot for evil; of that, I have no doubt. But perhaps this provides Serg and me the first opportunity to speak as brothers. We will see."

"Nick told me about the arrangement at the church in Jerusalem," Worthy said, addressing the Patriarch. "Pardon my candor, but the setup there, with these different groups controlling different parts of the church and with them having to coordinate their . . . their processions and services, well, that's simply a disaster waiting to happen. It's like three or four fraternities at some college sharing the same house."

"Don't apologize for your candor, Mr. Worthy. But monks should be better than fraternity brothers." The Patriarch sighed deeply. "If peace doesn't reign at the site of Jesus' victory over death, then our faith offers no hope for the world." He paused for a moment before asking, "As a detective, what advice would you give Pope Gregorio and me?"

Worthy sat silently for a moment before replying, "The best case scenario is that the riot is the product of what we might call spontaneous combustion. Some monk offends another monk, and things escalate from there. In that case, things might die down as quickly as they exploded. But I think the assassin we're chasing is behind what happened this morning, and that means my advice isn't so encouraging. I expect something else to happen, probably again in Jerusalem."

✝

JULY 17: JERUSALEM: THE CATHOLIC HOSTEL

"Is it true, Aiden? Am I here in Jerusalem because that's what the Vatican wanted?" Margaret Cleery asked.

Aiden could feel her staring at him with a new look. *She's wondering if I'm the Vatican's agent. Not to worry; my mask won't be breached by a reporter's lucky guess.* He reached over to clasp her hand. "Margaret, that reporter was just trying to get a reaction."

"Then she succeeded," Margaret said. "When she said that, I felt my world turn upside down. Maybe I've . . . maybe I've been played all along."

Aiden squeezed her hand. "We're in this together, Margaret. I hope you know that."

Margaret nodded slowly. "I'm sorry, Aiden. I know you're loyal. But that note—how do we explain that? Whoever left it knew what I'd said in Rome and knew how this riot might connect with those messages."

Aiden saw immediately the need to redirect her mounting suspicions. "Margaret, the simplest explanation is that the note came from someone with us in Rome. If so, I might be able to find that out. But it's possible we have a mole, someone acting on behalf of the Vatican. That person or persons could be in our group, or they could be someone stationed here in Jerusalem."

Margaret stood up abruptly and walked to the window. "Aiden, is it possible that the reporter and cameraman knew we were coming and were waiting for us?"

Aiden recognized the danger in Margaret's growing anxiety and knew he had to say something to keep her suspicions in check. "Margaret, I think it's far more likely that the BBC reporter was simply at the right place and the right time. If we go down that 'what-if' road too far, you're going to end up thinking the Vatican was behind the riot. Or," he said, pausing as she studied her profile at the window, "you're going to wonder if I'm a spy for the Vatican."

Margaret turned toward him, but because she was backlit by the window, he couldn't see the expression on her face. *Did I make a mistake in saying that?* he wondered.

After a moment, Margaret spoke in a calmer and steadier voice. "No, Aiden, I don't think that. I say that not only because I've never questioned your loyalty but because I know you don't have any greater love for the Church's hierarchy than I do. Yes, I know that you're a faithful priest, but I know that even a whiff of Vatican politics disgusts you as much as it does me. And Aiden, please don't feel as if you have to deny that."

For a moment, Aiden felt his own world turn upside down as a giddy thought floated through his mind. *Is it possible that I've been wrong all along? Is it possible Margaret Cleery isn't a fraud?*

The thought flew out of his mind as quickly as it had entered. No, this woman could fool her gullible followers, she could even fool the press, but she hadn't fooled him. Everything she'd ever said or done in his presence had been scripted; that he knew. She might be the best actor he'd ever known, but he had, from their first meeting, been slowly putting into focus the person behind the role she was playing.

The real Margaret, he reasoned, was someone with a great deal of pent-up anger at life. She'd been chafing at her assigned lot in life perhaps since she was a child. She'd had a smart mouth in her not-so-smart family and had been punished for that repeatedly. Now, as an adult, she was too bright to manage a laundromat, but bright women with no credentials in Greystones, Ireland, had few options.

Aiden didn't doubt that Margaret Cleery was brilliant; in fact, he didn't doubt that she was more than one person. She was many persons, and he'd seen several of her personalities since meeting her in Rome—the sacrilegious Margaret; the weak, fainting Margaret; the dependent Margaret; and now the pious Margaret.

Aiden considered that Margaret Cleery was like other female so-called mystics over the centuries—women who'd found a voice in a Church that didn't allow them to stand at the altar. In their desperate attempts to escape "normal" lives, such women had circumvented the rules but damaged themselves in the process. Margaret Cleery was certainly not the first woman, not the first narcissistic self-proclaimed mystic, to develop paranoid fantasies about the Church that wouldn't accept her.

Margaret Cleery had returned to the window and was looking down on the same walkway that Aiden had viewed from his room. Aiden wondered, *Does she care about the history that surrounds her? Or is she interested only in the present, the Jerusalem that will be the next act of her performance?*

LENA ACCEPTED THAT SHE'D CROSSED A LINE as an unbiased researcher in leaving the note at Margaret Cleery's room about the riot at the church of the Holy Sepulcher. She accepted that she'd crossed another line by waiting, head covered by a scarf, in the square, hoping for a chance to see Margaret Cleery in action.

The morning phone message to her room from the Catholic headquarters in Jerusalem had simply informed her of the riot at the church and warned her to stay clear of it. So, why had she informed Margaret Cleery? She reasoned that no one would ever know of her leaving the note, but she felt a need to explain why she'd given up her objectivity, her detachment.

She told herself that her study of the woman was being obstructed by this very detachment. Reviewing film and news reports would mean that her evaluation for the Vatican would be filled with words like "perhaps" and "it is likely, or it is unlikely." She told herself that she needed to see the woman in person.

She dismissed the notion that her actions had caused the confrontation between Margaret Cleery and the Israeli official that the BBC had covered. No, she'd only made the meeting possible. Margaret Cleery provoked reactions wherever she went, as she'd proven in Rome.

But Lena couldn't avoid the questions surfacing in her mind. Was there another motive behind her inserting herself into the drama, something she hadn't done in Rome? Did her decision have anything to do with missing Worthy? Had she crossed the line of academic detachment because she wanted to push Margaret Cleery into the open so that she could return to Rome as soon as possible?

She couldn't deny that she'd resented the Vatican's request to follow Mother Cleery to Jerusalem, if that was even fair to the word "request." And she also couldn't deny that if Worthy hadn't walked into her life, she'd have jumped at this chance to be in Jerusalem with this assignment.

In the end, Lena decided such self-analysis was pointless. What she did, she did for a whole variety of reasons. Yes, she would be more careful, more circumspect in the future. But the task now wasn't to lay blame but to summarize what she'd learned about the woman from the confrontation in the square.

Under the heading "physical appearance," she wrote the following: "Margaret Cleery is slighter than she appears in photos, though she was formidable when she was confronted by the reporter and the Israeli official. She appears to be in reasonable health, despite having diabetes."

Under the heading "impressions of emotional state," Lena typed: "Margaret Cleery showed a wide range of emotions at the church and all seemed appropriate to the situation. She was clearly surprised by the BBC reporter and cameraman, but seemed less so by the Israeli officer and soldiers. Margaret Cleery seemed to be in touch with the reality of the situation, showing no signs of dissociation."

Under the heading "evidence of mystical characteristics," Lena typed: "Her followers are intent on hearing every word from Margaret Cleery's mouth. Her reactions to the reporter and the Israeli officer could have been taken by her followers to be mystical messages, but were more likely the quick-witted responses of a bright person under stress. Whatever Margaret Cleery is, she is no fool."

CHAPTER TWENTY-SIX

---◆---

JERUSALEM. IN HIS EARLIER LIFE, THE CHESSMASTER would have had as much interest in going to Jerusalem as he would have had traveling to the South Pole. But now, he realized that his entire life had been leading to this city, this time, for this purpose.

He had found it surreal to pack his bags, knowing that his was a one-way journey. He wouldn't be returning to his estate and his isolation. He felt no nostalgia, no sense of farewell on his final walk on the moors. How could he feel attached to his small portion of an entire world, an entire universe that would soon be passing away?

His normal behavior when sitting in first class on his rare flights was to do what seemed to be expected of wealthier passengers. Seated first, first-class passengers would look down at their favorite newspapers as they cradled a glass of wine, all the time ignoring those who were walking through their privileged section for the cramped seats of economy farther back in the plane.

But on his flight to Israel, he couldn't help but watch the stream of humanity—young families, older couples in retirement, military personnel—that walked past him to their seats. None of them knew they too were on a one-way flight. He thought of the cartoons where a wild-eyed bearded man in shabby robes held up the sign "The End is Near!" He wondered how his fellow passengers would respond if he stood and announced, "The End of the World is Now!"

No, the End for his fellow-passengers, with their plans, hopes, and worries, would come as Jesus had said, "as a thief in the night." But, by the grace of God, he'd been chosen not just to know the time of the thief's appearance, but to play his part in ushering in the thief, the Coming King.

He arranged to stay in Jerusalem within walking distance of what he considered Ground Zero. Within a few hundred yards were the three points of a sacred triangle: the Western or Wailing Wall, the Temple Mount with its two mosques, and the church of the Holy Sepulcher.

He'd studied the maps of Old Jerusalem so thoroughly that he felt, as he walked the Old City, that he knew the streets as well as he knew the footpaths on the moors of his estate. Yet, he was surprised by how small the total area of the sacred triangle in the Old City was. Nevertheless, these few blocks of Jerusalem were destined to be, as one of the prophets had written, "the center of the earth."

As he walked the area, he reviewed the advice from his various contacts in the city about the best positions for their deployment. Three groups would carry out the operation, setting the spark that would ignite the fiery end of the world. Each team was under the assumption that its action was a solo performance, one meant to simply turn the wheel of history another degree, but no one other than the Chessmaster knew that the actions of the three teams, taken together, would herald the world's end. And then the entire universe, including these three holy sites, would evaporate, dissolve, and disappear to make room for the New Jerusalem descending from heaven.

While he knew that thousands, maybe millions, were praying for the End, he had trusted no one with his plan. Would he be thought insane? Yes, certainly by non-believers. Would he be arrested if the world knew what he had already engineered? Without a doubt.

But ever since he was a young chess protégé, a recluse in a country's capital, he'd scorned the way others viewed him. As his chess mentor had drilled into him, why should he care if others, who would never accomplish anything in this world, ridiculed or shunned him?

So, to the End, the Chessmaster would be alone with his thoughts and his knowledge. He smiled as he walked the crowded streets of Jerusalem, surrounded by waves of humanity heading for different religious or historical sites. They did not know it, but, in a second, all would be gone.

The one exception to his self-imposed isolation was his sense that he was being used by the avenging God, the warrior Christ to come. He felt this Christ very near to him, and that was the only relationship he needed. And he felt this Christ was as pleased as he was with the riot at the church of the Holy Sepulcher. The incident at the church—the riot and its aftermath—had come off nearly as planned. The presence of Margaret Cleery at the church had been unexpected but something he took as proof of divine providence. And yes, the beating of the Armenian monk had gone further than he'd approved, but better to err in that direction, he reasoned.

When the riot began, he'd been nearby in the guise of a European, possibly German, tourist, who, dressed in cargo shorts and with a Nikon around his neck, had stopped to shoot photos of the melee. He'd obeyed when Israeli soldiers arrived and shooed him away.

Thirty minutes later, he'd returned, without camera and shorts but in a light sports jacket and a notebook. He melded into the small group of news crews and acted the part of a journalist who'd been called to the scene by a media outlet.

In that way, the Chessmaster had been able to observe Margaret Cleery and Aiden O'Malley for the first time. He watched as she dealt with the reporter and then the Israeli officer, her angry and reddened face reminding him of a pug dog ready to attack. He made a note of this weakness in her that he could exploit later if needed.

As he watched her performance, he was pleased that his manipulation of Aiden O'Malley had brought the Cleery woman so easily to Jerusalem. She would play a minor, but important, role in the drama ahead.

He also studied Aiden O'Malley. Photos often revealed little of a person's character and even the priest accepting the money sent by him revealed only one aspect—greed—of Aiden O'Malley. As an outsider himself who'd grown up assessing chess opponents, he saw something he recognized in the movements of the little priest. While the priest was trying to deflect the advances of the BBC reporter, he nevertheless turned his body—an unconscious "tell?"—so that he invited the reporter to come closer to Margaret Cleery. And when the Israeli officer and Margaret Cleery were wrangling, the Chessmaster was sure that he detected a slight smile on the priest's face.

In that instant, he realized something he hadn't guessed before. The little priest hated Margaret Cleery. So, why was he helping her? Or was he? He jotted a note: "AO—can be used, but not trusted."

Yet the most surprising and troubling aspect of the scene was the presence of another person, a woman wearing a too-Western dress to make her headscarf believable. She stood off to the other side of the square but kept inching forward to hear Margaret Cleery. The more he observed the way this new woman never glanced up for more than a few seconds, the more he sensed that she was another version of himself. *She's spying*, he thought, *but why? And for whom?*

He wondered for a moment if she was one of his agents in Jerusalem. If so, the woman without knowing it was one of his pawns, on his payroll, and doing his bidding. But even if that were true, it bothered him that he didn't know what she was trying to accomplish. He'd have to find out who she was and, if she were a new threat to his plans, how to deal with her.

Waiting until the Cleery group left the square, the Chessmaster too departed. He needed to temporarily put aside his thoughts about the unknown woman and concentrate on the next step in his plan. What would follow would be another penultimate move on the chessboard, a move to engage the bigger players, the bishops and knights, who needed to come to Jerusalem before the endgame could occur.

JULY 19: ROME: MAXIMILLIAN KOLBE HOTEL

WORTHY AWOKE THE FOLLOWING MORNING to the sound of cars honking on the streets surrounding the hotel. As had been true the past four days, he awoke in a blissful state of amnesia, but after a few seconds, he remembered that Lena was gone. He groaned as he sat on the side of his bed and opened his laptop.

Lena obviously rose earlier than he did, for Worthy found today, as was true the past two days, that she'd sent an early morning email.

"Chris, will you be my priest? I left Margaret Cleery a note at her hostel encouraging her to make an appearance at the church of the Holy Sepulcher. Don't worry, the riot you've undoubtedly heard about was over by the time Margaret arrived. I was waiting for her, as I wanted to see her in action. Maybe I'm becoming a bit of a detective. If so, it's all your fault.

I know you came to Rome on the same plane as Mother Cleery, but I don't remember if you ever said what impression she made on you. Anyway, I find her quite normal, at least as mystics and frauds are usually described. She reminded me of a student of mine at Notre Dame who was a field hockey player—short, Irish, and clearly not one to pick a fight with.

Is it wrong for me, an Italian professor trained in objectivity, to hope Margaret Cleery is on the level? I liked how she took on an Israeli officer—couldn't tell if he was police or military. They all carry automatic weapons, but she stood up to whoever he was.

Anyway, missing you,

Yours, Me"

"Yours." What did that mean? Was it short for "yours truly" or for "I am yours?" And as was true of an earlier email, this most recent one focused on work. To this point, neither of them had shared their feelings other than to say each missed the other. And despite that admission, they both had steered clear of talking on the phone.

In his return email to Lena, Worthy shared the news from Rome that related to the riot in Jerusalem. In the past, when battles between monks at the church of the Holy Sepulcher had occurred, the pope; the patriarch; and the catholicos, the head of the Armenian Church; had sent separate pleas for peace to their respective monks serving in the Church. The response to the latest battle at the church was different. Pope Gregorio and Ecumenical Patriarch Michael had appeared together on a video, sitting side by side to demand, rather than plead, that peace be restored immediately. Both stated firmly that the guilty parties who assaulted the Armenian monk should be punished regardless of which community they belonged to.

When Patriarch Michael had earlier asked for Worthy's opinion about the joint video communication featuring Pope Gregorio and him, Worthy had agreed that such an approach might be sufficient if the riot was the result of a misunderstanding and an overreaction.

But Worthy remained troubled. The riot in Jerusalem fit perfectly with the contents of the file that Lena had left with him, as well as with the bombing in St. Peter's Square and the attacks at the Phanar in Constantinople. The pattern was troubling. Maiming a monk in Jerusalem and provoking a riot at a holy site wouldn't be sufficient for the assassin. The next attack would be deadly, more like the bombing in St. Peter's Square.

CHAPTER TWENTY-SEVEN

———— ◆ ————

JULY 20: JERUSALEM: A SECOND NEED TO CONFESS

USING ONLY HER INITIALS, MARGARET CLEERY signed up for confession in the chapel of the Catholic hostel. She'd hoped that her angry nature and smart tongue had somehow been conquered over the past week. But when the BBC reporter tried to trap her, she felt her hackles rise, as in the old days. And when the Israeli officer bullied her, her life-honed capacity to bully back had been unleased.

For the umpteenth time since yesterday, she asked herself if she truly wanted to change. In Rome, after Jesus spoke to her in the church of San Teodoro, she felt not just the desire, but the need for a new life. She still wanted that desperately, but changing her instincts when feeling threatened would take time. She remembered her grandmomma's words: "When you fall down, bounce right back up and punch the bastard who pushed you down."

But how do I push back on myself? she wondered, before realizing that confession was the only way the question could be answered. Her Protestant friends in Greystones had often teased her that she was lucky to be a Catholic, someone who could confess her sins one day and then go out to do them all over again the next. But it wasn't until now that she realized what bothered her about that teasing. Now she knew that the most difficult part of confession wasn't sharing with another human being what you had done, said, or thought. No, the challenge of confession was in the promise of repentance, the vow to not commit the same sins again.

In Rome, she had thought—perhaps naively—that if she truly meant it when she told Jesus she wanted to change, then the change would occur. She now saw a future of struggle, of confession after confession, of endless contrition, of promises to try again, to be followed by more struggles. She imagined her soul being a limb of her body broken many years before and left untreated. How many resets would such an arm or leg need to undergo before it would be whole again? And why did it seem each reset was being done without anesthetic?

Until her experience at the church of San Teodoro, she'd felt at odds with Rome. Maybe the truth was that before that visit, she felt at odds with her life. She felt both crushed and lightened by the experience in the tiny church of San Teodoro, and now vaguely understood that God brought her to Rome not only to proclaim his message but to face herself.

She didn't feel at odds with Jerusalem, however. The city was so similar to how she had imagined it from the flannel-graph boards in her Sunday School classes of her youth. It took so little imagination to picture Jesus or any of His disciples walking these narrow, rough stone streets and walkways. Perhaps He carried His cross on the very street below her window.

Her favorite childhood memory from Sunday School had been studying the story of Jesus angrily cleansing the Temple of the merchants and moneychangers, a story she would retreat to when she lost her own temper and wounded someone with her sharp tongue. But now she remembered that only four days after Jesus cleansed the temple in anger, he'd stood silent before Pilate. What would it be like, she wondered, to feel anger rise from wherever it arose and choose not to release it?

Via Dolorosa—the way of suffering. Aiden had suggested that Margaret and her group walk the fourteen stages of the cross later that afternoon, once the worst of the sun's heat had passed. Yes, she would walk as millions of pilgrims had done before her and would no doubt after her. But first, she would offer her confession.

✝

JULY 20: ROME: ST. PAUL'S OUTSIDE THE WALLS

WORTHY AND FATHER FORTIS WAITED FOR the Vatican's black sedan outside their hotel. They'd been notified of the time but neither the destination nor the purpose of the trip.

Over the past days, Worthy's thoughts alternated between the assassin and Lena. Reading her emails was painful, and he could only imagine how he would feel hearing her voice when they talked. He missed Lena teasing him, calling him her "one great exception to the rule" of avoiding American men.

But what future can we have? he asked himself again. Lena had made it clear she could never live in the US again, and Worthy knew that living in Rome would be much different from loving it as a tourist. Unlike his daughter Allyson, who was fluent in Italian, Worthy had a tin ear for language. He hardly knew enough Italian to order an espresso.

All that raised the question of how their love could continue if they lived apart. He thought their relationship could limp along for months, maybe a year communicating with one another online, but his fear was that such a long-distance relationship would eventually cool.

Father Fortis poked Worthy and pointed out the window to a street sign. "We're on the Via Ostiense, my friend. St. Paul walked this very road when he was brought to Rome for trial. In fact, if I'm right, you're in for a treat. I think we're meeting at St. Paul's Outside the Walls."

"Does 'outside the walls' mean what I think it does?"

"Probably. Rome has several important churches that were constructed outside the city walls of the time. St. Paul's is one of them. It houses the relics of the apostle."

"I thought you told me Paul was beheaded at another place," Worthy said.

Father Fortis nodded. "Yes, you're right. According to tradition, he was beheaded at Tre Fontane, but his body was moved to the church I think we're going to. I've only seen pictures of the place—truly spectacular—so . . . well, I'm more than a bit excited."

Worthy was puzzled. "So tell me why we're meeting at a church dedicated to St. Paul instead of at St. Peter's."

"St. Peter's isn't exactly a neutral site, Christopher, in terms of Church politics. Plus, there are always too many paparazzi around the Vatican. I've read that the place we're going to is much more isolated."

The destination was St. Paul's, just as Father Fortis had speculated. What surprised Worthy was how new it looked, until the Vatican official accompanying them explained that the present church had been practically rebuilt after a massive fire in the 19th century.

After St. Peter's, St. Paul's was the largest church that Worthy had ever seen. And the scarcity of visitors made the church seem even bigger. Their footsteps echoed as they walked through the enormous nave of the church until they came to the altar where Father Fortis knelt in prayer before the remains of St. Paul. From there, the Vatican official directed them through a series of doors that led into a charming cloister. Both Worthy and Father Fortis stopped as they entered the cloister, as if some hand held them back. Worthy imagined that what arrested Father Fortis' progress was the fragments of Roman ruins that covered the walls on all four sides. But for Worthy, what caught him and made his heart ache was the overpowering smell of boxwood which reminded him of being with Lena.

"Beautiful, yes?" the Vatican official asked. "The columns, they are very precious. Sometimes I come here to walk in the cloister."

"So ironic," Father Fortis observed, taking a moment to absorb the quiet. "St. Paul had to be the most strident voice in the early Church. And yet here there's such a feeling of calm—maybe even a bit of the peace of Eden."

The Vatican official, clearly more interested in the roses than in Father Fortis' musings, motioned toward another door on the opposite side of the cloister. Leading the two men into a well-lit library with shelved books from floor to ceiling and, in the middle, a polished mahogany table, he said, "Please wait here. The Holy Father and the Ecumenical Patriarch will be joining us shortly." With that, the man shut the door behind him.

Worthy sighed. "I don't know if I can take more theology, Nick."

Father Fortis shook his head. "They asked you to be here, which makes me think this meeting will have more to do with our investigation. You did say that you forwarded your suspicions to both the Vatican and Patriarch Michael, Christopher."

"Yes, I sent it to both of them. We'll see what they think of my Jerusalem idea."

Father Fortis sat down in one of the chairs. "I hope you're wrong, my friend."

Worthy shrugged. "I hope I'm wrong as well. I hate to think of Lena being caught in the middle of something worse than a bunch of monks rioting."

The two men were silent for a moment before Father Fortis spoke. "When you began to focus on Jerusalem, I remember what you told me back on our first case together, your theory that a murder is the result of a killer and a victim being on a collision course for some time. But that's what's bothering me. If you believe more killings will happen in Jerusalem, doesn't that give us a chance to prevent that?"

"Ideally, yes. But if I'm right and the person behind all the attacks that are mentioned in that file is also behind the bombings in Rome and Istanbul and now the riot at the church of the Holy Sepulcher, all we can be sure of is this: the assassin has never returned to a previous site."

"Yet you think the next incident will still be in Jerusalem," Father Fortis said.

Worthy nodded. "If I'm right, that the person or group behind these attacks is convinced the world is about to end, wouldn't Jerusalem be the ultimate site? But how many religious sites are there in Jerusalem—hundreds?"

"At least," Father Fortis replied. "It's not called the Holy City for nothing—holy for Jews, Christians, and Muslims."

"But which religious site—Jewish, Christian, or Islamic—will be the target?" Worthy asked. "I'd say the chance of getting ahead of this person and intervening remains slim. But if, as I believe, the killer wants to be present in person for the attack, we do have something no one has had before. He or she is pinned down in a city that we know in advance."

The thwack-thwack of a helicopter engine halted their speculations. *That's no doubt the Pope or the Pope and the Patriarch together*, Worthy thought. The meeting would begin shortly, and he could predict the questions put to Father Fortis and him about the investigation. And the answers they could give, would they be anything more than speculation? If he was right and the assassin had shifted his attention to Jerusalem, the Pope and Patriarch would once again be safe. That would be good news to share even if it meant he'd be leaving Rome without seeing Lena again.

JULY 20: JERUSALEM: ON THE VIA DOLOROSA

AT THE SEVENTH STATION OF THE CROSS, the commemoration of Jesus falling a second time on His way to Calvary, Margaret Cleery experienced a moment of clarity. For the first six stations, she'd listened to Aiden read the appropriate meditations, and she'd knelt at the proper time, even as she felt she was somehow acting.

Her confession back in the Catholic hostel two hours before had been disappointing. The priest's command of English was poor, and he offered nothing when she confessed her doubts that she could ever overcome her anger. She felt she was a generic sinner, someone who'd stopped by to drop off dirty laundry.

But by the seventh station of the cross, Margaret's frustration with the morning's confession was ebbing. It was unfair, she realized, to expect every confession to provide the release that she'd experienced with the Ethiopian priest in Rome. Now, as she knelt in the street outside the seventh station on the Via Dolorosa, she remembered that Jesus had fallen not just once or twice, but three times.

She started to apologize to God, to condemn herself because she would fall not just twice or three times in the future, but perhaps a thousand times. She would fall because of her quick temper and even quicker tongue, while Jesus had fallen for a different reason—He fell because of her sins and the sins of the world.

As her knees began to complain about the rough edges of the cobblestones, she heard a familiar voice within her say, "Margaret, stop. You don't understand." She was aware that the others in the group had risen from their knees, but she was helpless to move. Her followers began to whisper to one another, but she hardly heard them.

"What don't I understand?" she said aloud, not to her followers, but to the voice. She waited for an answer, praying it would come if she remained quiet. Softly, the voice returned. "I chose the cross. I chose to fall, and I would choose that all over again if I could. Don't wallow in your guilt. Instead, know that I fell so that you would know how much I love you."

She remained on her knees as tears began to flow. After a moment, she felt a hand on her shoulder. She looked up to see Aiden looking down on her.

"What is it, Margaret?" he asked.

She accepted his help in rising from her knees. Surrounding her were her followers, waiting to hear what she would say.

"Jesus said He would fall and die all over again if He could—because He loves us."

She looked around the circle slowly, noting how everyone continued to look at her expectantly. She didn't know if the words made any sense, but she noticed that most of her followers made the sign of the cross when she stopped speaking. Behind her followers were a few people, locals or tourists she did not know, who were attracted to the odd scene.

Her eye ended up focusing on someone behind her group, the only person not looking at her. Instead, the man was staring at Aiden. *Does he know Aiden?* she asked herself. Despite the heat of the day, she felt a chill run down her spine. Then, the middle-aged man, probably European, tall, thin, and with receding sandy hair, seemed to sense that she was looking at him and turned to walk slowly away. Not once did he look back in her direction, but as he came to a corner, he raised his hand to wave up to a set of windows high above the street.

Margaret heard the burst of gunfire at the same time that bullets whizzed by her head. A split second later, she felt a sharp pain in her shoulder that spun her around before throwing her to the ground. She heard screams from those around her as well as bodies falling. The gunfire continued for no more than five seconds before suddenly stopping. As she raised her head to look around, she saw bodies lying inertly on the ground. Her eyes scanned the scene until she saw Aiden lying in a pool of blood. His body was twitching uncontrollably, like a fish floundering out of water. She heard a voice call out, "Oh, God, no," but didn't know if the voice was Aiden's or hers.

As the pain in her shoulder give way to a numbness that began to branch out throughout the left side of her body, she wondered if she were dying. If so, she felt no fear. But her last thought before losing consciousness was of the man who'd waved to the windows. The voice she heard in her head as she drifted into darkness said, "Margaret, you've seen him before."

JULY 20: ROME: ST. PAUL'S OUTSIDE THE WALLS

POPE GREGORIO AND PATRIARCH MICHAEL SAT next to one another in the room, facing Worthy, Father Fortis, and the others who sat around the mahogany table. Father Fortis thought that both the Patriarch and Pope looked troubled, and he wondered if a new burden had been added to what they both already bore.

Pope Gregorio spoke first. "Mr. Worthy, we wish to thank you for your report, as incomplete as it is at this point. If you are correct, whoever is behind these attacks believes that his actions are part of some divine plan. It that a fair summary?"

Worthy cleared his throat. "It's too bad that the priest who first spotted a pattern to these seemingly random acts has died. He deserves the credit."

The Patriarch sat forward in his chair. "But you were the one who proposed that these events are linked to some group or person who believes the world is about to end. May I ask on what basis you made this connection?"

Worthy shot a glance at Father Fortis, who nodded for him to proceed. "Everyone knows this kind of thinking has grown since 9/11. And with all the unrest in the world, pessimism is contagious."

Pope Gregorio tapped the table with his index finger. "In every century of the Church's existence, there have been people who believe they can decipher the 'signs of the times.' It's a belief that has always led to disappointment or tragedy. But that's the kind of group you believe is behind the attacks in Rome, those at the Patriarchate, and now the ongoing crisis in Jerusalem?"

"Yes, that's exactly what I'm saying," Worthy said. "We're looking for a person or a group that's quite a bit different—not poor, certainly not uneducated, and able to pull together the support of very diverse apocalyptic groups."

"What do you mean by 'very diverse?'" one of the Vatican security officials asked.

"When I analyze all the recent attacks and those mentioned in the file I was given, I'm convinced that there is more than one end-of-the-world group involved, and these groups are, in fact, from different religions," Worthy replied. "A Christian alt-right group could have carried out one of the attacks, but not others. The same with Islamists or Zionists."

Father Fortis heard the murmur of disbelief from some of the Vatican officials present. "We keep close track of the groups you're referring to. These groups hate each other. The last thing they'd do is agree to work together. Just look at their internet sites."

Father Fortis watched as Worthy sat calmly, his gaze remaining on the Pope and the Patriarch. "What if one person is coordinating the actions of different groups, groups that don't know the others exist?"

Father Fortis couldn't hide the look of surprise crossing his face. He'd seen that calmness on his friend's face before, when Worthy made an intuitive leap in a case. What Worthy had just stated was just such a leap, based on, but beyond, what the two of them had talked about. If Worthy was bluffing, his gamble was a dangerous one. His theory that one person was behind all the attacks placed the two of them at the end of a very shaky tree limb. Now Worthy had gone to the end of that limb and thrown himself into the air, in the direction of an even higher branch that only he could see.

When the Patriarch looked at Father Fortis and asked, "Do you agree, or is Lieutenant Worthy getting ahead of the evidence?" he realized his face must have registered his reaction to Worthy's confident assertion. Father Fortis took a moment to collect his thoughts before speaking. In their cases together, he'd seen Worthy do what the Patriarch had asked about—running ahead of the evidence. But he'd also witnessed his friend seeing an opening when others saw only a wall.

"Christopher is ahead of the evidence, but that doesn't mean he's wrong. What he said makes sense of everything that's happened."

"So where do you think this mastermind is now?" Pope Gregorio asked.

Father Fortis sat forward to take some of the focus off Worthy by answering the question. "What Lieutenant Worthy is saying is that the person behind all these attacks is likely in Jerusalem."

"Doing what?" the Patriarch asked.

Father Fortis turned to Worthy to answer the question. "I hope I'm wrong, but I think he's readying his groups for another attack. We should expect something even bigger—and soon."

The Pope and the Patriarch looked at each other, and Father Fortis could feel the electricity in the air. Looking around the room, he asked, "Has something else already happened?"

The Vatican official who'd earlier verbalized his skepticism spoke. "Less than an hour ago, there was a brutal ambush of a group of Catholic pilgrims in Jerusalem; in fact, the attack was on the Via Dolorosa. We know that some of the pilgrims have been taken to hospital, but others have died."

Father Fortis, joined by others in the room, bowed his head and made the sign of the cross.

The official continued. "What makes this attack even more serious is that the group targeted is one associated with Margaret Cleery, who, as we all know, was in Rome until a few days ago. We don't know her condition or the names of the other victims."

Father Fortis glanced quickly at Worthy, whose face was ashen. *Lena is following Margaret Cleery and her group in Jerusalem. Is Lena one of the casualties?* Father Fortis thought.

Worthy coughed and in a wavering voice said, "I assume no one has taken credit for the attack."

One of the Vatican officials nodded. "It's early, but no, you're right. And we cannot be sure that there's a connection between the riot at the church yesterday and the attack today."

Pope Gregorio stirred, "However, if Lieutenant Worthy's theory is correct, a connection of some sort is certain."

Worthy seemed unaware of the Pope's support. He was looking down at his hands as if they held an answer.

"Unfortunately," the Pope continued, "the monks at the church of the Holy Sepulcher are acting as if the two events are connected. More shouting at one another and some threats. We've received word from the Office of Religious Affairs in Jerusalem that all services at the church have been suspended for the next forty-eight hours."

No one said anything until Patriarch Michael spoke. "Holy Father and I have made a decision. It's a decision not open to discussion, but we want you to know of it because the decision involves a few of you. As many of you know, Holy Father and I have committed to begin treating one another as brothers. When we can act together, we will."

The Patriarch paused, as if to let his words sink in. "In light of this tragedy, Holy Father and I intend to act with one accord. The possibility of further battle between Christian monks in Jerusalem must be avoided at all costs. We are also aware that Margaret Cleery and her followers might have been targeted because of her messages, messages that have called for reconciliation between our two Churches. We cannot distance ourselves from these events. Therefore . . ."

Father Fortis sensed how the sentence would end, but the boldness of it still shocked him.

"Therefore, Holy Father and I will be traveling to Jerusalem tomorrow, as soon as the Israeli authorities permit. We will meet at the church of the Holy Sepulcher with the Orthodox Patriarch of Jerusalem, the various Catholic cardinals, and the Catholicos of the Armenian Church. There, together, we will pray for the peace of Christ's Church universal and for the peace of Jerusalem. In the days following, we will speak directly with the monks at this most sacred site to see what can be done to avoid this kind of tragedy in the future."

The same Vatican official who'd spoken before jumped to his feet. "Holy Father, no, no! Your safety is my responsibility, and I forbid this . . . this foolish plan." His words brought a stir to the room. "Excuse my language, Holy Father, but I cannot allow you to go to Jerusalem until this crisis has passed."

Pope Gregorio raised a hand, and the room quieted. "We understand your concern, but we don't believe this crisis will pass until we go to Jerusalem. In terms of security, the maximum number of guards allowed by Israeli security will travel with us."

"And Father Fortis and Lieutenant Worthy will also be with us," Patriarch Michael added. "We pray that with God's help, the two of them will discover where and when another attack could occur. It may not be too late to apprehend the culprit or culprits."

The Vatican official was not prepared to surrender. "I'm opposed because Lieutenant Worthy's theory appears to be . . . to be correct. Isn't going to Jerusalem in the wake of these attacks just what the perpetrator wants?"

Father Fortis couldn't help but notice the irony. First, the official had ridiculed Worthy. Now, he agreed with him.

"Lieutenant Worthy," the Pope said, "what's your assessment of our decision?"

Worthy's finger was tracing a line on the polished surface of the table. "Going to Jerusalem might not be the wisest step. It could be a trap."

The Patriarch smiled. "The wisest step? Surely, the wisdom of what we decide depends on the outcome. Is it safe for us to travel to Jerusalem? Probably not, although Rome and the Patriarchate haven't proved to be safe either. The reach of this group or person is impressive, don't you agree?"

"Oh, yes, I agree," Worthy said, but then fell silent.

"If there is a chance of an even more serious battle between Christian monks in Jerusalem," Patriarch Michael, "then the wisest step is surely for us to do as we've decided. The animosity among Christians at this most holy site is toxic. If our coming together as brothers in Jerusalem to meet with the Armenian Catholicos can bring peace, then we must try."

"We must," the Pope repeated for emphasis.

The Pope and Ecumenical Patriarch stood, bringing everyone in the room to their feet. Pope Gregorio turned to Patriarch Michael and asked him to offer a prayer for guidance and for God's will to be done. The Patriarch did so, first in Greek, then in Italian, and finally in English. Following the prayer, the two men embraced before walking to the door.

"Everyone I've named should be ready to depart tomorrow," the Pope added from the doorway.

Father Fortis and Worthy stayed in the room after the others left. As he watched his friend continue to draw a line with his finger on the table, Father Fortis understood what the gesture meant. On one side of the line was hope, and on the other side was despair. Which would be Worthy's future depended on whether Lena was alive or dead.

At that moment, Worthy's phone rang.

CHAPTER TWENTY-EIGHT

---◆---

JULY 20: JERUSALEM: AT THE HOSPITAL

Margaret Cleery regained consciousness, though her eyes had trouble focusing. Behind an old-style hospital room partition, she could hear men and women talking excitedly in a language she didn't understand. Occasionally, she heard the sound of feet running.

So, I'm alive, she thought almost with disappointment as she turned her head and felt pain radiate from her left shoulder. She had a vague memory of kneeling and then falling to the ground amidst screams and moans.

"He waved," she muttered. "I saw him wave."

Thoughts began to bounce around in her head. *What did you do to deserve this?* she heard her mother's voice say. From her grandmother, long dead, she heard, *You're always getting yourself into trouble, so it's your own damned fault, my little missy.*

"No, no, no," she moaned, trying to clear her head of the unwelcome visitors. "I need to talk to Aiden. He understands me." As dread seemed to descend from her head to her feet, she yelled, "Where is Father Aiden?"

A nurse came from around the partition. "Ah, you are awake. This is good, but please, do not move," he said as he leaned over her bed and shone a light into each eye. He spoke in that unfamiliar language to a woman who also appeared and came around to the other side of Margaret's bed.

"Is my friend here?" Margaret asked the doctor, hoping she also understood English.

"Yes, yes, later we will see what we can do," the doctor said as she looked from Margaret's face to a machine with numbers running across the screen. "Do you know where you are? Do you know what happened?"

"Did someone shoot me? What did I do to deserve it?" she asked, aware that her speech was slurred.

"Yes, you were shot, but the bullet entered and exited your shoulder very cleanly. The bullet tore through muscle, so yes, painful, but nothing to worry about."

"What about my friends? I was with my group," she said, grabbing the doctor's arm with her right hand.

The doctor said something to the nurse in that unfamiliar language and then shook her head.

"Do you know what city you're in, Mrs. Cleery?"

"You know my name? Am I in Rome?"

"No, Mrs. Cleery, you are in a Jerusalem hospital."

"Jesus died in Jerusalem, but He spoke to me in Ireland. Did you know that?"

The doctor frowned and spoke again to the nurse. "We're going to give you a sedative, and when you wake up, everything will be much clearer. You're still in shock, Mrs. Cleery. Do you understand?"

Margaret shook her head. "Yes, shock. My friend's name is Aiden, Father Aiden. When I wake up, ask him to come see me."

The hospital workers once again looked at each other even a young nurse came around the partition with a syringe and inserted it into a plastic tube running into Margaret's arm. The funny-sounding words of the two grew softer and softer until Margaret felt a black cloud fall on her like a heavy blanket.

JULY 20: ROME: ST. PAUL'S OUTSIDE THE WALLS

"Yes, it's really me," Lena said.

Worthy's head slumped and, for a moment, he couldn't speak. "Say it again," he said. He could feel Father Fortis' hand on his shoulder. "She's okay, Nick. She's okay."

"Thank you, God," Father Fortis said, making the sign of the cross.

"When we heard that Margaret Cleery's group had been targeted, I . . . I . . ."

"I know, Chris, I know. I've made a friend—actually a person I paid—at the reception desk at her hostel. She let me know when the Cleery group was on its way to the Via Dolorosa. I knew they'd end up at the church of the Holy Sepulcher, so that's where I was when I heard the shots."

"How close?" Worthy asked, his voice still wavering.

"About two blocks. I got there just before the ambulances, so I saw the carnage."

"Too close, Lena, too close."

"Really, Chris, I'm okay."

"I know, but I don't quite believe it yet. If I lost you . . ."

"But you didn't, love."

Worthy closed his eyes. Lena's going to Jerusalem had been painful, but that pain was nothing compared to the hole that had opened up in his heart when he feared she might be dead. In that moment, he experienced the same panic he'd felt four weeks before when he feared that Father Fortis had been killed in the bombing. Did he regret that he'd let Nick and Lena into his life at such a deep level? No, after his divorce and before he met Nick, he realized what hell was. Hell is being alone, unloved, and forgotten, a place he never wanted to be stuck in again.

He wanted to tell Lena that he'd never be separated from her again, but he knew now wasn't the time. Now was the time to focus on the task at hand. Finally, he said, "Did the shooter target Mother Cleery?"

"She was hit, I could see that. I saw her in a pool of blood, but the blood seemed to be coming from her shoulder. How has the Vatican responded?" Lena asked.

Worthy explained that the Pope and the Ecumenical Patriarch had decided to go to Jerusalem.

Lena reacted immediately to the news. "Oh, my God. Is that safe?"

"No, it's hardly that, but their going could flush the perpetrator out."

"But doesn't that make them bait? If I weren't so worried about what might happen here in Jerusalem, Chris, I'd wish that Nick and you could be here to protect them."

Worthy paused a moment, hoping to sound calm. "Actually, Lena, Nick and I have been asked to accompany the Pope and the Patriarch. The good news is that we'll see each other tomorrow."

JULY 21: JERUSALEM: IN THE HOSPITAL

MARGARET CLEERY DIDN'T WAKE AGAIN until the next morning, and after she had breakfast, the attending nurse asked if she felt up to having a visitor.

Oh, good, Aiden's here, she thought, though the person who entered her cubicle was a woman she didn't recognize. *What a pretty face*, she thought, as the visitor smiled at her.

"Do I know you?" she asked, surprised to hear her own voice.

"My name is Dr. Lena Fabriano, Mrs. Cleery. I'm from Rome."

"Rome, yes, Rome. But someone told me I'm in Jerusalem. Or did I just dream that?"

"No, you're in Jerusalem. There was a shooting, and you were wounded."

Margaret Cleery pointed with her right hand at her left shoulder. "Just here?" she asked.

"Yes, just there. Are you in pain? Should I call for the doctor?"

Margaret Cleery shook her head and then winced. "It's like a bad toothache in my shoulder. Except that doesn't make any sense, does it?"

Lena nodded. "I think that makes perfect sense."

"Were you there . . . at the shooting, I mean?" Margaret asked.

"No, I was waiting for you at the church. But I heard the shots."

Margaret licked her dry lips. "I wanted to go into that church, but they wouldn't let me."

"Yes, I know. I was in the square a couple of days ago when you tried to go in."

"Are you one of my followers, then?"

"In a way, I guess."

"I don't understand. Do I know you?" she said, repeating herself.

"Mrs. Cleery, I was asked by the Vatican to study you. Your messages from Jesus . . . well, they interest the Vatican."

Margaret tried to raise her head, but she immediately laid it back down.

"I asked Aiden if the Vatican had tricked me into coming here. Did they?"

"No, I can assure you that isn't true. I won't lie to you. Some Vatican officials hoped you'd go back quietly to Ireland while the rest of us wanted you to stay in Rome where we could . . . understand you better. Nobody from the Vatican wanted you to go to Jerusalem," Lena said.

"'Understand me better.' That's a polite way of saying they think I'm nuts. I can't remember your name, but you tell me. Am I crazy?"

"My name is Lena Fabriano, but just try to remember Lena. And no, I don't think you're crazy, Mrs. Cleery."

"Okay, Lena, call me Margaret. Mrs. Cleery is my mother and my grandmother, and they didn't particularly like me."

"Ah, yes. You must have been quite a different child growing up."

"Not in the way you might think. I didn't hear any messages until just a few years ago. Before that, I was just a sassy kid who went her own way, and then I became a sassy Mom with sassy kids. Now, I guess, I'm a sassy grandmomma as well."

Neither talked for a moment, before Margaret looked over at Lena. "Do you know my friend, Aiden, Father Aiden?"

Lena looked down for a moment. "I know who he is. From Ireland as well, right?"

"Yes, another little Irish priest, just like in the movies. All Irish priests seem to be little, but then again, we women are often taller than our men— also heavier." She searched her visitor's eyes. "Can I see him—Aiden, I mean? I know he was wounded. I remember seeing him on the ground."

"That will be up to your doctors," Lena explained, pausing before continuing. "Are you too tired to answer a few questions, Margaret?"

Margaret shook her head. "No, go ahead. Maybe they'll keep me from thinking about what I don't want to think about."

"I understand. I want to ask you about your time in Rome. Did something happen there? What I mean is, the way you acted when you first came to Rome—at the airport and then in St. Peter's Square—seemed to change. Am I right, and would you be willing to talk about that?"

"You mean I came to Rome as a smart ass, and then all of a sudden, I wasn't such a smart ass."

"I guess you could put it that way," Lena replied with a smile.

"Well, dearie, I'll say this much for you, you don't miss much. To understand me, I guess you'd have to say that I've been a rebel most of my life. I'm not talking about doing anything criminal but just doing what I liked when I wanted. That was true, even when what I did hurt me—and others. So, you can imagine how I felt when Jesus started speaking to me."

"Actually, I only study mystics. I've never had an experience even close to what you're talking about. What was that like for you in the beginning?"

"A helluva shock, to put it mildly. I mean, if God chose a person like me, maybe my being a rebel all my life was, you know, part of the plan."

"So you felt special, then."

"Over the top special. Even when the experts called me a fraud or a faker, that just made me laugh. Since I knew I wasn't making the messages up, I felt smarter than they were. I was able to say, 'Screw them,' you know?"

"Still a rebel," Lena said.

"Still a rebel," Margaret repeated. "But now I was a rebel with a crowd of people who believed in me. That went to my head as well. At least, it did in the beginning. Then I became sick and tired of being watched every moment and being adored. Sometimes, I just wanted to slap the people around me—a good hard slap across the mouth. Did any of the mystics you've studied ever feel like that?"

"I don't think we'll ever know. If they had feelings like that, their stories were sanitized. Whatever normal emotions they had were probably removed."

"Oh, God. I couldn't bear it if people turn me into something I'm not."

"So what happened in Rome?" Lena repeated her question.

"After my fainting spell—which probably looked fake to my detractors—I was laid up for a few days. But I felt trapped in my room, so one day, when Aiden took my group on one of his fieldtrips, I snuck out and found myself in this little Orthodox church."

"San Teodoro," Lena added.

"Yes, that's the one. Anyway, I went in, and I was alone in this little sanctuary. It was very dark, very dark. What I say next, please know I can't explain. I just was overwhelmed; actually I felt crushed, by how self-centered I've been my whole life. Maybe the death of the two deacons got through my thick skin.

Or maybe it was seeing the chains in that other church, St. Peter's chains, I mean. There was just this feeling of great sacrifice by others, by all these martyrs who I knew nothing about. I felt like a fraud. Not a fraud like my critics have accused me of, but a fake as a person."

She looked up to see tears in Lena Fabriano's eyes. "I don't think a fraud would ever confess to feeling like one," she said.

Margaret Cleery closed her eyes for a moment and didn't say anything.

"Is this tiring you too much?" Lena asked.

Shaking her head, Margaret Cleery continued. "So the next time I snuck out from my room, I went to this church in one of the backstreets near the hotel. As luck would have it—but then again, I don't think it was luck—an African priest asked if I'd come for confession. I felt like running out, but then it struck me that maybe I'd never given an honest confession. Anyway, the long and short of it is that I ended up admitting some feelings I've had toward God for most of my life. I like to be in control; do you know what I mean?"

Lena nodded.

"I can't believe I'm telling you all this, but you seem to know me," Margaret Cleery said. "Anyway, God chopped my legs out from under me in Rome. Here I was, in Rome to share these messages—so I thought—and then I realized that I was in Rome for another purpose—to give up control. For the first time in my life, I didn't have a clue about the future. I still don't, if you want to know the truth. So, do I go back to my laundromat in Greystones after this—with my arm in a sling?"

"It sounds like you don't have to know that right now. If this isn't too painful to talk about, can I ask what went through your mind when you were shot?"

"I thought I might be dying, and this is the truth—that didn't scare me. Then, I remember seeing Aiden on the ground. I guess you could say he was convulsing." Margaret paused, trying to bring back another image.

"There was something else," she continued. "What was it? Now, I remember. I saw this man, this man just beyond my group who wouldn't look at me. Even though he had sunglasses on, he was facing Aiden and seemed to be staring at him. I thought that was odd."

"Then what happened?" Lena asked.

"Then what happened," Margaret repeated. "He seemed to know I was looking at him. He turned and walked away. But why would I remember that?"

"Did he do anything when he walked away? Did he walk faster or jog?"

Margaret Cleery was silent, her eyes closed, as she tried to bring back the scene. "He loped, if you know what I mean. On the balls of his feet. And, I think he . . . I think he waved."

"At you?"

"No, up to an open window. Yes, he waved to someone in a window. And as soon as his arm came down, the gunfire started."

"Margaret, this is very important. I have a friend—a police friend—who's just come to Jerusalem. He thinks the same person or persons who committed the drone attack in Rome is behind what's going on here in Jerusalem. Do you think you could describe this man?"

"I didn't get much of a look at him, but I had a feeling I'd seen him before. Oh, and we should ask Aiden. Whoever the man was—it was almost like he knew him."

JULY 21: JERUSALEM: READING OVER BRUNCH

THE CHESSMASTER LOOKED UP FROM HIS CUP of Turkish coffee and the English newspaper. He read the names of the two dead and the five others injured, including the one critically. As he well knew, sacrificing a pawn or two is a normal part of any chess match. He was relieved that Margaret Cleery was still useful to him—she was worth far more than a pawn—and there was still a slim chance that another significant chess piece, Aiden O'Malley, could survive. But his agent, the same sniper who'd been used before in Istanbul, couldn't be blamed; shooting into a crowd was hardly a precision sport.

In the confusion on the Via Dolorosa, his agent had gotten away, though he left rifle cartridges behind. It was a small matter, more an issue of neatness than anything else. He also knew, now that the game was reaching its final stages, that moves that would have mattered earlier in the match were now of no consequence.

As an example, his own role had changed, and he was enjoying it. In the past, he'd always prized anonymity and detachment above everything else, even the success of a mission. Now circumstances were different. The agent on the Via Dolorosa had seen his face, and he suspected that Margaret Cleery had recognized him from the day before.

But the truth was that he'd always planned, when the game reached its conclusion, to be present. He was, after all, the Chessmaster, still the one determining the moves, but now he was also a type of super chess piece on the board.

In any match he'd played or observed, he recognized the moment when he could see the end was six to seven moves ahead. Those less skilled in chess would miss the moment, but for the adept, the enlightened, the match was all but over.

That was how he felt as he finished his cup of coffee. His agents in Jerusalem, unaware of how their separate actions would bring down the curtain of history, had learned of their parts within the last forty-eight hours. And now the two key players for the last scene of the drama—the Pope and the Ecumenical Patriarch—were in Jerusalem, thanks to the tension he'd orchestrated at the church of the Holy Sepulcher. Every one of his agents knew that the signal could come at any time. All that was left was to attract the Pope and Patriarch to "ground zero" in Jerusalem, where, at the opportune moment, he would raise his hand to wave a final time, and then—the world's endgame.

Until that fateful moment, the Chessmaster's plan was to occupy himself with his favorite readings—the book of Revelation and a copy of the Dead Sea Scrolls. What better reading could there be for a person awaiting the End in Jerusalem? As he walked through various parts of the Old City, blending into crowds of tourists and pilgrims, he could quote the pertinent passages from memory.

"And I saw the Holy City, the new Jerusalem, coming down from God out of heaven, prepared as a bride adorned for her husband."

"And he carried me away in the spirit to a high mountain, and shewed me that great city, the Holy Jerusalem, descending out of heaven from God."

"And, behold, I am coming quickly, and my reward is with me, to render to every man according to what he has done."

How surreal, he thought, *to know how the world will end and not be able to share that with anyone.* Yet, in a matter of a few days, he knew that God's future would unfold. This ancient city of God, this Old Jerusalem, would pass away in an instant. The people he was passing in the narrow streets along with the billions in the history of the world, those who'd given God not a thought in their lives, would in a flash stand face to face before the Almighty. As he listened to the sounds of this ancient but lively city—the peddlers, vendors, teenage boys with soccer balls, mothers hanging out the wash above his head, and the beggars—he wanted to scream above it all, "You will be struck dumb with shock." He wanted to proclaim that those who had never bowed before the name of Christ, including most of his own agents and his own dead father, would be thrown to their knees when the Warrior with the flashing sword appeared.

And he? Would he hear, "Well done, thou good and faithful servant?" Would he be offered a white robe and crown? If it were possible, he wanted to say to the Coming Warrior that he'd already received his reward. He'd been chosen to turn the wheel of the world a final turn, a world that had always disappointed him. By the mercy of the Coming King, his whole life made sense to him.

CHAPTER TWENTY-NINE

⸻ ◆ ⸻

JULY 22: JERUSALEM: A SHORTAGE OF TIME

WORTHY STOOD WITH FATHER FORTIS AND LENA on one side of Aiden O'Malley's bed while Margaret Cleery sat propped up in a wheelchair on the other. Worthy had been in enough intensive care wards to recognize from looking at the monitor, with its wavy lines, beeps, and numbers, that the priest was barely hanging on.

Somehow, Aiden O'Malley had survived his most recent surgery, this one to deal with a massive brain bleed. He was expected to come out of the anesthesia at any moment, although his prognosis was dark. Before going into emergency surgery a second time, Aiden had asked to see Margaret Cleery if he survived the operation.

Worthy and Father Fortis were there, hoping to hear if the priest could add anything to Margaret Cleery's description of the assassin—dark sunglasses, tall, sandy hair, receding hairline, bald spot on the crown of his head, loping awkwardly up on the balls of his feet. With the exception of the sunglasses, Worthy realized that the Cleery woman was describing the back of the man as he walked away. What Worthy hoped was that Father Aiden, who the surgeon thought would not survive the day, could provide some details of the man's face.

Aiden O'Malley moaned softly as he opened his eyes. He looked confused as his eyes scanned the room until they rested on Margaret Cleery. He offered the slightest smile as he reached a hand in her direction. She took and held it.

"Margaret, Margaret," was all he said for a moment, and he said it very slowly, as though he were under water.

"Aiden, O Aiden. This is all my fault," Margaret exclaimed with a sob.

The little priest started to shake his head but then stopped. "No, no. All mine."

He closed his eyes, leading Worthy to wonder if he'd lost consciousness. If the priest opened his eyes again, Worthy knew he needed to use every moment.

"Father Aiden, can you hear me?" he asked.

The priest answered by opening his eyes and looking at Worthy.

"Aiden," Margaret Cleery said, "this is an American policeman, and he needs to ask you a few questions. Only a few, I promise."

Aiden gave the briefest nod.

"On the Via Dolorosa, your group was shot at. Do you remember that?" Worthy asked.

Again, Aiden nodded.

"Do you remember a man standing at the back, not part of your group? He was tall and wore dark sunglasses."

For a moment, Aiden didn't respond in any way.

"Aiden? It's Margaret again. This man was looking at you after I fell. Then he walked away. Do you remember?"

After a moment, Aiden nodded again.

"What did he look like?" Worthy asked.

Aiden seemed to frown. Then, very slowly, he raised his hand and tapped at his ear.

Worthy tried to decipher the gesture. Aiden tapped a few more times, his frown continuing.

"He had something in his ear?" Father Fortis asked.

Aiden's hand fell to the bed as if the gesture had drained all his energy. But the frown was gone.

"Probably a transmitter," Worthy offered. "Anything about his face, Aiden?"

The frown returned. Again, his hand rose slowly from the bed and this time rested on his nose.

"His nose, something about his nose?" Worthy asked.

Aiden offered a brief nod before letting his arm fall again.

Worthy realized he might have no more than five minutes. "Let me make some guesses, Father. If I'm right, just raise your finger, okay?"

There was no response from Aiden.

"Was the nose long? Is that it?"

Aiden frowned.

"Did it look crooked, like it'd been damaged in a fight?"

This time Aiden raised a finger.

"Good, good, Aiden. Mrs. Cleery also said this man was tall, with sandy hair and a receding hairline. He also walked in a peculiar way. Is that the man you're remembering?"

Again, Aiden raised his finger slightly.

"That's great, Aiden. Was there anything else you remember?"

Aiden frowned, then closed his eyes.

The room was silent for a moment until Aiden opened his eyes and looked in Margaret's direction. "Margaret, only Margaret," he muttered.

"I think Aiden wants you all to leave," Margaret Cleery said, nodding in the direction of the three.

Aiden raised his finger slowly to confirm Margaret's suggestion.

"I'll wait outside for you, Margaret," Lena whispered as she rose from her chair.

"Just Margaret," Aiden managed to repeat.

OUTSIDE THE HOSPITAL, WORTHY AND FATHER FORTIS hailed a taxi to take them to the church of the Holy Sepulcher. "Now what?" Worthy asked. "Two attacks, so close together. Our man is moving quickly, and I have a bad feeling that what's happening now is part of some sequence. So how do we get ahead of him?"

"Tall, sandy hair, and a crooked nose," Father Fortis replied. "That's not much to go on."

"Don't forget the loping walk."

"Is that important?"

"It could be important, or it could be something to throw us off. If he really walked that way, it could help us. I worked at a halfway house when I was in college, and I remember that a loping walk can be a sign of extreme social anxiety."

"And that tells us what?"

"That this person is isolated. He's had difficulty forming relationships, maybe never having had a friend."

"And angry about that?" Father Fortis asked.

"Angry and frustrated. This type doesn't ever feel they fit into this world."

"How about intelligence?"

Worthy shrugged. "That's what makes such a person's life so miserable. They tend to be very intelligent, especially at solving complicated problems and puzzles. But forming relationships is the one problem they can't solve."

"So empathy would be impossible?"

"Probably. A person like this could kill and feel revenge or satisfaction, but rarely remorse. And here's another thing, Nick. If my arm-chair diagnosis is right, our man can figure out problems that others can't, such as secret codes, strategy games, difficult crosswords, that sort of thing. He will likely have a great sense of superiority."

"And he'd be attracted to apocalyptic thinking about the world coming to an end?" Father Fortis asked.

"Numerology, the Kabbalah, the books in the Bible about the end of the world, our man wouldn't be able to leave that kind of material alone. For him, decoding the signs of the end of the world might be the ultimate puzzle."

Neither man said anything for a moment until Father Fortis said, "There is a bit of good news, Christopher, something Patriarch Michael shared with me on the flight from Rome. One of the Orthodox monks stationed at the church of the Holy Sepulcher has a doctorate in Biblical eschatology, the beliefs about the end of the world. He might be able to help us."

As the taxi meandered through the narrow streets of Jerusalem's Old City, Worthy realized what he was looking at. If Worthy had hoped one day to visit Rome, his father had dreamt of coming to Jerusalem, not to the present city of competing faiths and rituals, but to the city of Jesus, His crucifixion and resurrection, the city of St. Peter and St. Paul. In a strange way, Worthy felt that his coming to Jerusalem fulfilled his father's unrealized dream.

By the time they arrived at the door of the church of the Holy Sepulcher, Father Fortis had warned Worthy that Stephanos, the Orthodox Patriarch of Jerusalem whom they would soon meet, had on more than one occasion criticized Ecumenical Patriarch Michael. How Stephanos would feel in the presence of the Pope of Rome was anyone's guess, Father Fortis told Worthy.

Nonetheless, the elderly man with the flowing white beard who welcomed the two of them at the door expressed gratitude, in light of the recent riot at the church, for the help of the two Americans.

The other person present was introduced as Father Jarrod, the monk with the expertise in eschatology. The balding monk, who spoke with a Scottish accent, came up to Father Fortis' shoulder, which meant that he seemed to disappear into Father Fortis' thick beard when the two embraced.

Patriarch Stephanos led them into a small meeting room, its walls covered with icons. When they were seated around the table, Worthy took a moment to study the Scottish monk. He looked as if he were in his early twenties, and yet he'd already earned a doctorate. *Let's hope you're smart,* Worthy thought.

Patriarch Stephanos cleared his throat and addressed Worthy and Father Fortis, "His All Holiness Ecumenical Patriarch Michael told me that you might be able to help with our current crisis. And I'm sure Father Jarrod is happy to assist in any way he can."

"Thank you," Father Fortis said. "Let me start by sharing that Lieutenant Worthy and I think that the person behind the riot here at the church and the shooting yesterday on the Via Dolorosa is the same person who engineered the attacks in Rome and Constantinople last month."

"What would be the motive of such a person?" Father Jarrod asked, looking from Father Fortis to Worthy.

"There has to be more than one person involved," Worthy explained, "but we think there's a single person directing the attacks. If we're right, this person believes he's living in the last days of the world, and that's why we hope you, Father Jarrod, can help us."

"Good Lord," the young monk said, "another one of those crazy groups?"

"We don't think this person is crazy, Father, so much as dangerous," Father Fortis corrected.

"Well, well," the monk replied, the words sounding like "weel, weel" in his Scottish brogue. "I hope I can help. Yes, I very much hope so."

"Are you familiar with the way these groups think?" Worthy asked.

The monk shrugged. "A bit. My doctoral studies focused on apocalyptic groups from the end of the Biblical period of Judaism and the early centuries of the Church. So I must be honest with you. I'm less knowledgeable about modern groups that believe in these sorts of ideas."

"This person or persons may not be part of any known group," Father Fortis said. "Lieutenant Worthy and I think this person might be using a variety of apocalyptic groups, maybe even groups from different religions."

"Is that kind of cooperation possible? These groups hate one another," Patriarch Stephanos said.

Worthy nodded. "It's not just possible, but we think in this case likely. We think he or they are planning the groups' next moves as we speak."

"Good Heavens," said the young monk, as red blotches began to appear on his neck, "what do you want to know?"

"This might be an obvious question," Father Fortis said, "but can you help us understand the type of person who actually hopes the world is about to end?"

"No, Father, that's not an easy question to answer," Father Jarrod replied. "But in the ancient past, people who were attracted to apocalyptic thinking often despaired at what was happening in their time. Most believed they were living through an era that was increasingly evil. Often, such people were facing persecution."

"And that's why they despaired?'" Worthy asked.

"Let me put it this way: when people can't see a way forward, they might give up belief in the future itself."

"So, we're looking for people dissatisfied with the world as it is," Worthy said, glancing at Father Fortis.

"Yes, and maybe people dissatisfied with life itself."

"You almost make it sound as if these people are contemplating suicide," Worthy said.

Patriarch Stephanos raised his hand. "I'm sure Father Jarrod didn't meant that."

All were quiet for a moment before the Scottish monk cleared his throat. "Actually, there might be some truth in what the lieutenant is suggesting. I have never thought of apocalyptic fervor as a kind of death wish, but, of course, there is the idea that the present age has to die before the Messianic age can begin. I suppose that could be called 'geo-cidal,' the belief that the world is so terrible that it has to be destroyed."

"Destroyed by God or by themselves?" Worthy asked.

Father Jarrod sat in silence for a moment before responding. "People who are hoping for the end of the world are usually waiting and praying for God to act. They tend to be passive as they wait."

"But not always?" Father Fortis asked.

"Hmm, yes, I understand what you're asking," the Scottish monk said. "Most of the apocalyptic groups in the past believed everything was in God's hand, under His control. But a few took the belief in divine determinism in another direction. Imagine believing that God has determined every moment of history since the beginning of the world. That led some groups in the past to believe God knew, or foreknew, how many martyrs would die before the end. So these groups, instead of waiting patiently, believed they could hasten the end of the world by embracing martyrdom."

"So they thought they could force God's hand," Father Fortis said.

"Yes, and not just through martyrdom. Are you familiar with the First Jewish War?"

Worthy shook his head while Father Fortis nodded.

Father Jarrod sat even closer to the table. "In the first century, only forty years after Our Lord's earthly life, Jewish Zealots who'd grown tired of waiting for the Messiah started an insurrection against Rome, believing God would intervene by sending the Messiah. But instead of God intervening, the only thing they achieved was the destruction of much of Jerusalem."

"That's something I've been wondering about. I think whoever is behind these attacks believes the groups he's controlling can do the same thing—start the final battle," Worthy said.

Father Fortis frowned. "But all this person will achieve is chaos, injury, and more death."

Patriarch Stephanos shook his head. "Perhaps not. The Israeli security forces keep a close eye on such groups. It's a vital part of keeping the peace."

"This is no ordinary crazed person," Worthy explained. "This is someone capable of engineering the drone attack in St. Peter's Square, the killing of two men at the Patriarchate in Constantinople, and the shooting on the Via Dolorosa two days ago—all that, and never getting caught. No one has ever been apprehended."

The four men sat in silence until Father Fortis addressed the Scottish monk. "If you could imagine such a person in Jerusalem right now, someone who believed that he or his group could start the final battle, where do you think he'd focus the attack?"

"Well, I must say, Father, you have me rethinking the riot here at the church," the monk replied. "Maybe he thought that that would trigger the end."

"I don't think so," Worthy said. "If whoever ordered the gunman to shoot into the crowd two days ago was also behind the riot here the day before, he's working up to something—something bigger."

"I don't follow," Patriarch Stephanos confessed.

"Lieutenant Worthy and I think the two recent attacks had a different purpose—to bring Pope Gregorio and Ecumenical Patriarch Michael to Jerusalem. We believe this person sees their coming as fulfilling some end-time prophecy."

Patriarch Stephanos slapped a hand down on the table. "Then Pope Gregorio and Patriarch Michael have given this madman exactly what he wants," he said. "I was against the plan from the beginning."

"You're not alone in opposing their decision, but, as the two of them are here, they represent our best chance of stopping this assassin," Worthy replied. "But go back to Father Nick's earlier question. Where would such a person believe the final battle will begin?"

"My first guess would be Megiddo, the site of Armageddon in the Bible. That's about two hours from Jerusalem," the monk said.

"I thought about that, but I don't think the Pope or the Ecumenical Patriarch could be lured to that site. What about here in Jerusalem?" Father Fortis asked.

Patriarch Stephanos frowned. "I can tell you where the Israeli security forces believe a terrorist attack could happen someday, and that's on or near Temple Mount."

Worthy wrote down the response before saying, "Why there?"

"Despite the intifadas between the Israelis and Palestinians, the main worry for Israeli security forces is Jewish extremist groups, some from the region of Galilee. Many are followers of Rabbi Kahani. Perhaps you've heard of him—the American rabbi who preached that Israel should be for Jews only? The Kahanists, those who follow his teachings, also believe that Jews must retake Temple Mount before the Messiah can return. At their rallies, they often talk about blowing up the two mosques on the site and rebuilding the Jewish Temple there."

"But you're saying that Israeli security already has these groups on their radar," Worthy noted.

"What about Christian groups? Some in the States have a similar dream, don't they?" Father Fortis asked.

Patriarch Stephanos nodded. "Those are Christian fundamentalists. We see too many of them here in the city. Their way of reading the Bible tells them Our Lord cannot return until the Jewish Temple is restored. I don't know if any of those groups would go so far as bombing Temple Mount, but they might be sending money to Kahanist groups who share that dream."

Worthy nodded. "Okay, that's helpful, except you're saying that location is under constant security."

Patriarch Stephanos exhaled slowly. "Yes, oddly the safety of the mosques on Temple Mount is dependent on Israeli—that is, Jewish—security. What is said here in Jerusalem is that when a butterfly hovers over Temple Mount, the Israelis know where that butterfly received its flight instruction."

"How far is this site from where we are right now?" Worthy asked.

"Not even two blocks, Lieutenant," Father Jarrod replied. "Sacred sites are literally stacked on top of one another here in the Old City."

"Not even two blocks?" Worthy asked as he glanced at Father Fortis. "So the holiest sites for Christians, Jews, and Muslims are within two blocks of one another?"

Stephanos nodded. "There are no two blocks on the planet that have more technology and security personnel. Whoever would try anything near the Wailing Wall or on Temple Mount would have to either be crazy or a brilliant mastermind."

Father Fortis looked down at his hands. "We're afraid the person we're looking for could be both."

CHAPTER THIRTY

———————— · ————————

July 22: Jerusalem: The Final Confession

MARGARET ACCEPTED A CUP OF WATER from the nurse as she continued to hold Aiden's hand. The hand felt too light, Aiden's face so pale beneath his red hair that she felt her friend was already partially gone. From his doctors, Margaret knew his chances of recovery were non-existent. But until Aiden spoke, she didn't know if he knew his condition.

"The words are coming out . . . very slow. Pretty soon, they'll not come out at all," he said with an attempt at a smile.

Margaret couldn't get over the feeling that she should be the one lying in the bed, facing the certainty of death.

Aiden interrupted her thoughts. "I want you to hear my confession, Margaret."

She shook her head, thinking Aiden must be confused. "A priest can be here in ten minutes, Aiden, if that's what you want."

Now Aiden opened his eyes and looked at her. "No, to you."

Margaret nodded her consent. "Okay, Aiden, if that's what you want."

"I . . . betrayed you. I have always betrayed you." His voice trailed off as his eyes closed.

"No, Aiden. You've been my rock. Without you . . ."

She felt Aiden's hand grip harder. "Without me, you wouldn't have been shot. Others in our group would be alive, not dead . . . or dying like me."

"No, Aiden. You suggested we come to Jerusalem; that's all."

Aiden frowned, his eyes going right and left. "I thought the Vatican wanted you here. I thought they were the ones . . . paying me."

"Paying you?"

Aiden opened and closed his eyes. *He's trying to save his energy,* she thought.

"In Rome, I got money . . . to spy on you."

"Aiden, shh, now. Dr. Fabriano, the woman who was here a few minutes ago, assured me it isn't true. The Vatican didn't encourage us to leave Rome."

Aiden frowned and was quiet so long that she wondered if he'd slipped back into a coma. But then, in an even stronger voice, he said, "I've been . . . a fool." He paused again as if rallying his remaining strength. "Margaret, I hated you . . . so long. I was sure you were a fake."

"No, Aiden, you were always there, believing in me. You're delirious."

Again, she felt pressure on her hand. "I'm the fake, not you," he said. "I need you . . . to believe me."

"But Aiden, when did you hate me? No, I don't believe it."

"Oh, Margaret," he said with tears streaming down his face, "you must . . . you believe me. Otherwise, I can't ask . . . for forgiveness."

"But I've never had any grounds for doubting you, Aiden."

"Then . . . who was the one who paid me?"

Margaret Cleery could see Aiden sinking. "I don't know. What does it matter?"

Aiden's eyes went back and forth again. "Oh, God, I . . . saw him. I knew he . . . was the one . . . paid me. I've been . . . working . . . for the killer."

Margaret's mouth dropped open, but there was nothing she could say. Was Aiden saying that the person behind all the attacks—the one in Rome, the two in Istanbul, the two in Jerusalem—was the one to bring Aiden and her to Jerusalem?

Margaret suddenly gasped. "After we were shot, the Pope and the Patriarch came to Jerusalem. Are you saying . . . ?"

Aiden tried to raise his head but failed. "The killer . . . missed in Rome," he managed to say. "He'll try again. . . here in Jerusalem."

"You couldn't have known, Aiden. You never meant anyone to be killed."

"My heart . . . so full of hate. I wanted so bad . . . so bad to prove you're a fraud." He opened his eyes wide and looked at her. "But you're not."

Margaret couldn't stop her own tears from falling. "Maybe I'm crazy, or maybe I'm a mystic, but I'm not a fake. We both know I'm not smart enough for that."

"What you said on the Via Dolorosa . . . what you said . . ."

Margaret Cleery was confused. "What did I say? I don't remember."

"You said . . . you said 'Jesus would fall . . . all over again if He could because . . . He loves us.'"

"Yes, Aiden, that was the message." Margaret sobbed quietly, feeling Aiden's hand becoming lighter and lighter.

"Are you still here?" he asked.

"Yes, I'm here. I won't leave you."

A look of relief crossed Aiden's face. "If you forgive me, I believe . . . Jesus will forgive me."

Rays of pain shot through her shoulder as Margaret Cleery raised herself from the wheelchair and leaned over Aiden's bed. Between her sobs, she whispered, "I love you, my dear, dear boy." She gave him a kiss on his forehead, and, as she did so, she heard Aiden let out his last breath.

JULY 22-23: JERUSALEM: UNWELCOME DOUBTS

THE CHESSMASTER SAT IN THE OUTDOOR CAFÉ as the sun set in Jerusalem, and a faint breeze signaled a cooler evening. Ever since he first read the Book of Revelation, he'd thought of these last days. With nearly a decade to prepare, to recruit, and to train, he'd expected to feel at peace. But his mind was unsettled.

Nothing of the plan had changed. From the first time he contemplated the end of the world, he accepted that God wouldn't rely on human technology to bring that about. The God of the Universe could not be held prisoner to human advancements in science, engineering, or weaponry, and so he never imagined the final scene of the drama in Jerusalem would need drones, snipers, or even bombs.

His research into Israeli security around the Wailing Wall and Temple Mount had validated his decision. The Israeli security apparatus was as sophisticated as any on the planet, but he believed that sophistication was the security forces' vulnerability. Their instruments could pick up the sound of a mole tunneling below ground or detect the presence of anyone above ground with bombs strapped to his chest. There was only one weapon from which the security forces could not protect the Wailing Wall and Temple Mount—the unarmed human being. Hadn't God demanded David to use Stone Age technology—a slingshot and a few pebbles—to take down the mighty Goliath? All that was needed to bring down the curtain of history would be a human voice igniting centuries of pent-up frustration and hatred.

Of critical importance to his plan was the trick he'd played on the three participating groups. None of the three—the Jewish, the Christian, and the Muslim teams of agents—knew of the existence of the others. None knew how their actions would be carefully choreographed, the first triggering the second, the second triggering the third, and all three creating such a scene of chaos and panic that the Israeli security forces would, in fewer than thirty seconds, be frozen in confusion.

He considered the simplicity of the plan to be its greatest advantage. Act one would begin with men disguised as monks starting another riot at the church of the Holy Sepulcher. If all went as planned, the Pope and the Ecumenical Patriarch would intervene, trying in vain to quell the disturbance. What they wouldn't understand, until it was too late, however, was that the rioting crowd would be led down the narrow street, ending up in the square fronting the Wailing Wall. Ground Zero.

There, his Jewish agents would be waiting. Some, like Zealots of old, would shout in Hebrew "God is with us! To the top!" Other Jewish agents would use the confusion to work their way through the panicky crowd to the Pope and the Ecumenical Patriarch where they would stab them. At that point, Israeli security would be overwhelmed by rioters, both real and fake monks, and the Jewish agents storming Temple Mount.

On Temple Mount, the Chessmaster's Muslim agents, warned in advance about an attempt by Kahanists to attack the mosques, would throw themselves into the battle. At that point, he expected "all heaven would break loose."

His chess days had taught him not to underestimate his opponent, and tomorrow he wouldn't. The Pope and the Ecumenical Patriarch had not come alone to Jerusalem but were protected not only by their own security teams but also by the two Americans.

Until the last few hours, he'd felt he had nothing to worry about. No one, he remembered with pride, had connected the actions he'd initiated around the world over the past few years, so how could they know who they were looking for? He had no website, he'd founded no movement, and he'd taken no credit for the attacks. And, because of his careful planning, none of his agents had ever been caught.

Even his being recognized by Margaret Cleery three days before on the Via Dolorosa didn't concern him. The balding wig and the clay nose job had hidden his military-style crewcut and facial features.

Similarly, the prospect of Worthy or Father Fortis sensing a trap didn't trouble him. Even if the two Americans managed to pull the Pope and the Ecumenical Patriarch out of the mob, he had other of his agents, dressed as Israeli security personnel, who would direct the hierarchs and Americans back to the "safety" of the church of the Holy Sepulcher. There the four would meet their deaths.

All seemed to be in perfect order, yet he'd been awakened that morning by a disturbing thought. Others in the past, reading the same texts he'd studied, believed they too were instruments of God's vengeance, those who would usher in the Conquering Jesus. And God, being God, could have used any of them to end history. What if he were no different from these others? What if God, being God, had not picked tomorrow for the world's end? *What if I've been wrong?* he thought.

He countered these troubling questions by reminding himself of his special calling. He told himself that others who stood in his place in the past—the Essenes and Zealots at Masada, Simon bar-Kochba in this same city—must have misunderstood their calling. But couldn't the same mistake apply to him?

It wasn't until he accepted that his doubts were nothing more than normal anxiety that he'd been able to go back to sleep for another hour. When he finally awoke, his first thought was: *The devil is just trying to rattle me.*

That thought might have been enough to push the questions away if he hadn't, at breakfast the next morning, picked up the English edition of the *Jerusalem Post.* As he was eating the omelet and potatoes, he turned the page to find an interview with Mother Cleery. Later, he would chastise himself for not throwing the paper aside, but his eyes couldn't leave the two columns underneath the photo of the Irish woman with her arm in a sling.

The first part of the article focused on Margaret Cleery's reaction to the death of Father Aiden O'Malley. She called him "her friend and rock," which caused the Chessmaster to chuckle. Would she never understand that the priest despised her?

To the question "What will you do now?" Margaret Cleery said that she was not in control of her future. She would wait to hear from Jesus where she should go next.

"You're damned right you're not in control of your future," the Chessmaster whispered to himself.

Later, he would ask himself why his eyes insisted on reading further. She was a charlatan, a person who, in the final hours of the world, meant nothing. So, why had he continued reading?

The last question the reporter asked was if Margaret Cleery had a new message from Jesus. Any reader could sense the reporter's skepticism, but Margaret Cleery treated the question seriously.

"Yes, I have received a new message. The message is for the person who is behind the upsetting events of the past few days in Jerusalem. The message is that Jesus knows that you are having doubts. I am supposed to tell you that Jesus himself has sent those doubts. Jesus wants you to stop what you are planning. It's not too late for you to save yourself and others," Margaret Cleery replied.

The Chessmaster was instantly lightheaded, feeling an urge to hurry back to his room but fearing that he would faint if he tried at that moment. Again, as if against his will, he reread the message. The lightheadedness passed as anger took its place. *This is the work of the Americans*, he thought. He studied each sentence of the message and realized there were no specifics, only generalities. Margaret Cleery hadn't written the message. The American monk and the Detroit detective wrote it hoping that he would read the message and panic. For a brief moment, he regretted that his plan to kill Lieutenant Worthy in Rome had failed. *No*, he told himself, *now isn't the time to question the will of God.*

He read Margaret Cleery's words over and over until he was certain he knew the Americans' real message. "We don't know who you are, but we think you're still in Jerusalem and you believe you're doing the will of God. We're worried that you're close to doing something else, something that we can't stop. We're hoping you'll feel guilty about all the destruction you've caused."

As he walked back to his room, he no longer felt lightheaded, but the connection of Margaret Cleery's message to the questions that had robbed him of sleep that morning continued to bother him. *Why did I buy that newspaper? Why, why, did I read that article?*

Back in his room, he looked at his watch. It was ten-thirty in the morning, twenty-four hours and fifteen minutes before his plan would go into effect. What he'd imagined himself doing this day was keeping a low profile, avoiding the streets of the Old City as he watched CNN and BBC in his room. He'd imagined enjoying putting his meals on his room account, knowing he'd never have to pay the bill.

Instead, he found himself pacing the room, feeling trapped in it. The stories on CNN and BBC held no interest for him. His mind was fixated on Margaret Cleery and her so-called message for him.

What would I do if I could do anything? he asked himself.

The answer came immediately. *Make Margaret Cleery confess the hoax, and then kill her.*

JULY 23: JERUSALEM: LENA AND WORTHY'S HOTEL ROOM

LENA AND WORTHY SPENT EVERY HOUR TOGETHER in Jerusalem as if the world could, in fact, be coming to an end. They avoided speaking about their futures, but Worthy sensed, one way or another, that they were coming to the conclusion of the case. The sense of separation he'd experienced when she left for Jerusalem, followed by the panic when he feared she'd been killed in the Via Dolorosa attack, had been so awful that he'd made promises to himself that he knew he couldn't keep.

It wasn't until their third night in Jerusalem that they sat up late to broach the taboo subject of their future.

"If it's okay with you," Worthy said from the chair facing Lena on the edge of the bed, "I'd like to go first."

Lena looked down and folded her arms across her chest.

"I have to say something that will seem obvious, but I need to say it anyway. For nearly a decade, I've been a boxer down on the mat, knocked out in the ring. But I'm on my feet again, and that's because I love you."

Lena didn't look up, but he could hear her sniffle as she wiped her eyes with a tissue. "I think you know that I feel the same," she whispered. After a pause, she added, "I just hope you aren't sorry we met."

Worthy reached across to take her hand. "No, no, you're the best thing that's ever happened to me. I thought I was a hopeless case, a kind of leper." He paused as he thought again about her comment. "Do you wish you'd never met me?"

The longer she hesitated, the more the pain in his chest deepened.

"I've thought it once or twice, when I realize we have to live apart." She looked up, the tears coursing down her cheeks. "But when I'm not thinking about the future, I'm just glad I let you into my life."

They sat in silence for a moment.

"Anyway, about the Vatican," she said. "I've been asked to continue my study of Margaret. That means, when she returns to Ireland, I'll go with her."

For one crazy moment, Worthy's mind caught on the absurd possibility that he could make a living in Ireland. But the image faded as quickly as it had come into his mind. Ireland was just Italy with more English spoken.

"Why would they ask that?" Worthy asked.

"Probably because I wrote that Margaret Cleery doesn't seem to be a fake."

"Really?"

"I'm not saying she's the real deal. She might be a fascinating psychological anomaly, but I'll need more time with her to sort that out."

"Can I hate her for determining your future, while I cannot?" Worthy asked.

Lena looked up and offered a weak smile through her tears. "Yes, you can hate her for that. My contact at the Vatican described further study of her as a once-in-a-lifetime opportunity. So, Chris, please don't hate me for needing to do this, even if it pulls us apart."

Worthy tried unsuccessfully to smile in return. "Can I protest to the Pope, saying Margaret Cleery is too dangerous to be around?"

Lena squeezed his hand. "When—not if—you catch this killer, I'm sure Margaret is going to be quite safe."

There seemed to be nothing more to say. Finally, Lena rose and kissed Worthy. "Can we go to bed now?"

CHAPTER THIRTY-ONE

---◆---

JULY 24: JERUSALEM: EARLY MORNING VISITOR

MARGARET CLEERY WAS AWARE that the hair on the back of her neck was standing up as she awoke in the predawn hours of the day. *If this is another message*, she thought groggily, *then Jesus has changed His pattern.*

Reaching to turn on the lamp by her bed, she squinted in the resultant glare. No, there was no message, but the feeling of vulnerability, even danger, wouldn't leave. After her eyes had a chance to adjust, she looked around the room. There, in the only chair of the room, sat a man whom she didn't recognize. He was looking at her intently but with a blank expression on his face. She thought about screaming, but he spoke as if he knew her thoughts.

"Don't scream or it will be the last thing you ever do," he said calmly.

Her brain jumped into action. *What is that accent? Is it Scandinavian or Eastern European? What does he want? Is he bluffing, or is he serious?*

The intruder reached into his shirt and extracted a serrated knife. *No, this man is not bluffing,* she thought.

Accepting the threat to be real, she turned her attention back to herself. *Am I paralyzed with fear? No,* she realized, *I'm not. Do I feel that this stranger could kill me? Yes, he could. Then why aren't I terrified?* After scanning her emotions, a surprising thought surfaced.

"We've been waiting to meet each other for a long time, haven't we?" she said, surprised at how strong her voice sounded.

The intruder didn't respond immediately but then slowly nodded.

After another moment of silence, she said, "You're the one behind all the attacks, aren't you?"

"What makes you say that?" he asked.

"What makes me say half of what I say? I don't know what made me say it, but I see you're not denying it. Your hair is different, but you're the man I saw before . . . before the attack. I'm sure of it. Some people think you're the same person who was behind the attacks in Rome and Istanbul."

The man lay the knife in front of him on his lap. "That would be the Americans, right? Yes, that would be the monk and the detective," he said, in answer to his own question. Margaret realized that the man had just admitted being behind the attacks.

After another pause, he continued. "What did you mean by your comment in yesterday's newspaper?"

Margaret propped herself up in her bed. "As I said, what makes me say half of what I say? What was the comment?"

"You said that Jesus had given you a message for me."

"Oh, right. Jesus told me that He has sent you the doubts you're having about . . . what you're planning."

"You're lying."

"Why would I do that?"

"Because you're a fraud. The message printed in the newspaper yesterday wasn't even from you, was it?"

"Who was it from then?" Margaret asked.

"From the two Americans, of course, or Israeli security. It was a feeble attempt to make me feel guilty, to change my plans. You were just reading a script; admit it."

The stranger's face hadn't changed at all since Margaret had awakened. His face could have been described as serene, except that Margaret would have said vacant. *Whatever this man is feeling*, she realized, *it isn't guilt*.

"Do you have a name?" she asked.

"My name isn't important," he replied. "But my role is."

Margaret considered a smart reply about killing others being his role in life but restrained herself. "And your role is what, exactly?"

"Have you read the Book of Revelation?"

"I think that was the book my priest told our catechism class to skip."

"Are you trying to be funny?" the man asked, something new appearing in his face. Whatever it was, it reminded Margaret of the first breeze that would awaken the calm sea in Greystone's harbor.

"No, not trying to be funny. Just telling you the truth."

"Well, your priest was wrong, dead wrong."

"I'm not surprised. We all thought he was pretty lame."

The expression on the man's face was changing again, and Margaret could see that below the impassive mask was anger.

"You are what I think in English is called 'flippant,' Mrs. Cleery."

"Now you're being unfair. You know my name, but I don't know yours. Are you Swedish or Latvian or from one of those countries?"

"My background isn't important."

"I forgot. It's your role that's important, and it has something to do with a book in the Bible that I've never read," Margaret said. "So tell me what your role is, Sven? Yes, I think I'll call you Sven."

"Don't you realize that your life is in my hands?" he asked as he gripped the knife and held it up.

"Yes, I can see that. But what you don't realize is that I don't care that much about living or dying. I'm bloody exhausted, to tell you the truth."

The stranger narrowed his gaze. "Are you trying to convince me that you're suicidal?"

"No, Sven, I'm not that. I'm just confused about where my life goes from here. Maybe you and that knife solve that question for me. But you seem pretty certain about where your life is headed, so maybe I'm a bit jealous. Does that make any sense?"

For the first time, confusion peeked around the stranger's mask. "Don't you ever think about the world coming to an end?" he said.

"Can't afford to think about that. My kids, especially the grown ones, all got problems—mostly money and drink, if you want to know the truth. I run a laundromat in Ireland, but you probably already know that. So, putting the messages from Jesus aside, my life is pretty ordinary and pretty much a downer."

A slight smile began to form at the corner of the man's mouth. "Sounds like a good reason to invent messages that you tell people are from Jesus. You've got a pretty good scam going to this point, I must admit. You may be from a laundromat, but you ended up in Rome and now in Jerusalem." He paused before adding, "Now, Mrs. Cleery, I have a message for you. The game is over. I don't just mean your so-called messages, but your entire life. And not just your life, but the lives of everyone."

"You've lost me, Sven. I have no idea what you're talking about. I mean, you're only about the thousandth person who's called me a fraud, and believe me, I wish that were true. If it were true, I would have admitted it long ago, and, my friend Aiden . . . Aiden would be alive right now."

"Sounds like you're the one with the guilt," the stranger said.

"A shite-load of guilt, Sven," Margaret admitted, tears streaming down her face. "Those bullets you let loose, they should have killed me and spared the others. I just don't understand what you're hoping to achieve."

"The answers are all in the book you've never read, the Book of Revelation. Tomorrow, God willing—and I'm convinced He is—Jesus will return as the Conquering Judge, and you and everyone else will fall to your knees in homage."

Margaret looked down at her empty hands. "Fall to our knees," she whispered.

"What's that?"

"It's from the message that I received on the Via Dolorosa, right before you waved at your sniper."

"It'd be much better if you dropped your game, but go ahead; tell me, what was your message?"

"I'd forgotten it myself, but Aiden remembered it . . . just before he died. Jesus told me He'd accepted his death, and he'd fallen on His way to the cross, so that we'd know how much He loves us."

The stranger sat in silence, his eyes now looking at something on the wall. Margaret looked over and saw that it was a crucifix. She'd seen so many of those in homes in Greystones and in her parish church that she didn't even notice them anymore. A crucifix for her was as common as a light switch.

"I hate those things," the stranger said.

"The crucifix? Why?"

"He looks so weak. But he was just faking; I learned that from the book of Revelation. He was always the Conquering Judge, and He could have destroyed the lot of them."

"So why didn't He?" Margaret asked in a quiet voice.

The silence in the room was different as if both were groping to understand something.

"He let them kill Him so that, at the end of time, He could pay them back."

Margaret looked up at the cross again. "You mean, you think Jesus was winding them up?"

"Winding? What does that mean?"

"Sorry, Sven. It's an expression from back home. You're saying Jesus was just pretending, just fooling everyone?"

The stranger's eyes were still locked on the crucifix. "He was just letting his killers condemn themselves. Jesus was never weak."

"Ah," Margaret said, finally understanding. "So that message I received on the Via Dolorosa—yes, I know you don't believe me, but pretend you do—that message would make no sense to your Jesus."

"You mean about Jesus saying that He'd accepted the cross, and He'd chosen to fall, so that we'd know how much He loves us—that so-called message?"

"Wow, Sven, you are paying attention. You prefer a Jesus who hates us, right?"

"No, no. Jesus loves the righteous, all those washed in the blood of the Lamb. He hates all those who refuse to . . . to fear Him."

"And that number includes me and the Pope and the Patriarch and the two dead deacons in Rome and the others in Constantinople and now Aiden?"

The stranger took a moment, shifting his gaze from the crucifix to Margaret. "If you don't fear Him, you will very soon."

"But I don't fear Him, Sven. I really don't. Actually, I think it would be easier to be afraid of Jesus than to accept that he loves me—and you—this much," she said, nodding toward the crucifix.

The intruder looked from the crucifix to Margaret. "Love is weak, Mrs. Cleery. Power is strong, and fear is the proper reaction to power."

Margaret looked into the eyes of the stranger. The vacant look was gone. His eyes were dancing as if the man were on drugs.

"One time, I asked Jesus about this, about this end of world stuff you keep talking about. Do you know what he told me?"

"Oh, please enlighten me."

"My Jesus said, 'no.' He told me a spiritual change is coming, something good, something healing. And it's going to happen in this world."

The stranger shot back as if bitten, "Jesus will send angels to kill a third of the whole world. Then He will come on a white horse with a sword whereby He will smite the nations. He will bring birds of the air to feed on the flesh of humans. That's from the Bible, Margaret."

Margaret shuddered. "The Bible. Yes, the Bible. You know, Sven, we actually had a decent priest for a few years when I was growing up. I'm not sure where he'd read this, but he preached one time that if he had to choose between God and the Bible, he'd choose God every time. That's what I feel when you talk about 'your Jesus' and 'your Bible.' That's not the Jesus who speaks to me, and He's not the one who told me to tell you to give this all up."

The stranger looked again at the crucifix. Before Margaret could stop herself, she added, "You're going to die alone, aren't you, Sven?"

"Everyone dies alone, Margaret."

"Aiden didn't. He died with Jesus giving him a kiss on the forehead," she said, surprised at her own words.

"If I stabbed you right now, Margaret, wouldn't you be dying alone?"

Margaret thought for a moment, then took a deep breath. "No, you're wrong. You'd be here. And if I loved you in the moment you killed me, then Jesus would be here as well. That's why that crucifix is in this room."

The stranger jumped to his feet, and for the first time Margaret was afraid. She was afraid not of the knife or what the man might do, but of the unexpected change in the intruder. He walked to the window with a loping gait and looked out to the rising sun.

"In a few hours, Margaret, one of us will be right." He turned from the window and came over to the side of Margaret's bed.

Margaret knew these might be her last moments. But she had no desire to resist.

The man held the knife as if he were making a decision and then replaced it inside his shirt.

"Today, only one of us will be right," he said, and, for the first time, Margaret thought she detected sadness in his voice.

JULY 24: JERUSALEM: CHURCH OF THE HOLY SEPULCHER

THERE ARE ROOMS A PERSON ENTERS, Father Fortis thought, where the tension is like a dry forest just waiting for a spark. The large sanctuary of the church of the Holy Sepulcher was such a room. The three groups of monks and friars of the famous church were clustered with empty chairs separating them from one another. Father Fortis knew that centuries of distrust and suspicion within the church had left their mark, the monks and friars doing their best to pretend that their counterparts didn't exist, much less share the same air with them.

The time was six a.m., chosen to avoid the media's attention on what could be a bitter shouting match, or worse. In the front, sitting on three common chairs, were the Armenian Catholicos Nevres, Pope Gregorio, and Ecumenical Patriarch Michael. Father Fortis was struck with the fact that the leaders of the three churches had probably never sat in the same room together.

Opening prayers from all three communities had done little to diminish the tension in the room. Father Fortis had the feeling that each group of monks or friars paid attention only to the prayer from its own representative. If one of the prelates sitting at the front so much as frowned at one of the other two, Father Fortis expected the room to erupt.

He knew that this would be the first real test of the Pope and Patriarch's brotherhood pledge, and where the Catholicos fit into the picture was a mystery to him. *Is he also now a brother?* Father Fortis thought.

If any occasion merited the phrase "a trial by fire," Father Fortis judged, this was it. There was no history of mutual respect or reconciliation among the groups sharing the church, nothing on which to build. The room instead felt like separate caves housing three warring tribes.

Catholicos Nevres, a distinguished man in his seventies with a white beard poking out of the hood characteristic of the Armenians, stood to speak first. As he began in passable English, Father Fortis felt a wave of relief as he heard a passage from St. Paul's letter to the Ephesians.

"Now therefore ye are no longer strangers and foreigners, but fellow citizens of the saints, and of the household of God. And are built upon the foundation of the apostles and prophets, Jesus Christ being the chief cornerstone; in whom all the building fitly framed together groweth unto a holy temple in the Lord; in whom ye also are builded together for an habitation of God through the Spirit."

Following the reading, Catholicos Nevres described the animosities between the monks and friars as an "unholy inversion" of St. Paul's advice. "By the death and resurrection of Christ, honored at this very site, God has made everyone in the room equal members of God's household. Yet, over the centuries, those privileged to pray in this most holy site have treated one another as foreigners and aliens."

Someone shouted from within the Armenian ranks, answered by shouts from elsewhere in the room. The Catholicos raised his hand for silence, then nodded to Pope Gregorio and Patriarch Michael seated to his right. "These two are my brothers, as much as you, my monks, are my brothers. But we have made idols of our differences, and, in doing so, we have destroyed the unity that Christ desires." There were murmurs of dissent from various directions in the room.

"We have our rights," someone shouted from the back of the room.

The Catholicos waited for silence to return. "Are any of our rights more important than being fellow brothers in Christ?" he asked.

Father Fortis noted the word "brother" again and knew it wasn't accidental.

With that, the Catholicos sat down, made the sign of the cross, and bowed his head.

There was a buzz in the room as the Greek monks and the Franciscan friars gazed over at the Armenian monks. *They're trying to gauge the Armenian reaction*, Father Fortis thought.

Ecumenical Patriarch Michael rose next and gazed at the monks and friars assembled. "The Psalmist wrote, 'Lord, I have loved the habitation of thy house, and the place where thy honor dwelleth.' Each of you is blessed to serve at the holiest site of our faith, the site of Our Lord's crucifixion and resurrection. Everywhere in the world where the message of Jesus Christ is preached, that message has its roots in this place. Here, Our Lord destroyed the barriers between Greek and Jew, slave and free, male and female. Everyone who enters through this door," he said, pointing over his shoulder, "should be surprised, even shocked, at the absence of barriers between us. This would be the will of Christ."

Whether the Greek monks were holding their tongues out of respect or were letting the Ecumenical Patriarch's words affect them, Father Fortis couldn't decide. "I used the word 'should,' for what do tourists and pilgrims experience in this holiest of temples? They find the roots of the Christian faith, found here, to be rotting with rancor and animosity," Patriarch Michael said as he looked around the crowded room.

Grumbling was again audible, but now from a different section of the assembly. Nevertheless, the Patriarch continued in a firm voice. "This, my brothers, is not your fault alone. When have you witnessed the love of Christ between patriarchs, popes, and catholicos? Have we not acted as the heads of hostile tribes? My brothers, we who are seated before you share the blame."

As he said the last words, Patriarch Michael struck his chest. "Brothers in Christ, forgive us," he said as he bowed to those in the room before sitting down.

Father Fortis was moved by the humble gesture, and he could see from the faces of some of his fellow Greek monks that he wasn't alone in this reaction. *But would those words be enough to erase centuries of hatred, or would they be forgotten in a week or month?* he wondered.

Pope Gregorio waited a moment before standing to speak. "The Nicene Creed proclaims, 'and on the third day he rose from the dead.' How do we come to know this? Where is the proof of the resurrection?" he asked. "I ask you who stand vigil at this holy site of Our Lord's resurrection, is the marble, the hanging candles, or the ornate icons proof of the resurrection? I say 'No!'"

Several monks from around the room jumped to their feet, with one or two even shaking their fists at the Pope. Pope Gregorio paused, waiting for the reaction to subside. "Sometimes we—all of us—forget that the world yearns to believe in the resurrection. We forget that pilgrims who come to this sacred place desire more than anything else new life, the life found in our resurrected Lord. But what do pilgrims who kneel in this place find? Do they experience new life, or do they meet the old life described by St. Paul, a life of bitterness, wrath, anger, and fighting?

"My brothers, the proof of this new life is not in the marble, the gold, and precious stones of this beautiful church. So, then, where is the proof? The only proof of the resurrection the world can find is to be found in us, Our Lord's disciples."

From his sleeve, the Pope removed a pamphlet and held it up to the room. "You know this pamphlet, for your chosen representatives wrote it for the pilgrims who enter this holy place. But what do visitors learn from this pamphlet? They read the times when the Greeks have their processions, the times when the Armenians have theirs, the times when the Franciscans have theirs, and then the times when the other groups process."

"This is our ancient custom," someone shouted.

"We must all ask ourselves," the Pope replied, "if these ancient customs honor or offend our Lord. Pilgrims should encounter the living Lord here, but don't most pilgrims see each group boasting of its own Jesus, as if Jesus can be divided?"

Shouts of "no, no" and "it is our right" could again be heard. Father Fortis wondered if anyone else in the room realized that the Pope was paraphrasing what Mother Cleery had said outside this church only days before. "This is God's Church, His alone."

The Pope waited for the responses to die out before continuing. "Is there only one Lord, Jesus Christ, or many?" The room was silent until a Greek monk called out, "There is only one Lord, Jesus Christ."

"If there is one Lord, Jesus Christ, then there can be only one holy temple, a temple not made with hands, a temple made up of all Christ's disciples. I will close with Jesus' own prayer to the Father. 'And the glory which thou gavest me I have given them; that they may be one, even as we are one.'"

The Pope sat down as the room became eerily silent. Father Fortis knew that what had been spoken would be remembered and recited by future historians. But he wondered, would these words change the hearts of those in the room? Would some not return to the old patterns of suspicion and jealousy?

Again, Catholicos Nevres rose and spoke as if he had sensed the fragile peace hanging in the air. "We have not come to speak fine words and then leave. The three of us will remain here today to meet with the heads of all the orders represented. Tonight, we will pray together in this church. We welcome all who wish to join us as we pray. May we together enter into Our Lord's crucifixion, crucifying the flesh and its anger, its desires for revenge, and may we together experience the new life in Christ as brothers."

✝

JULY 24: JERUSALEM: THE HOTEL

AN HOUR LATER, WORTHY KNOCKED on Father Fortis' door. As he entered the room, Worthy saw a candle burning in front of an icon of Christ.

"I've interrupted your prayers, Nick. I apologize."

"Not to worry. I know where I left off," Father Fortis said with a smile, before he seemed to realize this wasn't a social call. "Sit, sit. Something's happened, my friend."

Worthy shook his head, preferring to stand. "Oh, yes. I just spoke with our contact in Israeli security. I did that right after talking with Margaret Cleery."

"Mother Cleery? Why?"

"Our man, the assassin, paid her a visit early this morning. Yes, I know he's breaking his pattern. Apparently, something she said in an interview with the *Jerusalem Post* really rattled him," Worthy said.

"Could she give a description?"

"Yes. He had dark wiry hair, military-cut, and he seemed agitated. Also the loping gait."

"He's taking more risks, Christopher."

"From what she told me, our guy doesn't seem to care. He said whatever is going to happen is going to happen sometime later today."

"Where?" Father Fortis asked, grasping his pectoral cross in his hand.

"That he didn't say, but I told the Israeli security to focus especially on the Wailing Wall and Temple Mount. As they reminded me, they always have maximum security there, but now they have at least a description of our man. I suggest we head there as soon as you're ready, just in case."

"Give me a minute. What else did Mother Cleery say about him?"

"About him?" Worthy asked.

"Who else?" Father Fortis asked.

"It's nothing," Worthy replied, choosing not to reveal, before he left, that Margaret Cleery had received a message for him as well. Worthy had started to tell her he had no time for her nonsense, but waited to hear what she said. "Mr. Worthy, I'm supposed to tell you that though you don't believe in Him, Jesus will always believe in you."

Worthy dismissed her comment, her words seeming like something found in a fortune cookie. No, he wouldn't share this with his friend, Nick, at least not at present.

"What else did she say about him?" Worthy repeated Father Fortis' question. "Just what I said, that he was agitated."

"That's not good, is it, Christopher?" Father Fortis said from the bathroom.

"It's not how I've pictured our guy. He's always seemed so calm, even detached." Worthy looked at his watch. Seven-fifteen.

"I'm ready, Christopher," Father Fortis said, stepping out of the bathroom.

"Great, but ready for what?" Worthy asked, as they left the room.

July 24: Jerusalem: The Mount of Olives

The Chessmaster paced his room. How different he felt from what he'd imagined and planned for this day.

Planned. Planning had been his life, perhaps the one trait he'd inherited from his father. Chess was an exercise in planning. Not just the next move, but, as he improved at the game, six, seven, even ten moves ahead. Matches between high-level players were one planner pitted against another. The victor wasn't the one who controlled the opponent—a worthy opponent had too many options to ever be controllable. No, the victor was the player who saw how the opponent's best move could become a part of one's own winning strategy.

So why can't I do that now? the Chessmaster asked himself. Margaret Cleery was a new kind of adversary. Did she really welcome death, or was she bluffing in the face of a knife? And how was it that by the time he'd left her room—fled her room would be more like it—he felt she knew him better than he knew her—even with his thorough files?

The problem was that Margaret Cleery had forced a door open in his mind, and the more he tried to close that door, the heavier and more immovable it became. On the other side of that door was a room in which he could see a blurred assortment of faces. He tried to look away, to think about what he considered the only critical issue—the unfolding of his plan that morning—but he felt his energy being sapped moment by moment.

He moved to the window and gazed out at what he knew from Bible maps was the Valley of Kidron. Across the valley was the Mount of Olives from where the Messiah was predicted by the prophets to come on the last day—this very day. The Chessmaster had chosen the hotel and requested this room precisely for a view he thought would give him strength. Then why was the view failing him?

The faces swirling behind the door in his mind became clearer with every passing moment, despite his efforts to block them out. He recognized Aiden O'Malley, followed by the faces of the two deacons killed in St. Peter's Square, as well as the archdeacon from the Patriarchate, and a host of others.

What did the parade of faces mean? He had thought little about his victims, viewing them as expendable pawns in the game. But now he saw them differently, as those who'd suffered for a great purpose. He found brief moments of solace in thinking that soon, those who'd died would know their lives had not been wasted.

But their faces returned, and he saw that they were writhing in agony, their faces contorted in pain, their voices screeching.

"It's almost over," he said, but whether his words were addressed to the faces or to himself, he couldn't say. He closed his eyes and imagined pushing against the door with all his might. But nothing happened, except that the voices grew louder.

He looked at his watch. *Nine-thirty, one final hour*, he encouraged himself. He thought back over his life. At the age of three, he lost his mother; in school, he was ostracized; by the chess master, he was badgered and physically beaten; and by his father, he was never loved. *Sixty minutes more—what is that to withstand?* he told himself.

Yet, he felt as if his skin was slowly being torn off. Every thought, every image, every sound felt like acid being splashed on bare tissue.

"I have to do something," he said to the room. "I can't stand this."

He left his hotel and headed in the direction of the Wailing Wall and Temple Mount. It was not yet time for him to get into position, to enter the room near the square from where he would track the progress of the rioting monks. From there he could hear the shofar being blown and could watch as his Jewish agents rushed to ascend Temple Mount.

He walked down a narrow street and told himself that if he kept to the right at every intersection he would return to this same spot. Somehow, however, after the first two turns, he found himself on an unfamiliar street.

He stopped and thought about retracing his steps when, out of the corner of his eye, he saw a door with wooden crosses on it.

A small church. Before he could ask himself why, he tried the door and found it unlocked. He ducked into the dark room and waited for his eyes to adjust. Slowly, to one side he made out several candles beneath a statue of a woman whose heart was pierced with a sword.

Another weak, suffering figure, he thought, expecting to feel disgust. But nothing seemed to be as it had been and as it should be. Looking down the central aisle, he could make out an altar beneath a suspended crucifix. He felt his breath clutch in his throat. Was there no relief from this sight? Blood made by red paint flowed down from the figure's brow, hands, and feet.

He realized that he hadn't been in a church since his teenage years, when, in coming home from school to the chess master's house, he'd occasionally stopped in one to warm himself. But that had been a Protestant church, one without these horrid crucifixes.

He steadied himself on the back of a wooden pew before looking at his watch. Ten minutes after ten o'clock. *So soon,* he thought, *then no more doubts.* He felt a breeze from somewhere and turned to see if someone had followed him in. Seeing no one, he turned back and saw that the breeze had caused the suspended crucifix to sway first away from him and then directly toward him.

He closed his eyes, remembering how the book of Revelation had helped him make sense of the image. Jesus had died, but He had died in rage at the injustice, with vengeance on his lips. That was the Jesus—the coming Judge with a sword—whom he knew and feared.

Yet, even as he tried to keep his eyes shut, he could no longer control them. They were locked on the swaying image, and coming back to mind was Margaret Cleery's comment—"If I have to choose between God and the Bible, I'll choose God." Absurd? Yes. Heretical? No doubt.

He walked to stand directly beneath the image. Looking up, he could see that the artist had carved Jesus' eyes half-open even in death. Margaret Cleery's words echoed in his head—*He would go to the cross all over again for us.*

Don't look anymore, he told himself. Instead, he rechecked the time. Almost fifteen minutes after ten. Only ten minutes more before he would be in position, just six hundred seconds. His agents dressed like monks were no doubt ready to pitch the church of the Holy Sepulcher into chaos once again.

Waves of panic gave him shortness of breath. *What am I doing?* He did not so much hear the question in his mind as feel that the question expelled itself with a force that nearly dropped him to his knees.

Frantically, he looked around the church and saw a door with a red light burning beside it. The darkness of the church was so great and the light so weak that he wondered why anyone bothered with the candle. But he lacked the ability to fight anymore, either physically or mentally. His body, as well as his mind, seemed to be controlled by another force.

He ran to the door with the wavering light and opened it. Inside, he saw a sleepy, elderly priest sitting behind a desk.

"Quick," the Chessmaster shouted. "I need you." When the priest didn't respond, he reached and grabbed hold of the priest's sleeve. Dragging as much as pulling the priest, the Chessmaster brought him into the church to stand beneath the crucifix.

As the Chessmaster pointed to the crucifix, he noticed that his watch said twenty minutes past ten o'clock.

"What did he say? What did he say before he died?"

The priest shook his head and looked confused.

The Chessmaster repeated the words slowly and loudly. "What . . . did . . . he . . . say . . . before . . . he . . . died?"

The priest's eyes brightened, and he smiled. "Ah, what did he say? He said, 'Father, forgive them; they know not what they do.'"

The Chessmaster fell to his knees, the empty room echoed with screams—not only his own but the screams of all who'd died at his hand in the last month. He banged the floor with his head, perhaps hoping to lose consciousness. After a moment, he quit screaming and, staggering to his feet, raced for the door. He began running in what he hoped was the right direction. For he knew now what he had been avoiding—that this Jesus, the Jesus who spoke to Margaret Cleery, would never destroy the world that He had forgiven.

The time was ten twenty-five.

CHAPTER THIRTY-TWO

———————◆———————

JULY 24: JERUSALEM: THE FINAL ACT

MARGARET KNOCKED URGENTLY ON LENA'S DOOR. "Lena, Lena, please be here."

Lena opened the door. Margaret's hair was a fright. She looked as if she'd been wrestling a bear and lost. "What is it?"

"We have to go. We have to go back to the church."

"Which church? What do you mean 'we have to go?' Has something happened?"

"The church of the Holy Sepulcher. Something horrible is about to happen."

"Calm down, Margaret. Worthy and Father Fortis are down by the Wailing Wall. If something is going to happen, it's going to happen there."

"No, no. It will start at the church."

Lena grabbed her camera and handbag. "You've received a message, haven't you?"

Instead of answering, Margaret Cleery turned and ran ahead downstairs and onto the already hot street. "I forgot the way to the church!" Margaret exclaimed, her voice sounding panicky.

"It's three blocks this way," Lena said.

Again, Margaret took off running, or at least trotting. Her red hair bobbed up and down with each jerky stride, her arm in the sling flailing. In two blocks, Margaret stopped to catch her breath. "Do . . . you . . . hear . . . it?" she gasped.

Lena tried to calm her own racing heart. "The commotion? Yes. Can you keep going?"

Not wasting energy answering, Margaret began trotting again with Lena in her wake. With every step, the shouts and banging grew louder as the sounds rebounded off the stones of the ancient city. By the time they came to the court-yard in front of the church of the Holy Sepulcher, Lena knew that another riot was taking place.

Monks in different robes were screaming at one another and throwing stones, their numbers being joined every second with others streaming from inside the church. Lena estimated over a hundred monks were fighting one another, some on the ground, bloodied by the rocks, others picking up the projectiles and returning fire.

Worthy's at the wrong place, Lena thought, even as she became aware of a sight that horrified her. From the church doors came Ecumenical Patriarch Michael, Pope Gregorio, and Armenian Catholicos Nevres. For a moment they looked at each other before linking their arms. The force of the monks behind them caused the three prelates to flow forward into the melee, and Lena feared they'd fall and be trampled.

She turned to say something to Margaret, but Margaret had launched her-self in the direction of the three hierarchs. Her bad arm was now out of the sling, and she was tossing monks to the right and to the left as if they were laundry bags. Lena pushed ahead and entered Margaret's wake, and slowly the two moved through the crowd at an angle that would bring them to the three prelates. But then the crowd surged forward, and Lena realized that everyone was being sucked out of the courtyard onto the street that led to the Wailing Wall and Temple Mount.

For a crazy moment, Margaret reached out and grabbed ahold of Patriarch Michael's sleeve. He turned to see who held him and saw Margaret. For a split second, Lena thought the Patriarch looked at Margaret as if he recognized her. But then the contact broke, and the Patriarch, Pope, and Catholicos were being pushed ahead.

Lena and Margaret, now pummeled by bodies on all sides, fought to stay on their feet. Words Lena recognized and words she didn't floated above her head. All she could think about was Worthy and Father Fortis who, no doubt hearing the riot, would be standing in its path.

Suddenly, a sound of some kind of horn could be heard above the commo-tion, followed by yet another commotion coming from the square itself. Lena held on to Margaret as if they were heading for a massive waterfall. Sirens now began to blare from the square ahead and from the streets behind them. She jumped up to see if she could find Worthy, but she failed.

The rioting monks spewed out into the square fronting the Wailing Wall. Ahead, somewhere, were the three Church leaders as well as Worthy and Father Fortis. Lena felt waves of anger rising in her as she thought of the man who'd stolen into Margaret Cleery's room. He'd gotten his wish. He'd created a firestorm.

Margaret veered to the left, pulling Lena in her wake. For a few moments, they made no progress, but slowly the two reached the edge of the crowd where they encountered less resistance. Ahead of them, Lena could see the three hierarchs and then Worthy and Father Fortis standing as a shield in front of them. *Thank God Nick is huge,* she thought. Worthy, however, was struggling to push back on the throng that continued to flood in their direction.

Margaret and Lena were now no more than ten yards from the three prelates when Margaret rose to her full height and began yelling in Worthy's direction, even as she pointed toward a man who'd broken from the main stream and was heading their way.

"It's him! It's Sven!" she shouted. Lena could see Worthy looking in her direction with a puzzled look before their eyes met.

"The killer is here!" Lena also shouted in Worthy's direction.

Beside her, Margaret Cleery called out. "He's the man with the crewcut. He's coming for you three!"

Worthy nodded as he turned to where Margaret was pointing and scanned the mob surging his way. Lena saw Worthy move to position himself between the man and his targets.

The man too was shouting, but whatever he was saying was being drowned out by Margaret's screaming, "It's him! It's him! Stop him!"

Lena could see Worthy brace himself for the man's attack. As the man lunged toward Worthy, Lena feared she would see the man she loved die before her eyes.

The man broke though the last circle but then stopped. Over the din, Lena could hear him yell to Worthy, "They will try to stab them. Get them to safety, but not back to the church! Don't trust anyone."

The man turned, and Lena could see his eyes meet Margaret's. For a moment, he seemed to go limp. Seeing him unarmed, Margaret reached out and drew him to herself.

"You were right. I was wrong," was all the man said before he slumped into her arms, and it was then that Lena saw three widening circles of blood on the back of his shirt.

"We have to go," Worthy shouted in Margaret and Lena's direction.

"I can't leave him," Margaret shouted back.

"You have to," Worthy said. "He'll be dead before you can get him out of here. I need you both to help us save these three."

Lena watched as Margaret gently released her grip and let the man, already unconscious, slide to the ground. Even though Lena knew Worthy was right, she could see Margaret fighting to stay, to not leave the stranger to die alone.

The four of them encircled the Pope, Patriarch, and Catholicos and made for a side street that ran off the square. Progress was difficult, not only because

of the crowds, but because Worthy and Father Fortis had to be looking back-
ward in case another attack was coming.

It was no more than seven or eight minutes, but it seemed like hours, before
the tight group gained the side street and distanced themselves from the rioters.
Worthy led the way, turning right and then left before stopping abruptly before
a door with wooden crosses on it. The seven of them ducked into the dark
space and waited for their eyes to adjust. Finally, Lena could make out a candle
in front of an icon of the Virgin Mary, a sword piercing her heart. "You're safe
here," the figure seemed to say. Margaret moaned as she fell to her knees before
the icon, her face buried in her hands as she prayed, "Father, forgive him."

CHAPTER THIRTY-THREE

JULY 25: JERUSALEM RESTAURANT

A FULL DAY OF INTERVIEWS WITH ISRAELI SECURITY FORCES, Jerusalem newspapers, and international media was interrupted for Worthy only once, by a phone call from his daughter Allyson.

"What Father Nick and you did is all over the news, Dad. Is it true that you saved the lives of the Pope and the Orthodox Patriarch?"

"It was a lot more complicated than that, Alli, and it would be wrong to give too much credit to Nick and me. It's fairer to say that we were involved."

"Sounds like the same old Midwestern humility to me," Allyson said. "But there was something else in the news. They've thrown out the case."

"Who is the 'they,' and what case have they dropped?"

"The lawsuit, Dad, the lawsuit in Detroit. The one against you and Father Nick. The judge threw it out."

"Did the judge specify why?"

"She mentioned a letter she'd received several weeks ago from Patriarch Michael. Here's what she told the media: 'The Ecumenical Patriarch of the worldwide Orthodox Church, after a thorough review, affirms that the actions taken by Lieutenant Worthy and Father Nicholas Fortis in the tragic death of one of her priests in Detroit five years ago did not violate Church policy on congregant-priest confidentiality.'"

Worthy didn't say anything for a moment. "You said Patriarch Michael sent this letter weeks ago?"

"July 1. Wasn't that the day you flew to Rome?"

"Actually it was the day before I arrived," Worthy replied. "I wonder why the judge released her judgment on the lawsuit today?"

Allyson laughed. "Think about it, Dad. She announced her decision the day after Father Nick and you are credited with saving the lives of the Pope and Patriarch. The city can't have its hero return under a cloud."

That evening, as Lena, Father Fortis, and Worthy sat in a booth in the back of a crowded restaurant in Jerusalem's Old Quarter, Worthy shared Allyson's news.

Father Fortis clapped his hands before putting his arm on Worthy's shoulder. "Thank you, God. Looks like we have a lot to be thankful for tonight, my friends."

A commotion in the restaurant drew their attention to the restaurant's widescreen TV where they saw their faces alongside Pope Gregorio's, Patriarch Michael's, Catholicos Nevres', and Mother Cleery's. Patrons at other tables turned and smiled, a few toasting the three of them.

"I suppose this is our fifteen minutes of fame," Lena said in a low voice.

"It'll take more than fifteen minutes for some people to forget us," Father Fortis said as he brought out a folder and laid it on the table. He took out two sheets of paper bearing different ornate letterheads. "After our interviews with the police and security this afternoon, Patriarch Michael asked to see me. That's when he gave me these." As passed one of the sheets to Worthy. "This one is for you, Christopher."

Worthy glanced at the sheet of paper and started to fold it as if to put it into his pocket.

Lena laid her hand on Worthy's. "No, Chris. I want to hear it."

Worthy shook his head as he nodded toward other occupied tables. "Not here; not now. Maybe later in the hotel."

"Just read it quietly, Chris," she said. "No one will hear but us. Besides, how many of the people here understand English, anyway?"

Worthy looked from Lena to Father Fortis. "Then Nick has to read his."

Lena smiled at Father Fortis. "That sounds fair."

Worthy shrugged as if he was obeying under protest. "Well, mine is signed by Pope Gregorio. It says, 'Lieutenant Worthy, Without Father Nicholas Fortis' and your persistent efforts to identify the assassin and protect us yesterday, a tragedy would undoubtedly have occurred. This tragedy would have been far greater than the loss of Ecumenical Patriarch Michael's life and mine. Your efforts along with the quick response of Israeli security forces prevented an international incident that would have had untold ramifications on the Jewish, Christian, and Muslim communities throughout the world.

Because of your intervention, Patriarch Michael and I are now able to remain safely in Jerusalem to join with Catholicos Nevres in pursuing peace in the first church of our faith, the church of the Holy Sepulcher.

I will close by adding two thoughts. Catholicos Nevres, Patriarch Michael, and I, Pope and Bishop of Rome will always believe that God brought Father Fortis and you to Rome and now Jerusalem to be our guardian angels.

And on a more personal note, I hope you will be willing to return to Rome if the Holy See needs your gifts and services in the future.'"

Worthy looked up and cleared his throat. "Your turn, Nick," he said.

Wiping a tear from his eye, Father Fortis asked, "Can't we just agree that my letter is much like yours?"

"No, Nick, fair is fair," Lena said.

"Okay. My letter is from Ecumenical Patriarch Michael. 'Dear Nicholas, you have been my constant companion and supporter over these tragic weeks. Somehow you have managed to fulfill your duties for me, for which I am grateful, while partnering with Lieutenant Worthy in identifying and stopping what the man we now know as Per-Olaf Johannsen had planned. God in His rich mercy brought a change of heart to this sad man, but Catholicos Nevres, Pope Gregorio, and I know how close Jerusalem and the religious world came to being thrown into chaos by what he had meticulously planned to unleash.

My dear friend, Nicholas, I want to reward you for your service, and I realized the only appropriate reward I can offer a monk is the opportunity to serve Christ's Church once more. I humbly request that you remain with me in Jerusalem to work with Catholicos Nevres and Pope Gregorio as we continue to pray and work together as brothers to bring peace to the church of the Holy Sepulcher. It is time for the site of Jesus' crucifixion to experience the new life, peace, and joy of the resurrection.

Your fellow servant of Christ, Michael.'"

Father Fortis looked up and saw Lena staring at Worthy's wrinkled forehead. "Why the frown, Chris?" she asked.

"Lena, I think I know what's troubling Christopher," Father Fortis said.

"Well, if you know, Nick, I don't," Lena said. "Everything in those letters is the truth."

Worthy and Father Fortis said nothing for a moment. "It's not the whole truth, Lena," Father Fortis said. "Right, Christopher?"

"Right, Nick. I expect we'll know more about Johannsen after Interpol combs through his home, but there's one thing we already know. And that is that neither you nor I changed his mind."

"I agree," Father Fortis said. "What changed Johannsen's mind was the message Margaret Cleery gave to him through the newspaper article. Instead of killing us in the square, Johannsen sabotaged his own plan. I can only imagine what his followers are thinking."

"Does the world have to worry what his disciples will do now?" Lena asked.

Worthy shook his head. "There are good grounds for thinking they'll be lost without Johannsen pulling the strings."

"Remember, if Christopher's theory is right—and I think it is—none of those groups knew about each other," Father Fortis added.

None of them said anything for a moment before Lena said, "You both give Margaret Cleery credit for changing Johannsen's mind, but if she were sitting her with us, she'd say that that message was from Jesus, not her. And I know what you're going to ask me, Chris. Does this mean she is a genuine mystic? Was that message a miracle of sorts, or did Mother Cleery intuit what someone like Johannsen might be feeling? I can't say, but maybe there's still time for me to find out," she said. "I've already told Chris this, Nick; the Vatican has asked me to fly back to Ireland with Mother Cleery and continue my research."

"When do you leave?" Father Fortis asked.

"Our flight leaves tomorrow evening, Nick. But this isn't goodbye, exactly. I'm hoping we'll see each other again. You see, I'm going to be visiting Chris in the States. And Chris loves Rome, so I know he'll come back to the city he loves—and me—whenever he can."

Father Fortis glanced at Worthy, knowing his friend would find the news bittersweet. Yes, Worthy would see Lena again, but he knew the weeks and months of separation in between would be hard on him. Offering a smile, he said, "Then that's another miracle. I remember you said you were through with America, Lena."

Lena returned the smile. "I have a good reason to give the States another chance."

CHAPTER THIRTY-FOUR

July 26: Jerusalem: The River Jordan

WORTHY AWOKE THE NEXT MORNING to find Lena no longer by his side. In a panic, he sat up and listened for any sound of her presence in the bathroom. *There it is,* he thought with relief, *the sound of the shower running.*

After dinner with Father Fortis the night before, Worthy and Lena stayed up, resisting sleep as the thief intent on stealing their last hours together. No doubt other rooms in the city were talking about Per-Olaf Johannsen, described by the media almost as a martyr, a man from the border of northern Norway and Finland who'd prevented a catastrophe by alerting Israeli security about an imminent attack on Temple Mount only to be stabbed to death in front of the Wailing Wall. But instead of talking about those events, Lena and Worthy talked until four in the morning about their future.

As dawn rose over Jerusalem and awakened Worthy, he knew they were facing the same impasse, that neither of them could ask the other to give up her or his life. He thought back on what Lena had said before they agreed to grab a few hours of sleep. "I remember reading something that could have been written for us," she'd said.

Worthy had sat silently, exhausted and hoping what she'd say next wouldn't be sentimental.

"As I remember, it goes something like this. Love doesn't always mean being together, looking into each other's eyes. Love is there whenever two people are looking out to the same horizon."

He remembered asking her to repeat that. Lena did, and he'd slowly nodded.

"Can you see what it means for us, Chris? We won't always be together physically."

Worthy had tried to say something, but the words hadn't come.

"Neither of us knows if seeing one another online and calling one another will hurt more than help. But no matter where we are, I know that we'll be just that, 'looking out to the same horizon.' And that's more important for our love than anything . . . even seeing each other every day."

Now, as the morning sun streamed through the window, Lena came out of the bathroom from her shower, her wet hair hanging in strands down to her shoulders. He couldn't help but stare at her.

"What's that look for?" she asked.

"I'm just taking mental pictures. Lena coming out of the shower, Lena dropping her robe, Lena—"

"Okay, you can stop there," she said, even as she came over to the bed, bent down, and kissed him. "Look, Chris, I refuse to spend our last hours together in this sad little room, being sad, and saying all the sad things we've already said. I want us to do something here, in Israel, something that will balance all the pain and grief of the past weeks, something that we'll always have as a good memory. Something good, something worthy . . . Yes, that's it. I want us to do something worthy, just like you're Worthy." After a pause, she continued, "So, I think we should drive down to see the Jordan River. We still have eight hours before I fly out with Mother Cleery."

"The Jordan River? Why?"

"Trust me. I'll explain when we get there."

In the cab ride from Jerusalem to the Jordan River, their driver, Muzaffar, delivered a lecture on Arab-Israeli history and politics over the blast of the cab's air conditioner. *Just as well*, Worthy thought. Lena and he simply held hands and looked out the window.

At the river, Muzaffar stopped in a parking lot to let his passengers off. He pointed across the river and told the two of them that not that many years before, what they were looking at was part of Jordan. "Now, it's part of the West Bank controlled by the Israelis. I had relatives who used to live there," Muzaffar said matter-of-factly.

Worthy handed Muzaffar enough money for two trips and contracted for the driver to return in an hour. "For you, my new friends, I will buy falafel from Jericho for our trip back," he said as he sped off.

The sun was reaching full strength as Lena took his hand and led him to the rocky edge of the river where she took off her sandals, put her feet into the water, and invited Worthy to do the same.

The water was delightfully cool, its temperature slowly overcoming the heat beating down on them.

"So tell me why we're here," Worthy said.

For a moment Lena didn't answer but stood and swished her feet so she could splash his legs. "Do you feel that, Chris? Do you feel what that is?"

Worthy stood in the steady current and splashed back, causing Lena to laugh. "Let me guess. It's a very old river," he said.

"This is the Jordan River. We are standing with our feet in time."

"Time?"

"Abraham walked across this river. Joshua certainly did, and I'm sure King David and King Solomon did as well. John the Baptist baptized Jesus near here. Some of my ignominious ancestors in the Crusades probably cooled their feet here. Suleiman the Magnificent must have as well," she said.

"Like I said, we're soaking our feet in a very old river."

"No, no, much more than that, Chris," she said, reaching over and clasping his hand. She moved toward him until their bodies were touching. "We're standing in time. Time is our biggest problem and our biggest gift. Today, the minutes and hours are flying by. We'd give a fortune to buy even an hour more of it, even ten minutes, as long as we could be together. Tomorrow, I'll be in Ireland with Margaret for Aiden O'Malley's funeral, and you'll be on a flight back to the States. Tomorrow, time will hang like a weight around our hearts."

"I already know how that's going to feel, Lena. I just don't understand how this river or anything can change that," he said. "I'm asking, because I hate time right now—how fast it's passing and how slowly it'll pass once you leave."

"And hating time, more than the distance separating us, more than lonely nights, more than anything else, is what could destroy our love, Chris. We need to be thankful for time," she said, squeezing his hand even as she teared up. "Time brought us together, you from your world, me from mine. Because of time, we're two lovers standing together in a river. How can we hate time? The water flowing around us *is* time. It's been passing over these rocks for tens of thousands of years, and, unless those apocalyptic end-of-the-world types are finally right, water will pass over these same rocks for thousands of years to come."

"So, you're saying, 'Don't fight the river?'" Worthy whispered.

Lena kissed him lightly on the cheek. "That's it. When I come to Detroit to see you and you come to Rome to see me, I want us to remember this moment, this standing here together. When we're apart and we're tempted to hate being apart, I want us to close our eyes and feel this water passing over us, just as it's passed over the feet of millions before us."

Lena drew Worthy's face toward her and looked deeply into his eyes. "Whether time is our friend or our enemy is up to us, Chris. It will always be up to us."

EPILOGUE

---◆---

THE DAY AFTER MARGARET CLEERY AND LENA flew back to Ireland was humid with bright sun, the air of Jerusalem still. Worthy and Father Fortis, with an hour before Worthy would leave for the airport, walked the short distance from their hotel to the church of the Holy Sepulcher. Broken furniture, filing cabinets, and reams of paper lay strewn throughout the courtyard, now strangely quiet.

They found two chairs still intact and set them down under the shade of a solitary cypress tree. "Two riots in a matter of days," Worthy said. "Makes me wonder if anyone can bring peace to this place."

"We both know Pope Gregorio and Patriarch Michael plan to try," Father Fortis said, "but given everything that's happened here in Jerusalem—from what Johannsen and his agents tried to incite on Temple Mount, to the riots here at the church, to the Palestinian-Israeli problem—I'm not surprised people think religion is the problem, not the solution."

After a moment, Worthy said, "Faith and wrath."

"What?"

"It's something I thought about after we learned what Johannsen said to Margaret Cleery in her hotel room. After he pulled a knife on her, he kept quoting scriptures about vengeance and blood, about God's wrath."

Father Fortis sighed as he looked at the police tape draping the church's doors. "People think idolatry is a sin from ancient times, but one of my professors in seminary insisted that idolatry happens every day. He wasn't talking about idols of gold or silver but the mental gods people create, the gods who are versions of themselves. People of all religions pore through their sacred scriptures, and, plucking a verse from here and there, they piece together gods who mirror themselves."

"Like Johannsen devoted to a god hungry for vengeance, a god as angry as he was," Worthy said. "Johannsen reminds me of those religious zealots who stormed the Capitol in Washington back in 2021."

Father Fortis made the sign of the cross. "Yes, Johannsen was another fanatic until Mother Cleery, bless her, made him reconsider. I believe what she said saved his soul."

Worthy turned to face his friend. "What about Margaret Cleery? Is she doing the same thing, listening to her own voice and thinking it's Jesus talking to her?"

Father Fortis looked down at the ancient cobblestones. "No doubt her critics would agree with that."

"But not you, Nick, right?"

"No, not me, and I don't say that because I'm a monk. God knows that monks can also create gods in our own image. Maybe that's what the monks and friars in this church have done over the centuries. Each group has an image of god it's comfortable with.

"But Mother Cleery is a different story. The voice she hears is anything but a mirror of herself. Based on what Mother Cleery told Lena, the voice she hears has steadily broken through who she thought she was. The voice she hears is inviting her to change . . . to become the person she was always meant to be."

Father Fortis paused before continuing. "Granted, her hearing a voice is unusual, but I've witnessed that same change in other people—many people, in fact. That change, that call for conversion, convinces me that God is at work."

The front door of the church opened, and an Armenian monk appeared with a broom. He ducked under the police tape, took one look at the two men, then began to sweep debris into a pile.

Glancing at his watch, Worthy started to stand. "Nick, it's time for me to leave. You'll let me know when you're back in the States?"

Father Fortis, however, didn't rise or answer Worthy's question. Instead, he said, "Do you realize this is our sixth case together, Christopher? We've worked together in New Mexico—twice, Detroit, Michigan's Upper Peninsula, Venice, and now Rome and Jerusalem. Six cases, each one different, yet all of them having us cleaning up a sorry mess—as that monk is doing. So much sorrow, so much violence. Sometimes, I can hardly believe all we've been through."

Worthy felt a lump in his throat. "A lot of pain and grief, but there's been something else. You said Margaret Cleery is changing, becoming the person she was always meant to be. Well, working with you has changed me. Maybe I'd even say I've become a better me, Nick. Without your friendship . . ."

Father Fortis laid his hand on Worthy's shoulder. "As your friendship has done for me. I thank God for our friendship every day."

"I know you do, Nick, and maybe in my own way, I do the same."

"I've never doubted that, my friend." Standing, Father Fortis said, "I don't want you to miss your cab ride to the airport. Here, let me give you a hug."

Worthy stood and, with a smile, faced his friend. "My ribs can't take one of your hugs, Nick, but here, let me give you one of mine."

Laughing, Father Fortis thought, *Another hug from Christopher. Will wonders never cease?*

THE END

GLOSSARY OF TECHNICAL TERMS IN *LIKE A THIEF IN THE NIGHT*

———◆———

Many readers will be familiar with **Roman Catholic** terms and titles. Here is a brief list of terms used in *Like A Thief in the Night*:

The Papacy. The papacy refers to the leadership of the Roman Catholic Church. The papacy occupies the Vatican or Vatican State, a separate political entity that exists in several areas in Rome, chiefly at the site of the martyrdom of St. Peter on the Vatican Hill.

Pope. The term literally means "papa" and designates the person who is the Bishop of Rome and who occupies the "chair of St. Peter" in the Roman Catholic Church. The appropriate term to address the pope is "Holy Father" or "Most Holy Father." The Pope can also be addressed as "His Holiness," but in *Like a Thief in the Night* the Pope is not addressed as such, as the similar titles "Your All Holiness" and "His All Holiness" are reserved for the Ecumenical Patriarch of the Orthodox Church.

Prelate. One who holds a high office in one of the various branches of the Christian Church.

Curia. The central government of the Roman Catholic Church. Under the control of the pope, the Curia oversees the various ministries and activities of the Vatican.

Readers might be less familiar with important **Orthodox** terms and titles:

Patriarch. A patriarch is the head of the Orthodox Church in an Orthodox-dominated country (e.g., the Patriarch of Moscow oversees the Orthodox Church in Russia.)

Ecumenical Patriarch. Considered the "First Among Equals ("equals" referring to other patriarchs)," the Ecumenical Patriarch functions as the head of the Orthodox Church worldwide. The appropriate form of address for the Ecumenical Patriarch is "Your All Holiness" or "His All Holiness." The Ecumenical Patriarch does not exercise the power in the Orthodox Church that the pope does in the Roman Catholic Church.

The Patriarchate. The headquarters of the Ecumenical Patriarch, which is in Constantinople (modern-day Istanbul, Turkey). The headquarters is also known as the Phanar. The Patriarchate is considered the "Mother Church" of the wider Orthodox community.

Significant term for the **Armenian** Apostolic Church:

Catholicos. The Catholicos (literally meaning "universal bishop") is the head of the Armenian Apostolic Church worldwide.

Franklin College in Franklin, Indiana, has been David's home for the past forty-three years. David has been particularly attracted to the topics of faith development, Catholic-Orthodox relations, and Christian-Muslim dialogue. In 2007, he conducted interviews across the country in monasteries and convents about monastic responses to 9/11. The book based on that experience, Peace Be with You: Monastic Wisdom for a Terror-Filled World, was chosen as one of the Best Books of 2011 by Library Journal.

In the past sixteen years, religious terrorism has become an area of specialty. Much of his time in the last ten years has been spent giving talks as well as radio and television interviews on ISIS, Al-Qaeda, and other terrorist organizations.

Now retired, David enjoys writing both non-fiction related to interfaith relations and the award-winning Christopher Worthy/Father Fortis Mystery series.

His wife, Kathy, is a retired English professor, an award-winning artist, and his best editor. Their two sons took parental advice to follow their passions. The older, Leif, is a Fine Arts professor and photographer, and the younger, Marten, is a filmmaker.

CPSIA information can be obtained
at www.ICGtesting.com
Printed in the USA
LVHW031509161021
700645LV00014B/408